PRA~~ISE FOR~~

"Finding Sheba is a thriller that will have you digging through your history books to learn the truth. But not until you finish every last page of this gripping story."
—*J. Scott Savage, author of FarWorld and Dark Memories*

"Finding Sheba is the perfect mix—excitement, action, tension-packed suspense, and a great, believable cast of characters. Add to that some of the greatest parts of the history of the Middle East, and you have a book that must be read. H. B. Moore has nailed it . . ."
—*Karen K. Christoffersen, producer*

"A story of secrets, mystery, and love. Passionate and filled with dangerous intrigue, Finding Sheba will keep you turning pages all the way to its breathtaking conclusion that will surprise as well as delight. A perfect book."
—*Julie Wright, Whitney Award–winning author*

"In Finding Sheba, H.B. Moore, a master at bringing biblical-based characters to life, has delivered a thriller that shakes readers to their core with the question: What if the Bible is false? Undercover Israeli agent Omar Zagouri is a perfect mix of Robert Langdon, F.B.I. Special Agent Pendergast, and Indiana Jones, and the novel will keep you on the edge of your seat until the very end, and maybe even beyond."
—*Lu Ann Brobst Staheli,*
author of The Explorers: Tides Across the Sea

"Fans of H.B. Moore's historical series will be familiar with Moore's meticulous research and accuracy and the exotic regions portrayed so vividly in each of her novels. But Finding Sheba takes history up a notch, combining it with current-day politics and an intriguing, potentially world-altering premise. Not for the faint of heart, Sheba takes readers on a thrill ride where time is only one of many enemies, and trusting the wrong person could mean death. An added dose of romance and dry humor makes the perfect combination for a great summer read."

—*Michele Paige Holmes,*
author of Counting Stars and Captive Heart

FINDING
SHEBA

An Omar Zagouri Thriller

H. B. MOORE

StoneHouse Ink 2013
Boise ID 83713
http://www.stonehouseink.net

First eBook Edition: 2013
First Paperback Edition: 2013

ISBN: 978-1-62482-082-3

Cover design by Cory Clubb
Layout design by Ross Burck

The characters and events portrayed in this book are fictitious. Any similarity to a real person, living or dead is coincidental and not intended by the author.

Published in the United States of America

For my father, S. Kent Brown, renowned biblical scholar, who brainstormed the plot with me. The rest is history.

FINDING SHEBA

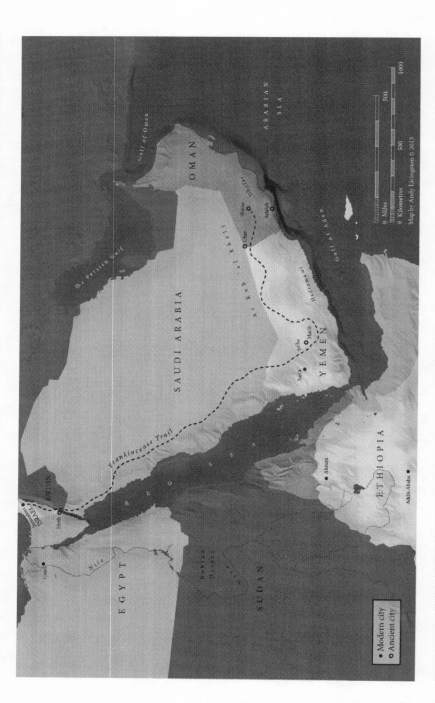

When the queen of Sheba heard of the fame of Solomon . . .
she came to Jerusalem with a very great train . . . And king
Solomon gave unto the queen of Sheba all her desire . . .
                                        (1 Kings 10:1–2, 13, KJV)

Chapter One

Brown University, Providence, Rhode Island

DR. RICHARD LYON'S HANDS trembled as they hovered above the keyboard, hesitant to write the email. He closed his eyes, flexed his reluctant fingers, and exhaled. He knew what had to be done, even if his life were put in jeopardy as a result. An assassination attempt had been made the day before on one of his oldest and dearest friends—the Coptic pope—His Holiness, Patriarch Stephanus II.

And Lyon had just discovered who made that attempt.

The revelation would rock the foundation of an already unstable government in a country that could not afford such a blow.

Only a select group of scholars knew the real reason why the attempt was made in the first place. A tomb had been discovered and on its walls, a map that would change the course of history.

Lyon opened his eyes and forced himself to type as the last glow of day peeked through the dusty blinds. Staying on at the university long past retirement age to continue his research had finally proved beneficial—although not entirely in the manner he expected. Recently, he'd found the final clue that would complete his lifelong study on the queen of Sheba. But first he must warn the others about the leak. His mouth pulled into a grim line as he typed the closing paragraph, then reread his words.

My fellow constituents,
There has been a breach of trust in our exclusive network
at DiscoveryArch . . .

As Dr. Lyon read, he leaned back in his worn leather chair, the stubborn wheels beneath groaning at the shifted weight. The computer screen cast its artificial glow upon the books stacked from floor to ceiling—books that contained the written works of ancient explorers and renowned world scholars.

Footsteps sounded in the hallway outside, and the professor turned in anticipation, expecting a student with questions about the midterm humanities paper. Instead, an envelope slid under the door. Lyon rose and picked it up. It was addressed to him. Curious, he opened his door and looked for the deliverer, but the short hallway was empty.

Leaving the door ajar, the professor settled into his seat and slid his index finger beneath the sealed flap. But there wasn't a note. In fact, within lay another white envelope identical to the first. Lyon removed it, squinting to read in the near darkness. Printed across the plain front were the words, *"VENITE, DILECTI FILII, EGREDEMINI IN HORTUM."*

He stared in horror at the Latin script—a quote penned by St. Thomas Aquinas on his deathbed. Blood rushed to the professor's ears as his face heated with disbelief.

They already know.

How had they found out? He hadn't sent the email yet. Lyon inhaled sharply, realizing that this single envelope had brought his life's research to a grinding halt.

Slowly he opened the second envelope, catching a waft of almond. Tiny particles of white exploded into the air, invading his nostrils and rushing to his lungs. The impact of the salt-like chemical was almost immediate, and Dr. Lyon felt his thoughts muddle together and blend into a fierce throb. He braced himself against his chair, trying to understand what was happening.

His gaze slid to the envelope he'd dropped on the floor, the contents spilled. The almond scent still hovered in his senses.

Cyanide.

Horrified panic constricted the professor's chest as he realized that just as St. Thomas Aquinas took his Latin invitation to his death, he would take the dead saint's revelation about the queen of Sheba to the grave. Within sixty seconds, his breathing became labored, and he gasped for air, air that was all around but that seemed to pulse away from him. *I made a . . . mistake.* If they had found him so easily, sending the email would make every person on that list a target. The room faded to black then, for an instant, it lightened again. One last thought of clarity made its way into the professor's mind.

Delete the email.

Dr. Lyon leaned forward, feeling the ground rock beneath his feet as his body started convulsing. Just as darkness collapsed around him, his finger reached the mouse and clicked on the small rectangle box: DELETE.

Chapter Two

North of Jerusalem
Five days earlier

I AM A LIAR . . . at least in their eyes, Omar Zagouri thought.

No other explanation could be given for a three-year-old Palestinian child flinging rocks at a car with an Israeli license plate—except that hatred was taught from infancy. *Hatred blinds men and justifies murder. But most of all, hatred lies.*

And I represent everything that oppresses them, everything they despise. All the more reason to finish this job and get the hell out of here.

Omar swung his pickax with renewed determination, putting his weight into the motion. He was wiry, but stronger than most men twice his size, and the stone wall crumbled like clay beneath his efforts. Sputtering as dust filled the stale, underground air, he wiped the perspiration from his face with a grimy sleeve.

"We're close!" said the laborer next to Omar. "Feel the cool air?"

Omar placed his hand against the jagged rock. Cold seeped through the cracks, causing the hairs on his arm to rise. He and several Palestinian laborers had been in this tunnel since daybreak. They had been forced to skip supper as their boss, Khalil, kept urging them on. And now, Omar felt excitement sear through his body. They *were* close.

Another foot or two, and the tunnel beneath the Israeli border would be complete. Government walls would no longer stop Palestinians from crossing the northern border at their convenience. Just a few days earlier, the wife of Omar's landlord died from internal bleeding because she had delivered a baby after curfew and couldn't be taken to the hospital for emergency treatment.

Omar gritted his teeth at the memory and swung the pick again and again with energized force. Although born Israeli and Jewish, he disagreed with some of the decisions made by the government to suppress his fellow Arabs. But the government was his paycheck. It had been an exhausting two weeks living in the small village, trying to talk and act like a native Palestinian. Omar felt an itch crawl along his upper lip, and he rubbed at his newly grown mustache. *That's one thing I won't miss about this undercover job.*

Or the digging.

The Israeli government wanted to monitor the tunnel for jihad leaders and weapon smugglers. The tunnel would not be destroyed, nor would Palestinians be prevented from using it. Omar's job was to gain the trust of the Palestinian villagers, volunteer for the workforce, and then install security cameras along the tunnel ceiling.

His pick pummeled against the rock, which collapsed into . . . black. Excited shouting erupted around him, followed by fierce shushing. He stared at the gap in the stone before him. The draft of cool air poured through as if it had finally found freedom, accompanied by a smell, dank and sour—almost putrid.

"Yalluh, yalluh!" Khalil shouted. *Hurry, hurry.*

The men swung their axes again, choking dust billowing around them. It was as if a dam had been broken—the rocky soil caved beneath their picks like goat cheese. Bits of earth pelted Omar, and dust stung his eyes. But he didn't mind. Caught up in the elation of his coworkers, he was the last one to relax his hold on the handle of his pickax. When the dirt and debris settled, he noticed the slumped shoulders of his friends and their open-mouth amazement. The muddled blackness of the gaping hole before them had dissipated into a soft glow.

But it wasn't moonlight.

They had broken into an underground cavern.

The flashlight beams bounced off a stone wall several meters away. Slowly the interior walls came into focus. They were covered in painted inscriptions, symbols, diagrams . . . Omar stared in disbelief, hardly breathing. In the center of the circular room sat a sarcophagus balanced on a pedestal.

"It's a tomb," he whispered.

Chapter Three

Southern Arabia
964 b.c.

TOMORROW MY FATHER WILL arrive with exotic gifts from the coast. Nicaula opened her eyes slowly, adjusting to the early morning glow filtering through the sheer linen of her platform bed. Thoughts of seeing her father, the king of Sheba, after many weeks of absence brought a smile. She listened to the muffled sounds about the palace. No doubt the servants were preparing for the arrival of their king.

The days had been quiet in the desert palace, broken only by the occasional passing caravan, contributing to the gifts of pearls, frankincense, tortoise shells, and gold that lined the walls of the treasury. In return, the princess had given the dust-covered Arabians fresh water and fodder for their camels and protection under her royal name. The travelers were content to gaze upon the splendor of statues surrounding the courtyard—statues that had been carved and carried from the limestone cliffs along the Gulf of Aden. Nicaula's favorite stone was a replica of the sun goddess, `Ashtartu, whom she hoped would bless her with many fertile years.

Rising up on an elbow, Nicaula rang the bell next to her bed. Seconds later, the female servant Azhara appeared, carrying a tray of fragrant oils. Her soft linen tunic swished about her legs as she approached the princess, eyes lowered, dark hair plaited and pulled away from her face. A single gold bracelet adorned her russet-skinned arm—a gift from the princess. Azhara bent on one knee and selected a vial of almond oil from the tray for approval.

The princess nodded. With swift strokes, the servant applied the balm to Nicaula's shoulders and arms.

Nicaula closed her eyes, allowing herself to relax with the massage. She hoped her father would bring the latest news of conquests and who flourished in commerce. He had always counseled his people to be generous to all nations and people, saying one never knew what enemy a new day would bring.

When Azhara finished, the princess thanked her and rose from her bed. Azhara helped Nicaula dress in a sheer under-shift and then started combing her hair, perfuming it with frankincense.

When satisfied with her appearance, Nicaula crossed to a wide basket she kept in her room. Unlashing the thin rope that held the lid in place, she lifted the lid. Inside the basket, a young cobra slept, and with the introduction of light, its eyes flashed open.

Nicaula began chanting in a low, lyrical voice words taught to her by her father.

We are from the Goddess
To Her we will gather

The snake swayed to the words, keeping rhythm with the chanting.

Like the grains of sand
Collecting on the dune

Just outside her sleeping quarters, the sound of running footsteps and shouting reached her. She paused, and the snake recoiled. She looked at Azhara, whose expression remained demure. Nicaula secured the lid before saying, "Go and see what's happening." She grabbed her outer robe as Azhara hurried to the far side of the chamber. Just as she opened the door, a group of servants burst through, each of them wearing traditional indigo turbans and white robes.

"Forgive us for intruding, O Highness," said a man with a scant mustache, bending low to the ground. "But the king has been ambushed."

Nicaula stared at the servant's bent figure, her mind reeling. Was her father all right? "How far away?"

"Not far—near the rocky hills past the first dune."

"We'll go to him immediately and take our vengeance on those who dare to waylay the king of Sheba," she said, trying to keep her voice steady. Azhara brought her headdress and fastened a woven silk rope about Nicaula's waist.

Nicaula looked at the assembled servants. "Prepare the horses, and alert the soldiers. We must leave this moment."

By the time the princess and her entourage reached the outer courtyard, several dozen soldiers were assembled, long daggers secured at their waists. They bowed their heads as she passed by them and walked to her favorite mare, a massive black horse, its muscles gleaming in the sunlight. The black horse pranced at the sight of its mistress. She stroked its face then, holding out a hand, she allowed the sentinel to help her onto the mare.

A small, stooped man approached. "I hope it is to your satisfaction, Your Majesty."

She nodded but remained silent, aware of the trembling in her breast that might betray her fear. She gazed across the desert toward the first rise of dunes. Then she turned to the rows of soldiers. "There's no more time to waste. Follow me." Without waiting for

Azhara or the others to mount, she leaned forward against the glossy
mare. "Aiyah!"

The horse jolted forward, breaking from the others, and Nicaula
tightened her grip as she blended with motion of the horse. The
hard-packed road leading out of the city seemed to melt beneath
the mare's hooves, and soon the princess's hair pulled free of her
headdress and streamed behind her as the hot wind tugged at her
clothing.

"Aiyah! Aiyah!" she called out. Her heart pounded in rhythm
with the powerful strides of her animal. Shouts echoed around her
as the others tried to keep pace. Any other day, she would have
enjoyed a race.

She expertly maneuvered the horse around the first dune just
above a dry wadi. The hot months had evaporated all signs of water
from the seasonal runoff, leaving a few scrub bushes in the water's
place. She urged the horse faster, her own chest heaving just as the
animal's sides struggled for breath. Then Nicaula saw the hills—low
and rocky. She lay against the horse, gripping its neck, her own
mouth dry with fear as foam sprayed from the mare's mouth.

They arrived at the base of the first hill, and the horse slowed,
fighting for sure footing among the jutting rocks. Then suddenly the
horse stopped.

"Move!" Nicaula shouted. She jabbed its ribs with her heels,
but the mare took a step backward. She stared at the sweaty beast
and its heaving sides; it had never failed her before. She climbed off
just as the soldiers and their horses reached her. Azhara was among
them; she dismounted and rushed to the princess.

But Nicaula held up her hand. Her mare's ears were back and its
nostrils flared. She turned to look up the slope. The horse refusing
to travel the hill could mean only one thing: it smelled destruction.
Nicaula pressed her lips together and gathered her robes, starting up

the incline. She moved as quickly as possible, followed by several soldiers, and picked her way along the rocky terrain. When she reached the pinnacle moments later and looked over the shallow valley, she nearly fell to her knees.

An array of lifeless limbs and dozens of twisted bodies stretched across the desert floor. The stench of death rose from the parched earth as if the sand were rejecting all that was foreign. No doubt the king's lifeless body lay among the dead. "Father," she whispered. Bile stuck in her throat as she scanned the body parts that lay desecrated across the desert floor and up the slope of the next dune.

Azhara joined her, crying out when she saw the bodies.

"Who would dare do this?" Nicaula moaned, holding her veil to her nose. Her heart twisted in disbelief and sorrow as she thought of her father journeying this way home.

She touched the necklace at her throat. "The ring of Sheba," she said, turning to Azhara. "Father has the ring that carries the Sheba symbol of the snake and lily, like my necklace. Search the fingers for it, and then we can truly know . . ."

Azhara took a brave step down the slope—toward the carnage. Within an instant, her knees buckled, and she sank against the rocky hillside.

Nicaula watched her maidservant violently retch. The other soldiers who'd followed Nicaula waited for her command, their faces ashen. She could never rest until she knew—*knew* her father had indeed perished. *Perhaps he escaped.* But the tremble of hope in her breast died almost as soon as it grew.

Carnage this great spared no one—not even royalty.

"Before the sun sets, I want each body searched for the ring of Sheba," she said. The men moved down the hill and methodically started inspecting the bodies.

Tomorrow the smell would be unbearable; this was her only chance to find out the truth. Touching Azhara's shoulder as she passed, Nicaula descended the slope and walked to the first fallen soldier. The young servant's head had been nearly severed, but his other limbs were intact. Without touching the corpse, she had full view of both his hands. No adornment could be seen. She walked on, stopping time and time again before each body.

The ambushed escort party contained at least one hundred members—respectable protection for any king. Most of the dead were servants in roughly woven tunics, and a few were courtiers—distinguished by their finely woven robes. Her father would not wear his identifying royal robes in case of a raid just like this one, but there had to be some evidence.

She passed a woman, whose face was thankfully covered with a mass of hair, when Nicaula felt the urge to pause. Something seemed peculiar about the maidservant. Nicaula stooped next to the body, and then she saw it. The woman's feet were much too big for any female. And her hands . . . one of them had been cut off. Nicaula rose and scanned the surrounding area, not seeing the missing hand anywhere. Why would the raiders take a severed hand? Unless . . .

A jolt passed through her heart. It seemed impossible, yet if the king had really tried to conceal his identity . . . With a shaky breath, she bent over the body and lifted the tresses from the dead woman's face. The heavy brows and prominent nose confirmed her intuition. Here lay her father, disguised as a woman. Kneeling next to him, Nicaula pushed back the heavy wig, revealing his tight, dark curls.

Her tears came fast, splashing onto his peaceful face. "They took your hand," Nicaula whispered. "They took the ring—our symbol of royalty." She moved her fingers to her father's face and touched his claylike cheeks. "I'll find the ring, and it will never leave my finger. Then I will make them pay."

The soldiers quietly gathered around their new queen as Nicaula bent close and kissed her father's forehead. "Good-bye, my father, until we meet in the afterlife."

Nicaula rose, her gaze settling on the assembled soldiers. She was now the queen of Sheba. As she spread her arms wide, the scarlet robe fell away from her forearms, revealing bracelets of gold. "Here the king of Sheba lies in death's repose. Here we begin our journey of vengeance."

Chapter Four

Northern Jerusalem

OMAR'S HEART POUNDED AS he lay on a seedy mattress in the bunk room. The other Palestinian laborers had fallen asleep over an hour ago, but he couldn't relax.

He peeled off his undershirt then climbed off the bed and dropped to the floor. Fifty push-ups should do it. *One, two, three* . . . His job had come to an end even though the tunnel was not complete. Most likely it never would be. *Fourteen, fifteen* . . . Like the Israelis, the Palestinians respected the deceased with great reverence. The project would be halted and the tunnel excavation discontinued because of the unexpected detour in discovering a burial site.

Twenty-two, twenty-three . . . On his night rotations at guard duty, Omar had been able to slip into the tunnel and install six security cameras along the crevassed ceiling. But now his mission had been foiled.

When he filed his report, the Israeli government would learn of the discovery. *Thirty-four, thirty-five* . . . How long before the rest of the world found out? Teams of archaeologists would start crawling

all over the area—and Omar would be reassigned. *Forty-nine, fifty.*
Breathing hard, Omar still didn't feel relaxed. He reached for
his backpack tucked beneath his mattress and removed the false
bottom, locating his satellite phone.

It would take only a minute to transmit the details to
headquarters. Then the news would spread. The media frenzy would
be insane. Omar sat on the bed and typed his message as he leaned
back on his pillow, waiting for the instrument to transfer the data.

*Job progress impeded. Ancient burial site discovered. Will
attract national interest. What are my next instructions?*

One minute passed, then two. He imagined the frantic
discussion taking place at headquarters between his boss, David
Levy, and his superiors. After a full ten minutes, the phone vibrated,
and a reply appeared on the miniature screen.

*Remove the security cameras, and report to your post.
Transportation will be waiting.*

He dressed in dusty jeans, a light green button-down shirt,
and work boots. Then he shoved his meager belongings into his
backpack—a change of clothing, a phone, a flashlight, a water
bottle, and a couple of protein bars. Omar glanced about the room as
he skirted the beds filled with slumbering men. He'd miss their good
humor, lively conversation, and their eyes—filled with generations
of sadness. But it was better this way. He didn't want to see their
betrayed expressions when, or if, they ever discovered his true
identity.

It had been a pleasure living among them, and several times
he'd felt their pain as if it were his own. Decade after decade, bad
seeds had been sown, and now those seeds uncontrollably sprouted
hate throughout the community. Foolish moves by the government,
such as a bombing raid that killed innocent civilians, only multiplied
and justified the hatred. *Learned hatred that could easily be directed*

toward me if they knew my real identity.

Once outside, he made his way through the quiet village and stood on the outskirts of town where the heavy brush concealed the tunnel opening. From his position he saw the night guard crouched on the ground and a trail of smoke coming from a cigarette.

In less than an hour, the second shift would begin, and another guard would come. Omar had to remove the cameras, be out of the tunnel, and then safely on his way to headquarters before then. He strode toward the guard and raised his hand in greeting. "Khalil sent me."

The Palestinian squinted upward, his eyebrows together. "Why?"

"Giving you a break, I suppose."

The man released a lazy trail of smoke between his lips then twisted the glowing stub into the dirt. He stood and let out a huge yawn.

Omar chuckled and slapped the man's back. "Sleep well."

The Palestinian grinned and walked away, whistling into the night.

When the guard disappeared into the village streets, Omar moved to a group of ragged palms. Three paces south of the first one, he knelt in the cool sand and began to dig. Moments later he removed a waterproof pouch containing miniature security cameras and installation tools.

He slipped the pouch into his backpack and hurried to the tunnel entrance with a quick glance behind. Everything looked quiet. Hoping Khalil wouldn't discover the guard change until Omar was long gone, he edged his way around the spiky branches at the tunnel entrance and flipped on his flashlight. As he walked along the narrow passage, he remembered his friends' voices reverberating off the stone walls. Laughter, song, and whispered conversations all seemed to haunt the place.

Omar stopped about ten paces in and shone the beam on the low ceiling. Nestled into a shadowed crevice was the first camera. He clenched the flashlight between his teeth and used the Phillips from his pouch, knowing he'd likely scratch the camera, but time was of the essence.

He wriggled the Phillips between the stone and the cement anchor that secured the camera. When the cement didn't give, Omar searched around for a rock to use as a hammer. Then he started the process again—separating the anchor from the ceiling—trying to apply just enough pressure so the camera would be released, but not so much that the stability of the carved ceiling was compromised.

His arms ached as blood drained from his fingers. He kept his eyes closed to a slit while dry earth rained on his head. "Come on," he urged as frustration began to choke him. Bit by bit, he chipped the cement away until the camera was released from its bondage.

"Finally," he muttered, hoping the next five proved easier. Gripping the flashlight again, he aimed it in front of him and walked along the tunnel, searching for the second. The damp air crept through his cotton shirt, cooling the warm perspiration on his chest. The tunnel narrowed to one meter in width, the height remaining just centimeters below Omar's height.

He spotted the second camera, removed the rock from his pocket, and started chipping. The camera worked free.

Omar wiped his face with his shirttail and moved on. The dank air grew thicker as he continued through the tunnel. Number three. He took a gulp from his bottled water and began the chiseling. The Phillips slipped and clattered to the floor. Omar cursed and bent to retrieve it. Then he noticed the dampness of the ground. He placed his hand over the moist earth, heart hammering. Possibilities floated through his mind. Perhaps they were near an ancient well. It made sense.

A tomb, a well, a buried civilization.

Omar straightened and continued the pounding. The camera released its hold unexpectedly and shot against the tunnel wall. "So much for recycling that one."

He checked his watch, seeing he'd already used up thirty minutes. Omar scooped up the camera and hurried along, knowing the fourth one was just around the next protruding boulder. His boots splashed in water as the damp earth turned into a trickling bed.

He was no geologist, but water running through a tunnel didn't seem like a good thing—especially in a tunnel with only one entrance.

By the time he'd reached the sixth and last camera, the water had soaked his boots. Omar steadied the flashlight in his mouth and balanced the Phillips against the anchor. With each strike, the pounding echoed back at him.

He paused, disconcerted by the sharp echo, and then remembered.

The tomb.

The hammering was reverberating off the tomb's walls.

Another strike, and the camera released. He turned in the direction of the tomb and shone his light through the eerie darkness. Omar hesitated; the hairs on his arms rose. If he hurried back, he'd have about five minutes to spare before the new guard arrived—just enough time to sprint out of sight and be well on his way to the border station.

Five minutes.

A tomb that had seen no life for centuries, perhaps millennia.

Five minutes.

Omar plunged toward the tomb opening. The rocks shifted

below his feet as he climbed through the gaping hole. He removed his boots before stepping onto the venerated ground. Placing a foot onto the cold earth, a shudder passed through his body as if he had been welcomed and forbidden to enter in the same instant.

He walked toward the center of the room and stopped before the stone sarcophagus. No doubt royal remains lay beneath the formidable lid, and for a moment, he wondered which king or queen it might be. "Who are you?" he whispered into the inky black.

The musty air gave no answer. He placed a hand on the pocked surface of the encasing, trying to remember any snippets of the archaeology journals he had read. He had no way of knowing if this tomb were five hundred years old or three thousand. Omar arced the flashlight beam along the walls. As he stepped around the sarcophagus, his foot kicked at a piece of wood, then another.

Looking down, Omar saw that the pieces he'd been walking on were not wooden. He stooped and turned over a yellowish fragment. *A bone.* Too big for an animal. *Human femur.* But why was it not in the sarcophagus? Had the tomb been raided? He swept the light across the littered ground. Dozens of bones lay strewn about.

Mind reeling, he sidestepped his way to the nearest wall and stared at the paleo-Hebrew writing upon the walls. If he could claim knowledge of one thing, it was languages. Born in Canada to a Jewish mother and a Moroccan father, Omar knew Hebrew, Arabic, and English from his youth. Once in college, he'd mastered several more languages, including Greek and Latin.

Omar walked slowly along the perimeter, trying to make out the meaning of the crude drawings that also decorated the walls. They were similar to those he'd seen in a documentary on King Tutankhamen, but different too. The figures were rounder, and their clothing consisted of long tunics. Some of the heads were tilted forward. Schooled in biblical Hebrew as any boy with a Jewish mother was expected to be, he scanned the drawings for anything familiar.

Moving his light upward, he searched for any familiar names, perhaps Solomon or his father, David. The paleo-Hebrew script predated Hebrew, and the letters were difficult to decipher quickly. His beam stilled. "Who's Melech Turug?" *King Turug.*

Below Turug's name was another. *Melech Amariel.* Omar moved the light across the wall. *Melech Tambariah.*

Who were these three kings? Pulling out his phone, he snapped several pictures, panning through the room. He hesitated as he saw an ornate inscription through the photo screen. Raising his flashlight, he peered at the unusual assembly of seven palm trees. The center palm was different from the others: instead of having a slender trunk, it looked like a snake intertwined with a flower. Something was familiar about the strange symbol. He zoomed on the center tree and took a picture. Then he checked his watch. Four minutes had passed. He took one more glance about the chamber, wondering what secrets had been preserved for so many centuries— or had it been millennia?

Jamming his feet into the boots, Omar hoisted the backpack over his shoulder. Adrenaline in overdrive, he ran through the tunnel, boots splashing in the water. His breathing was labored by the time he reached the entrance.

Omar knelt in the dirt and crawled upward, pushing silently through the dried foliage. *Please be late.* His stomach dropped when he saw a man pacing several meters away. The man turned, and in the waning moonlight, Omar recognized Khalil. No doubt the boss had been surprised to find the other guard absent. Or had the guard already told the boss that Omar had taken over? If Khalil suspected Omar was in the tunnel, why didn't he follow?

His questions were answered almost immediately. Two jeeps

with blazing headlights roared around the corner of the nearest
building.

Khalil had been waiting for backup.

Omar reached into his pack and pulled out a smoke bomb.
He removed the pin and chucked the metal ball into the air.
Khalil turned with surprise and shouted, which was soon replaced
by coughing and sputtering. Pushing back his remorse, Omar
scrambled to his feet and plunged through the billowing gas.
He knew Khalil would be fine, but he had been instructed to do
whatever it took to maintain his cover, no matter the damage.

Omar sprinted across the cracked earth toward the border
station. In order to prevent being shot by Israeli patrol, Omar dialed
the station's number from his phone.

"Shalom?"

"It's Matan, number six-one-four. I'm coming in." Omar
covered the last several hundred meters. The guard stepped from the
station and unlocked the metal gate, where a sedan waited. Omar
hopped in, barely noticing the driver, and leaned against the cool
leather. *It's finally over.*

The dark landscape sped past as the car plunged ahead. Omar
had just started to catch his breath when his phone buzzed. "I'm
finished for good this time," he announced into the device.

"Like hell you are." The voice on the other end was cold.

The last thing Omar cared about was impressing his boss,
especially since Omar was quitting. "These people deserve better.
They're treated like small children. Pretty soon they'll have to get
permission to piss."

"Save it for someone who cares, *Matan*. When will you be
here?"

Omar released a breath of air and glanced out the window. "Ten
minutes."

"I'll be waiting in my office."

The phone glowed: *Call Ended.*

Omar squeezed his hands into fists. It would take all his willpower *not* to punch David Levy out.

Chapter Five

Cairo, Egypt

CAIRO. SO THIS IS the place where legends are made, Jade thought as she stepped into Terminal 1. Free at last from hours of cramped travel, she inhaled the furnace-hot air. Seconds later, cigarette smoke assailed her eyes, and she blinked against the stinging. She pulled up one end of the silk scarf from around her neck to cough into it. What had seemed fashionable in the States was obviously out of place here—the Egyptians wore scarves around their heads, not their necks. And from the stares she received from the men, she realized her blonde highlights and pale green eyes were also incongruous with her surroundings.

Following the other passengers, Jade halted in front of passport control, where she unzipped her backpack and handed over her passport. The female official in a neatly pressed uniform looked closely at Jade's picture, then back to Jade. The woman turned the page, stamped the passport, and said in a heavy accent, "First time?"

"Yes."

The official returned the passport. Jade thanked her and broke into a half-jog to keep up with the passengers streaming toward baggage claim. Everyone seemed to be in a frantic hurry. A German woman on the plane had advised Jade to exchange money *after* going through customs, but a few passengers stopped to exchange currency at the banks. Jade more clearly understood the haste when she entered the claim area and saw that long lines had already formed for the distant customs counters. As soon as she jockeyed into the baggage arena, she scanned the conveyor belt for her floral-printed suitcase.

If it hadn't been for the death of her beloved professor, Dr. Lyon, she wouldn't have come alone. For a moment, she wondered if she'd made the right choice in following through with this trip. Instead of going home to face her mother—the trivial lunches at the club, tennis matches with the guys, and endless summer parties— she had chosen a summer internship in Cairo to research her thesis on the queen of Sheba. Jade had a lot of work ahead of her since the evidence was thin on the queen being the daughter of an Egyptian pharaoh. Yemen and Ethiopia believed she lived and reigned in *their* countries.

At twenty-four, Jade had completed her first year in the master's program at Brown University and was well on her way to the associate teaching career she hoped to land upon graduation. Her thesis was due in December, so this trip came at a perfect time to meet her deadline. She came from "good stock," according to her father, yet the disappointment in his eyes was evident when she hadn't shown interest in the fields of medicine or law. This was her chance to prove to her parents that she could be successful on her own accord. History was her true passion, and when Dr. Lyon selected her to serve as his intern, she had said yes without hesitation.

But that was before he was found dead in his office. And now, she would meet a colleague of his to fulfill the internship. In her professor's honor, Jade would aid in Dr. Lyon's quest to find the remains of the queen of Sheba and reveal her fabled wealth.

As Jade waited for her luggage, she punched a few notes into her phone: the heat, the smell, the different hues of skin surrounding her—all a product of history, a history that might have once been shared by the queen of Sheba. Then Jade texted her parents that she'd landed safely. She spotted her luggage. The newly dented floral suitcase stood out in the company of the plain, dark suitcases and taped boxes surrounding it. She pocketed her cell and slid between two veiled women to snatch her suitcase. Once in line for the customs desk, Jade allowed herself to look around. She had read about the airport's recent renovation, and to say the least, it was an impressive building.

Massive windows separated the cool interior from the suffocating heat outside. The pilot had announced Cairo temperature just before landing—45° C. Jade mentally calculated the conversion in her head: 113° F. *Climbing or dropping?* Lounges with luxurious armchairs and elegant couches dotted the polished floor. Cafés emitting enticing aromas lined the corridor, the chairs occupied mostly by men. The ceiling reached two stories high, letting in the orange blush of the setting sun.

A few paces in front of her, a woman began arguing in German with an official, and most of the surrounding crowd quieted. "Was tun Sie? Es gibt nicht dar." *What are you doing? There's nothing there.*

Jade craned her neck until she could see what was happening. It was the woman who had been seated across the aisle from her on the flight. The German lady's suitcase lay open, clothing and underwear strewn upon the long metal table. The woman's husband tried to shush her, but she refused to comply. "Ich habe nicht die Zeit." *I don't have time for this.*

Two female security personnel grabbed the woman and forced her into a curtained enclosure behind the customs desk. "Verschieben Sie Ihre Hände weg von mir!" *Move your hands away from me!* By the continued loud protests, Jade knew the woman was being strip-searched. "Bitte! Nein!" *Please! No!*

Jade clutched her backpack against her chest as if she could somehow protect herself from such an invasion.

Pulse pounding, she tried to breathe normally. As the line inched forward, she silently repeated the vague Arabic expressions she'd recited on the plane. "Ahlan was Sahlan." *Welcome.* Perhaps speaking the language would appease the customs officials. She looked at the mood ring on her right hand. *Gray.* She was definitely nervous. *Ahlan was Sahlan*, she repeated in her head as she gripped her backpack tighter.

"American?"

Jade snapped her head up and looked into the two very black eyes of a security guard. "Yes, I'm American."

A slight smile twitched the security guard's mustache. "Your passport, please?"

His English is quite good. She sifted through her backpack for a moment before realizing she'd put her passport in her front pocket. The same German woman who was now being thoroughly searched had advised her to keep it as close as possible. At least the woman's protests had stopped. Jade handed over the document and watched as the official spent a moment leafing through the mostly blank pages. Then he gave it back.

"Thank you." He waved her through.

Relieved, she hoisted the backpack onto her sweaty shoulder and lifted her suitcase. Exiting customs, she scanned for the nearest exchange counter. She pulled out one hundred dollars in traveler's checks to exchange for about seven hundred Egyptian pounds. Once she had changed her money, she moved through the exterior doors, where the cigarette smoke was replaced by dust—and a hot breeze. Jade hesitated for a moment, barraged by the temperature change, when a young boy pressed against her arm.

Flies danced around his face as his eager eyes looked into hers. "One dollah?"

Instinctively Jade reached into her backpack, but then immediately regretted her actions as half a dozen kids swarmed her, each one more earnest than the next.

"Yalluh! Yalluh!" one wiry boy shouted.

Confused, Jade looked around. *Yalluh* meant "hurry" and was one of the few Arabic words she understood.

She held up her hand. "Stenna." *Wait.* She fished out some quarters and handed them to the children. Just as quickly as the children had gathered, they were gone. Jade pivoted and saw two policemen rushing toward her then passing to follow the children.

Jade scanned the taxis that lined the curb. Several drivers raised their arms and waved, calling to her, all of them with a cigarette hanging out of their mouths. She tried not to smile at their open shirts, revealing dark chest hair and thick, gold chains. *The '70s never left this city.* Honking came from all directions, as well as rapid shouting in Arabic. Jade was just about to select a taxi when a man stepped in front of her.

"Ms. Holmes?"

The faint odor of spicy aftershave reached her nose. She looked up, startled to see amber eyes in a city of dark. The man's face was deeply tanned and narrow, but rugged-looking—*the kind of face described in romance novels.* His sandy hair was slightly shaggy, and a couple of days' growth stood out on his cheeks and chin. For an instant she was reminded of a lion until the man offered a half smile. His teeth were even and white, nothing like the fangs of a wild African beast. "Mademoiselle Holmes?"

How perfect. He spoke with a French accent. *Another romance novel cliché.* Then she realized he was waiting for her answer. "Yes, I am . . . she . . ."

"It's all a little overwhelming at first, isn't it?"

"And you are?"

"Dr. Lucas Morel, Egyptologist and devoted follower of the late Dr. Lyon. It looks like we'll be spending the summer working together." An almost imperceptible lift of his eyebrow told Jade he was sizing her up.

So this was the scholar Dr. Lyon had told her so much about. She wondered how old he was and decided he was in his late thirties. She glanced away, feeling uncomfortable with his open stare.

"Come on," Lucas said. "I'm parked over here." He lifted her suitcase and walked away from the taxis.

Devoted follower? What an odd thing to say—as if Dr. Lyon were the leader of some cult. She decided she was at least intelligent enough to match up with this shaggy guy in severely pressed khakis. Any intimidation she'd felt earlier about meeting a renowned Egyptologist was gone. She just wished he didn't have to be so good-looking. He probably had a gorgeous wife and three kids in a villa along the Mediterranean coast.

She followed him until he stopped next to a silver Mercedes— older model—and popped the trunk. Jade hesitated for a moment, noticing that the front wheels were perched on the edge of the curb—a green curb. About a foot from the passenger door was a bus sign. *Illegal parking.* She caught Lucas looking at her with an amused expression.

A blaring horn made her flinch.

Lucas chuckled. "Jump in, or we'll get run over."

Jade eased through the passenger door and sat, glancing behind her. The driver of the bus was shouting. She looked over at Lucas as he maneuvered his way into the traffic. "Aren't you afraid of getting a ticket?"

"The police don't care. In fact, look behind you."

The bus horn continued to blare as Jade turned. Sure enough, another midsized car had slid into the space Lucas had just vacated. The driver jumped out and shook a fist at the bus, receiving a honk in return.

Jade leaned against her seat. "Wow."

"You'll get used to it."

She nodded, swallowing against her dry throat. Lucas seemed to drive effortlessly through the heavy, noisy traffic.

Lucas suddenly swerved the car to avoid a motorbike, sending her careening against him. "Sorry," he muttered.

She straightened in her seat. Then she gazed out the window at the brown-high rises, the littered sidewalks, and the barefooted children running from car to car, trinkets dangling from their hands.

"If you acknowledge just one of them, our car will be mobbed," he said. Traffic thinned just enough that Lucas found an opening and moved onto a side street, again causing her to bump into him. His hand touched her arm, supporting her, for an instant longer than necessary. A juvenile thrill entered her skin. *Here I am, in the middle of Cairo, sitting next to an extremely handsome French man.* She tried to ignore the warmth his touch had brought. After all, it was over one hundred degrees outside. *That explains it.* She glanced at his hands, looking for a wedding ring, but saw nothing. *Well, he probably has a woman in every city from here to Paris.* She wanted to laugh at herself. Really, she wanted to ask Lucas a thousand questions, but most of all, she wanted a shower.

The car slowed, and Jade peered out the window. "This is it?"

They were passing a courtyard festooned with palms, where beyond the fountain and gargoyles rose a monument, topped by a bust standing guard in front of a stone building. "It looks ancient." She rolled down her window, letting the hot air strike her face.

"If you consider 1910 ancient."

Jade glanced at him, very aware of their close proximity in the small Mercedes. She wondered if he always kept his window down while the air conditioning was blasting. "1910? I thought it was founded by Marcus Simaika in 1914."

"*Morcos Smeika Pasha* founded the Coptic Museum in 1910. Tomorrow you can read all about it on his monument."

"Tomorrow? Why not this afternoon?"

"We have early dinner reservations."

She was just about to reach for her phone to check the itinerary outlined by Dr. Lyon when the car lurched forward. Lucas maneuvered into the unforgiving traffic as several horns blared. Sticking his head out of the window, he shouted something in Arabic.

In front of them a car had come to an abrupt halt, nearly plowing into another. Lucas slammed on the brakes. Behind them, tires screeched, and the sage scent of burnt rubber filled the air.

"What happened?" she asked, her breath coming in gasps.

"The light turned red, and someone decided to stop," Lucas said through gritted teeth.

Jade glanced at his profile. His eyes were focused straight ahead, unblinking. "Is there a problem with that?"

He released his grip on the steering wheel. "It's just unusual in this part of town. Typically it takes a police officer to halt the traffic. So if someone suddenly decides to stop for a red light, well . . . you see what happens."

Looking behind, Jade saw angry drivers climbing out of their vehicles, several of them shouting. Lucas pounded his palm against the steering wheel. They waited in the nearly suffocating heat, and she absentmindedly twisted her mood ring, noticing it had changed to pale amber. *Anxious.* "Maybe we could just go back to the museum until the traffic clears."

"No, I've got a better idea." He threw the gearshift into reverse then turned and placed a hand behind her seat. "Hang on." With his other hand on the steering wheel, he gunned the engine, sliding neatly between two cars. Amid more honking and Arabic expletives, Lucas deftly wove his way into the oncoming traffic.

"What are you doing?" Jade gripped the sides of her seat, thankful for her seat belt as her nails dug into the soft leather.

Lucas ignored her above the roar of the Mercedes and the frantic beeping of angry motorists. Jade's body jerked to the right then the left. She squeezed her eyes shut and suddenly . . . it was quiet.

"Here we are," Lucas said. He opened his door and unfolded his long frame.

They had parked in a dark alleyway. Large cardboard boxes lined the dirt-covered walls. With trembling hands, Jade unlatched her seat belt and reached for the door handle.

"One dollah," a voice said outside her window. A young man opened her door. His white shirt and tan pants hung on his body, at least two sizes too big. If nothing else, his thinness was apparent in his gaunt face. Climbing out, Jade turned, searching for Lucas.

"This way," Lucas called from several paces away. "Ignore the boy. I already paid him to watch the car."

Jade flashed a halfhearted smile at the young man's eager face. Then she moved past him. Trying not to wrinkle her nose in disgust at the alley's rancid stench, Jade reached Lucas's side. "Where *are* we?"

"Quiet," he whispered. He gripped her arm in the near darkness and walked briskly down the center of the alley. Then he leaned close, his breath hot on her ear. "There are plenty of beggars living in these alley houses. We don't want them all to come out at once."

Jade stole a glance along the walls of the alley. *Houses?* They were *boxes*. "Why—"

"Shhh!" Lucas hissed, steering her toward a short flight of stairs that ascended above the street. At the top was a small courtyard, and at the far end was a door framed with a thin line of light. He knocked, and within seconds, the door opened. He pulled Jade along with him into the glittering interior.

Delicate lamps with dangling beads were scattered throughout the room. Brocade cushions served as chairs at low tables, and heavy tapestries hung on the walls. Blue smoke hung thick in the air and was unlike any Jade had ever smelled. It was sweet, almost intoxicating.

"Frankincense," Lucas said.

Jade nodded, looking about the room. The men and women sat huddled together on the cushions, eating with their hands from large platters filled with steaming rice and meat.

A squat man approached, wearing a neatly pressed white chef's uniform, arms nearly as large as his torso. "Ah, Monsieur Morel, we are delighted you could join us this evening. Will it be just the two of you?"

"Yes," Lucas said, slapping the man on the shoulder. "And we're hungry."

A deep chuckle bubbled from their bearded host, and they followed him to an alcove where cushions had been propped around a miniature table. "Satisfactory?"

"Very." Lucas pressed several pound notes into the man's hand and then turned to Jade. "After you."

She sank into the cushions, feeling the tenseness from the traffic congestion and near accident begin to diminish. She realized she was famished. "I could eat a goat—"

"Be careful what you say."

"Why? Because they serve goat?"

"No." His eyes scanned the room.

"What are you looking for? You're acting like we're on some sort of a spy mission."

He rotated his tan face until his eyes locked with hers. At this close distance, there was no doubt that part of his irises were gold. *Simply smoldering.* Jade shifted against the cushions with increasing uncertainty. Lucas looked like a tiger—ready to pounce. *I've got to kick the romance novel habit.*

Two steaming platters of barley and meat were delivered, along with a pot of dark tea. Jade looked at the food and let the spicy scent engulf her. As Lucas started to pour a cup of the tea, she said, "Water's fine."

He shook his head. "Don't try the water. Soda's much safer."

"All right," Jade said, looking around. "What do they have?"

When Lucas didn't answer, she turned her focus back to him. His eyes were lit with amusement. "I believe you call it Coke."

Why is he looking at me like that? Doesn't he ever drink soda? "Perfect."

He signaled the waiter, and within seconds, a chilled bottle was set before her, opened, with a straw. After the waiter left, Lucas leaned toward her, ignoring his food. "We're the ones being spied on," he said, his voice barely audible.

Jade suppressed a smile. "Who would want to spy on a research assistant and an Egyptologist?"

"The same people who murdered Dr. Lyon."

Murdered? She gaped at him. "What do you mean?"

"They knew he was close to discovering Queen Nicaula's burial place, and they killed him for it."

Jade stared at him across the table. She knew Nicaula was another name for the queen of Sheba. The cushions beneath her felt stiff and hostile, the frankincense stifling instead of inviting. Instinct told her that no one could possibly be capable of harming a man such as Dr. Lyon. Yes, different nations claimed Nicaula as their queen, but the monarch had been dead for thousands of years. "How could the location of her burial place matter so much? All the artifacts will belong to the country in which it's found."

His gaze locked with hers. Lucas said, "It matters to three nations. The Yemenis profess Bilqis was their queen, ruling over the region of Sa'ba. The Ethiopians claim her as their Makeda and say that her son was a product of her union with King Solomon. And of course there's the thesis you're working on—that the queen was the daughter of an Egyptian pharaoh." He dug into his food.

Jade followed suit. After a few minutes of thinking about what Lucas had told her, she said, "Even though three peoples claim her as their queen, it's not as if the course of history would change if one country were proved wrong."

Lucas leaned forward, the soft light throwing irregular shadows on his near-perfect features. "A common misconception. Dr. Lyon had been studying an ancient site on satellite photographs of Oman—a site some scholars refer to as Ubar, hundreds of miles west of Yemen. In recent conversations, he claimed to have spotted evidence of the legendary city. In addition, he also made an astonishing observation: Ubar was the birthplace of the queen of Sheba. Ancient cultures buried their dead in the land of the deceased's birth."

Ubar was just a legend—a city spoken about only in fables by the likes of Marco Polo, Jade thought with irony. "That's impossible. The news would be around the world if Dr. Lyon discovered Ubar and purported the queen of Sheba was buried there." She paused, seeing the conviction on his face. "In all my classes with the professor, he never mentioned this. Impossible." She wriggled against the cushion, feeling exceptionally hot all of a sudden.

"Not at all," Lucas said with a self-satisfied smirk. "According to Lyon, evidence—now suppressed—has been found in a tomb in Jerusalem that the queen never knew Solomon, let alone conceived his heir. That rules out the Ethiopians, and possibly the Egyptians. So the Yemenis are the top contenders. And with Dr. Lyon's theory, the country of Oman just burst into the arena."

At this, Jade stopped eating, losing awareness of the restaurant around her. Her mind reeled at the importance of what Lucas said, but she couldn't grasp the significance until he spoke again.

"You know there's no archaeological evidence that King Solomon or King David ever existed." He lowered his voice. "Finding her tomb will prove once and for all that the key stories in the Bible are true. The Jews' claim to Israel will be solidified."

She stared at him, her chest tight. Now *this* was something someone might kill for.

"But that's not all," he said. "Something else was found in that tomb—something that will lead us to the queen."

"What?"

"That's what we need to find out."

Chapter Six

Israeli Intelligence Headquarters—Northern Command

"WELCOME HOME."

Omar stared at his hands, avoiding his boss's penetrating stare. He hated the man's pointed face, close-set eyes, and groomed mustache. *A weasel.* Omar sat in a hard, plastic chair on the other side of the desk while David Levy enjoyed the comfort of a new leather version.

"Talked to your girlfriend lately?"

Omar jumped out of his chair, anger pulsing through him.

"Relax. I'm only kidding." David raised a hand, half in defense and half in what might be an apology, but the smirk didn't leave his face. As Omar sat down again, David said, "I could take that personally, you know, and write you up."

"I'm already on 'plan.'"

David chuckled. "I know. I know. Just trying to prevent a scrimmage, although it might be interesting to see who wins. Not enough room in this office anyhow."

David very well knew that this office was better than the cube Omar was assigned to. He should have been promoted from his humble assignment as Special Agent for the Preservation of Cultural Heritage and Ancient Artifacts, but instead the intelligence department brought in this hotshot six months ago. And Levy's first assignment? To flirt with Omar's girlfriend—well, *ex* now—and just like clockwork, within a couple of months, she'd broken things off with him.

Omar couldn't get Mia to tell him if it was because of David, partly because she wasn't speaking to him, but he still had his suspicions. Omar folded his arms, wishing he could find anything . . . *anything* that would prove David stole her. Then he'd beat the man till he couldn't—

"Your new orders arrived," David said.

"In the last *five* minutes?"

"Yep. Quite amazing how fast we work, isn't it?" David kept his gaze level, challenging.

"Too late. I'm putting in my two weeks' notice."

David sat unmoved. "Don't you even want to know where? Or with *whom*?"

"Nope." Omar stood and extended his hand. When Levy didn't respond, Omar dropped the invitation. "Well, it was nice, uh, working for you, and I'll just clean out my desk."

"Nice try," David said, but the tips of his ears reddened.

Omar hid a smile. *That got to him.* He walked out the door, hearing David's voice sail after him. "We're sending you to Yemen. Flight leaves in twenty-five minutes."

Stopping midstride, Omar hesitated. *Yemen.* That's where *she* was. With a groan he turned and walked back to David's office. He stood in the doorway and faced the idiot.

David stood, chuckling as he smoothed his weasel mustache. "Thought that might change your mind. Before you get too excited, though, you're on a separate mission from Mia. If you can find a way to contact her, maybe you can meet for . . . coffee . . . although I'm sure you'll try to get a lot more out of her than that."

Deep breaths, Omar commanded himself. "My two weeks still stands."

"All right," David said, waving him off. "Two weeks, and you'll never have to listen to me again. You'll get the orders on the plane." His gaze hardened. "Just don't screw this one up."

Omar left before he did something that might land him in the slammer. His fingers itched to snake around the man's neck until the absence of air erased all glimmer of life.

Chapter Seven

Cairo

IN HER RENTED APARTMENT in the Cairo suburb of Maadi, a strand of hair tickled Jade's neck each time the fan rotated in her direction. Between the odd splay of honking coming from outside and thinking about Lucas's conversation the night before, she wondered if she'd slept more than an hour.

A wailing sound came from outside, and Jade rolled over in bed, listening to the haunting melody. *The call to prayer.* The Muslim world had awakened and begun its holy ritual. She had not paid much attention the night before to the towering mosque near her stacked apartment building.

She glanced at the digital clock next to her bed. *5:30.* Stifling a yawn, she shuffled across the floor and dug through her suitcase for a sports bra. Even though she'd be exhausted by the afternoon if she went running on so little sleep, she couldn't just sit in her room for two hours until Lucas came to pick her up at "seven thirty sharp."

Changing in the morning light that cut gently through the shadowy room, Jade donned her Lycra pants and running shoes and then grabbed a sweatshirt just in case the outside air held a chill. Her cell phone beeped. She sat on the bed and checked the message—a text from her mother. *Glad you got in safe. Call me, dear.* Instead of calling, she sent a text. If she picked up her phone, the conversation, or more accurately, the interrogation, might go for a while. She left the room and found the halls empty, except for the dust swept into the corners. Jade volleyed down the stairs, using them as her warm-up.

Once on the sidewalk, she settled into an easy jog. The air was cool and dry, with a taste of dust, holding the promise of a scorching day. Past the row of apartment buildings and a run-down outside theater, she noticed a few shops with lights on as the owners prepared for opening. Large posters in their windows advertised cola products, written in both English and Arabic. Lucas had mentioned that drinking soda was typically safer than drinking the water.

Lucas. She could almost picture the intensity of his eyes and hear his urgent whispers from the night before. She'd made notes on her phone about most of their conversation as soon as she had returned to her room.

They knew he was close to discovering Queen Nicaula's burial place, and they killed him for it. Lucas's words resounded in her head as she increased her pace to a regular jog.

Her research for her thesis had revealed numerous articles written by archaeologists about the possible locations of Ubar, but none had linked it to the queen of Sheba. The queen was happily settled in Marib, the heart of Yemen—according to the Yemeni people. Jade had also done some reading on the case the Ethiopians made for the queen to be their own, yet she'd never paid close attention to those history details. Maybe now she should.

Jade's breath came harder as Lucas's words repeated themselves in her head. *Something else was found in that tomb—something that will lead us to the queen.* The idea was very unsettling, to say the least.

She wriggled her sweatshirt off and tied it around her waist. She turned the corner, running full face toward the rising sun. As she squinted against the glare, Lucas's words spun as Dr. Lyon's rheumy blue eyes leapt into her memory. Two weeks before, she'd volunteered for the summer internship. So much had changed since then.

Perspiration dripped into her eyes, and Jade lifted a sweatshirt sleeve to wipe it off. She checked her phone. *6:10.*

Her breath growing short, she reversed her direction, wondering about the itinerary Dr. Lyon had given her. Various visits to archive centers, a meeting with the Coptic patriarch—now living in exile because of a recent assassination attempt—scheduled field trips to Alexandria and the Red Sea coast . . . all to document the Egyptians' belief that the queen of Sheba was the daughter of an Egyptian pharaoh. Then she remembered something—a comment Dr. Lyon had made when he handed her the packet. "We'll update the itinerary when we arrive in Cairo."

Until now, Jade had assumed some of the scheduling might change, depending on the availability of those they were to meet. Now she sensed this research trip was something altogether different, but what? Was Dr. Lyon leading her on a mission far beyond simple research for a college thesis?

She ran past a row of Dumpsters and tried not to inhale too deeply. When she cleared the last one, someone grabbed her arm. A rush of panic drove through her as she tugged away. She twisted from the firm grip as a dozen instantaneous thoughts flashed fear, but before she could cry out, a voice spoke in her ear. "It's me."

Jade spun around and nearly collided with Lucas. She covered her hammering chest. "Lucas?"

"I didn't mean to scare you," he said. "I've been looking all over for you."

"I—" Jade stared at the relief forming on his face. "What are you doing here so early?"

"I brought you breakfast. When you didn't answer the door, I started looking around." He nodded toward the apartment.

"I almost . . ." She hesitated, feeling sheepish.

"Screamed?"

"Hit you." She tried to keep the smile from her face.

"You can never be too careful."

Was he referring to himself or to a random attacker? He continued to stare at her until Jade felt self-conscious. *Those tawny eyes.* She tucked flyaway strands of hair behind her ear and hoped her shirt wasn't soaked too much with perspiration—unless it was just enough to look like the women on Reebok commercials. "I should have brought Mace," she said.

His eyebrow lifted. "Now that would have been interesting." His gaze trailed downward. "It might be a good idea, if you plan on wearing *that* in public every morning." His eyes locked with hers for a moment, and Jade forgot to breathe. Then he turned and started walking in the direction of her building.

Jade stole a glance down and saw her sweatshirt had slipped below her hips, and her cropped T-shirt sat just above her navel. She sighed and retied the sweatshirt around her waistline, hiding all exposed skin. *I'm such an idiot.* Then she hurried to catch up to Lucas. Seeing his hands empty, she asked, "Well, where's breakfast?"

"In your apartment." His brow creased. "You left the door unlocked."

Jade followed him up the stairs, wondering how she could have left the door unlocked. They passed a young man coming down, who cast admiring glances in Jade's direction. She instinctively wrapped her arms about her torso.

"You might want to make sure nothing's missing," Lucas said as they reached the third landing.

Jade's heart skipped a beat as she considered the possibility. Stopping in front of her room, she turned the handle on the door and stepped into the quiet apartment. First, she checked her bag for her wallet. Still there. Nothing was ruffled, nothing disturbed. The senses in her nose tingled, and she glanced at the newspaper-wrapped sandwich on the nightstand.

"Falafel," Lucas said from the doorway. "It should still be warm."

She nodded and then took a breathless peek underneath the bed. She straightened and turned toward Lucas. "Everything looks fine."

"Good. I'll wait out here while you change." He took a step away from the door, hesitating. "Oh, and Jade? My friends call me Luc."

He pulled the door shut, and Jade found herself standing alone in the dim room. "Am *I* your friend, Luc?" she whispered as she crossed to the windows and opened the blinds. Sunlight burst in, revealing dancing particles of dust. She turned and searched through her bag, pulling out two romance novels. The covers looked trashier than what was on the inside. *Cheesy marketing*, she thought. She tossed both of them into the garbage, knowing she couldn't afford to ogle Lucas any longer. It was time to focus on her thesis, and if that meant blocking everything else out, so be it.

She made her way into the bathroom, stripping off the sweat-drenched clothing, then placing her mood ring on the corner of the sink. It was red. Excited. *No, energized. And that's because I just worked out.* Then she opened the mottled shower door and gasped as two rust-colored cockroaches scuttled across the stained tile and disappeared down the drain. She backed out of the bathroom, wrapping her nakedness in her arms, and slipped on her sandals.

Once her feet were safely protected, she entered the shower again. Letting the water trickle across her shoulders, she pushed thoughts of "Luc" from her mind and how much time he might have spent in her apartment during her absence.

Chapter Eight

Qam al Asad, Yemen

PERSPIRATION SOAKED THROUGH ALEM'S thin cotton shirt until the sun's heat scorched his black skin. Raising his eyes to scan the clear sky, he cursed. *My luck that Yemen is having its biggest heat wave ever.* Fresh from Ethiopia, Alem Eshete had signed on with a Yemeni excavation crew for the chance to earn money for next fall's tuition at Addis Ababa University. At least that's what he'd told his parents. Premed wasn't cheap. Neither was his father's ailing health, and his track scholarship covered only 50 percent.

"*Yalluh!*" the crew boss screeched.

Alem increased his pace, loading the broken cement into a wheelbarrow. He had the body of an athlete and could probably outrun any man on the crew, but the heat was a fierce taskmaster. He glanced at the man who worked next to him: Omar, a quiet man in his mid-thirties. They had become fast friends.

"Tonight," Omar whispered. "We'll break out the flask."

Alem cast a furtive glance at the crew boss then grinned at his friend. "It'll be a welcome treat after today." Omar had impressed him with his command of English and Arabic. He even spoke a little

Amharic, Alem's native tongue. "The others will be envious."

"That's why we'll wait until they're all asleep," Omar said.

Something to look forward to in this hellish heat. Alem grunted as he lifted a large slab, filling the wheelbarrow to capacity. Then he guzzled water as Omar wheeled the cement to the sorting yard. Trying to justify why he stood in scorching heat, digging up rocks and broken cement, Alem thought back three months ago when his grandmother sent him a letter. Before he'd had the chance to ask her about it, she'd died. His grandfather had given him some of her books, but it was the letter Alem cherished the most.

He kept the letter in his traveling bag, tucked between the pages of his well-worn Bible. One line in particular continued to haunt him: *Find Queen Makeda; she will redeem our past.* The letter even included a strange poem about the queen. Wanting to grant his grandmother's wish, he applied for the excavation job as soon as the semester ended.

The unmerciful heat blurred his vision for a moment as he closed his eyes, thinking about his heritage—the legends he'd been taught since birth. He was a descendent of the great Queen Makeda—known at the queen of Sheba to the rest of the world. In another country, he might be considered a prince, but his family had branched far and wide, diluting him to one of dozens. Regardless, a movement throughout the country by government loyalists decried any "inherited" power that a royal descendent might obtain.

Although some Ethiopians insisted the queen was buried in their homeland, increasing evidence supported that her burial site was located somewhere in Yemen. If that could be proven, scholars would set out to disclaim that she ever lived in Ethiopia, and the entire royal dynasty would be in question.

And the government loyalists would win. Since receiving his grandmother's letter, Alem had started reading archaeology journals with great interest. That's when he learned one thing—finding the queen's tomb was a long shot.

But what if he did? What if he discovered evidence that she was a native of Ethiopia and his family was proved to be the true royal descendants? Well, his financial burdens might be eased a little— to say the least. He looked about him, scanning the other crew members. He'd yet to learn all their names, but he sensed they were starting to trust him for his hard work. Soon, he'd ask them about the biblical queen.

I'll find her, somehow. I owe it to my people.

His friend returned and picked up his chisel. Omar was on the thin side and five foot ten at the most, but his strength was far from lacking. They continued working in silence so as not to attract the attention of the crew boss. *Tonight, I'll ask Omar what he knows.*

Omar dropped his chisel, and Alem turned. The man's mouth hung open, and saliva dribbled down his chin.

"Sit," Alem urged, easing him to the dusty ground. The excavation of the ancient church site had taken more time than the cranky crew boss had forecasted. Already tensions were high among the workforce, and any illness or mishap would only add to the delay. Omar's head lolled against the stone wall, his eyes staring ahead, focusing on nothing.

Alem pressed a water bottle to Omar's lips. "Drink this."

A shadow crossed behind his back.

"What's wrong with him?" the crew boss asked in broken English.

"Overheated . . . He'll be fine soon."

The boss hesitated, and Alem braced himself for the worst.

"Find him some shade," the boss said.

"Thank you," Alem said, and then turned to Omar. "Let's go, my friend." He wrapped Omar's arm around his shoulders and helped him stagger to his feet.

Reluctantly, Alem left Omar propped against an acacia tree and returned to the work site. His worry for the man outweighed even the irritation of the constant flies that vied for position on his flesh. The work was tedious as he chiseled away the loose rock and cement, loaded the wheelbarrow, and then pushed the barrow to the sorting site and sifted through the debris in search of anything valuable. Bits of pottery, the shaft of a dagger, remnants of cloth— all had to be turned in to the boss. Every so often, Alem craned to see how his friend fared, but as the sun settled behind the cragged horizon, Omar still remained in one position.

A shout reverberated through the ruins, signaling the end of another work day. Alem wheeled his half-loaded wheelbarrow up the temporary slope. It was then that he saw two men carrying Omar's limp body to the truck.

Abandoning his wheelbarrow, Alem stumbled forward. "Wait!" But just as he reached the truck, the bald tires spun, and a column of dust separated him from his friend. Shaking his head, Alem walked toward the group of acacias that had so recently shaded Omar. Alem reached out his hand and placed his hand on the gnarled trunk, staring at the ground with regret. *I should have demanded immediate medical attention.* Then he saw a thick leather pouch nestled in the spiky grass. After a quick glance over his shoulder, he picked up the bag and opened it, anticipating a couple of pictures and maybe an identification card belonging to Omar.

Passports. There were at least a dozen of them—all male, all Arab. *Were they stolen? Or maybe Omar held them for the crew.* But the passports all contained different pictures of Omar—all with different names. Something still rested at the bottom of the pouch. Reaching in, Alem removed the metal object. He was surprised to see an ornate Christian cross. *Omar is Muslim, isn't he?* Alem turned the relic over in his palm. The cross was similar to the Greek Orthodox emblem.

A commotion erupted near the tents as the boss commanded everyone to gather their things. Alem pocketed the pouch, passports and all, and then he hurried to the tent he shared with a couple of other men. They'd already cleared out, so he grabbed his duffel bag and bedroll, then helped strike the tent. Everyone worked at a feverish pace. "What's going on?" Alem asked one man.

The Arab adjusted the glasses on his nose then shrugged and lifted a heavy bundle into one of the trucks. An engine backfired, and Alem's pulse jump-started. One by one, the trucks started pulling out. He sprinted to the last remaining truck and climbed into the back, taking his place next to the other crew members. He tried to catch his breath as he wondered about Omar's true identity.

Suddenly the truck veered north, away from the main city. "Where are we going?" he asked the skeleton of a man next to him. He figured his lousy Arabic was better than the crewman's nonexistent English.

"New job."

"What about Qam al Asad? We just leave it torn apart?"

"There are no bones here."

"Bones? *Whose* bones?"

The other crewmen stared at him now, and the Arab laughed, showing gaps between his yellowed teeth. "Bilqis—the queen— who else? She is all we ever search for."

Excitement pulsed through Alem. Bilqis was the Yemen name for the queen of Sheba.

The other men turned their solemn gazes toward Alem as the Arab continued, "And when we find the queen, we'll all be executed."

"Executed?"

"You think we get paid this well for pottery?"

Alem opened his mouth to answer, but nothing came.

The Arab slapped his leg and laughed. "You will learn. Very, very soon."

"What will I learn?" Alem asked. The others looked away, and silence ensued over the roar of the engine. The truck sped along the rocky ground, jostling the workers together.

If I had anything left in my stomach, it would have been purged by now, Alem thought with contempt. At least he was better off than Omar. Where was his friend? But his question went unanswered as the hours passed, and by the time darkness settled, a couple of the men had fallen asleep.

Alem felt panic building in his chest. With the dark came his fear of cramped quarters. Suffocating . . . he felt as though he would go ballistic, or at least injure someone. His fist involuntarily flexed—open, shut, open, shut—as if he craved to smash someone in the nose. He could almost feel the collapse of the delicate bones beneath his knuckles.

The truck lurched to a stop, slamming Alem into the man next to him. Those sleeping were knocked awake, and bodies jostled on top of one another. Alem made his way through the men and stumbled out of the truck, grateful he'd incurred only a few bruises. He stretched his tired limbs and looked up at the moon.

Then a gunshot rang out.

His heart stilled. The men around him dodged for cover under the truck. Some started running to nowhere.

Another gunshot sounded.

Adrenaline sliced through him as he scrambled beneath the truck, where he huddled with a few of the men. Fierce whispering surrounded him, but the Arabic was too rapid for him to understand, though there was no mistaking the fear.

When several quiet moments had passed, some of the men moved from their hiding place and started walking around the truck. It took another full minute before Alem scooted his way out. Groups of Arab workers stood clustered together.

Moving past the truck, Alem saw a figure lying on the ground near the lead vehicle. The man's light-colored shirt was stained scarlet, his limbs eerily still. Nobody knelt beside the body offering medical aid. One man stood a short distance away, and in his hand was a rifle. The moonlight splashed against his features. It was Rabbel, the crew boss, an AK-47 cradled in his arms.

"You!" Rabbel strode toward him. "Get in the truck!"

Alem climbed obediently into the cab and slid over the parched vinyl upholstery. *Grandmother*, he thought, *I'll bet you didn't think your request to find Queen Makeda would turn out like this. Am I to be a martyr even before the journey begins?* The crew boss rounded up the remaining men and forced them inside their respective vehicles. Suddenly Alem's door flew open, and Rabbel pointed at the steering wheel with his rifle.

"You drive."

Chapter Nine

Cairo

NOT YET OPEN TO the public for the day, the courtyard of the Coptic museum was deserted, and Lucas led Jade to a small side door. "I'll be able to show you around with no interruptions," he said as he inserted the key into the lock.

Jade shifted her backpack from one shoulder to the other, grateful to have the place to themselves.

"You can leave that in my office."

"It's all right. I'll keep it with me." She stepped into the museum and waited as Lucas turned the lights on. When the fluorescent bulbs flickered to full strength, she crossed to a display case filled with ancient weavings. One drew her attention—its red cloth contained two seminude dancing figures.

Lucas stepped up behind her. "The angel and the saint."

His breath tickled her neck, but she ignored the sensation. She leaned closer to the case and read the description. "Made during the sixth or seventh century B.C." She looked at Lucas. "Too late for the queen of Sheba."

"Most of these textiles are from the same era." He moved along the case. "Here's the 'flying angel,' dated a century or two earlier and done on linen instead of wool."

"Both depict grapes." Jade made notes on her phone about the polychrome color designs showing a flying angel who carried a red garland and about the vine leaves and bunches of grapes in the right-hand corner of the textile.

"Food for the gods." He stopped before another textile piece, pointing. "This shows a musical celebration centered on the god Pan. The queen of Sheba would have been more than familiar with him in his Arabian form."

Jade moved to his side and studied the third-century artifact. "Do you believe the queen worshipped pagan gods?"

"At least until she met Solomon. His explanation of an almighty God may have converted her, which was ironic because in his later years, Solomon returned to his pagan worshipping." Lucas looked at her for a moment.

His eyes were warm today. *Welcoming.* She tried to focus on the textile square.

"I think it's reasonable to reject the idea that she became a goddess herself, as some believe," he said.

"So you don't think she had visionary powers?"

"Perhaps, perhaps not. Regardless, she was the second most powerful ruler in antiquity. The question is, *where* did she rule?" He scratched at the stubble on his chin, which Jade noticed was longer.

She was suddenly aware that they were *very* alone in the museum. She continued walking and paused in front of a seventh-century St. Antony icon. "Who else knows about Dr. Lyon's theory on Ubar?"

"The members of DiscoveryArch," Lucas said, leaning toward the St. Antony icon as if to read its plaque.

"DiscoveryArch?"

"An exclusive online community of scholars from around the world—many of them archaeologists." He let out a low breath and straightened. "I was accepted into their private organization a year ago. It's quite a remarkable group—the only one of its kind. Most of the ideas shared don't create much of a stir. But when Dr. Lyon proposed Ubar as a location for the queen of Sheba's tomb, quite a bit of arguing erupted." He hesitated. "I'm only telling you about this now because I think someone from the group leaked information . . . and it turned out to be dangerous."

"Dangerous? How?"

"I suspect that Dr. Lyon was close to the truth—too close." His eyes bore into hers. "But his was just a theory, right?"

"Right."

"Right *and* wrong." Lucas shoved his hands in his pockets with a shrug. "The Ubar theory may have rattled some nerves, but no one would kill over it. Unless . . ."

"What?" she prompted. An odd look came into his eyes, and she felt a slight chill spread along her arms and back.

"Have you ever read the Bible, Jade?"

"Uh, most of it, I think," she said, more confused than ever.

"Dr. Lyon told me he'd read the Bible several times in the last year. It seemed he was looking for something . . . something more than just Solomon's story about the queen of the South." Lucas offered a plaintive smile. "No matter. Perhaps Dr. Lyon sensed he was near the end of his life."

Jade wasn't convinced, and she knew Lucas didn't believe that either. An old man suddenly finding religion?

He placed his hands on her shoulders. "Our association with Dr. Lyon may put us both at risk, mademoiselle."

Jade swallowed against the dryness in her throat. His scent was very musky this morning, as if he were on the prowl.

"Don't trust anybody," he said in a low voice.

One part of her wondered if she should trust *him*.

He removed his hands and checked his watch. "I'm expecting a fax, if you'll excuse me. Then we need to get out of here."

Jade was about to ask where they needed to go, but he turned and hurried away, leaving only his scent behind. *Like a large cat.* She twisted her ring—it was bronze. *Restless.* She continued looking through the artifacts, stopping to read the accompanying information and periodically jotting down notes—her mind on the man who'd just left.

She moved through the rest of the museum until she couldn't focus anymore. *What is taking him so long?* The museum opened, and a few tourists wandered in through the front entrance. She exited through the side door and stepped into a courtyard, making her way to the offices on the north side of the building. Nearby a train blared past, its tan color almost white in the morning sun. The passengers, mostly men, leaned out of the windows, and a few even rode on the top of the cars.

Just as she reached the first office, Lucas surged out of the door. He barely looked at her as he thrust keys into her hands. "Drive the car around back," he practically growled.

Jade opened her mouth then shut it again, noticing the sheen of perspiration on his forehead. Turning on her heel, she strode away, nodding to another group of tourists as they exited from a taxicab. She tossed her backpack in the rear seat and climbed in. She turned on the ignition as a dozen possibilities entered her mind. Perhaps one of their interviews had been cancelled, or maybe DiscoveryArch was still arguing about Ubar. Did he find out something more about Dr. Lyon? She drifted into the light traffic, receiving only one honk for her invasion.

Moments later, navigating the narrow, rubbish-strewn alley,

Jade pulled behind the museum, where Lucas paced along the wall. On the ground sat a computer and two boxes. She slowed to a stop, and he popped the trunk and loaded the supplies. She watched his jerky movements in the rearview mirror. *He's definitely upset.*

She climbed out of the car as he slammed the trunk. "What's going on?"

Lucas just shook his head and jumped into the passenger seat. "Turn around and take a right at the end of the alley."

"Aren't you driving?" Jade asked, knowing how poorly she'd fare on the maniacal Cairo streets.

With a brief shake of his head, he swore under his breath. He started fiddling with the radio, hitting the dash when only static came through. Giving up, he turned off the radio.

Jade drove to the corner and stopped, waiting for a donkey cart to pass.

"Start pulling out," Lucas said, his irritation sending a jolt through her. "Someone will let you in."

Inching her way into the oncoming lane, she waited for the right opportunity.

"Now!"

Jade flinched and stepped on the accelerator. One car had slowed, but it hadn't seemed enough. She sailed into the flowing traffic and gripped the wheel with both hands. "Where now?" she asked, trying to keep her voice steady.

"Right at the next intersection. Then keep it straight."

A couple of miles down the next road, the traffic started to thin, and the apartment buildings grew less dense. Since Lucas stared blankly out the window, Jade hoped his temper had cooled. "Luc, I don't like this. At least tell me where we're going."

Lucas rubbed his temple as he scrunched his face. Then he leaned to the side and pulled a piece of paper from his pocket. "This came from a fax number somewhere in Israel." He tossed it onto her lap.

Jade looked down at it, trying to decipher the words as she drove.

Say good-bye to the tomb in Jerusalem. You'll soon be joining Lyon in hortum.

"*Hortum* . . . Latin for *garden*?"

Lucas snatched the piece of paper. "Correct." He turned on the radio again. This time the static had cleared. The announcer spoke rapidly in Arabic, obviously excited about something important.

A minute later, Lucas turned down the volume. "Someone just bombed the tomb in Jerusalem."

Jade stared at him. "The one Dr. Lyon was trying to contact the patriarch about?"

"Whoever murdered Dr. Lyon did this."

After a deafening pause, Jade asked, "And they sent *you* a fax?" Fear pounded through her chest.

"At first I thought the message was a play on words. Lyon is dead, in heaven, or buried, in the garden—if you can consider a cemetery a garden of grass. But now, I think 'garden' means something other than a graveyard."

"Like what?"

"Like the most famous garden in history."

It took her a second. "The Garden of Eden?"

He nodded curtly, then wadded the paper and tossed it at the windshield, where it fell against the dash. She thought hard. Biblical scholars placed the Garden of Eden in Iraq, though there were other famous gardens and oases throughout history. Her mind listed them as she recalled her history studies, but nothing stood out. As she continued driving, the balled paper kept sliding along the dash, baking in the sunlight.

When they reached the outskirts of the city, Lucas said, "Just follow the 01 to Alexandria. It's about three hours."

"We're going to see the patriarch *today*?"

He nodded but kept his head turned toward the window, seemingly staring at nothing. *Mysterious and moody.* Jade gripped the steering wheel, trying to disperse the annoying commentary that kept popping into her mind.

Her neck ached, and she realized she was clenching her teeth and tensing her shoulders. *Relax.* Letting out a breath of air, Jade tried to settle in for the long drive, doing her best to ignore the way Luc's perfectly sculpted hands rested on his still-crisp pants. *Strong, capable hands.*

The minutes passed as they sped by the towns and farmlands. Lucas's breathing suddenly deepened, and a quick look told her he'd fallen asleep. Jade's shirt was cemented to the leather seat, the perspiration from driving all afternoon long dried. A monastery in Alexandria. That's where they were heading. To see the Coptic patriarch who lived in exile away from his own people—a man who had nearly been assassinated just a couple of weeks before.

When she'd been driving almost three hours, she said, "Lucas?"

He opened his eyes a slit, and then he checked his watch. Shifting in his seat, he exhaled a huge yawn. "Needed that nap." He glanced at her. "Thanks."

Jade nodded, feeling her own eyes sting with exhaustion. An upcoming road sign announced the town of Al Bayda. "How close are we?"

He studied the road for a moment. "Not much farther. Let's stop at the food stand up ahead."

Jade slowed the car, parking in front of a lean-to that doubled as a fruit stand and a house, by the looks of the clothesline in the back. A young girl with matted pigtails wearing a bright pink dress ran out from behind the structure. She flashed them a wide grin and started yelling something in Arabic. A moment later, a man appeared, his face deeply lined. He shared the girl's grin and welcomed them profusely.

Peeling herself from the seat, Jade climbed out of the car. Her thighs and knees ached from lack of use. Lucas wasted no time in collecting a half dozen pieces of fruit and a couple cans of Pepsi.

After selecting a mango, Jade peeled a section and sank her teeth into the fruit, relishing the sweet burst of flavor. The Egyptian watched her eat, as if her enjoyment of the fruit dictated his happiness. When she smiled, he grinned and thanked them again and again. Lucas took over the driving, and Jade watched the fruit stand in her side view mirror until it was out of sight.

Lucas's satellite phone rang, and with one hand, he answered it. "Yes?" He threw a glance at Jade. "That's unbelievable." He paused. "Well, try harder." He ended the call.

"What's wrong?"

"The editor from *Saudi Aramco World* can't find Lyon's article submission on the queen of Sheba." He drummed his fingers on the steering wheel.

"Why do you need it?"

"Because hours before the professor's death, he sent me an email about finding the last bit of evidence connected with the Jerusalem tomb. He said he was completing a study to send to *Saudi Aramco*—with information that would detail the final link to the queen's tomb. I asked him to email me the draft, but I never heard from him again."

Oh, Jade mouthed. She thought about the press release she'd read on the professor's death. There weren't many details disclosed. A stroke or heart attack was suspected. She wondered if there'd been an investigation or if his office was searched. Maybe his article was still on his computer. Without realizing it, she started twisting the ring on her finger. Lucas placed a hand over hers.

"Are you all right?"

"Uh, yes," Jade said, relieved and disappointed at the same time when he removed his hand. She was probably getting on his nerves. "Sorry."

When he didn't respond, she felt even more embarrassed. She wasn't used to just sitting, but she had nothing to read since her romance novels were gone. *Good riddance. I can't afford to notice the definition of his forearms as he drives.*

"The patriarch is not an ordinary ecclesiastical leader," he eventually said.

Not that she knew any ecclesiastical leaders personally, but Jade was curious. "What do you mean?"

"He's a former professor of the University of Alexandria. Years ago, he left the professional life for the ecclesiastical. You could say he has a deep interest in ancient tombs. He's the one who began DiscoveryArch." His eyes flickered with excitement. "He's also one of the most brilliant scholars I know . . . next to Lyon, of course."

"Maybe he's seen Dr. Lyon's article."

"Maybe."

Fifteen minutes later, Lucas left the main road and drove along a furrowed lane framed by date palms. The late-afternoon sun couldn't penetrate the healthy shade, and Jade leaned back in her seat, relishing the cool wind from the nearby sea riffling through her hair. According to the map, they were on the outskirts of Alexandria, which bordered the Mediterranean.

Lucas took a sideways glance at her. "You might want to do something with your hair."

Jade's face heated, and she turned to him, ready to argue.

"We're meeting a *pope,* Jade."

Chagrined, Jade unzipped her backpack and located her hairbrush. "If you didn't insist on having the windows down . . ." she muttered as she took the brush and stubbornly yanked it through her windblown hair.

"It doesn't bother me personally, you know," Lucas said.

Surprised at the softness in his tone, she wondered if he liked his women a little on the natural side, since he didn't seem the kind to put up with the high-maintenance type. And the way he had said her name—with that French accent. *Stop. He says everything with an accent.* She smoothed her hair behind her ears and found some lip gloss in her backpack.

Seconds later, Lucas pulled up in front of a large gate, and a burly guard crossed to them. Other security guards were stationed at lookout posts along the high walls surrounding the compound. After the guard checked both their IDs, he ordered them out of the car and conducted a quick weapon search. Jade climbed back into the car and turned to Lucas. "Wow."

"I didn't want to scare you, but since the level of security speaks for itself . . . this is due to the assassination attempt."

"Wasn't it around the same time Dr. Lyon died?"

"The day before. I want to find out the last time the patriarch was in contact with Dr. Lyon."

At the end of the long driveway was a low building—what seemed to be another guard post. A man wearing a military uniform came out and directed them to a courtyard, where they parked.

The guard and Lucas exchanged a few words, and then the guard left.

"It might be a while," Lucas said.

Jade wandered around the desert garden, inspecting the low shrubs and cactus-like plants while Lucas perched on a stone wall beneath the shade of a palm, watching her. She tried to ignore his stare, but when she was bold enough to glance at him, it seemed his eyes were half-closed. *He's not really watching me.*

At least thirty minutes passed, and Jade worried they'd be denied an audience. On the drive, Lucas had explained how important it was to get the patriarch's sanction for their research project. He told her the Copts had more developed knowledge on the queen of Sheba than perhaps any other religious group.

"Monsieur Morel?" a voice sounded from the far side of the court.

Lucas moved to his feet and motioned for Jade to join him.

A man wearing a tan-colored uniform and black beret bowed before them. "His Holiness, Pope Stephanus II, will receive you now."

Jade followed the men into the cool interior. They walked down a short hallway, and then stopped in another courtyard with a roof extended overhead, giving the feeling of being inside. At a round table sat a man in his early sixties. His embroidered robes and rounded hat made his office clear. Lucas strode forward then bowed his head in greeting.

After meeting Lucas, the patriarch extended his broad hand toward Jade, and she took it. "Welcome. Please, will you have some tea?" His face was weathered in a gentle way, as if his days had been spent pouring over the philosophies of man. Splays of graying hair curled beneath his cap line.

"Thank you," Lucas said, but Jade shook her head. He threw her a glare.

"I'd prefer water or a soda . . . if that's all right."

The patriarch waved his hand, sending his servant scurrying away.

Lucas's eyes held hers briefly, and Jade realized she'd have to explain later. It appeared she'd broken some *cardinal* rule, and in front of a pope, no less.

The men exchanged pleasantries while Jade took in her surroundings. The tiled floors were magnificent, the likes of which she'd seen only in photographs. Marble columns extended from floor to ceiling, and live palms dotted the spacious room.

After the drinks were served, the conversation began. Almost without taking a breath, Lucas relayed the news about the bombing of the tomb.

The patriarch raised his hand, stopping Lucas midsentence. "Yes, a serious misfortune to the archaeological world. It will take months to piece together the remnants."

"Dr. Lyon was writing an article about evidence inside that tomb, but it was never sent out," Lucas said.

The patriarch nodded. "As you know, my people take a unique interest in the theories of Dr. Lyon. If the queen's remains can be found in neutral territory such as Southern Arabia, our political standing will be strengthened. Disputes between my people and the Ethiopian clerics in Israel will cease. Our interpretation of the ancient biblical text will be validated. But we will accept what comes—even if it's in Ethiopia." The patriarch paused, taking a sip of the steaming tea. He leaned forward. "There has been another discovery—something that may offset our losses from the Jerusalem tomb."

Jade felt the skin along her neck tingle. *A real archaeological discovery had just been made?*

"A statue has been excavated in Aksum, Ethiopia." The patriarch's eyes danced with Christmas morning pleasure. "It's a sculpture of a queen. The style and form date to about 950 B.C. There's an inscription at the base of the statue with the name of a woman."

"What is it?" Jade burst out.

"That's what you're going to find out," the patriarch said. "A flight from Alexandria will leave tonight. You'll arrive in Addis Ababa around 2:00 a.m., where everything has been arranged for your convenience."

Chapter Ten

The Empty Quarter

THE WANING MOON COMBINED with the dim headlights to provide just enough light to guide Alem along the rutted road. He gripped the metal wheel as unrelenting potholes grated his joints, coupled with the pressure against his ribs from the barrel of the gun. Although he'd never driven such a beast of a truck before, it hadn't taken him long to figure out the gears and get the convoy moving at top speed. The gas gauge now hovered just above empty. They had already gone through the two five-gallon cans of gasoline kept in the back. Glancing at his crew boss, Alem was surprised to see the man half-asleep. But he knew better than to be fooled into thinking he could catch Rabbel off guard. The man could probably sleep standing up and not miss a thing.

In the past couple of hours, Alem had deduced enough Arabic to understand that the boss had killed his assistant over a disagreement of direction—northeast or northwest? The argument about a map had led to the man's death. And now they were heading northeast, the apparent "right" direction. In the near distance, Alem saw the familiar shape of a toll building.

"We stop here for gasoline," the boss said.

A young Arab, not more than sixteen, exited the toll building holding a rifle. Barefoot and wearing a too-big blazer over a long tunic, he jogged to the lead truck and poked his head in the window. He grinned at Alem, qat on his breath. "Fifty riyal."

Rabbel said, "Forty."

"Fifty." The boy drew back from the window and whistled. Three other teenage boys appeared, each armed with a Kalashnikov.

Rabbel fiddled with the fanny pack strapped about his waist, keeping the gun propped against his knees. "Oranges?"

"Ten riyal," the boy said.

"Seven."

The boy leaned toward his constituents and spoke in a fierce whisper. "Nine."

Counting the money, the boss grumbled in Arabic. Alem kept motionless as the bills changed hands.

Twenty minutes later, the caravan of trucks pressed forward. Oranges eaten, bladders relieved, and no one else shot—Alem felt he was better off than an hour ago. With a pang, he wished he could be in the back of the truck. At least then he could catch some sleep.

Rabbel relaxed his grip on the shotgun and even propped it against the passenger door. He noticed Alem's glance. "No place to run or hide out here."

Alem stared into the scattering darkness. It was nearly dawn, and the neighboring shapes slowly took form. Dunes, many hundred feet high, towered above the truck. *So this was the Empty Quarter.* The infamous stretch of sand—legendary for its ruthlessness. At the university, he had read the accounts of Bertram Thomas and Wilfred Thesiger, the first white explorers to cross the desert and live to tell about it.

And when we find the queen, we'll all be executed. The words of the Arab resounded in his mind. Alem gripped the grooves of the steering wheel. "Are we looking for Bilqis?"

"What do you know of the queen?"

"Only what my country believes."

"Ah. Your people claim her as their own." Rabbel chuckled. "We'll soon prove the Africans wrong. The queen of Sheba was born in Arabia. She ruled here and died here."

Indeed, Alem thought as he kept his gaze straight ahead. The noble heritage of his ancestors would be cruelly trampled if anyone could prove the queen's reign began and ended in Arabia.

"When we find her bones," Rabbel said, "the world will be forced to recognize the truth. The city of her burial will become the new Mecca. Jews and Christians and Muslims will flock to southern Arabia—bringing us prosperity and many, many tourism dollars."

But at what cost? And when we find her, will we all be executed?

The truck crested a ridge, and the sun burst over the horizon, throwing its sphere of light across the golden sand. Rabbel pointed to a dry wadi that ran perpendicular to the road. "This is it."

Alem slowed the truck, staring at the emptiness—only a few scrub brushes, a sparse mangrove, and an abandoned wooden structure designated the site. On the north side of the road, the sand multiplied until it formed a dune. They were at the edge of the Empty Quarter.

If Alem had grumbled about the last site or the terror of the ride through the desert, he had yet to understand real misery. The temperature was hellish, and by midday, it was 48° C.

He would do anything to feel a drop of rain—a large, cool drop. The thin clothing he wore was thoroughly soaked with perspiration. Even the tops of his ebony hands glistened with beaded sweat. He lifted his shovel again and plunged it into the dry wadi, turning over a shovelful of silt.

Alem gazed up at the rising slope of the Mahara Plateau. Little vegetation could be seen from this angle, but the Yemenis had assured him of the grasses and flowers that grew there in the winter season. It seemed almost impossible that a place as desolate as this harbored any sort of greenery.

Walking along the bed, Alem kicked his foot against loose rock and sand. Would this foolish search for the queen's tomb ever produce anything of significance? He surveyed the desolation. Who would want to live here anyway? It was hard to imagine that any of the miles of dunes they had passed could have ever supported a kingdom or even a single palace.

Alem shoveled the parched earth. Around him, the Yemeni workers had settled into a rhythm. Periodically, Rabbel shouted a command.

Alem's shovel struck a rock, and he stooped to lift it. It was rough, maybe limestone. He knew that along the coast of Yemen and Oman, limestone cliffs towered at least one thousand meters in height. Odd it should appear this far north. Then he thrust his shovel into the earth again, and another rock stopped his progress. Shaking his head, Alem pulled the offending stone from its place. Just as he was about to toss it aside, he paused. It was metal. He glanced behind him and saw Rabbel at the other end of the wadi.

Alem turned the piece over then rubbed it against his shirt. The tarnished metal was dull in the stark sunlight, obviously a handle of some sort. Alem licked his thumb and rubbed off some of the crusted sand. He drew in a breath. It looked like the hilt of a sword.

Alem rubbed along the length of the handle until an intricate design appeared. It was a snake intertwined with a plant or flower. Something about it was familiar, and Alem squeezed his eyes shut for a moment. Maybe it was a tribal emblem on a flag from one of the villages they had passed. Then a feeling of disquiet settled over him. He remembered. He had seen this symbol before . . . etched on his grandmother's headstone.

Chapter Eleven

Yemen

THE BUZZING GREW CLOSER until Omar felt as if the fly had actually entered his ear. He shook his head wildly against the annoying insect, wincing with pain in the process. Still, he didn't open his eyes. One was swollen shut, the other too tired, and the returning itch of his mustache only compounded the discomfort. Since his hands were tied behind his back, he rubbed his cheek against the straw-filled mattress. The friction relieved the itch, but at the same time aggravated his injured face.

He didn't remember anything much until he awakened in this cramped place—a former storage room, as evidenced by the scavenging rats that had run across his feet during the night. *How long have I been in this room? An hour? A day?*

After spending the night in a small hospice several kilometers from the work site, Omar had returned to find his former crew gone. Not that he was surprised, knowing that the glorified grave robbers wouldn't stay in one place for long. But he needed to finish gathering information on the crew boss, Rabbel.

At the abandoned site, Omar had made his way back to the tree

Alem had placed him under. After a cursory search for his missing bag, he sank to his hands and knees and began to search more thoroughly. He ran his fingers through the stiff desert grass, finding nothing. If his ID badges fell into the wrong hands, it wouldn't take long for someone to figure out his real purpose in Yemen.

He could be jailed, exported, or worse.

Omar hadn't heard anyone approach, but his throbbing head was a reminder of the terrific blow he'd received. His next memory had been waking up in this dark place, and now, stuck in the storage room, he still felt the pulsing pain in the back of his head. It was a perfect way to end a long week of working himself nearly to death, not being able to make any contact with his ex-girlfriend, Mia, and being captured by a bunch of no-name insurgents.

Omar had been close to infiltrating Rabbel's confidence. The man had admitted three things so far: they were searching for the queen's tomb, they had been sending any relevant findings to the National Museum of Yemen in San'ā', and their expedition was privately funded. This told Omar that the Yemen government wasn't sponsoring the trip, which probably meant that Rabbel's group was operating illegally.

The Israeli government was also convinced that Rabbel was behind an assassination attempt on an important religious figure—the pope of the Coptic Church. This pope apparently had information about the queen of Sheba's tomb that Rabbel's group desperately wanted. *So why try to kill the guy? Couldn't anything be purchased for the right price?*

Omar suspected that Rabbel was linked to an organization called Ancient World Piracy, AWP, which was just a fancy title for modern-day scavengers—or, more accurately, thieves. International bylaws mandated that any ancient ruin or artifact discovered was the property of said nation, even if the finding was made on private land.

The black market was glutted with stolen artifacts, some of which Omar had been able to track down—the starving Buddha statue in Pakistan, an ancient Peruvian burial shroud, a rare chert tool that was ten thousand years old. So when David Levy sent Omar to Yemen to join an excavation crew, he was quite intrigued—until he was kidnapped. *A minor detour.*

It was imperative for Omar to find out if there was bribery between Rabbel, AWP, and the Yemen government, then pin Rabbel for the assassination attempt. *Killing two birds with one stone, my specialty.* Israel would love to be recognized for saving a Christian pope's life and, as a bonus, hold an entire country responsible. Even better, all of Europe and America would be devoted forever, and the free weapons and military power would just keep coming in.

From somewhere outside, Omar heard voices. He knew that as soon as he let on that he was awake, he would be questioned and, most likely, brutally tortured. He'd heard the stories from others in his field who had been hostages, and some joked that it was only a matter of time before it was his turn.

Apparently it had come.

Omar tried to wriggle off the mattress, deciding there had to be a way out of this mess. His tied ankles slipped to the floor, thumping loudly. *Damn.*

The voices stopped, and he held his breath. Then the lock in the door slid open, and a waft of fresh air passed over his face. A man stood in the entryway, and beyond, Omar saw the figures of several others.

"Water?" Omar asked in a hoarse voice.

A chuckle sounded. Then someone called for water.

Suddenly hands gripped his arms and jerked him up until he was sitting awkwardly on the bed. A cold metal cup pressed to his

FINDING SHEBA | 83

mouth, and as he gulped the stale liquid, he studied his captors with his one good eye.

Khafiya-swathed men surrounded him, their black eyes peering between layers of checked cloth. Rifles gripped in their hands, the four men pressed forward as a unit as rapid Arabic hurled in his direction.

"Your name?" a gangly man on the right demanded.

"Where are you from?" another said, raising his rifle. "What are you doing at Qam al Asad?"

"I'm Omar. I was left behind by my work crew."

The captors exchanged doubtful glances. "Who's your boss?" one asked.

Omar relaxed a little. These men had nothing on him. "Rabbel." Instinct told him they weren't the ones who found his IDs. If so, he wouldn't be alive to answer so many questions.

Two of the men left the room and argued fiercely with each other while the other two trained their rifles on him. By mentioning Rabbel's name, Omar was settling his fate—for better or worse. Was the crew boss their friend or enemy?

"What did you find?" the first man asked.

"Nothing," Omar said.

The man gripped the nape of Omar's neck. "How long have you worked for Rabbel?"

"A few days."

The other two men came into the room and stared intently at Omar. The first Arab let go of Omar's neck. "Why were you left behind?"

Omar winced at the pain in his neck. "I fainted."

The men looked at each other and laughed. "He fainted," one said, and the laughter started again.

The first man leaned toward Omar. "You do not have

permission to step on Bilqis's land."

Omar hung his head, feigning contrition. "I didn't know. I was just waiting for my crew."

After a moment of discussion, one of the men announced, "We will feed him until Rabbel pays."

I guess I'll be here a while. Omar watched them leave. He didn't trust the insurgents. Just as he didn't trust David Levy—and *he* was supposed to be the good guy. Omar stared at the water-stained ceiling above. He had to return to the campsite where he'd buried his satellite phone. It was the only secure way to contact his superiors and learn his next instructions. It also had a GPS tracker, which would come in handy about now.

A commotion arose from outside, and Omar tensed. The door burst open, and one of the men entered, holding a plastic container.

"Eat." The man left the bowl on the mattress.

When the door shut, Omar rotated to his knees until he knelt over the bowl. *Couscous.* It was still warm. Hands tied behind his back, he devoured the food like a common animal, acquiescing to the fact that his dignity had fled the moment of his capture.

As the shadows in his room deepened into night, Omar kept his gaze on the high window covered with chicken wire. It was too small to crawl through, but watching the moonlight splash in gave him some connection with the outside world. When the noises from the other room stopped, he began the laborious task of contorting his arms against the ropes, hoping to loosen them.

After several moments, he rested against the ticking, his arms and wrists throbbing. He had two choices: wait to see what happened or try to escape.

With renewed determination, Omar wriggled against the ropes, wishing he'd studied Houdini's tactics to fit his body through his looped arms. He slid to the ground, eyeing the thin bulge in his

pocket below his knees. His carpenter-style jeans might prove
useful after all. Since his patch days, he'd kept the last lighter from
his final cigarette. It had become a badge of achievement . . . a lucky
memento now.

It's time to cash in the luck. Rolling onto his side again, he
stretched his leg back toward his tied hands. His hand groped
frantically at his pant leg, but he could touch just his lower calf . . .
not high enough. Omar worked his way into a sitting position and
pulled his knees to his chest. Leaning forward, he used his teeth to
open the pocket. Then he rocked onto his back, lifting his leg in the
air and shaking it. The lighter slid out and landed next to his head.

Please work. It hadn't been used for six years. Omar lifted
the lid and then flicked the tab over and over. He wasn't certain
when the first flame ignited, but he knew when it started licking
his skin. He gritted his teeth against the searing pain as the flames
gnawed the rope. Finally he could no longer stand it, and he leaped
toward the bed and pressed his hands against the mattress. In an
instant, the fire extended its grasp, and the mattress started to burn.
He fell against the floor and rubbed the knotted rope in the layer
of dust, putting out the last of the flames that singed his wrists.
He scrambled to his feet and delivered a kick at the door, yelling,
"Naar! Naar!" *Fire!*

The door shoved open, and the captors stared in confusion at
the burning mattress. Shouting erupted. Omar eased his way past the
chaos. Just as he reached the outside door, he managed to work one
hand free from the charred rope. He moved through the opening and
groped his way through the courtyard.

For a breathless instant, he stood behind a tall, wide palm,
expecting one of the men to appear. Then Omar eyed the heavy
metal gate that separated the living quarters from the street. He
was certain it would screech when opened, but climbing would

take precious time—time in which a bullet could make his body its home. As smoke billowed from the storage room, Omar moved to the gate and slipped out.

"Stenna!" *Stop!*

Omar scurried across the street and plunged into a narrow alleyway. He sprinted along the road, the unpaved rocks stabbing his bare feet. The pale light from the moon cast unearthly patches throughout the alley as shouting reverberated off the walls, telling Omar his captors followed. Up ahead he saw something looming—a garbage bin—and not far from that, the street opened into another courtyard and another gate.

He draped his shirt over the top of the metal prongs then returned to the garbage bin. Climbing inside, he pulled a soggy piece of cardboard over his head. While footsteps rushed past, Omar fought the bile rising in his throat as he tried not to inhale the smell of rotting food.

Don't retch.

The gate squealed open, and the footsteps faded.

Now.

Omar climbed out of the Dumpster, wincing as his hand slipped on the oozing grime. He turned away from the courtyard with the open gate and ran back along the alleyway. It would take them only a few seconds to realize they'd missed him.

Suddenly something crashed against the side of his head. The sound pummeled his ears as pain simultaneously burst through his temple, and for a split second, he wondered if he'd been shot. He whirled around and saw his attacker holding a raised AK-47.

Omar lunged forward and wrestled for the rifle. The man was strong, but he was not desperate like Omar. He jerked his elbow and pummeled the man underneath the chin. Gasping, the man fell to his knees. Omar grabbed the gun with two hands and thrust the butt into the Arab's stomach.

"No offense, but I have someplace to go." Omar pulled the rifle away and moved into the street. A quick scan told him it was deserted. He turned north and started a dead run, but over his footfalls he heard shouting. The Arabs had discovered his trick.

Then he saw it: a rusted jeep.

Omar volleyed into the vehicle and tossed the rifle onto the passenger seat. He deftly hot-wired the starter and then waited for the spark. *At least my field training is becoming useful in my last week of employment.* Perspiration trickled down his face while he waited for the spark. The jeep started with a roar, and Omar cranked the wheel to the left. With one glance behind, he floored the accelerator.

Chapter Twelve

Ar Rub' Al Khālī, Arabia
964 b.c.

NICAULA HELD THE SCEPTER above her head, and the royal caravan came to a halt. More than a hundred camels traveled in the party, carrying baggage. Servants walked on foot alongside an army of fifty soldiers riding on horses. The queen tipped her head in reverence toward the western sun—goddess 'Ashtartu. Nicaula turned and scanned the direction from which her caravan had come, catching a glimpse of the oasis they had left that morning. Then her gaze moved to the north.

The party stood along the edge of the High Sands—a wasteland bearing the secrets of thousands of years. Nicaula knew this part of Arabia, for she had traveled here with her father. It was a land without rain where men and beast died an equal death, a land that was no respecter of persons. Only the cold marked the sand's drift into winter and the heat, the frail bloom of summer.

As she gazed at the rising dunes, ranging in color from pale saffron to deep scarlet, her heart hardened like the cruel desert. Just like the parched Arabian sands, life had taken nourishment from her.

She touched her necklace, reminding her of the price her father had paid.

Three servants moved from the front of the caravan and stood before her. For one moon, they had been tracking the marauders who had taken the king's life. "O Queen," one said. "What is your command?"

What would my father do? "Look out there." Nicaula moved her arm in a semicircle. "Is it not unusually quiet? Not even a crow, nor lame hare, moves about the landscape."

One of the servants crouched to the ground, squinting at the markings in the sand.

"Rona, how long ago did you lose them?" Nicaula asked.

Rona slowly rose, keeping his head lowered and his gaze beneath the queen's penetrating stare. "The oasis. The tracks ended there."

"If you are lying to your queen, you will lose your life," she said, not bothering to mask her vehemence. "Down!" she commanded her camel, and it obediently lumbered into a sitting position. She climbed off the animal and strode toward the desert rise as her maidservant, Azhara, fell into step behind her. Bending forward against the slope, Nicaula climbed the first dune.

The sand fell away beneath her sandals, creating rivulets of moving grains from each step. Several dozen soldiers skirted the base of the dune, but she kept climbing, setting a fierce pace. Once the queen crested the top, she knelt on the soft precipice. Azhara caught up to her, her breathing labored.

"There." Nicaula pointed eastward. "That oasis contains the last evidence of the marauders. To the north lies the endless desert, and to the south, the Mahara Plateau," she mused. "They couldn't have traveled too far north. Perhaps they make their camp near a wadi on the south side."

Azhara touched the queen's arm. "Look." As the sun made its final descent behind the horizon of dunes, a shimmering form appeared against the ginger sky. "Smoke."

Blood rushed through the queen's limbs until she thought her heart would boil in its own anger. "It is *they*." Rising to her feet, she stood for a long moment, staring, touching her necklace, and tracing the flower-and-snake etching with her finger. "They are foolish—foolish to make fire and lead us to their hiding place. Fools to trespass on my land. And fools enough to kill a king."

Azhara looked past the queen, her expression abandoned to thought.

"What is it, woman?" Nicaula asked. "Speak at once."

"Perhaps they want to be found."

"Perhaps. They may thirst for blood. Nevertheless, they will meet Maniya—goddess of death—tonight."

Hours later, Nicaula ordered her men to prepare for battle. All activities were hushed. Even the beasts seem to respect the need for quiet. The queen paced outside her tent, then moved through the soldiers, checking on their preparations.

Then Nicaula saw him—the unusually tall soldier who had caught her attention the day before. He bowed his head as she approached. She took note of every detail from his laced leather sandals to the curved dagger at his waist and the worn turban neatly tied about his head. A few ebony curls had escaped it, his full cheeks betraying his youth.

The soldier made a move to sink to his knees, but Nicaula reached her hand out to stay him. "What is your name?"

"Batal, son of Asad."

Nicaula recognized the name Asad—he had been a loyal servant to her father. "Your father was a great warrior."

Batal dipped his head in acknowledgment, still not meeting her gaze.

If she could trust this man as *her* father had trusted *his* father
. . . She now knew why this young man had piqued her curiosity.
Her father had often told her that the most precious resources
might come in the form of one stalwart servant. *Choose him, Nica,*
she could almost hear her father say. *Trust him.* She looked at the
soldier, liking what she saw. "Follow me."

Silent as an ibex, Nicaula wove her way along a narrow pass
that divided a row of dunes—straight for the marauders' camp. If a
surprise attack occurred, only one man would be there to defend her.
The scent reached her before the sounds did. She slowed her step,
and behind her, Batal paused, his nostrils quivering.

Chanting accompanied the rank odor, low and heinous.

With each step, the chanting grew louder until it pulsated
through her blood and thumped its way into her heart. For an instant
she regretted bringing the young soldier, wondering if the upcoming
sight would be too much for him to bear.

Nicaula stopped, compelled to say something to Batal, but when
their eyes met, she saw the determination in his eyes—neither life
nor death mattered.

They continued until they saw an orange glow ahead. Nicaula
turned to the nearest dune and began to climb while Batal kept pace
with precision. The chanting seemed to surround them, possess
them, and soon the queen reached the mountainous summit of sand.

At first Nicaula could barely distinguish the dancing forms that
appeared to be half men, half beasts surrounding the great fire. Then
she recognized the dark ridges of the curved horns, the reddish-
brown fur, and the white markings on the lifeless faces—the men
wore decapitated heads of gazelle. In the firelight, the marauders'
skin glistened with fresh blood, either from self-mutilation or from
the recent sacrifice of the beasts.

The chanting rose in pitch and frenzy, and a jolt of dread passed through Nicaula. She remembered seeing such a scene with her father when she was but ten years old. She turned to see Batal, whose eyes widened.

"What are they doing?" he whispered.

"See the skewer?" She pointed toward the fire where heavy smoke billowed from a blackened carcass. "They thank their gods for their meal."

"But the gazelle should smell sweet when it's cooked."

"Yes, but they aren't cooking a fallen gazelle. These men are cannibals."

Saying the words, her stomach churned. The tribesmen who had killed her father were cannibals. And the fact that they left the murdered people of Sheba to rot on the desert floor was a powerful blow. Their message to the queen was clear—the king of Sheba was not even worthy of their palate.

ॐ

NICAULA MOTIONED FOR BATAL to follow her, and they descended the face of the dune like sidewinding snakes. The scent of burnt human flesh diminished, and she hoped to purge the images and smells from her mind during the next worship revelry to the sun goddess. At the base of the dune, Batal hesitated, holding his arm in front of the queen.

"What is it?"

He brought a finger to his lips and remained motionless.

Then Nicaula heard it too. The chanting had changed from praise and celebration to angry cries. "They prepare for battle. They must have discovered our presence."

Batal nodded, his gaze locked with hers.

"We will return and inform the others." Nicaula took the lead and began to run toward the camp, desperately hoping their warning would be in time. As her feet slapped against the crusted sand, she knew she should order Batal to run ahead and inform the others. But fear pierced her heart at being left alone.

As they plunged forward, the rise and fall of chanting grew closer. It was difficult to gage the distance of the marauders, but Nicaula knew it couldn't be long before her caravan's footprints were spotted. A sharp cry from behind startled her. The queen slowed and looked around to see Batal heaped upon the ground.

She ran to him then knelt at his side, seeing the shaft of an arrow protruding between his shoulder blades.

"Run!" he said.

Nicaula hesitated, but then moved to her feet and ran, hunched over, to the base of the next dune. Perched along the ridge of that dune was Batal's assailant. The man's bare chest glistened with smeared blood in the moonlight. He removed an arrow from his sling and placed the notched end against the bowstring, taking dead aim at Batal.

I have to stop him.

Just as the man released the arrow, she leapt through the air and shoved him from the side. He cried out then jumped to his feet again, but Nicaula was ready. Her dagger drawn, she gripped it steady as the marauder landed on top of her.

His groan was cut short as Nicaula's dagger plunged into his throat. Blood burst from the wound, spraying onto the queen's face and clothing.

With great effort, she wriggled out from under the dead man and returned to find Batal nearly unconscious. The chanting had ceased, and the battle cries echoed through the dark. Surely her people had heard the approaching warriors. They needed no warning from her now.

She smoothed the black curls from Batal's face. "Forgive me," she said as she removed her bloodstained headdress and wadded the cloth. In one motion, she shoved it into the soldier's mouth. Then with a swift jerk, she pulled the first arrow from his back. His cry was muffled, just as she intended it to be. She reached for the second arrow lodged in his side. With the same resolve, she yanked it from his flesh. "Feign death," she whispered into his ear.

She rolled onto the ground and covered her legs in sand, quickly burying her entire body. By holding a hand over her nose and mouth, she reserved an air pocket.

Several moments passed before she heard them. These desert marauders might notice anything out of place, even on the darkest night. The ground vibrated with their pounding footsteps. With each second, Nicaula's pulse increased in tempo. She had escaped the first onslaught of warriors, but how would her people fare? The cannibals had likely reached her camp by now.

The cool sand weighed against her limbs, filling in around her. Behind her closed eyes, she could easily imagine the worst of the battle that must be taking place. Her men were strong and well prepared, but the desert had a way of throwing hostility at friend and foe alike.

Tears wet her eyes temporarily, evaporating as soon as they formed. If Batal died, and her people fled from the marauders, what would be her fate? Her father had taught her many things—how to serve her people and rule as queen—but not how to survive alone in a harsh desert. Her throat ached as she longed for water. The sand had crusted around her mouth, nostrils, and eyes.

The passage of time meant very little to her, and she relied solely on sound. She prayed to the gods—pleading, making promises. Then she beseeched her dead father. *Protect our people. Deliver them from this evil.*

Only when stillness completely surrounded the queen did she
move her arms. Slowly, she dug her way through the sand and rose
to a sitting position.

All was quiet and empty.

Nicaula examined the tracks that ran near her hiding place—
they had come so close. She snapped her head up and searched for
Batal along the dark desert floor. His body was still there.

Half-crawling, half-stumbling, the queen made her way to the
soldier's side. She touched Batal's cheek. Cool. Then she moved her
palm to his lips. They were still warm, and she felt the gentle release
of air coming from his nostrils.

Nicaula brushed the sand from his eyelids and lashes. Her gaze
trailed to his back where his tunic was stained dark with blood,
but when she touched the soaked linen, her fingers came away dry.
The bleeding had stopped. Then she noticed that his dagger had
been removed from his belt. The marauders must have stolen it.
Instinctively, the queen reached for her own dagger and clutched it
in both hands, settling next to the soldier.

The night air was cold, and she shivered against the soft breeze.
She pulled her knees up to her chest and wrapped her arms about
them. Never had she felt so alone. Not even the sun goddess seemed
to be protecting her. But she would remain at Batal's side until she
knew his fate. After all, he had just taken an arrow meant for her.

As the night deepened, Nicaula carefully curled against his side
so as not to disturb him. His body warmed her shivering skin. She
held her breath for moment, curious about the balmy sensation that
spread through her body. It was strange to lie next to him, for she
had never been close to a man in this manner. If she were not queen
. . . She squeezed her eyes shut against Batal's pleasing features.

Her father told her that as queen, she'd always have to put the
kingdom before her heart. A man could snatch everything from her

if she wasn't careful. The only way to keep her full power was to marry another king or prince. Touching her necklace, she renewed her vow to avenge her father, but as she closed her eyes, she found herself praying for the life of the man beside her, hoping, and then dreaming.

When the pale sunlight peeked over the dunes, casting its silvery reach across the immeasurable grains of sand, a voice called in her dream, "O Queen."

Batal! Her eyes opened with a start. She rose to an elbow and turned her head, searching. He crouched only a few paces from where she'd slept, his black eyes watching her. Beneath the courage, she saw pain.

Nicaula stood and walked to the soldier. With silent understanding, she examined his wounds. "I have some herbs at our camp that will relieve your pain." *If there is anything left now.* "Come, the others will think we were carried off by the marauders."

The pair began the trek back to their camp. Nicaula exhaled relief, knowing the gods had smiled on them this day—for both she and the soldier were still alive. They remained silent, listening for any sounds, and as they rounded the final dune, the queen found she was holding her breath, waiting to see the carnage.

As she halted, she placed a hand on Batal's arm, prepared for the worst. But instead of dead bodies strewn about the desert battleground, there was no one.

"Where are they?" Nicaula dropped her hand and walked into the camp. "Did they fight the battle elsewhere, or did they flee before the marauders?"

Batal walked next to her, his face scarlet.

The queen expected that even he, a young soldier, understood the disgrace of fleeing before an enemy—especially a personal enemy to the queen.

"Perhaps they search for us," he said.

The queen gazed at the deserted tents dotting the landscape as her tunic flapped in the warm wind. Her hair, free from its scarf, tangled and spiraled liberally down her back. "Not even a dagger or a bow," she marveled. On the far side, her tent still remained, its goatskin panels slapping against the poles in the forlorn wind.

Nicaula pushed through the tent opening and stepped into the shady interior. The rugs, the bedrolls, and the vessels of food and water remained untouched. Nothing made sense. If her army had abandoned camp, the marauders certainly would have ravaged the site. If there had been a battle here, the evidence would be obvious. But there was nothing. It was as if everyone had simply vanished.

When she exited, she came face-to-face with Batal. "Nothing's been looted. Even my bag of healing plants remains. We should eat."

He made a move to enter the tent and prepare the food, but she stayed him. "You need to rest. I'll prepare the food and make a poultice for your wound."

Although he looked hesitant, she saw the silent gratitude. They entered the tent, and the queen spread out a rug for him. She filled a clay drinking cup with stale water and offered it to the soldier. Nicaula located her herbal pouch and extracted dried *remram*. She pounded the leaves into a powder, then added water, making a poultice.

She knelt by Batal's side. "This will burn," she said, lifting the back of his tunic so the wound was exposed to the open air. Nicaula dabbed the paste on the wound sites, hoping they wouldn't fester. Rising to her feet, she left the tent and walked the perimeter of the camp, looking for signs of a struggle, but she found no evidence of blood or torn clothing.

It was as if her men had left in great haste. Had the marauders pursued her men and overtaken them? As the sun topped the dunes,

Nicaula returned to the tent. Batal slept, so she settled onto a rug. Soon she allowed herself to sleep through the oppressive afternoon.

The air in the tent became stifling, and Nicaula woke, bathed in perspiration. She rose and pushed her way out of the structure, welcoming the light breeze as it lifted the damp strands from her face and neck. The desert air was quiet—too quiet. The queen moved around the side of the tent, watching and waiting.

Within moments, she spotted a dark figure traveling in the shimmering heat. The man, swathed in indigo clothing, urged his camel forward at a rapid pace. Just as suddenly, he came to a halt, couched the camel, and climbed off. He rushed toward the tent, and Nicaula pressed herself against the panels.

She gripped the dagger she kept at her waist as she watched the man move inside. Nicaula heard him call out, "Batal?"

Her body relaxed. She moved along the perimeter of the tent then peeked through the flap. "Rona."

Instantly, Rona turned and bowed. "O Queen, the gods be praised that you are alive."

Batal stirred. "Where is everyone?"

Rona lifted his head and looked from the queen to Batal. "They are on their way back."

"From where?" Nicaula asked.

"We pursued the marauders until Sa'ba." Rona lowered his voice. "We thought you had been killed."

"Batal took my arrow," Nicaula said. "Tell me everything that happened."

"Azhara came to me and said that you had left the camp. She thought you'd gone to seek the marauders." Rona cleared his throat. "She thought you had gone mad in your grief. She told us you took Batal, but not long after, we heard the war cries. We thought they were victory cries—we believed the tribesmen had captured you and . . ." His voice broke.

"Did you flee before the warriors?" Batal asked.

"No!" Rona protested, his eyes narrowing. "We were angry, ready to enact the most severe revenge. We gathered in a single line, every man with his weapon drawn. The sight was such as I have never seen before. The marauders looked like savages—death in their eyes—as they screamed their way into our camp." He wrung his hands. "We thought the queen dead, and we wanted revenge."

"Tell us what happened exactly," Nicaula said.

"Azhara . . ." He looked at the ground. "The maidservant ran in front of our line. She wore one of your royal robes, and she told them she was the true queen in case they had killed you. Azhara said she would willingly go with them if they would spare her soldiers." His eyes shifted to Batal.

"And?" Nicaula said.

"She made us promise not to follow. They took her with them, like an innocent lamb." Rona choked on his words. "Arguments broke out among the soldiers. Some believed you were still alive and wanted to search. Others wanted to pursue the marauders."

"And you?" Batal asked. "What was your choice?"

"I thought the queen . . . dead. So I rallied the men, and we set off after the tribesmen. We pursued them until Sa'ba. But they called in reinforcements, numbering at least one thousand." He hung his head. "It was then we were forced to retreat."

The queen started to pace, anger and sorrow battling for position within her breast. Her father had warned her that some decisions would be very difficult. She took a deep breath and stopped to face the two men. "From this day, the entire civilization of Sa'ba shoulders the guilt of my father's murder and now of my maidservant's abduction. We will form a great army and claim Sa'ba as our own."

Chapter Thirteen

Yemen

A COUPLE OF LUCKY turns prevented Omar from being pursued, but that didn't ease his anxiety. Trouble seemed to follow him everywhere, especially since David Levy became his boss. Was it possible that an actual person could be bad luck? Even with the seat belt firmly attached, his body bounced off the leather seat with each rut along the road. And despite the fact that he had only a vague idea of where he was going, he drove with skillful maneuvering—not something learned in training but during a mandatory two-year stint as a government soldier.

Omar knew he had to drive northeast past Marib to the campsite where he'd buried his satellite phone. He could only hope there was enough gasoline to get him there. He suspected that David Levy knew how dangerous the job would be and wasn't worried in the least about putting Omar in the direct line of fire. In fact, he doubted Levy had lost any sleep over the fact that an agent had been missing for several days.

The angled form of a tollbooth took shape on the road ahead. Yellow light spilled from the interior, making the booth look like a lopsided beacon in the night. Omar slowed the jeep. He recognized the booth, a crooked Pepsi sign hanging from the roof and the red on the slogan bleached pink by the desert sun. At least he was on the right road, but he had no cash, so whether he was going in the right direction didn't matter much right now.

A man exited the toll station, his ample form clothed in a dingy, white tunic—true to a desert dweller. A curved jambiya knife was strapped to his girth, and a rifle was slung casually over his shoulder. "ID?"

Omar reached into his pant leg and withdrew the faded card from a pocket.

The man examined it briefly. "Where are you going?"

"To Marib."

The guard studied Omar for a moment, and then walked around the jeep, kicking each tire. He stopped next to Omar and leaned toward the dash, peering at the gas gauge. "Do you have room for a passenger? If so, the fee is waived."

Omar leaned back as far as possible. The man was inches from his face, and Omar could smell his pungent sweat mixed with qat. "Of course."

Another man emerged from the station, much slighter in figure. He moved to the guard, thanked him, and climbed into the back of the jeep.

"Many thanks," the guard said.

The tires spun as Omar accelerated, speeding along the darkened road. His passenger didn't move or speak. *All the better*, he thought. *No questions, no answers*. After several minutes, he asked, "Where do I drop you off?"

"I'll let you know when we get there."

Omar recognized the voice—*her* voice. He slowed the jeep to a stop and turned. "Mia?"

Removing her head scarf, the woman shook her dark curls free. "You're quick, Matan."

"What are you doing here?" It felt strange to hear her address him by his real name. Even in the field, she was supposed to call him by his undercover identity. He stared into familiar brown eyes framed by heavy lashes and carefully tweezed brows.

"Looking for you," she said.

Omar shrank against his seat. They'd sent someone because he'd screwed up. Of all people, it had to be *her*. He hadn't seen her since, well, four months ago on New Year's—the day she moved out of his apartment.

Now, in the moonlight, he detected her smug expression. "Sorry I troubled you," he said.

Mia smoothed a curl from her face and offered a nonchalant shrug. "When your reports ceased, they suspected something was wrong. So I put out my feelers and discovered that someone with your description was being held near Qam al Asad." She met his gaze. "I was on my way to rescue you."

"Oh . . ." Omar glanced away, feeling angry and stupid in the same instant. She had been an agent as long as he had, but already she'd moved up in the ranks. Her dialects were perfect, her disguises flawless, and her methods of reconnaissance unmatched. "How long have you been in this area?" He couldn't help staring at her again, wondering if she regretted breaking up—even for a moment.

"Just long enough to find you. They pulled me from my translator assignment at AWP."

Not surprising, Omar thought. Not only could Mia jump into any assignment and blend right in, she always managed to strike at the heart. "So they think I'm dead?"

"Hardly," Mia said, a smile lighting her eyes. "They just

thought you had some . . . trouble. What happened?"

"Well . . ." An uncomfortable warmth spread to his neck. "I became dehydrated, was kicked off the crew, lost my passports, ended up with a gash on my head, and then was stuffed into a storage room by bitter, angry men."

Mia's smile broadened. "Sounds interesting. How did you make it out?"

"Started a fire and stole this jeep."

Mia threw back her head and laughed. Omar felt his stomach tighten as her laughter tickled his skin. If there was one thing he'd missed about her . . .

"Hey," she said, her voice suddenly urgent. "I see headlights."

He turned, hearing the rumble of an engine. "And they're coming this way," he muttered, throwing the jeep into gear.

Just like old times, Omar mused as he gunned the engine. Except there was one significant difference—they were no longer a couple. She'd ended their relationship four months ago. He was getting too intense, she'd told him. Too dependent. *No*, he thought with irony, *I had just fallen in love*. That and he couldn't stand the way Mia let David Levy flirt with her. It was as if she enjoyed it.

He tried to expel the tangible memories. But the throbbing in his head wouldn't erase the ugly New Year's Eve scene—David dancing with Mia, his hands all over her, Omar standing on the sidelines, his fingers wrapped around a small ring box, helpless anger consuming him. He'd started drinking . . . a lot. The next thing he knew, a group of men were pulling him off red-faced David, and someone had called the police.

"They're gaining," Mia yelled over the roar of the tires. She catapulted into the front seat and flashed a look of warning in his direction. Omar pulled his thoughts into the present.

"The camp isn't far," he shouted. "I just need to ditch these guys so I can get my stuff back. Then you can go back to your real assignment."

"Is there anything there to protect us?"

"No." He took a quick glance behind and saw that the other vehicle was getting too close. Its headlights distorted the ground around them.

"Then stop! We won't be able to lose them. Look around us. There's nowhere to hide."

He scoffed. "Have you written your obituary?"

"I mean it. *Stop!*" Mia grabbed his arm. "I have a plan."

"A plan to get us killed . . ." Omar said, not letting up on the gas.

Her grip tightened. "Trust me."

"Funny you should ask *me* to trust *you*." He released his death-like hold on the steering wheel and coasted the jeep to a stop. He turned to Mia, taking in her windblown hair and fiery eyes. "This better be good."

"It is." She pulled her backpack from the rear seat and stuffed the pack underneath her shirt, stretching the cloth over the bulk. She adjusted the backpack so her belly looked very large, then slumped against the door. "I'm pregnant."

Bewilderment shot through him. "What?"

Mia covered her mouth and stifled a laugh. "*Pretend* I'm pregnant and I'm about to deliver your baby. Demand a doctor."

He waited for the battered truck to reach them. Three men piled out, all armed.

Omar raised his hands and yelled, "My wife is having a child! My wife is having a child."

Mia started to moan, playing the part well.

One of the men stepped cautiously forward and peered at Mia. He nodded to his companions then looked at Omar. "We'll find a midwife to help."

"Yes, that's where we are going."

Mia cried out, and the man jumped back, looking at Omar. "You come with us. You should not be around a woman like this."

Omar grimaced. Foolish desert traditions. How was he going to get out of this one? "Uh—"

"No!" Mia screamed, real perspiration on her face. "He stays with me. The djinns will take my baby if I'm left alone."

What in the—? The men drew back, their eyes wide at the mention of djinns. All Omar knew was that djinns were spirits that supposedly haunted frankincense trees and protected ancient ruins. *But hey, if it worked . . .*

"All right, all right," the man said. "We'll be back soon with the midwife."

Omar stared at the receding truck as it hurtled bits of sand and dirt into the night air. He turned to her and mirrored her contagious smile. "Djinns? How'd you come up with that?"

She ignored the question, gazing at him, lashes half-lowered. "You thought I was serious about being pregnant."

A witty remark died on his lips. "Just caught off guard." He tore his eyes from hers and started the jeep. *It wouldn't have been mine anyway.* Thoughts of what it might have been like if they were still together tossed inside his head, knowing they would have shared more than a simple smile at their success.

"How far now?" Mia asked.

Omar pointed toward the horizon. The silhouette of an oasis could be distinguished in the distance against the moon.

Mia nodded and clutched the backpack against her chest as if to protect her from the night air.

They neared the campsite, its scraggly palms bending in the desert wind. As Omar remembered, the outhouse stood prominently at the center of the camp. Not far from that was an old well—with stagnated water hardly fit for an animal. He brought the jeep to a stop. "After you," he said, motioning toward the privy. Without hesitation, Mia hurried toward the small building. *Like a true veteran.* Not even a squat pot could deter this woman.

After he took his turn in the rank facility, he joined Mia at the side of the jeep, where she handed him bottled water.

"Thanks," he said then gulped nearly half of the bottle in one swallow. His throat wanted more, but he decided to hold off and save it for later. "I'll start digging." Next to the first tree, he stooped and began to dig with his hands.

"Want to use this?" Mia asked, standing over him.

Omar glanced up and saw a small utility shovel in her hand. "Where—"

"Just part of my standard supply pouch . . . that every agent should carry."

He grasped the tool and dug, feeling his face heat. Maybe being kidnapped hadn't been so bad. He didn't know which was worse—being tied up in a small room or being chastised by his ex-girlfriend. They were about equal in torture, he decided. "Don't you have someplace to be?"

"Very funny. How about we let headquarters know you're still alive? Then you can worry about my plans."

Omar's shovel reached two feet, but still there was nothing. He sat back on his heels and wiped the gritty perspiration from his face.

"Are you sure—" she started.

"Yes. Just use yours to relay the good news. Then you can take the jeep back to Yemen."

"And leave you here alone with *nothing*?"

Omar rose and folded his arms. "I'll hook up with another crew." He knew it sounded ludicrous, but he wanted to see her reaction. "And I'll enjoy some peace in the meantime."

Mia's eyes flamed. She turned away and started toward the jeep, hair bouncing against her shoulders in defiance. "I want the shovel back when you're done!" she said over her shoulder.

"The sooner I finish, the sooner you can leave," Omar called after her. He started to dig again. *Quiet at last.* She didn't have claim on his feelings anymore, so he didn't care if he'd sounded rude. He glanced in her direction. She sat in the jeep, arms crossed, waiting. The shovel struck something solid, and soon he'd removed the waterproof case containing his things. But instead of returning immediately to the jeep, he leaned against a tree and waited for the connection. After a minute, his phone chimed. He typed his message: *Separated from the crew. Mia found me. What are the next instructions?*

Several minutes passed before the reply from David Levy came. *Don't get too excited. You lost her long before she left.*

Omar's hand tightened around the phone, threatening to crush the innocent device. Just as he was about to reply with every curse word invented, the coordinates for his next assignment popped onto the tiny screen. He stared at the message. "Unbelievable."

He straightened and walked slowly back to the jeep. Mia kept her head turned the other way, but he saw the same location flickering on her handheld instrument.

"I guess we're in this together," he mumbled, starting the engine.

According to the coordinates on the GPS feature, they were only a half day's drive from the edge of the infamous Empty Quarter—but that wasn't close enough. He was driving a stolen jeep, and any moment, the Arabs could be returning with a midwife in tow. And there were at least a dozen toll stops to slow them down.

"Got any money?" he asked.

"Of course," Mia replied in a tight voice, keeping her eyes averted. "Let me guess—yours was stolen, lost, burned, or shredded."

"Something like that."

It was going to be a very long ride.

Chapter Fourteen

The Empty Quarter

STARING INTO THE MURKY darkness of the tent, Alem let out a frustrated sigh. After he'd discovered the sword hilt the day before, the digging turned into a frenzy. Stray pieces of discolored metal were found, but nothing so specific as the decorated hilt. An archaeologist arrived in the early evening hours and estimated the artifact to the eighth or ninth century b.c. If the man was right, the discovery could be a major find indeed. When Alem had asked the archaeologist about the symbol of the snake and flower, he'd confirmed it might represent the pagan goddess `Ashtartu. The archaeologist also pointed out that some thought the queen of Sheba was a reincarnated form of `Ashtartu.

It doesn't make sense. Why would his grandmother's headstone depict the same symbol? He wished he could call his grandfather and ask him. His family had professed Christianity ever since Queen Makeda had been converted to Solomon's god. His grandmother had told him the story of how Makeda had cast her nature worshipping aside when she realized the sun could not be so powerful if it could be blotted out by a flock of birds.

Most of the lore surrounding the queen of Sheba was too fantastic for even a man of religious faith to believe. *Let alone me.* Her supposed goat legs and cloven feet led to other myths depicted in art around the world. A statue at Dijon's Saint-Bénigne cathedral showed the queen with goose-like feet. Even more preposterous was the claim that Solomon had the hair removed from her legs before bedding her. What Hebrew man, ancient or modern, cared about hair on a woman's legs?

Alem heard the arrival of another vehicle. A second expert in ancient artifacts? He exited his tent. At the edge of the camp, the crew boss stood next to a Land Rover with a man dressed in a police uniform.

Maybe his boss would be arrested for the murder of his assistant. Then Alem saw that the conversation was friendly. When Rabbel noticed Alem, he and the officer moved toward him. Introductions were made, and the officer heartily shook hands with Alem. "You are the one who made the discovery?"

"Yes." Alem looked from one man to the other, not sure if being the object of their interest was a good thing.

"Very nice." The officer looked at Rabbel and gave a brief nod.

Rabbel said, "You will come with us tomorrow—to another site. We've just received permission to excavate in Oman. The rest of the crew will remain here."

Alem stiffened. The last thing he wanted to do was travel to another country with these men. "My visa is good only for this country."

The officer winked. "Don't worry about that."

As Alem walked back to his tent, fear gripped him. He had no defenses against a man who killed and an officer of the law—or the lawless. Desperately, he thought of stealing a truck and leaving—or even taking a bag of food and jogging away in the moonlight. He'd be able to clock at least ten miles before sunrise, but common sense told him he'd be fine as long as he did his job. He shook his head at the thought of another wild ride through the desert. He'd come across the sword hilt by chance, and he didn't want to be singled out from the other workers.

Entering the tent, he settled onto his hard bed. He closed his eyes, thinking about his grandmother's letter. *Find her.* If one good thing came from this new change, it might be that it would bring him closer to the discovery of the queen. If nothing else, at the end of it all, he hoped the paycheck would be worth the trouble.

☙ ❧

MORNING CAME TOO SOON, and Alem felt a boot at his side, rousing him from sleep. Rabbel stood over him. "Pack your things. We leave immediately."

As the boss left, Alem scrambled to his feet and shoved everything he had into his duffle bag. He rolled his sleeping bag and secured it, with the pillow tucked beneath the ties. He glanced at the Yemeni who shared the tent. The man's snores indicated that his dreams hadn't been interrupted by the disturbance.

"Good-bye," Alem whispered with a half-hearted wave in the man's direction. He moved to the campfire and gulped down a cup of bitter coffee. He grabbed a flat pita and gnawed at one end, feeling sand grate against his teeth. *No matter how long I stay on the crew, I doubt I'll ever get used to the bleak menu*, he thought as he moved to the waiting Land Rover.

Alem settled against the already warm seat in the back of the Land Rover as they traveled into the rising sun, speeding across the desert floor. The dunes continued to tower on the north side, and a collection of wadis rushed by on the south. Time passed in a blur—hot wind preventing any real conversation. Hours into the drive, he sank against his duffel bag and tried to nap. The lull of the humming tires and the driving wind eventually gave him rest.

As the evening sun pushed at their backs, Alem woke and noticed the changed landscape. A few palms dotted the terrain, and groves of brush had crept up. The SUV slowed, and Alem straightened in his seat. He leaned out his window, trying to make out the curious shapes in the distance.

"Shisur," Rabbel shouted over the engine by way of explanation. "An oasis with structures built thousands of years ago."

"We're already in Oman, then?" Alem asked.

"Yes," the officer said. He slowed the Land Rover another notch. His voice carried easily into the backseat now. "This oasis is part of the region of Ubar. And here, because of your good fortune in finding the ancient sword, you'll be able to scare the djinns from their hiding places and discover their secrets about the queen."

Alem stared ahead. His grandmother had told him that djinns could be evil spirits or demons that protected sacred ground. They lived in frankincense trees, and the superstitious used to make offerings to the spirits before they collected the resin. Fables alleged the queen of Sheba had a djinn for a mother. "How am *I* to do this?"

Rabbel's eyes glinted. "By performing an ancient rite."

It was probably lighting some candles and saying prayers, Alem decided. Or a maqyal ceremony, and they'd sit around chewing qat.

When they stopped at Shisur, the three men set to work raising a tent. From across the collection of ruins, Alem saw a cluster of homes, forming a small village of sorts. Those in the settlement paid no attention to the men setting up camp on the other side of the ruins.

Darkness advanced over the ancient land as Rabbel built a fire. Dinner was a light fare, consisting of dried meat, pita, and a few nearly spoiled tomatoes.

"Tomorrow we start digging?" Alem asked, surveying the men across the glow of the fire.

"It depends," the officer said.

"Are we waiting for others to show up?"

Rabbel stood and the officer followed. They walked around the campfire toward Alem. He started to rise too, but the officer pushed him to the ground.

"Hey," Alem said, "What's going—"

The officer's hands clapped around his neck. Alem tried to twist away. Grabbing the officer's wrists, Alem clawed at the man's hands, looking to Rabbel for help. But Rabbel was suddenly on top of him, pinning him to the ground. Alem struggled, but the pressure on his neck increased, and soon his vision went black.

When Alem regained consciousness, the first thing he was aware of was the aching stiffness and cold in his limbs. He stared wildly into the darkness, trying to gain his bearings. He couldn't see the moon or stars, so he concluded he was inside the tent. Ropes dug into his mouth, wrists, and ankles. He wriggled against the bindings, feeling the pain radiate from his neck to his mouth. Moaning, he tried to sit up, but he had no way of supporting himself. He felt cool sand beneath his skin and realized he'd been stripped to his underwear.

Something pricked his leg, and Alem stiffened. When the sensation passed, he wondered if it was his imagination. He'd heard enough tales of scorpions and snakes.

A forlorn melody, sounding like a flute, floated from somewhere. He smelled smoke—probably from a campfire. A maniacal laugh rang from outside, blending with the melody.

Then a gust of wind burst against his exposed skin, and his senses screamed into action.

"Look. He's awake." Rabbel's voice.

Hands gripped Alem's arms and dragged him out of the tent. He twisted, using a burst of energy, but Rabbel and the officer laughed.

Alem struggled with fury. "Let me go!"

Rabbel laughed again. "Tonight you'll be our gift to the djinns, and in return, we'll find the queen."

The men dragged him toward the fire. The melody grew louder, and Alem craned his head to see where it was coming from. Beyond the reach of the firelight sat a row of straggly Bedu men—inhabitants of the desert—their faces mere skeletons, skin stretched tight over their prominent bones. Wiry hair grew from their chins, reaching to the middle of their chests. The lyrical notes soared into the air, becoming more pronounced, more frenzied.

The officer held a flaming torch close to Alem's face, and he felt his eyebrows singe. He cried out, but the other men just laughed.

Then in one motion, he was dropped to the ground, face up. Hands seemed to come out of nowhere, pinning him down. "Don't move," the officer growled. He removed the long dagger from his belt and pressed it against Alem's neck. With a sharp pain, Alem's skin sliced open beneath the pressure, and warm blood slipped along his collarbone. The knife moved to his shoulder and cut again. Alem tried to scream, but a piece of cloth was shoved into his mouth. Haziness clouded his eyes as he hovered between consciousness and unconsciousness.

Before Alem passed into oblivion, he saw Rabbel's face inches away, a smaller knife in his hand.

The cutting had already begun.

Chapter Fifteen

East of Sa'ba, Yemen
963 b.c.

AS THE FINGERS OF dawn stretched across the horizon, Nicaula adjusted the leather breastplate against her torso. Her army of three thousand was in position, stationed around the low-lying hills just outside of Sa'ba. It had taken nearly two moons to assemble her militia, but even if Azhara had perished, the revenge would reach gloriously toward heaven, where the maid's soul dwelt for suffering a martyr's death.

The city of Sa'ba still slept, its night guards sluggish at their posts. Through her spies, Nicaula had learned the guard change occurred just before daybreak—when they planned to infiltrate the city. The queen mounted her mare, then adjusted her headdress, since she wouldn't wear her crown until victory was assured. The delicate silk weave of the scarf was intertwined with fine pearls, but her real treasure would be rescuing Azhara—with the marauders found and punished and the ring of Sheba recovered.

Guiding her mare, Nicaula approached the front line where Batal sat on his horse at the helm, perfectly poised, his expression

filled with all the seriousness his youth could muster. After
his fearless protection of her, the queen had elevated him to
commander. The other soldiers bowed their heads as she rode
among them, inspecting their uniforms and their beasts. Win or lose,
the sight of her army would be great to behold.

She paused when she reached Batal's side. The lightening sky
warmed the ebony locks framing his moist face, and a flicker of
tenderness registered in his gaze when their eyes met. Her breath
caught for an instant. Recovering, she said, "It's almost time."

"I'll stay to protect you, O Queen."

For a moment, she wished it could be so. No, she ached for
him to stay, but she pushed away any selfish desire. "I have guards
aplenty to accompany me. You're commander now and must lead
the men to victory."

Batal held her gaze. The queen couldn't take her eyes from him,
noticing flecks of concern in his eyes. She guessed him to be in his
seventeenth or eighteenth year, and while she was close to his age,
she felt a motherly protection for him. That explained the seed of
fear in her heart. It was just concern that any mother might have, yet
she longed to reach out and grasp his hand. "Go and conquer in my
name."

She turned and urged her horse behind the line of soldiers
before she did anything unbecoming to a queen. She waited
breathlessly to witness Batal's first command. He raised his
steel sword for silence. With one motion, he brought his sword
downward through the air and heeled his horse. By order of the
queen, no cry went up, but it was as though three thousand hearts
shouted in unison as the army surged forward—one goal in mind.

Moving her horse to the crest of the hill, Nicaula watched
the men flow toward the city. She could well imagine the guards'
astonishment. She wondered if Azhara would be able to hear the

battle from her confinement and know that vengeance had arrived.

In the distance, the resonance of a conch shell pushed through the air—the warning had sounded. Blood rushed through Nicaula's veins in anticipation as the army neared Sa'ba. She'd given strict instructions that the women and children be left alone and for the fighting to cease at the first sign of surrender. Perhaps the chieftain of the region was a reasonable man upon defeat.

The day wore long and hot, and each moment seemed to stretch into an hour as Nicaula paced the camp. She'd commanded that a flag should be raised upon victory. But there was still no sign.

The soldiers who had stayed to protect her stood huddled in groups. They had wished to fight with their comrades, but their task was even more important. No matter what happened to the soldiers at Sa'ba, the queen must be preserved.

In the late afternoon, the man from the lookout post cried, "Someone approaches!"

The queen gathered her robe and ran in that direction, and immediately, several soldiers fell into step beside her. Nicaula reached the rise just in time to see a soldier on horseback plowing toward them. In his hand, he held a stick with a crimson flag attached.

"Batal!" She stood braced against the heated wind and blowing sand, watching the horse and its rider approach. Satisfaction swelled within as she saw his triumphant face and his firm grip on the flag.

The other soldiers in the camp surrounded the hillside as they waited for the first news. Reining the horse to a stop, Batal grinned through the dust covering his face. "In the name of our queen, we have captured the marauders, and the land of Sa'ba belongs to Sheba."

Nicaula cried out then brought her hands to her mouth. In a flurry of flowing linen and silk, she ran to Batal and gripped the horse's reins. "Well done." She took a deep breath, steeling herself. "And Azhara?"

"She lives."

The queen bowed her head for a moment as gratitude flooded through her. Batal removed a folded cloth from beneath his tunic and presented the item to the queen. She unfolded the cloth to find the ring of Sheba. Meeting Batal's smile, she felt as if their hearts were joined for an instant.

Then sense of duty claimed her better judgment, and the queen turned to face the other men. "We'll prepare for our victory ride through the city roads."

The men fell into action, striking tents, gathering food supplies, and loading the camels. Nicaula walked to her horse, surveying the activity. Several of the men gathered around Batal, jubilant as he told of the successful battle. His bloodstained clothes were inspected, and someone brought him shrub tea. The queen smiled and turned from them, hoping no one had seen her glistening eyes.

When everything was nearly prepared, Nicaula climbed onto her horse and met Batal at the front of the procession. His face and hair had been bathed, and he wore a clean mantle about his shoulders. He masterfully controlled his horse that still trembled from its run, the heaving muscles of the beast nearly matched by its master's.

"We have avenged your father, O Queen," Batal said, his voice confident.

"Yes," Nicaula said, catching the triumph in his youthful eyes. "The king's death has been honored at last." Slowly, she felt the weight settle on her shoulders as she turned and saw all the men waiting silently for her next command.

A new city to add to her kingdom, a new people . . . and she'd be doing it without her father. The ring had taken its rightful place of honor on her finger.

She held out her jeweled hand toward Batal. "On this victorious day, as commander of my army, you will lead this procession."

When they reached the city, Nicaula guided her horse through the dusty lanes. Mud and rocks made up the walls of the squat homes within the defeated walls of Sa'ba; dried palm fronds provided inadequate shade. Death still hovered among the residents and high-pitched wailing permeated the neighborhoods: women, grieving for their men, gathered in front of their homes, tearing their clothing and smearing their faces with ashes. The queen sat stiffly on her animal, feeling the wails pierce her back with ferocity.

She tried to ignore the emotion building in her throat. These women were not guilty of the crimes their men committed. She turned toward Batal, who rode beside her. "How many killed?"

"A few hundred. All military leaders fled or were killed."

"And where are the marauders being held?"

"Under guard at the palace."

Nicaula focused ahead again, ignoring the open stares that followed her presence. Some of the women even stopped in their cries to watch her pass. "Where is Azhara?"

"She waits for you at the palace. She'll not speak until she sees you." Batal glanced at the onlookers. "The people are curious about the queen. They see a woman has come to rule, and they think you must be a goddess."

The queen snapped her head around and looked at the commander, a smile curving her lips. "A *goddess*? Is that what you told them?"

Batal's face flushed. "I told them nothing. I've only heard the soldiers talking."

"And the chieftain? Is he under guard too?"

"He fled before we reached the city. And he will not be back."

Nicaula looked at the soldier in surprise. A chief who wouldn't fight? "He doesn't care for his people?"

"The people do not care for *him*." He raised a bronzed arm and pointed down the road. "We are very close now."

The queen squinted against the gathered gloom. The sun had just set, bringing cool shadows to the path. Up ahead, she saw a crumpled form in the middle of the road. A young child was on the ground, his mother crying over him.

"Halt," Nicaula said.

One by one, the surrounding soldiers reined their beasts. Batal climbed off his horse, and when the queen extended her hand, he helped her down. A few villagers, who had been following them, gathered as closely as they were allowed. Nicaula moved to the small body and stooped. The mother looked up, grief in her eyes.

The queen watched the boy's chest rise and fall with jagged breaths. A long gash adorned his small arm. Nicaula stared at the pale face and the dark lashes spread against his thin cheeks. He couldn't be more than five or six years of age.

The queen stood. "What happened to this child? No children were to be harmed."

Batal took a step forward, his mouth drawn tight. "I issued the command myself. Every soldier was informed."

Nicaula let out her breath as she held the commander's gaze. "Bring this boy with us. He will be attended to by *my* physician. Allow the mother to follow." She turned to the villagers. "And let it be known that I am a merciful leader."

Climbing on her horse, Nicaula spurred it forward. Once she reached the dilapidated palace, she dismounted and led the others inside. The dead bodies had been removed, but the stench of death still remained. Torches lined the walls, their fiery light making the entrance hall look somewhat welcoming. "More light," Nicaula said. "And we need water and food for the child."

She sidestepped a puddle of drying blood and noticed it streaked along most of the hall. "Where is Nabil?"

The healer ran forward, and Nicaula studied the shrunken man, wearing battle garb that overwhelmed his thin frame. "You should not have gone into battle. Your healing skills are more valuable than your combat skills."

He bowed his head.

"You may attend the boy now." The queen turned and scanned the room, assessing the disarray, from the broken tables, the trampled food, and the bits of clothing and armor, to the collected dirt and hay. Batal was in conversation with another soldier. He was a natural leader, and the other soldiers respected him. She knew she'd made the right decision in making him commander. It would also mean that she'd have more interaction with him.

She crossed to his side. "Take me to Azhara."

Batal led her past the great hall and through a silent corridor. He kept a respectful distance from her, and suddenly she longed for the privacy they'd shared after the dunes. They stopped at a locked door, and he knocked. "The queen is here."

After a moment, the latch clanged, and the door opened.

Nicaula blinked against the dimness. A skeleton of what used to be a vibrant girl stood there—feet bare, legs and arms bruised, clothing torn, and most of her head shaved with the remaining hair hanging in ragged clumps. "Azhara?"

The servant hung her head as tears dripped to the floor.

"What have they done to you?" The queen stepped forward and took the girl's hands in hers. They were scratched and scarred as if she had been in many fights.

"We found her chained to that wall," Batal said.

Nicaula's eyes strayed to the far corner, where ugly, metal

shackles protruded from the stone. The surrounding wall and floor were soiled with urine, feces, and blood.

"We released her from the chains," Batal continued. "But she refused to leave the room until you came."

"Poor girl," Nicaula said, cradling Azhara's face. The queen's own tears formed and joined with the servant's. Then Azhara fell against her queen, trembling as pitiful sobs broke through. The queen stroked her shorn hair, which looked as if someone had hacked it off with a sword. Festering cuts on her skull were visible through the stubble.

When the girl's sobs faded, the queen drew away and examined Azhara's ruined body, not missing the dried blood on her thighs. She turned to Batal. "Where are the marauders?"

"In the outer courtyard behind the palace."

Nicaula nodded, a hot flash of rage pulsing through her. She leaned over and kissed Azhara's forehead. "Call in the women."

Moments later, two servants entered the room, their eyes taking in Azhara's appearance.

"Draw the girl a bath," the queen instructed, and both women bowed. Nicaula turned to Azhara. "The healer, Nabil, will attend to you after you bathe. Do not be afraid."

The maid nodded, her lips trembling.

Nicaula backed out of the room and joined Batal in the hallway. "Take me to the marauders."

They walked in heavy silence back to the grand hall, where Batal gathered four other soldiers. The men led the queen through the maze of corridors with low ceilings. When they reached the final door connecting to the outer courtyard, she took a deep breath before stepping out into the night.

There were at least a dozen of them: hardened desert dwellers. They wore ragged shifts around their waists, torsos bare and nearly blackened by the sun. Raised welts of self-mutilation covered their arms and chests. Nicaula saw no fear in their gazes. No respect. No allegiance. No human soul.

Batal and the other soldiers flanked the queen's sides, but seeing the hungry looks of the desert raiders, she felt as if she stood alone and naked. These men were guilty of abominable acts toward Azhara.

Nicaula wasted no time asking about the servant girl. Instead, she walked straight toward the leader. The only change in his expression was the glint of his black eyes. "You have the evil heart of Onuris," the queen said. "You are like the forsaken war god who delights in bloodshed and death, but not for this will you die."

She looked at the men surrounding the leader, feeling their bloodthirsty eyes roam over her body. "You have murdered my father and left our people to rot on the desert floor, yet you will not die because of my desire for vengeance." She kept her gaze steady, ignoring the foul stench permeating from the men. "You have taken a young girl and destroyed her virtue—which is graver than taking life itself."

The queen lifted her chin, rising to her full height. "And for *that* you will all suffer a robber's sentence. At sunrise, both your hands will be cut off, and you will live the rest of your days begging for that which you can no longer steal."

Her gaze traveled over the other men. "All of you will suffer this mercy."

The leader chuckled, and Nicaula turned away from him. She heard several men spit and curse her name. Her soldiers rushed forward and clobbered the offenders. She exited the courtyard without a backward glance, feeling as if fiery arrows had pierced her soul, while the other soldiers remained outside, defending the queen's good name.

Once inside the palace walls, her knees weakened. She stopped in an empty corridor and tried to calm herself. Batal followed and stopped, standing so close that she could almost feel his breath on her neck. Almost . . .

She turned and leaned against him. He stiffened for a moment, and then slowly his arms encircled her. His chest was warm, reminding her that a good heart beat inside *this* man and that not all men were capable of such horrors.

After several deep breaths, she pulled away. Looking up at Batal, she saw the question in his eyes, but she wasn't ready to come up with an answer. She turned and walked to the grand hall, ready to announce the punishments to her people. Hearing Batal's footsteps following her, she wondered if perhaps her father had been wrong. Perhaps a queen could marry for love.

⚬ᣟᏇ Ꮗᣟ⚬

DAYBREAK TRAVELED SLOWLY ACROSS the arid plain, and as the glow touched Nicaula's chamber, she opened her eyes. She burrowed beneath her rug, imagining the bedcover like Batal's arms—securely wrapped around her. Then her mind flooded with the monumental task ahead of her. Suddenly the rug became cold and unwelcoming, and the image of Batal's caress faded into obscurity.

Nicaula threw aside the cover and climbed off her bed. She was disgusted with herself. Thinking of a man while Azhara—tortured and bruised—slept at the foot of her bed. Nicaula watched the girl sleep, only imagining what images of terror existed behind the servant's restless eyelids.

But this morning, it will all end. Then I'll forget my foolish heart and be the queen I was born to become. The queen pulled her robe about her shoulders, shivering in the morning cool. Her stomach was empty, but she'd enjoy no food until the unpleasant task was completed.

For a wild instant, Nicaula wanted to wake Azhara and escort her to the scene of torture. The girl would be able to see her vengeance enacted.

No, she should never have to see their faces again. Instead of waking the girl, Nicaula performed her own toilette with the water brought in the night before. Then she picked up an ivory brush and combed through her dark tangles. A few long strands of black hair fell at her feet, curling like snakes on the floor. The queen twisted her hair and fastened it high on her head with two gold pins. Then she donned her headdress and adjusted the veil so it concealed her entire face. Those demonic men would not see her almond eyes in the light of day.

Unlatching the door, the queen moved silently into the hallway, where two soldiers stood at attention, bowing their heads upon seeing her. Nicaula was slightly disappointed not to find Batal among them, but, of course, he would be attending to more important matters. "The girl still sleeps within," Nicaula said. "Continue to guard the room from any disturbance."

Both men nodded and maintained their positions.

The queen walked to the main hall where Rona, Batal, and several other soldiers prepared for the morning rite. When they saw her, they bowed their heads. Nicaula's gaze halted on Batal's dark curls for an instant too long, so when he raised his head, he caught her staring at him.

Her face heated, and she spoke more harshly than she'd intended. "Are the bindings prepared?"

Rona rose from his place. "You want to bind the wounds?"

"Yes," the queen said, trying not to look at Batal again. "I don't want any of them to have the luxury of bleeding to death. Their souls will remain on earth with their miserable bodies."

The men returned to sharpening their daggers against a large stone. As each man finished, they silently assembled and waited for the queen's instruction. "No one man will be required to perform the order. The vengeance will be on all of your hands as we unite as one voice and denounce their murderous and torturous traditions."

The queen took the lead, and the men followed. They reached the courtyard just as the sun's rays tipped the outer wall. The gray shadows warmed, and the stench of the night before had dissipated with the morning breeze.

Most of the marauders were already awake, and the others stirred to life as the soldiers surrounded the courtyard. One prisoner in particular shook violently.

"We will start with the leader," the queen said.

Batal nodded once then called for the leader to be brought. Two soldiers flanked the man's sides as he passed by the queen. With a fierce grunt, he lunged and Nicaula drew back, narrowly avoiding contact. The man spat and cursed. Batal fell upon him, pressing his dagger against the man's neck. "He should die for this," Batal said, his muscles tense, waiting for the queen's permission.

"No! Death would be a reward," she said.

Batal forced the prisoner to kneel and place his hands on a slab. A shiver moved along the queen's neck, but Batal's gaze was distant, unnerving, as he held the man's arms by force. Rona took a step forward and gave the command. A soldier moved into place and brought down his blade against the marauder's wrist. The clang of metal against stone reverberated through the courtyard. The man screamed so loud that the second strike could not be heard. The queen kept her head turned toward the other prisoners, seeing the horror in their expressions.

Two soldiers rushed forward and bandaged the leader's wrists as he continued screaming and struggling violently against them. But after a moment, his body went limp. As the next prisoner was brought forward, again Nicaula couldn't watch. Pity and rage mixed together, creating a hole of nausea in her stomach. When the last man had met his fate, the queen nodded her approval in Rona's direction. Then she left the courtyard with Batal close behind. His quiet presence was comforting, but she didn't turn to him as she had the night before. Her mind was clearer now—her focus more sure.

She left Batal standing outside her chambers as she entered and crossed to Azhara's mat. The servant still slept, her breathing steady. The queen moved toward the basin, removing her veil and headdress, and splashed the tepid water onto her face. She placed her still-wet hands against the table and took a deep, trembling breath. *It is finished.*

The queen removed the small statue of the sun goddess from the side table and placed it on the windowsill. The sun pierced its way through the narrow opening, casting a fiery glow around the miniature body. Nicaula knelt on the rug, then raised both hands and quietly chanted. "O `Ashtartu," she whispered. "Our victory over Sa'ba comes from your grace. Our avengement for our king comes from your mercy. Our union with Azhara comes from your honorable compassion."

Azhara stirred fitfully in her sleep.

The queen fell silent again, mouthing "O `Ashtartu" again and again.

Chapter Sixteen

The Empty Quarter

OMAR STRETCHED HIS ARM over the back of Mia's seat. Despite the furnace-like air blowing full strength, she slept deeply. The sun had risen, peaked, and now made its slow jog to the west. They'd burned through more than half of Mia's cash at the various checkpoints and toll shacks along the desert route.

As far as Omar could see, there was nothing, unless he counted the occasional scrub brush or spooked hare. *Why would anyone want to live in such a desolate place?* The expeditions of explorers had been over-romanticized, he decided.

He maneuvered the jeep along the bumpy road, surprised that Mia continued to sleep through all the jostling. He glanced at her aquiline nose and full lips, noticing with a painful lurch how her lashes seemed to flutter above her cheeks. Peeling his eyes away, he stared at the bleakness ahead. He didn't actually need to look at her to remember every curve of her body.

Omar flexed his sweaty palm against the steering wheel, cursing the heat, the sand, and the woman whose heart had turned cold toward him. Up ahead, against the shimmering desert floor, he saw another checkpoint. At this rate, they'd be broke before they reached their destination. And he was starving. Nothing made him crankier than an empty stomach.

Mia released a huge yawn, and her eyes opened as he downshifted gears. She straightened and leaned toward the bug-splattered windshield. "Looks like trouble."

Omar arched a brow, noticing how her perspiration-soaked shirt clung to her slim waist. "How so?"

"See their head wraps?"

"Grayish—one flap hanging over the shoulder. So?"

"They're the Bargusoi tribe, originally from the coast of India, and they are known for their fierce tempers. Even if I really were in labor, we wouldn't be getting through this checkpoint unscathed."

"Are their guns bigger than ours?"

"It's not funny," Mia snapped. "I'm not worried about their guns. It's their appetites."

"So they're a little hungry? Me too."

"As hungry as a cannibal?"

Omar nearly slammed on the brakes. "What?" He stared at Mia for an instant then looked back at the road. "Let me guess—they watched *Hannibal* or *Survivor* one too many times and decided it was a great way to save on living expenses?"

Mia let out a disgusted snort. "I see you haven't changed." She pointed to a dry wadi that sloped away from the road. "That's your best chance. They won't be expecting it."

"We'll also get shot at least eight times before the jeep overturns because of its dead driver."

An exasperated sigh escaped Mia. "Their ancestors—the Hippioprosōpoi—believed true power came from the consumption of another's blood, preferably the blood of their opponents. By eating the flesh of their enemies, they would take their enemy's strengths."

"So did it work?" Omar asked, then cried out as Mia struck him in the arm. She reached over and swung the wheel to the right.

"Here we go! Step on it!"

Omar elbowed Mia aside and took control of the steering, maneuvering the vehicle down the steep incline toward the wadi. He couldn't see the checkpoint any longer, but his body tensed as he anticipated a shower of shells piercing his arms and back. For several seconds, he concentrated on avoiding potholes and a few sparse acacia trees.

Mia extracted her Kalashnikov rifle from the back and knelt on the seat. Bracing one foot against the dash, she pointed the weapon to the left as she scanned the road that ran parallel to the wadi.

"Faster!"

Omar jockeyed their speed to nearly fifty kilometers per hour. He knew this would throw off the accuracy of any extra-hungry cannibals, but he hoped it wouldn't break down the shooting accuracy of the non-distressed damsel at his side.

"Are they coming after us?" he shouted above the roaring engine.

"Yes."

Omar craned his neck to see above the ridge. Still nothing. "All I see is flying sand."

"That's because you're seeing their dust. They're going to try to head us off."

"Should we turn around?"

"No! I've got an idea."

"This better be good," Omar yelled just as they hit a particularly deep hole.

Mia bounced hard enough that she slammed against the windshield with a thud. Not missing a beat, she straightened and repositioned her rifle. "It's good." She grabbed the steering wheel again. "Stop the jeep now."

"You're kidding." He kept the pressure on the gas pedal, but Mia slid her foot beneath his leg and reached the brake.

"We can play footsies later." He cranked the jeep to a sudden stop, and Mia jabbed him in the ribs. He threw his hands in the air. "All right, all right. You hold them off, and I'll run the other direction."

"Very funny." Mia stepped out of the jeep, her face and upper body caked in sand. With her gun propped against her left side, she put her finger to her lips then pointed to the ground.

Omar noticed a few patches of mud. It must have rained in the past couple of days. He shook his head. Was she going to pelt mud chunks at them?

"Where there's mud, there's almost always a snake." She crouched and lifted her finger. Only a few paces away, a dull-red snake, etched with a black-and-white pattern, lay beneath a rock. "Ah-ha. A saw-scaled viper." Mia ignored the whine of the approaching engine as she moved stealthily closer.

The viper moved, creating a rasping sound. Mia used her gun to pin the reptile to the sheltering rock and reached for the snake with one hand. "Got him. He's small but deadly." Straightening, she held up the writhing snake like a trophy. Her dusty smile confirmed her accomplishment. "Let's see if they're as scared of snakes as their ancestors were. Drive behind me, slowly."

She moved out in front of the jeep and walked toward the truck barreling along the wadi toward them.

"I hope she knows what she's doing," Omar muttered as he trailed her. The approaching truck showed no signs of slowing. Despite all the heartache she'd put him through, he couldn't help admiring the woman.

The gray-clad pursuers came to an abrupt halt, and the men

barreled out of the truck. *Eight men.* Omar braked quickly and jumped out of the jeep, his assault rifle in hand.

"Must be a slow day in the Empty Quarter," Omar said as he sidled up to Mia's snake-less side.

She held the limp snake in front of her.

The driver was just climbing out when he noticed the snake, apparently for the first time, for he shimmied right back behind the wheel. He shouted something in a panicked voice to the other men, who stopped—hearing the warning and seeing the snake at the same time.

"Hare Krishna, Hare Krishna . . ." Mia chanted.

Omar stared at her. He didn't know she had such melodic talent. It sounded like some oldie playing on Saudi radio.

"O Krishna! O Radhe . . . O Caitanya Mahaprabhu . . . O Nityananda Prabhu . . . Please be merciful!"

The men stood still, seemingly mesmerized by Mia's voice. Her words grew in strength and rose in pitch. Suddenly the snake jerked awake as if it had been sleeping.

The men pushed and tripped over each other as they stumbled to their truck. They flung themselves into the bed with a few grunts and yelps. The driver wasted no time in stripping the gears into reverse, turning the truck around, and creating rising billows of dust in farewell.

Omar turned, openmouthed, to Mia. She squatted near the ground and released the snake, which slithered away as though it didn't mind the brief interruption. Mia brushed her hands together and straightened. With one hand shielding her eyes, she glanced at the sky. "We should make it before nightfall."

"And you became a snake charmer . . . when?"

"My stepfather was a herpetologist, remember?"

"Uh, yeah. But I didn't realize you had such a knack for

reptiles."

Mia flashed a grin as a breeze lifted the damp tendrils from her face. "No big deal. I'm glad it was useful."

He smiled back. "Yeah. Me too. And the whole chanting thing? Also learned from your dad?" He remembered something about her father's scientific interests, but now he wished he'd paid a little more attention.

"My mom." Mia climbed into the jeep. "Remember she taught ancient Arabian studies at Hebrew U? On the side, she threw in a little belly dancing and snake charming. That's how my parents met; he saw her charm a snake."

"Makes sense. I don't know any herpetologist who wouldn't fall for a snake charmer."

Mia lifted a brow. "That's what you said last time I told you."

"Ah," he said as he settled into the driver's seat. "I'm seeing the larger picture." *I am an idiot.*

"I knew you'd come around."

He fought the incredible impulse to apologize for being a possessive jerk, an idiot, a moron . . . but stopped himself just in time. "What do you mean by 'come around,' exactly?"

"What do *you* mean by seeing the larger picture?"

"Just that I'm beginning to realize that maybe you were a little right."

"Only a *little*?"

He cast a sideways glance at her, turning the key in the ignition. "If you weren't so standoffish, I'd show my gratitude with more than saying thanks."

Mia propped her heavy boots on the dash. "Keep dreaming—"

The engine sputtered to life, drowning out her last words, but Omar detected the slight hint of a smile.

Chapter Seventeen

Ethiopia

JADE SETTLED AGAINST THE leather upholstery in the first-class cabin with a sigh. The last hour had been a whirlwind as she and Lucas were escorted by the patriarch's bodyguards through airport customs and into the first-class section of EgyptAir.

Lucas sat across the aisle from her. He fished in his pocket and brought out a folded piece of paper. "Read this."

She read the printed email from Dr. Lyon, written to the patriarch, about a tunnel excavation in northern Jerusalem. Palestinians had dug the tunnel to escape harassment at the Israeli guarded border. "A diagram was found. Very confidential. Call me as soon as possible." She looked at the date. Then a chill spread across her arms. It was written the same day Dr. Lyon died. "Did the patriarch call him?"

"Yes, but he said there was no answer."

"How much do you think the patriarch knows about what Dr. Lyon wanted to tell him?"

"I'm not sure."

"Maybe the queen was buried in Jerusalem."

Lucas chuckled. "Quite possible, mademoiselle."

A shiver warmer than the cool plane touched Jade.

He took out a notebook from his bag and started to sketch a timeline with his pencil. "Let's start with what DiscoveryArch revealed about the Jerusalem tomb. The inscriptions on the tomb walls omit any reference to David or Solomon."

Jade leaned across the aisle, watching him draw. "Well, it wasn't their tomb then."

"It wasn't Solomon's tomb, but the king buried there lived during the same era as Solomon." Lucas printed the word *Amariel*. "A king by the name of Amariel apparently ruled Jerusalem from 960–949 B.C. Before him, his father ruled for fifteen years. And after Amariel, his son and successor, Tambariah, ruled from 949–936 B.C." He wrote the names of David and Solomon and circled them. "Some on DiscoveryArch have suggested that the kingdom was divided, or these new kings ruled over Babylonia."

"Not possible," Jade said, noticing how his tanned fingers wrote the words in elegant script. "Solomon is considered to have ruled from Syria to the borders of Egypt as early as 980 B.C. to as late as 950 B.C."

"Right." Lucas continued drawing, inserting numbers as he went. "These years overlap Amariel and Tambariah, creating evidence that cannot be discredited so easily."

"So that doesn't leave much room for David or Solomon."

"Right again. After all, the tomb in Jerusalem proves that these kings existed. And proof of existence is something we don't have for either David or Solomon."

Jade entered the names of Amariel and Tambariah into her phone. "What about the Ark of the Covenant?"

He closed the notebook. "It's always been anyone's guess . . . at least for those who consider the Bible to be historical gospel."

"It *is* gospel." Jade noticed how relaxed he seemed, as if he'd spent many hours debating this very topic. His expression was open, amused. Like a predator, waiting for his prey to fall into his trap. *So smooth, so patient.* She twisted her ring, feeling her face heat.

A hint of a smile rose to his lips. "Not everyone has such conviction as you, mademoiselle, and they'd like to see that conviction destroyed."

"Why?"

"Money."

Jade fought not to roll her eyes. "All right. Beyond the *money*, what benefit is there to prove David and Solomon never existed?"

"How many nations recognize Israel as a state?"

"Most of them, except the Arab ones—"

"Not necessarily." Lucas folded his arms. "The major dispute in Israel between the Jews and the Arabs is not about religion but land, or, more specifically, *ownership* of what they consider sacred land."

"Of course, that's understandable."

"What do the Jews call Israel?"

"The Holy Land."

"Yes. But they also call it their *homeland*." Lucas crossed his legs. "They claim Israel as their homeland because they are descendants of the great kings David and Solomon." He lowered his voice. "If Solomon never existed, where does that leave the Jews?"

"Without rightful claim to Israel."

"Correct." A triumphant smile spread across his face. "As we speak, someone is desperately trying to line up all the appropriate evidence to prove Israel's statehood illicit. And Dr. Lyon knew it. And the tomb in Jerusalem cast enough doubt—"

"So they bombed it."

Lucas nodded. "Dr. Lyon's theory about Ubar may be only a theory, and perhaps he came up with it in defense of the tomb excavation in Jerusalem, to explain the line of three kings. The Yemenis in particular would love to believe the professor is right, and nations will spend millions to uncover any threads of evidence."

Sighing, Jade jotted a couple more ideas into her phone. "What's *our* role?"

"We're going to Ubar right after Addis Ababa—to finish what Dr. Lyon started."

"What about my thesis? I can't hop from city to city—"

"Ubar isn't a city. It's a region. Your thesis will be better than anything else written on the subject. Forget the theories out there of the queen living in Egypt. We're going right to the heart of her birth land."

Staring at him, she shook her head. "Isn't it all just a big desert?"

Lucas chuckled. "That's an understatement. The dunes in the Empty Quarter reach over two hundred meters, and man can travel only in the night during the hot summer months. Thesiger once called the desert of Southern Arabia 'a bitter, desiccated land,' but it wasn't always that way. In the early 1990s, Nicolas Clapp discovered an entire civilization beneath the sand, with a little help from NASA. In antiquity, what we now know as a desert bloomed like a garden—fertile valleys, monsoon seasons, and cultivated farms dotted the region. A lot has changed in three thousand years."

"A *garden*," Jade said. "Could it be the *hortum* spoken of in the note?"

His hands fell into his lap as he stared at her. "Brilliant. Very possibly a garden." He linked his fingers behind his neck, looking over at her. "I'm not going to look at that note as a threat, but as an invitation."

"Where do we start?"

"We might be going to Oman. The patriarch received special

permission from the Omani government to visit. Quite easily, I might add. It makes me wonder if Yemen is already up to something, and Oman wants to beat them at their game."

"What do you mean, *game*?" Jade asked.

"There will be some competition once we get there," he said. "Underground organizations such as AWP—Ancient World Piracy—will be vying for possession. They have been at odds with the patriarch for a decade. He has thwarted several of their undercover digs, costing them millions. Wherever we go, we're bound to run into some . . . complications. Don't forget that millions of dollars and lasting fame will be the lot of whatever lucky man makes the find."

"Or *woman*."

His gaze turned inquisitive. Jade's pulse quickened, and she focused on the ring on her finger. It had flamed orange. *Daring.* "You don't think a discovery will be made?"

"*Something* will be discovered." He reached over and tapped her hand. "The most important thing, *ma chérie*, is to trust me. No matter what happens."

A flight attendant stopped in the aisle, offering drinks and pastries. Jade selected a pastry and took a bite of the honeyed baklava. The exotic flavor burst on her tongue, and she closed her eyes for an instant, savoring the flaky sweetness.

Lucas stirred the ice in his drink, seeming to be lost in thought.

"Tell me more about that pirate group—AWP?" Jade asked.

He stopped stirring, the ice cubes clinking together. "Ancient World Piracy is a tradition handed down from antiquity. It's become a worldwide organization, although it's very private. In fact, some governments deny its existence."

"It began in *antiquity*?"

He nodded. "The concept of piracy emerged in 800 B.C., but the actions of warfare and piracy were evident at least a thousand years before that." He leaned back in his seat, his head turned toward her. "The advent of boats on water brought the birth of the pirate. The actual word *pirate* comes through the Latin *pirata,* as translated from Greek, meaning 'attacks on ships.'"

I know the root of pirate, Jade wanted to say. But she was mesmerized by the details and didn't want to interrupt Lucas's story.

"From the earliest establishment of wealth on the earth, there have always been those who aren't willing to earn their living, but would rather pillage for it." He took a sip of his drink.

"So what sets these guys apart from any other modern-day thieves?"

"AWP sees itself as a group of pirates searching for ancient treasure," he said. "They put on a façade of preserving artifacts, but they use coercion, bribery, and sometimes murder to collect their goods. They also worship pagan deities and perform ancient rites, which bind them together stronger than most blood relatives."

"Ancient rites?" she prompted. She took another bite of the pastry. The tiredness pressing against her temples eased a little as the sweetness of the baklava warmed her senses.

"Warding off evil spirits of the desert—the evil djinns—by singing and dancing around frankincense trees, treating their women as no more than slaves of pleasure, and performing human sacrifice."

Jade swallowed, not feeling hungry anymore. She didn't know which should appall her more—women as objects or human sacrifice. "Do they still practice sacrifice?"

He hesitated. "There've been rumors . . ."

"What do you think?"

"They were doing them a hundred years ago—why change now?" He signaled the flight attendant and gave her his glass. After the stewardess headed down the aisle, he looked at Jade again. "You should catch some rest. Tomorrow will be a long day." He reached up and switched off the overhead light.

Jade switched her light off too, but stared at the darkened window, twisting her ring. It looked amber in the dim light. *Anxious.* Lucas fell asleep almost immediately, his soft snores barely audible above the engine. Her thoughts still tumbled. She pulled her phone from her bag and summarized what Lucas had said about djinns and human sacrifice. It made her shudder. When she finished, she reached for a blanket and pulled it around her shoulders. It seemed that just as she reclined her seat and closed her eyes, someone spoke to her.

"Yes?" Jade blinked with bleary eyes at the woman above her, and the neat uniform came into focus.

"Madam, your seat belt for landing."

Jade fumbled for the belt and clicked it into place. As she readjusted her blanket, she glanced in Lucas's direction.

He held a small instrument in his hands—something that looked like a cross between a PDA and a cell phone. With the other hand, he methodically ate a peeled and quartered orange. A slight frown crossed his face, but his tiredness had vanished, and the light was back in his eyes.

Lucas looked up and smiled with those dazzling teeth. "Sleep well?"

Jade returned his smile with a nod, suddenly very aware of how long it had been since she'd showered or brushed her teeth.

The plane began its descent to Ethiopia's Bole International. When the seat belt sign turned off, Lucas packed his things, and Jade folded the blanket she'd used.

Once off the plane, dry heat assailed them, even though it was 2:00 in the morning. The main terminal was under construction, so they took a shuttle to baggage claim.

"Welcome to Addis Ababa," the shuttle driver said in clear English.

"Thank you," Jade mumbled, feeling exhaustion deep within. Her mind was fuzzy, and she knew if the shuttle ride were any longer, she'd fall asleep again. She found a cloth-covered seat and sank into it, Lucas taking the one next to her.

"Where are we staying?" Jade asked through a yawn as the shuttle lurched forward.

"We'll bypass the hotel and take a taxi directly to Aksum. It's about nine hundred kilometers."

Jade rubbed the back of her neck. "Can't we leave after some sleep?"

"This inscription might be the first real evidence that ties Ethiopia directly to the queen of Sheba," he said in a quiet voice. "If it is, the Ethiopian legends will become documented history. If there is a leak from DiscoveryArch to AWP, they'll undoubtedly be on their way. As soon as they find out about the statue, they'll concoct a way to take over the site and twist things to their benefit. Their financial stability depends on proving that the queen lived and died in Yemen, since they seem to have so much influence with the Yemen government."

"How can *any* government allow this treachery to go on?" she asked.

"Just as any government has since the beginning. It's the vicious cycle of money. AWP gets a private donor, and then offers money to the government for exclusive digging rights, secretly sharing any profits. The artifacts attract private collectors and more donors . . ."

Jade squeezed her eyes shut for a moment. She didn't know if Lucas's theory about Lyon's murder was correct, but after learning about AWP and the bombing of the Jerusalem tomb, she was beginning to believe him.

After they collected their sparse baggage and found a taxi, Lucas said, "You can take the backseat and sleep."

Jade didn't remember much else about the early morning hours, except for the random bright lights of an oncoming car, a few exchanged words between Lucas and the taxi driver, and the occasional lurch as the car turned. Jade drifted in and out of sleep and tried not to think of the bed she was missing in an Ethiopian hotel.

When a waft of fresh air blew over her curled up body, she lifted her head. The taxi was parked, and Lucas had unloaded their things. Her door stood open, and a pleasant spicy smell entered the vehicle. Sitting, she tried to smooth her hair, feeling the thickness of her dry mouth and dreading what her face must look like.

Lucas leaned into the car. "We'll eat at this café then walk to the site."

She climbed out of the backseat, her aching limbs paying for the cramped position. "What's that smell?"

"It's coming from that grove of frankincense trees over there." He pointed to a wide field of gnarled trees. "Gold of the desert."

"Gold?"

"Anything worth fighting over is gold in someone's eyes," he said, steering her to a table.

An elegant woman, wearing a white dress with elaborate honey-colored stitching, greeted them and took their order. Lucas ordered one of the local dishes for both of them.

After a quick meal of a chicken dish called *doro alicha*, they set off across the fields, skirting the frankincense trees. Jade's sluggish body was slow to keep up with Lucas's brisk pace.

The call of exotic birds caught her attention as they hiked along the rugged ground. Eventually an outcropping of rocks appeared, and Jade realized they were tumbled ruins, not natural rock formations. Lucas stopped and waited for her to catch up.

He swept his arm across the expanse of ruins. "The queen of Sheba's palace."

Jade stared in disbelief at the broken-down walls topping a deep foundation. "*This* is it?"

"According to Ethiopian tradition."

She surveyed the landscape and pointed to the northern end at a parallel row of stones. "A drainage system?"

"Correct," Lucas said. "Come on, I'll show you the best part."

They descended a slight ridge and saw a flagstone floor still intact in its earthen floor. Jade knelt beside it. "Wow. How old is this?"

"Some say it's as old as the queen of Sheba."

She laughed. "Really?"

"At least that's what everyone thought until it was excavated in the '60s. That evidence convinced some people this place was built long after the queen would have died."

"Maybe it was built for one of her heirs, or as a tribute."

A smile flashed across his scruffy face. "You sound like a hopeful."

She straightened, aware of their close proximity. "What do you think?"

"How can I say it . . . Possible until proven otherwise?"

Jade smiled. "I like that."

He held her gaze for a few seconds then broke away. They spent the next several moments inspecting stairwells, bathing areas, and even a kitchen with preserved brick ovens.

Jade looked beyond the mass of ruins to a collection of stone edifices. "What are those?"

"Granite stelae—obelisks. No excavation had been done in the area until this week." He rubbed his hands together against the chill of the morning. "Dr. Maskel and his crew should be here soon. They're the ones who discovered the buried statue."

Jade scanned the area for signs of recent digging. "Where is it?"

"On the other side of the ridge. It's probably been moved—"

The whine of a truck cut into Lucas's words. They both turned and saw a yellow Land Rover skirting the ruins. The vehicle came to a stop, and two Ethiopian men jumped out, leaving the truck idling. They rushed across the uneven ground to Lucas and pumped his hand.

The taller man spoke first. "Welcome, Monsieur Morel."

Then they turned to Jade—all smiles. "Welcome, welcome. I'm Dr. Maskel, and this is Dr. Shum."

Jade shook his hand, liking the tall man immediately. He wore colorful robes of silver and blue, topped by a cloche-style hat of the same fabric.

"You made good time," Dr. Maskel said with a wink.

"We took a taxi straight from the airport," Jade said.

Dr. Maskel laughed and glanced at Lucas. "That's the Monsieur Morel I remember."

The other man, Dr. Shum, stepped forward and bowed to Jade. "Welcome." He was shorter than his colleague, but his tan robes were equally luxurious.

A few more pleasantries were exchanged, and then Lucas cleared his throat. "Well, let's see this thing."

With a chuckle, Dr. Maskel motioned them into the Land Rover. Jade was offered the passenger seat, while the other two men folded themselves into the backseat. Maskel maneuvered along a dirt road, past the free-standing obelisks and stopping at a low tent on the other side of the ridge.

"No guards?" Lucas asked, his expression pointed.

"Oh yes, we have guards," said Dr. Maskel. "They're probably still asleep."

Lucas let out a snort, and Dr. Maskel rang with laughter. "It will be several days yet before the rest of the world gets wind of this. By then I promise I'll have armed guards around the clock at every corner of the field. But first, I want your opinion."

A shuffling sound came from the tent, and a bleary-eyed man wearing a rumpled robe appeared. "There's our guard, alert as ever," Dr. Maskel said. "Now if you go to the chapel where the Ark of the Covenant is, you'll see a completely different caliber."

"Nothing gets by those monks," chimed in Dr. Shum.

"Follow me." Dr. Maskel quickened his long strides.

The four of them entered the tent, and Jade was immediately drawn to the female statue lying on its side. Beneath it was a coarsely woven rug, protecting it from the dirt floor. Lucas walked slowly around it. Every so often he stooped and inspected a detail. Dr. Maskel rocked back on his heels, obviously straining to keep his silence. Finally, he burst out, "There's an inscription at the base."

Lucas nodded absentmindedly as he inspected the crudely formed hand of the woman. He let his gaze trail the length of the statue's bare legs, arriving at the engraved letters. "Mid–950s," he said to no one in particular. "This statue could very well have been created during the queen's lifetime."

Dr. Maskel clapped his hands together and let out a high-pitched squeal. "I knew it! The moment we unearthed the thing, I *knew* it would be significant."

Jade suppressed a laugh at the archaeologist's reaction.

His grin remained plastered on his face as Lucas traced the writing with a finger.

"These two letters form a harsh *a* sound in most early Semitic languages." Lucas moved his finger to the next letter. "Wait."

The other men sobered, and Jade held her breath.

"*A-s* or *a-z* . . . then a hard *h*—"

"Do you see the *ma*?" Dr. Maskel asked. He looked at Jade and mouthed, "For Queen Makeda."

"It looks like the *r* to me, an *ra*." Lucas looked up, his face strained. "The name of this woman is not Makeda."

Dr. Maskel visibly flinched, and Dr. Shum crouched next to Lucas. "Are you *sure*?"

"Well, she's obviously royalty, and the question now is, who is Azhara?"

"Azhara?" Shum straightened, his knees cracking in the audible silence.

Dr. Maskel just stared at the statue, disappointment plain on his face.

"I don't understand it," Shum said. "The statue dates to the queen's era. It has to be her. Who else could have been queen?"

"Maybe Azhara was a title they gave her, a nickname," Dr. Maskel spoke rapidly. "Or a version of Makeda . . . maybe a new language she developed, something that died with her reign—"

"I don't think so," Lucas said.

An uncomfortable heat climbed up Jade's neck as she sensed the tension between the men. She searched her mind for any place where she might have heard the name Azhara, but nothing biblical or historical came to mind. She typed the name into her phone notes and waited for the men to continue.

"What about the second word?" Maskel asked.

"It's another name."

"Not the woman's title?"

"*Ta . . . m . . . ba . . . ri . . . ah*," Lucas sounded out. His face seemed to pale slightly.

"What's the origin of Tam-ba-ri-ah?" Dr. Maskel asked in a glum voice. He looked from Lucas to Dr. Shum.

Lucas's expression was placid, but Jade had been around him nonstop for nearly three days now, and she sensed he knew more than he was telling. With a slight lift of his shoulder, he simply said, "It's not Arabian or Ethiopian."

"Egyptian?" Jade suggested.

Lucas shook his head. A thin sheen of perspiration had popped onto his forehead. "Hebrew is my guess."

"Ah-ha!" Dr. Maskel said. "Hebrew it is. Very promising indeed. After all, the queen did travel back and forth to Jerusalem, so it would make sense that Hebrews traveled with her in the party. Azhara might have been another child begat through Solomon, conceived when he came to visit the Ethiopian palace."

Lucas stepped away from the statue and looked at Jade. His face had reddened. Dr. Maskel's theories were growing more and more wild. She was curious at the apprehension in his eyes. "Are you all right?" she asked.

Lucas shook his head slightly. "Let me finish showing you the ruins. Then we can discuss these names over tea."

She followed him out of the tent, noting the difference between the cool interior of the tent and the warmth the sunlight brought. "Let me show you the best preserved obelisk out of the lot," Lucas said loud enough for those inside the tent to hear. They walked over the rocky ground, and at one point Jade's toe caught, and she almost fell. Lucas grabbed her elbow and held it securely. He steered her toward a shady spot beneath a frankincense tree. Then he turned and said, "We need to leave as soon as possible."

"Why? We just arrived."

Lucas rubbed his forehead. "This is probably not the summer internship you expected."

"I didn't mean—"

"Look," he said. "Remember where you saw the name Tambariah before?"

Jade wrinkled her brow, staring into his dark golden eyes that seemed to contend with the blue sky behind. Without looking through her notes, the discussion on the plane came to mind. "The email. Tambariah was one of the names in the Jerusalem tomb."

"Exactly." Lucas's voice was flat. "And that's why we need to contact the patriarch as soon as possible and let him know about this development." He glanced around, as if he expected someone to discover them at any moment. "Don't you see? This changes everything. It seems as if Tambariah was every place King Solomon should have been . . . In fact, this evidence of Tambariah's existence might be the proof that Solomon never existed."

"This statue might be that proof?" Her mind reeled. A new discovery, and she was one of the first witnesses.

"There's more."

Jade looked at him expectantly.

"Thugs like those in AWP look for diversions like this. They send a few 'scholars' to any new discovery and make a lot of noise. Meanwhile, they're free to break international laws without the usual scrutiny."

"Do you think the statue is a fake?"

"Not unless it's a very good copy. But it may have been brought here from another location. Once this leaks to the press, this place will be a field day for experts of all kinds."

It was hard for Jade to imagine this quiet, serene site being a hotbed of controversy. "Can I take pictures before we leave?"

"Just a few. But we need to conceal our suspicions. We'll join the others for tea. Then after ten minutes, you need to claim some calamity."

"Like I have the flu?"

"Something like that." He looked around again. "Let's return and hurry this thing up."

Twenty minutes later, Jade sat in the front seat of the Land Rover, cradling her head against her alleged migraine. Dr. Maskel had offered to take them to the nearest taxi depot, and it seemed rude to refuse. The ride to the depot was silent, if not tense. After Lucas and Jade thanked Maskel, they climbed into the backseat of a taxi. Rosary beads hung from the driver's rearview mirror, and the radio played, a slow melodic tune teasing the air. Lucas reached over and patted her hand, flashing his white smile. "Great job."

Jade's temperature went up a notch, even though he'd done nothing more than praise her as a teacher might a student. As the taxi sped back to Addis Ababa, Lucas took out his phone and wrote an email to the patriarch.

"Are we still going to Yemen?" Jade asked.

Lucas brought a finger to his lips, motioning for Jade to speak quietly. He leaned close to her. "Everything will move quicker now. How many pictures did you get?"

"Six or seven." She pulled out her phone. Lucas inched closer and looked at the pictures with her.

"Wait, go back to the previous one."

Jade reversed direction and handed the phone to him. The picture showed a full-frame shot of the statue's profile.

"Why didn't I notice this before?" Lucas murmured. He tipped the angle to dispel the glare of the sun. "This statue is pregnant."

Though she knew what he meant, Jade smiled at the statement. Observing that an inanimate object could be pregnant sounded absurd. "If it's true, it's not very obvious."

"Look." Lucas rotated the phone toward her, and with his pinky, he pointed at a muted marking on the woman's bared belly. "First sign—her stomach is uncovered. The second—this circular marking represents the continuum of life."

Jade leaned close and peered at the image. "And her child?"

"Perhaps the answer is buried beneath one of the obelisks. But that excavation is out of our hands. Once word gets out about the Azhara statue, archaeologists will be pulling their government strings to lay claim on every square foot of that field."

"Do you think Azhara is the queen of Sheba?"

Lucas handed the phone back and glanced out the window. "It's always possible, although the Israelis and the Yemenis won't like it. Part of their national identities are linked to the queen's heritage."

A chime from his own phone interrupted him. He read the incoming email then looked at Jade. "Illegal excavation is underway in Oman in the same area that the patriarch secured for Dr. Lyon."

"By AWP members?" Jade whispered, her mind whirling.

"Yes, and it looks like we're heading straight there. We'll have to take our own guards with us, of course." Lucas lowered the phone and turned his full attention to her. "Five years ago, Dr. Lyon discovered some inscriptions on the ruins of Shisur—an ancient oasis in western Oman. Through carbon dating, they were linked to a mere century *after* the queen's era, but Lyon always believed the testing was done inaccurately."

"Do you think AWP is trying to cover up the evidence at this site too?"

"Possibly. AWP doesn't want the queen's tomb found in Oman just as the Ethiopians don't want the tomb found any place other than Ethiopia."

"So what can we do?"

"Raise a lot of noise and hope it scares off AWP. They won't take kindly to outsiders coming into their 'territory.' Regardless, we have permission to use the site and to inspect the inscriptions for ourselves." He paused, holding her gaze. "If any evidence can be linked to the queen's era, you're going to have one hell of a thesis."

Chapter Eighteen

Sa'ba
960 b.c.

THE MORNING AIR WAS frigid as Nicaula stepped onto the terrace that adjoined the bedchamber of her newly remodeled palace. Everything was peaceful, and the evidence of battle had long since faded. Weeks had melted into months, and with the passing of time, the kingdom of Sa'ba prospered. Her servant, Azhara, thrived in her safe surroundings, and Batal commanded the ever-training soldiers.

The sound of donkey carts clamoring over the flagstone below sent a smile to the queen's face. She remembered watching the activity from a similar balcony in another place, where as a young child she ached to play with the village children, but her father told her she was meant for something better. He had taught her to read, though he knew he could be punished for it. He had taught her military strategy, and he had whispered in her ear that someday she would be queen.

Now, in the dappled gold of the morning sun, Nicaula let her gaze stray beyond the browned buildings. In the past months, Sa'ba had become a major trading stop on the frankincense trail. Outside of the city, a trail had formed, bringing commerce in spices, incense, and exotic treasures. Caravans chose the city as a resting place to resupply their food and water, all for small fees to the government and offerings to the temples.

Nicaula looked at the merchants' campsites dotting the open desert. They would spend a week or two haggling with other vendors over the price of their wares, only to pack up and move on when disputes couldn't be settled. Often, Batal or another member of the high ranks interfered and offered a compromise—one that benefited both the merchants and the queen.

The sharp sound of horses' hooves grew closer, and Nicaula turned her attention to the street below. Around the bend, a rider came into view. *Batal.* The queen watched the commander expertly maneuver his horse around carts and people. His shoulders were broad and his confidence matured. In just a few months, Batal had become a man, and the queen felt a slight twist in her stomach as the light reflected off his ebony curls. From her perch, she saw the muscles defined in both horse and rider.

Bittersweet.

Footfalls sounded behind the queen, and she turned to see Azhara. Over time, the servant's body had become soft and womanly. The gentle folds of her simple tunic emphasized her mature curves. Her hair had grown back to its former luster, the plaited locks intertwined with strips of linen. The queen had noticed men watching Azhara—their eyes alive with interest. But the maidservant's gaze held only emptiness toward them.

Azhara bowed her head. "The court awaits, O Queen."

A rare flicker of warmth had passed through her eyes, and Nicaula smiled at her faithful servant. "The court may continue their wait. This day is too beautiful to spend beneath a palm roof." She turned and placed her hands on the cool wall. "Call for my horse to be prepared, and Azhara, I would like you to accompany us."

The shuffle of steps left the balcony, and Nicaula smiled to herself. Judgment and regulations could wait a while; today, she wanted to immerse herself in the people.

A short time later, she settled onto the back of her newest horse, its fine coat gleaming Arabian black, while half a dozen guards accompanied her as they rode through the streets. Merchants and villagers alike drew out of their way, bowing their heads in respect. Nicaula smiled at the eager children who ran alongside the impromptu procession, their teeth flashing against their browned faces.

By the time they reached the outer gate of the city, they had quite a following. Batal, on his usual patrol, had the gates swung wide. He glanced curiously at the queen, but she kept her gaze forward, ignoring the radiating heat that seemed to pulse between them. She knew that at any moment she could command him to come to her . . .

The people thought she needed to produce an heir before she grew too old, yet the tribal chiefs and sheiks who lived in the surrounding lands had not interested her enough. *Too old, too young. None compared to Batal . . .* The queen shook her head free of the permeating thoughts.

The desert air rushed against her face, its morning coolness belying the imminent heat. The outside market was already alive with aggressive bartering where makeshift tents sat in a wide circle, rugs displaying goods—frankincense, turtle shells, textiles, transparent gems. The queen stopped in front of a line of sewn goatskins filled with spices when a grizzled merchant stepped forward, displaying a nearly toothless grin. "From the East. Very fine, very pure."

Nicaula dismounted, noticing the hush from the surrounding vendors as she bent over a skin containing a coarse, red spice.

"Cinnamon," the merchant offered. "It adds sweetness."

The queen thrust her hand into the warm crystals and turned her arm until she could touch the base. No rocks.

She withdrew her hand and brought a pinch to her lips, the aromatic flavor bursting against her tongue. "I'll take the entire lot."

The merchant bobbed his head and thanked her over and over in a rapid dialect, but the queen waved him off and walked on. She stopped at the next display and inspected the soft nuggets of yellowed frankincense. The merchant sat huddled beneath his crooked shelter, rocking back and forth. Nicaula waited a moment, expecting the man to rush forward with a fervent greeting.

She bent and picked up a nugget, but still the merchant swayed in his tent. Silence fell around her as the guards waited her command. Disrespect would carry a heavy fine or even punishment. With the sudden quiet, Nicaula listened to the soft chants that came from the man in an unfamiliar dialect, short and rhythmic. The queen walked to the entrance of his tent as two guards flanked her, their daggers drawn.

The words were lyrical, as if the man spoke a tale or sang a poem. When her eyes adjusted to the gloomy interior, the queen saw that the figure was not a man, but a woman. "What are you singing?"

A young boy emerged from the shadows, standing protectively tall. "My mother cannot hear nor see you."

Nicaula appraised the boy, from his matted hair and huge dark eyes, to his cracked feet. "You brought this frankincense across the desert with an ill mother?"

"No." The boy's black eyes darted to the ground. "Yahweh helped us."

"Yahweh is your father?"

"Our god."

"Tell me of this god, Yahweh. Does he rule the night or the day?"

"Yahweh rules both the day and the night."

Nicaula arched a brow and stared at the young child. Something about him intrigued her—his assurance, his protection of his mother, and his somber eyes that were like the deep wells of the desert. "No god can rule both, or the elements will fall out of balance and bring destruction."

"My mother told me that our god is the supreme ruler over all," the boy said, his gaze straying toward his mother, his mouth pulling into a frown.

"What else did she tell you?"

The woman's chanting began again, her hunched form swaying back and forth. The guards gripped their daggers tighter.

"What's she saying now?" the queen asked.

"She tells the story of the great king of Jerusalem."

Nicaula's pulse rushed until it sounded in her ears. "How great is this king?"

"Greater than any king alive or dead. Yahweh speaks to him. My mother was his concubine."

"This king is your father?"

"Yes."

"How can a great king let his son live as a nomad and the mother of his son travel the desert alone?" Nicaula's gaze didn't miss the worn tent panels, the small stash of dates, and the threadbare rugs on which they stood.

"My mother left the kingdom when her face and ears were burned. The king demands perfection, and she was too ashamed to let him see her."

Nicaula looked at the chanting woman with renewed interest. It was difficult to see her face in the shadows of the mantel covering her head, but the queen noticed the woman's hands. They were not old as Nicaula had assumed, but smooth and slender. This woman was young and must have been beautiful once to attract the attention of a king. "What is your name, boy?"

"David. I am named after my father's father."

"Come, little David. Come outside and tell us this story of the great king and his god."

The queen's entourage gathered around the young boy as he told of the great king and his palace and many wives and concubines. Nicaula was captivated by the tales of Solomon's wealth and wisdom that came from the god Yahweh. Over the next weeks and months, the queen requested the boy's presence daily and asked for story after story until she had everything about the king of Jerusalem committed to memory. The queen learned of Solomon's vast amounts of gold and silver, and his throne of ivory with twelve lions on one side. David told her about the exotic animals such as apes and peacocks. She marveled that Solomon ate on plates of gold, and that he had over one thousand chariots.

Nicaula gave the young David and his mother quarters close to the palace and saw that the royal healer cared for his mother.

Batal seemed especially interested in the powers of Yahweh. When David spoke of his god, Batal's demeanor changed and his skin seemed to glow like fresh honey. Day after day, David's stories drew in his audience, and soon, Nicaula started to dream of the king herself.

And each night when she lay in her bed alone, she thought of the little boy with curly hair and dark eyes—and wondered how much he looked like his father.

Chapter Nineteen

Yemen

ANOTHER AIRPORT, ANOTHER COUNTRY. Jade slept fitfully on the plane ride from Addis Ababa to San'ā, the capital of Yemen.

As the plane taxied across the runway to the terminal, Lucas called the flight attendant over. With some cajoling, she produced a navy silk scarf, and Lucas gave her several bills for it. He motioned for Jade to wear it.

She turned the scarf over, unsure of what to do, when the Yemeni Air flight attendant came to help her. With a few deft strokes, the attendant secured the scarf around Jade's head.

She walked off the plane, conscious of every step as they moved with the passengers onto a bus—standing room only. Jostling for a place, Jade found refuge by Lucas and tried to avoid the male bodies that seemed to press too close. Instinctively, she held her bag tightly against her chest.

Through the lurching ride, she looked out the grimy windows. She expected an airport similar to the ones in Cairo or Addis Ababa, but the bus stopped in front of a rundown building. Even though it was five thirty in the morning, confusion reigned. She and

Lucas walked past a line of passengers waiting to board another plane when a static-filled announcement in Arabic came over the loudspeaker. The line immediately broke apart, and Jade watched the people shove and shout at each other. A few leaped over the barrier to get in front of the others. She instinctively sidled next to Lucas, and he put a hand on her arm.

"No assigned seating on the outgoing carriers?" she asked.

"Welcome to Yemen." Lucas chuckled. "Let's get some coffee—this city has some of the best in the world."

He ordered a large coffee, and Jade chose an orange juice. She took a sip. "This juice is really good—more tart than usual."

"Not how the Americans make it? No added sugar and preservatives?"

She smiled and continued to drink the freshly squeezed juice. The way he'd pronounced "preservatives" was absolutely charming, but she tugged her gaze from him, bent on thinking about something else. A man sat near them, dressed in a military-style uniform, his Uzi hanging casually from his shoulder.

Another announcement blared through the loudspeakers, and as the speaking droned on and on, Jade realized two different people were giving the announcement. "What are they saying?"

Lucas looked at her over the steam rising from his mug. "One announcer is talking to the other. They're planning to go to a football game later this afternoon."

"They're planning this over the intercom?"

He smiled. "It appears so." He set his cup down and leaned back, stretching his arms behind his head. "Don't worry. Once we leave the airport, things will seem relatively normal."

Jade finished her juice, and she scanned the walls for a sign that resembled a bathroom facility. "Where's the restroom?"

"It's just around the corner. You might want to take some

napkins with you."

She didn't want to ask Lucas the particulars, so she grabbed a few napkins and crammed them into her pocket.

Now that the frantic passengers were out of the terminal, the airport hummed quietly. Jade found the restroom and pushed open the door. A wall of stench hit her nose full force. She covered her mouth and pinched her nose as she moved to the nearest stall. There was no door, and the toilet was gone. She glanced in the second stall—no toilet, just a hole in the ground. The surrounding area looked as though it hadn't been cleaned for some time, if ever. Jade's stomach churned, and she rushed outside the bathroom. She leaned against the wall and tried to catch her breath. She inhaled deeply a few times, wondering if this was the only restroom in the airport.

As she debated whether she could wait, the fresh orange juice decided to torture her system. Back in the bathroom Jade went, holding her breath and hoping she wouldn't lose all sense of dignity.

A few moments later, she emerged from the bathroom, her stomach weaker, cold perspiration beading on her head, and an undeniable itch to wash her hands. There had been no running water in the sink. A few yards along the wall stood a drinking fountain. She hurried to it and rinsed her hands in the lukewarm water.

"Ready?" a voice spoke behind her.

Jade turned to see Lucas.

"Sorry about the restroom conditions," he said, eyeing her. "First experience with a squat pot?"

"Is that what the hole in the ground is called?"

He nodded, his eyes glinting with humor. "This airport is notorious for its awfulness, but when we reach the desert, it'll be even worse."

"It wouldn't be so bad if the facility were at least clean."

"We'll check into a hotel where you'll have a proper bathroom."

Jade was tempted to hug him or kiss him—something. A hot shower . . . soap . . . a clean towel. She might even feel like herself again. But the excitement wore thin as they passed through customs and then stepped out of the airport. Grubby hands pulled at their bags, calling, "Five dollah?"

Jade gripped her backpack. "No, thank you."

Lucas shooed the kids away and hustled her toward a taxi. The driver collected their bags, and Jade barely had time to notice his traditional attire—a long, white shirt extending past his knees, a vest, a blazer, a wide belt with the hilt of a knife protruding from it, and a wrapped turban. He had a ready smile topped by a trim mustache, his chin swathed in a short, white beard.

The taxi squealed from the curb, throwing Jade against the vinyl. Multiple hanging knickknacks adorned the dash, and a vibrant, upbeat melody blared from the radio. Lucas barked a few orders in Arabic, and the driver nodded with a grin.

Then it hit her—an odor so rank that Jade imagined herself cloistered in the airport restroom again. She covered her mouth, and she realized that Lucas had his collar pulled over his nose. "What is it?" she asked in a muffled voice.

"There's an open sewer nearby." Lucas motioned toward the window. "It'll pass in a few moments."

Jade's eyes stung, and she tried not to dry heave.

The taxi driver, who whistled off-key to the radio, didn't seem bothered in the least. Jade couldn't see how anyone, no matter how long they lived here, could get used to that smell.

Slowly the stench faded, and Lucas checked his phone. "Change of plans. The crew is already waiting for us—supplies and all. Looks like we won't be spending the night in a hotel bed."

Next internship—which will be never—I'm going to make sure there are allowances for sleeping and showering. She forced herself to say, "That's fine."

Lucas cast a sideways glance to her. "Uh . . . I have an idea. It'll just put our arrival thirty minutes out."

Thirty minutes for what? She sighed and turned to the window. The darkness had started to lift, and they were driving through an alley of sorts. Then she realized it was a two-way road, but the buildings were very tall. As the taxi turned onto a wider road, the rising sun reflected off the buildings, and Jade was stunned at the beauty.

"They're called tower houses," Lucas said.

The tall houses cast deep shadows over the next street they took, and the delicately arched windows and doorways were topped by intricate designs of stone. The buildings were brown, tan, and red, with white accents around the roofs and windows. Along the streets, dozens of men and young boys moved about their morning business. Jade also noticed how incredibly tall the lampposts were—at least twenty-five feet.

The driver halted in front of a hotel with a similar exterior to the surrounding tower houses, and Lucas hopped out. Then he leaned back in the taxi. "You'll have your shower in no time. Follow me."

Soon they stood at the front desk with their baggage. The elderly gentleman at the desk peered over his reading glasses at them, and Lucas greeted him in Arabic. The man's eyes kept shifting to Jade. Then a fierce argument started.

Both men were stubborn. Lucas grabbed Jade's arm and ushered her toward the front door when the man gave into Lucas's request.

As Lucas and Jade walked down the narrow hallway, she whispered, "What was that about?"

"He wanted to charge us for an overnight stay."

"How much would it have been?"

"Only a few dollars, but you'll see that everything has a bargaining price here."

They stopped in front of room ٢٠.

"Number twenty?" Jade guessed.

Lucas nodded then unlocked the door and swung it wide. "After you."

The room was sweltering, and Lucas crossed to switch on the fan. The place smelled of stale cigarette smoke, and an open pack of cigarettes still sat on the bedside table.

"You take a shower first. Then I will," Lucas said. "I'd wait outside, but the hotel concierge thinks we're . . . together." He cocked his head and smiled.

Jade let out a laugh, but inside she felt nervous. She turned and went into the bathroom. Then she shut the door and leaned against it, closing her eyes. *I am such an idiot.* Lucas wasn't like other men. He'd been a perfect gentleman since the day she'd met him. Regardless, she locked the door before slipping out of her clothes. The tile was quite worn and cracked, but at least it was roach-free. She turned the water to warm, soon discovering there was only one temperature: tepid.

Thirty minutes later, they were back in the taxi, Jade feeling refreshed, although she hadn't stopped perspiring. Lucas handed her an assault rifle. "Strap the Kalashnikov over your shoulder."

"You're kidding." Jade stared at the bulky gun. "I don't even know how to use it."

"No one else will know that," he said, strapping a second one around his shoulders.

Jade complied, though she felt uncomfortable wearing such a deadly thing. The morning sun brightened as they maneuvered through the traffic, and Lucas threw her a few quizzical looks as she twisted her ring furiously.

Moments later, they stopped at a gasoline station. As they climbed out of the taxi, a large man, clad in a long, white tunic, waved them over. He stood next to a jeep and a couple of pickups, the beds of which were loaded with supplies. Jade eyed the man's jambiya knife, extending from his belt, and wondered if the weapon was used for defense or merely decoration.

"Welcome," the Yemeni said in thick English, smiling at Jade. "I'm Ismail." He wiped his forehead with his sleeve. "I just returned from the desert."

Lucas greeted him in Arabic, and they exchanged rapid conversation.

When Ismail left them, Lucas put his arm around Jade's shoulder, pulling her close. "Act like you love me."

"What?"

"We're engaged to be married, *ma chérie.*"

Before she could reply, he kissed her cheek, and then released her. Jade stood for a moment, her thoughts tumbling against each other. Maybe she'd heard him wrong. When Ismail was speaking with another man, she moved to Lucas's side and whispered, "You told him we're engaged?"

"Ismail commented on how beautiful you are . . . I had to say something."

"So you said we're engaged?"

Lucas nodded, his concentration returning to counting the supplies.

"Now we'll have to pretend the entire time."

He straightened and cocked his head. "You don't understand. It's better they think you're not available for the taking." He winked. "You know you can trust me, right?"

Her voice caught. Did she? "I—"

Lucas touched her lips with his fingers. "Don't answer. Just ask yourself if pretending is really so bad."

Jade closed her mouth. Her eyes caught in his steady amber gaze. *Not bad at all.*

Chapter Twenty

The Frankincense Trail
960 b.c.

NICAULA'S SKIN TINGLED IN anticipation. His gold-and-ivory throne floated above the ground, supported by powerful djinns, and the six golden steps leading to the massive edifice were flanked by beasts and birds. Slowly, he turned his head, his face handsome and powerful, framed by tight copper curls. His eyes, the color of dark honey, focused on her. Beneath his gaze, Nicaula felt awed. This man ruled over the greatest kingdom in the world.

Behind the throne was the grand gallery, lined with at least one hundred women. All were dressed in colorful robes of silk, their skin and hair oiled, just as the boy had told her. The great king had many wives and hundreds of concubines. Here were only a few.

Suddenly, the king descended the stairs. As he reached the third step from the bottom, a pair of golden bulls bawled; on the second step, brass lions stretched their mouths open into a roar. Nicaula admired the king as he reached the final step, sending the bronze eagles' wings flapping.

The king stood before her, and Nicaula was immediately struck by his short stature. Upon the throne, he appeared the height of two men, but now . . . The queen bowed her head. He took her hand, and when she lifted her head, he leaned close, his lips nearly touching hers.

"O Queen." The distant voice cut through Nicaula's vivid dream. She opened her eyes, blinking against the fading light that seeped through the tent panel. She had dreamt the same dream in Sa'ba and many times along the trail to Jerusalem. It was a message from her soul that she was to meet this great king and his all-powerful god. "I am awake," she called out.

Azhara entered the tent, her skin browned to nearly black as they had been traveling for several moons. The queen pushed away the disconcerting thoughts of the foreign king's lips closing in on hers, wondering if her recurring dream was a vision—a premonition that she was destined to marry a king. Her father had taught her that the djinns spoke through dreams.

"Is the meal prepared?" Nicaula asked.

Azhara shook her head, and it was then the queen noticed the wild look in the servant's eyes. "What is it?"

"The horizon is black—a sandstorm is coming." The tent panels slapped against the crusted sand floor as if to answer.

The queen pushed past Azhara and stared at the dark mass moving slowly toward the oasis.

"We must take cover inside." Azhara's voice was unnaturally high as she joined the queen.

"Listen." Nicaula gripped her servant's arm, looking at the sky then back to the darkened form. "The wind blows the wrong direction, and the sky is unchanged." As the women stood in tense silence, the queen gradually distinguished a low hum.

"What is it? Rain?"

"Rain would be a gift. What is approaching is a curse." She

turned to the servant. "Find Batal."

Azhara rushed off, and moments later, she appeared with Batal. He hurried to the queen's side and bowed low.

"The beasts are hobbled, goods secured . . ." He looked from one woman to the other. "You've not followed my instructions."

The queen held up her hand. "Were it a sandstorm, I would agree. But this is much, much worse." She extended her arm toward the growing cloud. "Those are locusts."

Azhara gasped and covered her mouth.

The three of them stood in awed fascination as the massed bodies approached the camp. Hundreds of paces wide and dozens high, the cloud of locusts pummeled its way straight toward them. Cries and screams resonated throughout the camp as the others scrambled for cover.

"We must pray to Yahweh for protection as we journey to his land," Batal shouted.

As the first spindly legs touched Nicaula's skin, Batal pulled her to the ground and covered her with his body. Azhara burrowed against her other side.

The droning closed in, and despite Batal's protection, Nicaula felt the insects assail her flesh, one after the other. Her stomach recoiled at the touch of the locusts' wings and their pursuit of nourishment.

Were the evil djinns stirring the locusts against her? Could Yahweh protect them, or would she and her people die this way—devoured by insects of the desert?

An eerie sound reached her clogged mind. At first she thought it was the undercurrent of the swarm, and then she realized it was the sound of urgent praying. The voice grew louder, and through the pitch of the storm, the queen heard Batal praying.

His words were muffled, but his demands seemed clear. Nicaula added her voice to his, hoping that anyone—goddesses Al'Uzza, Allat, Menat, or even Yahweh—would respond.

The minutes passed slowly as the swarm continued on its relentless course. Nicaula's tears crusted the sand to her face. Her body had grown so numb, she was no longer sure she was a part of it, and Azhara's weight next to her offered no protection.

Finally, the furious beating of tiny wings lessened. The lifting came gradually, like the slow pull of a young root from moist soil.

The queen kept her tight position until she was sure—sure of what she heard.

Quiet.

Nicaula lifted her head, sputtering sand from her mouth. Everything was gritty—warm—sharp.

Almost as suddenly as it started, the wind quieted, and the sand softened. Slowly, Nicaula's senses returned. She felt the caked sand against her scalp, the fierce dryness of her throat, the stiffness of her legs and back, and the calloused flesh of Batal's hand on her arm. Without realizing it, she had buried her head against his chest, and his arms had wrapped around her.

She shut her eyes as she took comfort in the man by her side—one to protect her and care for her as no other could. Even with her eyes closed, she could see the features she'd memorized so long ago—his ebony curls, his eyes blacker than night, his high cheekbones, his lips that said her name . . . She let out a long breath then reluctantly pulled away from him and found herself staring into his steady gaze. Her heart pounded with relief over their safety, combined with the intensity of his expression.

He moved ever so slightly, so that their bodies no longer touched, and Nicaula released her gaze. His youth, passion, strong will, and devotion combined for a dangerous concoction.

"Are you all right?" he whispered.

She nodded, swallowing against the stiff lump in her throat. She wanted to touch his face and brush the sand from it. She wanted to feel his arms around her again. She wanted . . .

Batal stood and helped her to her feet. Her legs wavered like delicate oleander. She took an unsteady breath as his calloused hand released hers. As the warmth from his touch faded, she looked over at Azhara, who had sat up—her black hair wild and tossed.

Through bleary, itchy eyes, Nicaula gazed across the former campsite. Tens of thousands of hoppers had settled onto the palms of the oasis, breaking the branches, devouring everything edible. The decimated sight brought stinging moisture to her eyes.

The locusts moved on, but left devastation in their wake. Only bare branches and roots from former bushes were left. Slowly the people rose from their positions, throwing off rugs and robes, assessing the damage. Then the sound of bawling beasts reached her ears.

Instinctively, Nicaula knew something was missing. One more scan for the familiar form confirmed the truth. Her Arabian horse was gone.

Someone touched her arm, and she turned to see Batal. Past him, Azhara still sat in the sand, her head lowered. The soldier answered Nicaula's question. "Azhara is all right."

Batal let his hand linger for a moment, and the queen looked up, meeting his gaze. His expression was somber—but there was more. Concern and tenderness belied the surface.

Nicaula knew she should draw away, but she remained, savoring the commander's touch for a brief moment.

"Are you well?" he asked.

Pulling back reluctantly, the queen scanned the terrain. "The oasis is destroyed, and the Arabian is missing."

Batal took a step forward, closing the little distance that

separated them. "I am asking after *you*, not the horse."

The queen looked at him in surprise. "He was my favorite."

Batal turned from her and called out to several soldiers, commanding them to search for the queen's horse. When they'd left, he looked at the queen, letting out a heavy breath. "Yahweh heard our cries."

"But he took my horse," she said.

"No," Batal said. "The locusts frightened the horse, but Yahweh spared our lives."

"Perhaps you are right."

"When we meet this great king, I fear you will never look upon me with favor again."

A finger of trepidation traced its way along Nicaula's neck. *What can he mean?* "Meeting the king of Jerusalem will not change your position as commander, even if he bequeaths an army of men into our services."

"I hoped to be more than just a commander," he said.

"Commander of my army is the highest honor I can bestow on anyone." Nicaula squinted against the pale light, studying his features. "Why are you troubled?"

"During the swarm, I realized I must confess something to you." Batal avoided her direct gaze and looked past her shoulder. "I am young, and perhaps that makes me more foolish than other men."

Bumps rose on the queen's arms as a breeze wrapped itself around her tunic. *He is leaving. He wants to join the superior ranks of the great king and live in Jerusalem.* Anger replaced any endearment she might have felt for him—any attraction she'd wrongly indulged.

"It has been many months since your grief," Batal said in a quiet voice. "And because of that, I feel I can be bold in my request."

He would abandon her, just as all others that she'd loved. Nicaula tried to keep the fury out of her tone. "You have my permission to leave. I do not want a commander who is not pleased with his position."

"Leave?" Incredulity spread across his face. "I am not asking—"

"The king of Jerusalem is greater than I am, and because of that, you will not enjoy the same status. Perhaps your estimation of yourself is correct—you are young and foolish. Leave at once. I do not want to see your face again."

"Nicaula!" A firm hand gripped her arm.

The queen stared at him, shocked first at the sound of her name, then at the action that accompanied it. His eyes had darkened.

"Let go," she said in a low voice.

"Hear me out, before my valor fails me." His hand dropped to his side, but his eyes were filled with angst.

Nicaula folded her arms and waited, wondering why it was so important that he speak now.

"I do not wish to leave unless that is truly your wish. If you marry the king, you'll be numbered only one among his many wives. You deserve complete devotion."

The queen took a step backward, wondering how Batal could have guessed her very thoughts, and wondering what his words meant.

He pressed on. "I will always remain your servant until the day of my death. But if you ever desire that I fulfill a more intimate role, I will do so, and not because you commanded it."

Nicaula stared at him for a moment. Through the sand on his face, she could see perspiration shining there. Suddenly she felt like laughing. "Your desert poetry is feeble. Speak your words plainly."

Batal's gaze faltered. "I could never compare to a king or a prince, but I will remain faithful and devoted until death—"

"Death? Why do you keep speaking of death? If you choose to join Solomon, I will not seek your life." Nicaula bestowed a benign smile even though she wanted to rage at his betrayal.

"Join Solomon? I was speaking of *marrying you* . . ." His eyes searched hers.

Like a flower blooming after a desert rain, warmth ruptured in her chest and travel to her feet. "You wish to *marry me*? *A queen?*"

"No . . . Yes. But if you were not a queen, my love would be the same."

Her breath stopped in her throat, and for an instant, she didn't know if she should inhale or exhale. A groan interrupted Nicaula's faltering, and Azhara lifted her head.

"Thank you for your declaration of . . . loyalty," Nicaula said.

She moved from him, feeling her limbs heavy and reluctant as she knelt to check on Azhara. Nicaula wanted to tell him how she truly esteemed him, how if she hadn't been queen, she'd wish to make him her husband. But she could not become betrothed to a mere soldier, no matter what her heart said.

Chapter Twenty-one

The Mahara Plateau

"TAKE ME," ALEM SPUTTERED. A couple of dark-feathered vultures crouched nearby with their heads lowered, nestled against their beige breasts, beady eyes keen. One took a hopeful step closer. But when Alem shouted again, it stopped.

The sand was everywhere, in his mouth, nostrils and ears and beneath his fingernails and even toenails. His near nakedness only aided the sand's intrusion. He lay near a boulder with just his legs in the shade, the rest of his body burnt blacker than the night. Along his torso, painful blisters had reared up.

The hours had blended together, and he didn't know how long he had been out here. The day before, he'd crawled to this shady spot, using the last of his reserves to do so. Alem tried to lift his head to examine his body. At least the bleeding had stopped, though painful welts rose on his forearms and chest. He closed his eyes against the burning heat of the sun. Any perspiration had dried long ago, and he doubted he had a droplet of moisture left in his body.

"Bring me some water if you're just going to stare at me," Alem called to the birds. His throat burned with the effort of speaking. For the first few hours, he'd made good progress as he traveled along the wadi leading to a plateau. He remembered others in the work crew telling him about the vegetation in the highlands. But without food or water, his strength soon ran out.

"Never mind. I can't swallow anyway," he croaked. He cracked an eye open and was met by the unblinking stares of the vultures. His fist closed around a scoop of sand, and he tossed it toward the birds. They remained unmoving, ever patient.

"O God—Allah—Yahweh—Grandmother—whoever sees my plight . . ." Tears would have formed in his eyes if there were any moisture left. "I failed you, Grandmother. I tried to restore honor to our name, but here I am—about to die because of my foolishness." The heat seemed to close in on him, making it difficult to breathe. His skin literally continued to bake, and his throat—it was an entity to itself. He wanted to cut out his tongue and disappear from existence. Nothing in his training as a runner, or any physical ailment, could have prepared him for this torture—a torture worse than death.

"Let me die now," he cried out. He'd heard about people being stranded in the desert, seeing mirages, going insane. Well, he was heading toward that.

Mercy right now would be immediate death. He turned slowly to his side, not only surprised that he could do it, but also that he could still feel pain.

Pressing himself against the cool underside of the boulder, he slipped into a listless sleep. After a moment or two, or maybe an hour, he felt a sharp scratch on his shoulder. *Vultures.*

Disappointed that he was still alive, he used his final ounce of energy to swat the creatures away. "At least wait until I'm dead," he said, although his statement wasn't coherent. He drifted again, his consciousness hovering between wakefulness and dreaming, when he saw his grandmother sitting next to him. He watched her lips move, but he couldn't hear a word. She faded to white, and for a while Alem felt as if he were floating. *Maybe I am dead.*

A loud bray sounded above him.

With great effort, he looked up and saw the loose, hairy lips of an animal.

A camel.

"I'm still alive?" Alem whispered, letting the camel sniff him out. "Are you my answer?" If this was a nursing camel in the wilderness, its milk would be nectar from the gods. Wandering camels could survive a couple of weeks with no water, but how long had it been since this animal drank? How far away was the nearest water? Alem rotated his body into a sitting position, moaning. He squinted at the animal through blurry eyes. The camel looked wild, and no bridle or rope indicated that it had ever been tied or ridden.

He scanned the camel's belly, looking for engorged nipples. It was a male.

Alem rose to his feet, using the boulder for support as he staggered with dizziness. The camel's image faded before his eyes and then jolted back again. He reached out a hand and touched the animal's coarse fur. "Will you let me ride you, boy?"

The camel lowered its head and nuzzled Alem's arm. "I don't have anything to eat either, but you can still walk." He moved his hand to its neck and scratched the flea-infested fur.

Buoyed with temporary hope, he tugged at the animal's neck. "Come on, boy, sit."

The animal bawled—sounding like a cross between a roar and an elongated belch. Alem wished he'd paid more attention to the camel commands he'd heard occasionally throughout Yemen.

He pulled again. "Down." But the camel didn't budge. "Down, you scruffy thing!" Alem barked hoarsely. He tried to yank the camel's neck toward the ground, but it wrenched away and trotted off a few feet.

"No, you don't." Alem stumbled toward the animal. After several more tries, his energy was depleted. He would have to wait, hoping that the camel would stay close by and sleep. He staggered back to the boulder and leaned against it, keeping a sleepy eye on the camel's movements.

As the sun melted against the western horizon, the camel sank to its knees. Alem was ready. He moved unevenly toward the beast and hoisted himself onto it. The animal balked at the added weight and lurched to its feet. But Alem held tight, refusing to let his chance for life slip away.

"Now let's see about that water," he said, his voice barely above a whisper. The camel took a lumbering step forward, causing Alem to cry out in pain as the bristle of the camel's hair penetrated his open wounds.

Each movement was excruciating as he was jostled about, but he hoped that every step was a step closer to water.

This is for you, Grandmother.

Chapter Twenty-two

The Empty Quarter

"WE'RE HERE," MIA SAID, waking Omar from his hazy dream.

"As long as it's anywhere but the Empty Quarter, I'll open my eyes," he said, receiving an answer in the form of another slug against his arm. He moaned. "That's starting to hurt."

Mia shrugged, her gaze focused on her satellite phone. "The coordinates match up."

At least she doesn't seem quite as angry anymore, he thought as he rubbed the sting from his shoulder. *If physical violence can be considered a sign of softening.* He looked through the windshield of the jeep to see a row of billowing tents ahead. Smoke curled from a campfire, and his nose twitched as he caught the smell of dinner. "Hungry?"

"Starved."

"Me too. Even if it's a camel, I'll eat it."

"Ew. Even *without* kosher laws, I still wouldn't eat a camel."

"What if you were starving?"

"I *am* starving." Mia pressed her lips together in that familiar, stubborn line.

"Hunger is relative. A kosher law couldn't make me starve to death."

Mia shook her head, her dark curls bouncing at her shoulders. "I'd rather die with a clean conscience."

Clean conscience? Her words were like a punch in the stomach. *Does she really think she has a clean conscience after what happened with David Levy?* Omar eyed her as she stopped the jeep and climbed out.

Omar followed, his gun over his shoulder. Several of the Arabs stood, postures rigid.

"Salamu 'alaykum!" Omar called out. He saw the recognition on their faces, and two men rushed forward to greet him. Omar laughed when they asked him if he was all right. "Never better," he said, doing a quick scan of the camp. Where was the boss? He introduced Mia in Arabic to the men.

"I'm not your wife," Mia said in English.

"You'll be left alone if they think we're married."

"Give me a break. It's the twenty-first century."

"Not in Yemen."

"You just want to share my tent."

Omar opened his eyes wide, feigning shock. "We broke up, remember? Well, you left *me*, but I've moved on. Completely." He put an arm around her shoulders and squeezed. "You need to keep your fantasies to yourself, sweetheart."

Fists clenched, Mia smiled at the men, who all stood now. One of the men invited them to join the meal.

"Of course," Omar said, moving his hand to Mia's lower back. He steered her toward the food. "Besides," he whispered in her ear, "we won't be here long enough to share a tent. Just use your charms on the crew boss, and then we'll be gone."

"Charms?" she said. "I came all this way, so I'm taking him in."

"Easy. One thing at a time." He settled onto a mat and reached for a handful of rice and meat. After a few greedy swallows, he noticed that Mia had moved several paces away. "Come and eat."

She folded her arms. "I can wait."

"These men won't mind. Maybe I lied a little, and they aren't as traditional as you might think." He turned to the one who issued the invitation. "Can you eat with a woman?"

The Arab grinned. "Of course."

With reluctance, Mia settled next to Omar and scooped a palm of rice. The other men avoided her gaze, and two of them left. "Don't worry about it," Omar whispered. "You're starving, remember?"

Mia stifled a smile and nodded. "I remember."

After a few moments of eating in silence, Omar turned to the man next to him. "Where's Rabbel?"

"He left for another job. I'm the boss now."

"You know Alem?"

The man lifted a shoulder as he shoved greasy fingers into his mouth.

Omar scanned the other Arabs, catching the eye of one he recognized from his former crew. "The black-skinned man—is he still here?"

"He left with Rabbel."

The Yemeni rose to his feet and walked away into the darkness.

"What was that all about?" Mia whispered.

Omar stared at the receding back of the man. He leaned toward Mia. "Go back to the jeep. I'll be there in a minute."

She rose, bowing her thanks to the Arab men, and then slowly moved to the jeep.

A few moments later, Omar stood and thanked his new comrades. When he reached the jeep, he grabbed a half-torn map.

"Wait here, and fire a shot into the air if anyone approaches you."

"*Matan*." Her voice held a warning.

"It's Omar." It irked him how she was usually such a stickler for following procedure, but other times . . . Well, he didn't have time for an argument. He left to find the Yemeni. It wasn't difficult, as the orange glow of a cigarette pinpointed the man's location.

When Omar stopped in front of the man, the Yemeni held out a cigarette pack.

"No thanks," Omar said, though his mouth watered at the anticipation of nicotine. The combination of his ex and the desert made old vices tempting.

"You look for the African?" the Yemeni asked.

"Is he alive?"

The man shrugged and then nervously looked behind him.

"Did he *leave* here alive?" Omar pressed.

A nod. The man inhaled the filtered toxins slowly then released the heady smoke through his parted lips. "The boss took him to another work site."

"Ah, I see." Perspiration beaded on Omar's forehead as he tried not to focus on the cigarette smoke. If he had to smell one more delicious plume, he'd be smoking again.

"But he take only one."

The weight on Omar's shoulders increased. Not only did this delay his assignment, but worry for Alem crept into his chest. It also meant spending more days and nights in this hellish climate, looking for an ant on the largest mound of sand in the world. He blew out a frustrated breath of air. Only one thing could cheer him up now, but she wasn't cooperating.

Thanking the man, he started back to the jeep when he heard a faint beeping. Omar slowed, trying to figure out where the sound had come from. He glanced at the Yemeni behind him, who was still smoking. Something wasn't right. He continued toward the jeep . . . and Mia . . . and the argument they were about to have.

She sat in the jeep, waiting with rifle in hand, just as he'd instructed.

"Good girl."

She scowled. "What did he say?"

"Hang on." Omar climbed in the jeep and revved the engine.

"I thought we were staying here."

"I'll explain in a minute." Omar shifted the jeep into gear, headed away from the camp, and then turned west.

Mia crossed her arms, her dark eyes glinting. Omar knew her patience would last only so long.

After several minutes, he slowed the jeep and killed the engine. "That man is probably calling to report us on his satellite phone right now."

Mia shifted in her seat and grabbed her backpack. Pulling out her phone, she began to dial. Omar's hand shot out and snatched it from her.

"Hey. What are you doing?" she asked.

"*Who* was the Yemeni calling?" He narrowed his eyes.

Mia stared back, unblinking. "Well, he's not one of us, so that leaves only one option. He's connected with AWP, and he's about to rat out our location."

Omar turned over the phone and slid the battery out.

"You're completely mad!" She grabbed for the phone, but Omar held it out of reach.

"Maybe he *is* one of us," he said.

"You're nuts. David would have—"

"I trust a band of blood-crazed Arabs with AK-47s more than I trust *David*." He tossed the phone into her lap. "Turn it on, and you'll walk."

"Fine. I don't need an invitation." She picked up her backpack and climbed out of the jeep.

Omar watched her leave—walking alone—through the dark desert. He leaped out of the jeep and jogged to her. By the time he reached Mia, she stood with her arms folded.

"Sorry," he mumbled.

She whirled on him. "Can't you just forget?"

He was surprised to see her eyes wet. Had Mia—the toughest woman on the planet—been crying? He was glad no one else was around to see what an idiot he was.

"I tried." Now that he started, there was no turning back. "I drank for two weeks straight, trying to *forget*." He wanted so badly to erase the hurt on her face—the hurt that he'd put there. "Then I just existed. I tried to quit the job over and over, but I didn't have the heart to give up seeing you completely."

Her eyes softened. "You kept your job so you could see me?"

"It worked, didn't it? Here you are. Here I am, seeing you."

Mia stared at him for a long moment then dropped her gaze. "It's no use, Matan. We can't ever change what's happened, and I don't think I want to anyway."

"What *did* happen?"

"Nothing."

"Come on. I saw how you danced with David at the party."

Mia sighed. "You saw what you *wanted* to see. You always have. It doesn't matter what I say or what anyone else says. You believe the world runs according to your perception."

Omar stiffened. This was an old argument, and the warmth of anger renewed itself in his chest. "You didn't deny sleeping with David."

Mia's expression darkened. "You never listened back then, and you still don't. I should never have to answer that question." She turned away.

"If it didn't happen, why won't you just say it?" he asked.

"Because," Mia said, spinning around. Tears coursed along her cheeks. "If you think that's the only thing that could take me from you, that's the only thing we had between us."

She fled, running toward the jeep.

I was wrong. So wrong. And I just wasted four months trying to prove otherwise.

He hurried after her. Mia sat in the jeep, staring at her hands, her dark curls plastered to the sides of her wet face. He climbed in the driver's seat, wanting to explain, turn back time. . . "David was out to get you from the beginning. He made it clear and egged me on. In fact, the last time I reported in—"

"I don't care anymore." Mia's tone was flat. "Just shut up and drive."

He started the engine, swearing under his breath. He drove too fast at first, ignoring how easy it would be to get lost. When his heart rate slowed, he reduced speed and glanced at Mia. Her eyes were closed, but he knew she was far from asleep.

According to the GPS on his satellite phone, the Yemen-Oman border was very close. Mia lifted her head as he studied the GPS. "Don't be stupid," she said.

"Too late for that." Omar met her gaze, but she looked away. "But as for the border crossing, I have an idea. Since we're out of money, we'll be taking the feral desert detour."

No argument from Mia. *One point for me.* But there was no satisfaction. At all.

Chapter Twenty-three

Red Sea
960 b.c.

NICAULA GAZED AT THE coastal town of Eloth that spread along the shores of the Red Sea. Its ivory buildings shimmered alabaster in the morning sun, and a fleet of towering ships was anchored near the shoreline. As a town known for its shipbuilding, the queen was surprised to see the piers silent. Then she remembered. It was the seventh day for the Hebrew people—just as the young boy had told her. No work occurred on this holy day.

Just as well. Her caravan had traveled all night to avoid the harsh desert clime, and they were ready for rest. After the sun set, they would approach the fabled crossroads and purchase fresh fruit and legumes.

Nearby, Batal sat on his horse, studying the town below. Nicaula wondered at his thoughts—he'd kept silent in the weeks since the locust swarm. Oftentimes she wished to tell him her true feelings without regard for protocol or consequence, but her sense of duty held her back. If there was one thing her father told her must come first, it was *duty*—both a burden and blessing for a queen.

And her continued dreams about the king of Jerusalem had to mean something.

Nicaula raised her hand. "We'll rest here until the Hebrews' religious day is over." Azhara and several others unloaded the camels.

Batal approached her and bowed. "Some of the men would like to celebrate as the Hebrews do."

Nicaula studied him for a moment. David had told them about the customs and celebrations. And since the locust storm, she'd noticed that fewer of her soldiers worshipped the nature gods, turning to Yahweh instead. She hadn't felt compelled to stop them. What if it was Yahweh who'd protected them from the locusts? "You may worship as you please."

Batal thanked her and turned away.

Having traveled for a few months, establishing camp had become routine, and a short time later, the queen settled in her tent and enjoyed boiled barley, fresh camel's milk, and cooked ibex. Following the meal, she drifted into a dreamless sleep.

It was the odd light that woke her hours later. Lethargic and damp with perspiration, Nicaula rose and took a goatskin, drinking her fill of stale water. Then she trickled water along her head and shoulders. Feeling refreshed, she walked out of the tent, and Azhara rushed over and bowed. "Everyone wants to visit Eloth as soon as the sun sets."

A faint smile crept to the queen's lips. "All right. We'll begin the trek when the sun touches the horizon."

ﺔﻠﻤﺠﻟﺍ

ON THE SECOND DAY in Eloth, Nicaula sent a group of soldiers and several women servants, including Azhara, ahead to Jerusalem. They would prepare the king to receive the queen of the South.

Without her ever-present maidservant, Nicaula felt even more vulnerable around Batal.

She tried to avoid him and only ventured out of her tent when he was on one errand or another. But it proved impossible. Every hour, she felt drawn to him more and more. Even worse, she'd started second-guessing everything her father had taught her, and when Batal was near or inadvertently touched her, she found her pulse racing. She couldn't sleep at night, tossing on her mat. It would only take one command, and he would be at her side, holding her in her arms, taking her to a place she'd never been.

But she gripped her hands together and squeezed her eyes shut against the restless obsession. *I'm being foolish.* Yet even as she tried to deny it, she knew she was in love with Batal. *A soldier.* The commander of her army. A man who had not a piece of gold to his name that didn't come from her. Her heart was on its way to breaking.

At night she watched him. With the maidservants asleep before the moon sat high in the sky, Nicaula crept to the tent opening and moved the flap just enough so she could see him sitting around the fire with the men. He didn't have any tales of women or adventure to share as they did, but the queen listened to his every word. Yes, he laughed with the others and shared in their drink, but he also held a quiet air of authority. He seemed to be a man beyond his years, serious, intent.

The third night in Eloth, Nicaula dreamt of the king of Jerusalem. She saw him from behind, his broad shoulders, his skill upon the Arabian stallion, and the haughty toss of his head. When he turned the animal around to face her, he smiled, his lips full, eyes wide set. *Batal?* Nicaula walked toward him, slowly at first, and then she ran. When she reached the horse, she looked up and saw his face changing. It narrowed, and his eyes grew darker. She tried to call to the king, reach him. But the horse shied from her, and the man said, "You have betrayed me, O Queen of the South."

The queen woke to darkness surrounding her, finding the night still deep. Her clothing was damp from perspiration, and she tried to relax her breathing so as not to disturb the maidservants who slept in the next section of the tent.

Her stomach tightened into a sickening feeling as she remembered her thoughts of betrayal. "Forgive me, O King. I have let my heart wander." She sat up and pulled her knees against her chest as hot tears burned her eyes and splashed against her cheeks. She *had* betrayed her visions of the king. Her infatuation with Batal must end tonight.

She crept out of the tent and walked toward the doused fire. Several men slept around the dark, smoldering pit, their breathing heavy with wine. It took only a moment to find where Batal lay on his side a short distance from the others. His features were peaceful, perfect, in the light of the moon. And even though the night was cool, warmth seemed to radiate from him. She knelt beside him, her heart thudding.

She ached with desire as she watched his even breathing expand his chest. She wanted to touch him . . . but the image of the king's disapproving face flashed through her mind. She had come to say good-bye. Slowly she bent over Batal and inhaled his musky fragrance. Her face hovered next to his, her lips almost close enough to touch him.

Her willpower weakened. She was queen, after all, and she could marry whomever she chose. Batal was a good man and would not mistreat her or go against her wishes. The passion of their love would be worth sharing her reign.

She pulled away, seeing his face fully illuminated in the moonlight. Then suddenly, his eyes opened. Nicaula's heart nearly stopped. His gaze went from surprise to understanding.

The queen's pulse drummed madly. He knew why she was there. She could see the desire in his eyes—so palpable that there was no doubt. He reached out and touched her shoulder. She breathed in sharply—it was as if she'd been touched by fire.

"Nicaula," he whispered as his hand moved along her arm.

Her body trembled, responding to his touch. His hand continued its journey to her waist, her hips, her thigh. She couldn't breathe. She couldn't move.

He rose to a sitting position until their faces were level. His hand cupped her chin, his breath warm and sweet upon her lips. She let her eyes close as she inhaled his fragrance. She ached to touch him, to cling to him and never let go.

His lips touched hers, and a shudder passed through her entire being. He kissed her slowly, his mouth taking control, and for once, she was his servant. Her body seemed to melt with his, transcending, floating above the earth. Her hands moved behind his neck, and she pulled him closer, feeling his arms tighten about her. Their hearts seemed to beat the same thudding race.

"Nicaula," he whispered, the name sweet on his lips. And then they were kissing again, but this time Batal's mouth became urgent. His hands moved up her back, tangling in her hair, and she arched against him. At any moment someone could wake and see them, but Nicaula didn't care. Kissing Batal was like the sweetest potion— one that she'd never stop craving.

Then the image of an Arabian flashed through her mind, and the man on the horse turned, angry, scowling. His face was narrow, his hair—tight copper curls. *The king.*

Nicaula's thoughts collided. What was she doing? She pulled away from Batal. "I'm sorry," she whispered.

The confusion in his eyes twisted her heart, and she tried to smile but couldn't. She touched his face, and he leaned forward again, taking it as an invitation. "I've come to say good-bye," she said, wondering how one kiss could have already broken her heart. "You must forget me, dear Batal. I cannot marry you."

He caught her wrist, determination in his eyes. "In time—"

"You must forget me and find someone you can love."

"I can love only *you*."

"You are young, you are handsome . . ." Her voice caught as his hands moved to her waist, pulling her closer.

Batal whispered in her ear, "I will never say good-bye. I will always be waiting for you. Even if I die, I'll wait in paradise."

"I give you permission to break that promise." Tears burned against her eyes as she drew away and stood. "I didn't mean for this to happen. Forgive me."

He rose to his feet and grasped her hands. "One kiss from you is better than a thousand nights with another woman."

Sorrow consumed her body. She tugged her hands away from his, took a step backward, and raised her hand to her heart. "Good-bye."

She felt Batal watch her leave, but knew she'd made the right choice. In no time, he would find a wife, someone to keep him warm at night and dispel all thoughts of her.

Once inside the tent, Nicaula lit a fish-oil lamp, the glow barely illuminating one end of the tent. In the corner stood a small statue of the goddess `Ashtartu. The queen was grateful that the maidservants slept deeply in the next section while she collected a bowl of water, her dagger, and the lamp and set all three items at the goddess's feet. Slowly the queen removed all of her clothing, and except for her ring and necklace, she stood naked in the flickering light. Her skin prickled at the exposure to the air as she knelt on the rug and bowed to the statue.

"Cleanse me of my lust," she prayed. "Remove the seed of my desire, O goddess of fertility." She picked up the dagger and cut off a lock of her hair. Then she put it into the bowl of water and watched the black strands float. "Remind me of my duty—that my mind will rule my heart." She brought the dagger to the center spot between her breasts and pricked her skin. She inhaled sharply and bit her lip to keep from crying out as a rivulet of blood ran down, pooling at her navel.

She touched the bowl to her lower stomach and let the blood drop into the water. The dark crimson mixed with the hair and stained the water. "With my body and my blood, I make this oath of virginity. No man will rule my heart. Only the gods of the heavens are greater than me."

The blood flow ebbed, and Nicaula lowered the bowl. Then she removed her ring and necklace and dipped them into the water. "I sanctify this jewelry, and it will become a symbol of my new pledge." She replaced the dripping jewelry on her finger and around her neck. Then she lifted a corner of the rug, dug a shallow hole, and poured the contents of the bowl into the sandy earth. "This holy spot marks the birth of my new soul." She raked sand over the hole and replaced the rug.

Silently she dressed, leaving the stain of blood along her torso to remind her of her promise. The goddess `Ashtartu was her witness, and the earth was the keeper of her oath.

Chapter Twenty-four

Yemen

I'M ENGAGED TO LUCAS. The thought drifted lazily through Jade's mind as she tried to imagine what it would be like to travel to France with him, to be introduced to his friends and family, to sleep by him every night . . . The sun must be affecting me. She straightened, tugging her perspiration-soaked shirt from the seat. Their small convoy had traveled through the desert for nearly two days. The previous night was spent sleeping at a small hostel, which was, apparently, a luxury. Jade and Lucas were given a shared bunk room, with her at one end and he at the other.

Jade felt the slow burn of the glaring sun on her arm, and she tried to move out of its reach. The windshield offered little protection, and the only way to avoid the blazing heat was if she traded Lucas places. But that would sandwich her between the driver and Lucas. She glanced at him again with mock disdain. He'd been asleep for the past hour. How could the man sleep anywhere and at any time?

She gazed across the bleak terrain, noticing a few scraggly trees and small bushes. Not much plant or animal life in sight. The vast expanse of cloudless sky stretched overhead and Jade had the odd feeling of claustrophobia, except in reverse. The changing colors of the sand provided the most interesting view—it ranged from almost white to dark orange. The afternoon had deepened, the sky's blue matured. The driver steered the truck off the road into the sand, following the other vehicles, and he whistled idly as he stopped and jumped out. Jade opened her door and climbed out to stretch her legs while Ahmed knelt by each tire and released some air.

"What are you doing?" she asked him.

Ahmed flashed a grin and he sidled right up to her, standing so close that Jade smelled his sour scent. Jade took an awkward step back, leery of the advances that Lucas had warned her about.

The driver motioned to the northern horizon. "High sand."

In the distance, the landscape changed, rising and falling as small hills converged into large dunes. Ahmed moved closer, his grin widening, and again Jade backed away. She climbed into the truck and waited for Ahmed to finish. Lucas was still asleep, and Jade wanted to swat him.

Through the deep sand, following an almost invisible trail, the convoy continued. Up ahead was another toll station. So far they'd passed through several, and Jade had been surprised at both the hostility and the friendliness—hostility when they arrived, friendliness when they paid.

A group of about a dozen men stood in front of the toll building, all with machine guns.

Lucas woke. He turned to the driver and asked in English, "We've passed Al 'Abr already?"

"Yes. We're at the border of Oman."

"Who are all those men?" Jade asked.

"Military." Lucas adjusted his rifle and checked the ammunition.

Jade's sweating hands grew clammy. "Are we going to need the guns?"

Lucas's gaze moved from the scene up ahead to her. "I've never seen so many at this stop. Something must be going on."

As they grew closer, Jade saw the not-so-welcoming expressions on the faces of the men. "Cover your face with your scarf, except for your eyes, so they think you're married," Lucas whispered.

Jade pulled the scarf over her face as the truck rumbled to a noisy stop along with the two other vehicles, and the drivers climbed out. Ahmed extended a few bills to the closest military man, apparently a leader, but the offer was waved away.

Lucas gripped his rifle, and slid to the driver's seat, pulling her with him. "Keep your hands on the wheel, and watch for my signal."

"I thought women weren't supposed to drive in this area."

"Change of plans."

After he climbed out of the truck, she moved into his seat, trying to calm her trembling hands and listen, but she couldn't decipher any of the conversation between Lucas and the military men. By the sounds of it, they were arguing.

Suddenly one of the soldiers jerked forward and caught Lucas by the arm. Lucas pulled away, waving his rifle, and in an instant, a dozen rifles were pointed at him. The soldier ordered Lucas to his knees then made him lie facedown in the sand.

Is this my signal? Jade's heart pounded with fear. Her stomach recoiled at the thought of what they might do to him. *Or to me.*

Jade gulped for air. It was now or never. She popped open the door, and the hot wind slapped at her veil as she stepped out.

Lucas twisted his head and called, "Get out of here!"

She hesitated, her hand still on the door handle. She looked around at the other drivers and crewmen, but they stared back at her, their fear equaling hers. *Isn't someone going to do something?* A bullet pinged against the truck. Jade dropped to the ground. Popping noises erupted and she covered her head, hoping for a little protection.

Mayhem started as the crew wrestled the weapons in the soldiers' hands.

"Jade!" Lucas's voice.

She lifted her head. Lucas had somehow freed himself and was running full tilt toward her. Gunfire erupted in the sand around his feet, and behind him, the crew members had wrenched themselves free and were running toward their vehicles. Fierce fire was exchanged as the men reached their trucks and gunned their engines. Jade leaped into the driver's seat and turned the ignition, almost flooding the engine. Lucas jumped into the passenger side just as she shifted into gear.

Lucas reached over Jade's arm and jerked the wheel hard to the right. Several bullets hit the truck. Miraculously, none touched the tires or windshield. The vehicle flew off the packed road and bounced across a couple of wadis. "Follow the others! We're going *around* the border station."

Jade's teeth slammed together as they hit a large dip, and the supplies in the back jostled against each other. Her hair blew in mass confusion as she kept the pedal floored.

"They aren't following," Lucas said after a few minutes. "You can slow down."

Jade eased off the gas pedal. "What happened back there?"

"There has been a murder at Shisur—they suspect some excavators, and they've closed the border."

A shudder passed through Jade's heart. "What happened?"

"Remember when I told you about human sacrifice? The

military said a man was sacrificed, but his body is missing. When I told them about the Coptic patriarch, they laughed and ordered me to kneel. I guess the rest of the crew smelled an execution, and they snapped."

"No respect for the patriarch, I see."

"Oh, they respect him—just not when he's thousands of miles away." The dust, multiplied by the strengthening wind, billowed into the truck. Lucas rolled his window up partway. Jade did the same.

"Are you okay?" he asked.

Jade's heart still hammered, and she'd probably have no appetite for a while, but otherwise . . . "I'm fine." She stole a sideways glance at him. He was staring intently at her, his face roughed up from lying in the sand. "What about you?" she asked.

"Nothing that can't be forgotten tomorrow." He reached over and placed his hand on hers. A jolt passed through Jade, bringing back the terror she'd felt at seeing him held at gunpoint.

"But next time, don't get out of the truck."

Jade nodded, her throat too tight to answer.

"I would have been fine, but a woman like you . . . not so fine."

Dread shot through Jade. Life had become just a little too fragile for a moment, and she wasn't sure that now would be a good time to crumble. One minute she was fantasizing about marrying Luc, and the next she'd almost watched him die. She took several deep breaths and then asked, "Where are we headed?"

"Beyond that ridge—the edge of the Empty Quarter."

Jade squinted against the distance. She could just make out the dust from the lead vehicles along the expanse of rising hills. "Those hills are the Empty Quarter? I thought it would be a flat desert."

"When we get into the dunes, you'll wish it were flat."

Jade's mouth formed an *o* as she kept her gaze forward. With minimal conversation from Lucas, she drove toward the dunes, following the other trucks. She tried to push the border incident from her mind by thinking about normal things like her parents and school. But nothing seemed normal anymore. The things that used to matter—getting high honors in college or finding the right job—didn't seem so important anymore. The life of the man sitting next to her was all she cared about at this moment.

She glanced at Lucas. He was peeling an orange. When he separated the first section, he handed it to her. She took it and popped it into her mouth. The burst of sweet flavor seemed like manna from heaven.

With new eyes, she soaked in the beauty of the vast desert as the sun sank fast, casting its last glimmer upon the dunes ahead. It was as if time stood still. After thousands of years, the sand had preserved the quiet recollections of those who had lived and died there in generations past. A shiver traveled her spine as she realized that the very queen of Sheba may have cast her royal gaze upon these same dunes. What had she been thinking of? Who did *she* love? Had her heart ever been broken?

The dunes flashed by, some light yellow in color and others a myriad of red and orange in the wind-carved sand mountains. The truck protested at the change in terrain, and its tires fought to maintain grip on the sifting sand. But Jade felt strangely happy, despite her exhaustion and unkempt appearance. She couldn't help smiling.

"Want to share?" Lucas asked.

"Uh . . . this place is really beautiful."

He chuckled. "You've become a convert. People who've never visited this part of the world don't understand. They don't feel its intoxicating pull. All they see is the violence and poverty on their television screens."

She looked at him, and something pulsed between them. She tore her gaze from his mesmerizing eyes.

"They don't feel the openness, the freedom, and the stark beauty of a land virtually untouched, raw, and wild," he said in an almost-reverent tone. "They don't see the exotic traditions, the devout believers, or the honor of tradition. Those who don't venture far from their homes are rather . . . boring, if you will."

She grinned. "Are you calling me boring?"

"Not at all." Lucas's tone deepened, catching Jade off guard.

She swallowed hard, trying to reason above her throbbing pulse. "When I look at this country, I see what the queen must have seen thousands of years ago. It's truly amazing to think about it."

"That's because the queen still lives."

"What do you mean?" Jade asked, prepared for some far-fetched theory published in an obscure archaeology magazine.

Lucas leaned forward, propping his elbow on the dash and gazing at her. "The queen was a one-of-a-kind woman in her day. She had power, wisdom, and incredible wealth. Men feared her and adored her—it was difficult to separate the two. She was beautiful beyond a poet's description, and many scholars have been dumbfounded by her spiritual influence."

Jade's face flushed as he continued to stare at her. Of course, she knew all of this, but hearing it from him was somehow much different.

"In a world where women were treated no better than slaves, she was a forerunner of combining femininity with righteous power. Her story has been told in the Bible, the Koran, and the ruins of Arabia and Africa." He paused. "As long as her story continues to be told, she still lives."

Jade relaxed against the seat, not letting his penetrating gaze unsettle her any longer.

"But I believe that the spirit of the queen is present in at least one woman I know."

She glanced at him and saw that he was smiling. She laughed. "Is that a compliment, Monsieur Morel?"

He studied her before answering. "The highest one I could ever pay."

Her heart drummed as she turned her attention to the road.

Lucas leaned back in his seat. "We should be nearing a channel where the earth is hardened from years of rain and runoff."

"Rain? Here?" She was relieved that their conversation was casual again.

"Every so often. In the winter months, a few desert plants will even grow and bloom."

Jade followed the plumes of dust ahead of them, ignoring the hungry whine of her stomach. Dampness crept along every inch of her body, and Lucas's charming words hadn't helped one bit. She looked at her mood ring. Orange. *Stimulating.*

"We should be in Oman now," Lucas said after a while.

The sun had nearly set, illuminating the sand to a brilliant gold. To the south, Jade noticed the landscape flatten and then rise again.

"The Mahara Plateau," Lucas said by way of explanation. "Do you want me to drive? We still have a ways to go."

Jade nodded and brought the truck to a stop. She took in the surroundings as Lucas drove, following the other tire tracks. "Is this a road?"

"For the locals, but not many others."

"People live out here?" She stared at the barren territory. Just some scraggly brush and a few rather dry-looking trees dotted the area.

"The desert community comes alive at sunset, since not many people are foolish enough to travel during the day."

Jade stared at the passing landscape against the violet sky. She felt miniscule between the vastness of the sky and the stretch of unending desert. A form moved against the horizon, capturing her attention. Straightening in her seat, she pointed. "What's that?"

"Looks like a wild camel."

"Out here, by itself? What does it eat?" She searched for any vegetation nearby.

"The local Bedu take care of their animals better than their own children sometimes. That camel may be wild, but one of the tribes has claim on it." He slowed the truck as they grew closer.

"What's it carrying?"

Lucas slowed even more and peered through the deepening twilight. "I can't tell from here." Letting the truck idle to a stop, he scooted out.

Jade climbed out too and walked around the front of the truck to join Lucas. "Will the others know we stopped?"

"We'll meet in Shisur. There's only one road."

The camel didn't move as they approached. Its large lashes seemed to droop in the heat. The shape on its back came into focus.

"It's a man," Jade whispered. The black body was half-clothed, hanging across the camel's back, and the man's arms hung limp, his head twisted to the side, face crusted with sand.

Lucas reached the man first. With one hand, he grabbed the loose skin around the camel's neck and with a couple of sharp commands, cajoled the animal to sit. Jade winced at the sight of the man's blistered and swollen feet.

"Help me take him off." Lucas gripped the flesh beneath the man's arms, and they gently eased him to the ground.

Lucas knelt beside him and felt for a pulse. "He's alive." Mouth set in a grim line, he turned the man onto his back.

Jade gasped at the mutilated face and arms. Even through the sand and dried blood, she saw that the markings were no random slashes. She covered her mouth.

"He's been sacrificed," Lucas said, his voice grim.

Sacrificed? Hot tears pricked Jade's eyes as she imagined the torture this man must have undergone. "The soldiers at the border—"

"Apparently they didn't know he survived." Lucas spoke quietly, his words sending shivers along Jade's skin. "I've seen sketches of these gruesome markings before. They signify the release of an evil spirit called a djinn—a protector of sacred relics of the desert. Through these carvings on human flesh, followed by the draining of the blood of life, the belief is that an ancient secret will be revealed."

Jade dropped to her knees next to Luc. "Such as the location of the tomb?"

"Yes." He met her gaze. "This man needs help desperately. We need to get him in the truck."

She nodded. Together they lifted the damaged body, and moments later, they had the man lying across the seats of the truck.

"Know first aid?" Lucas asked.

"The basics." *Like how to put on a Band-Aid.*

"See if there's a first aid kit somewhere."

She found the kit under the driver's seat and handed it to Luc.

He gave her a water bottle. "Try to get him to swallow some, but go easy." He popped open the kit and rummaged through the contents, discovering a plastic bottle containing clear-blue liquid. "Let's hope this astringent takes away some of the infection."

The nausea in Jade's stomach intensified, and she tried not to concentrate on the man's deformed face as she lifted his head and poured a small trickle of water against his cracked lips. The precious water was wasted as it slid along his cheek and then pooled beneath his neck onto the seat.

"He's not responding."

Lucas looked up, his hands muddied with blood as he cleaned the man's torso. "Keep trying. We can always find more water."

Where? A noisy fly bullied its way into the truck, landing with morbid curiosity on the man's carved chest. Jade swatted angrily at the insect. "How close are we to Shisur?"

"It's nearly fifty kilometers to the north," Lucas said. "He's lucky to have survived at all, let alone travel this distance. We have to get him to a hospital. We'll backtrack to Thumrait, and if there's no medical help there, we'll continue south to Salalah. I'll ride in the back while you drive."

Jade's breath caught in her throat as her stomach muscles clenched. She didn't know how nurses kept their minds above the task at hand. "Why don't you drive?" It would be dark in an hour or so, and she didn't know how she'd do in the unfamiliar desert. "I'll be fine to ride in the back."

Lucas studied her for a brief instant and then acquiesced. Jade climbed out her side and scaled the tailgate. As she sat among the gas cans and stacked supplies, she stared at the bloodstains on her hands. The motion of the truck pitched her forward, but she soon regained her balance and settled in for the bumpy ride, keeping one eye on the patient.

Not ten minutes later, the truck slowed, and Lucas reached for his gun.

Approaching them was another vehicle.

Chapter Twenty-five

Eloth
960 b.c.

THAT NIGHT NICAULA FINALLY slept and dreamed again. Because of her farewell to Batal with both heart and soul, she now dreamed about the great king of Jerusalem—his gold-and-ivory throne. The six golden steps. The king's honeyed eyes. The hundreds of concubines. His lips closing in on hers.

When the queen awoke in the morning, she knew she'd been cleansed. The goddess and gods had granted her a new start, and she was free from Batal and her obsession. Dreaming again of the great king of Jerusalem could mean only one thing—he was her true destiny.

With the morning still young, Nicaula spent her time walking through the dusty streets of Eloth. She wore a veil, hiding her swollen eyes. With her maidservants at her side, the queen stopped from time to time to examine wares at the outside bazaar and the shipbuilding yards. Sporadically, the townspeople bowed and paid their respects to her, but for the most part, the people didn't know that a great queen walked among them.

Nicaula paused as she approached a group of boys huddled around a heating pot. They were stripping coconut husks and throwing the fibers into the water.

"What are you doing?" Nicaula asked.

One boy turned around and flashed a toothy grin. "This makes the thread to stitch the ship's planks together."

In her childhood, Nicaula had seen men sewing planks with ropelike fibers along the Gulf of Aden. She turned her attention to a group of men who sat nearby, spinning the softened fibers into coarse thread. Above their heads, black smoke billowed from the structure behind them. "What are they doing inside?" Nicaula asked.

The same boy answered. "They're fashioning copper and iron ingots."

The queen's gaze trailed down the street, following the half-dozen structures that emitted the same strain of smoke. Sharp sounds reverberated off the rough walls. The queen moved to the closest building and peered through the doorway, through which she saw the bare backs of men bent over fires as they pounded metal into shape. After a few moments, she pulled away from the suffocating heat and, instead of continuing in a straight path, she led her entourage along a windy street until they reached a massive structure of clay and palm fronds.

Inside, men carved wood planks by hand, and a man near the doorway looked up, greeting the visitors. His trained eye took in the appearance of the queen and her attendants, and he bowed low. "How can I be a service to such a great lady?"

"I am queen of the South," Nicaula said.

The man visibly started and bowed even lower to the ground. When he raised his head, his face was flushed scarlet. "Welcome to my shipyard. We are honored by your presence."

"Tell me, to whom do the ships belong that adorn your waters?"

A look of amazement crossed the wiry man's face. "To our great master, the king of Jerusalem."

"Ahh," Nicaula said, a thrill passing through her. This was yet another indication of her destiny. "I have yet the privilege to meet your king."

"Are you interested in purchasing a vessel of your own?"

"Perhaps on our return." The queen scanned the large room. Several workers had stopped in their tasks and stood staring. Her focus returned to the shipyard merchant. "May we visit one of your vessels?"

"Of course." Spots of perspiration beaded on the man's brow. "It will be an honor to tell our king that a queen from Arabia admired his ships."

"Very well," Nicaula said, restraining a smile. "I may tell him myself."

"You are traveling to the land of Jerusalem?" The merchant clasped his hands together.

"Upon the morrow, we will set out for the land of Jerusalem. Then we will pay a visit to the king's great city." Nicaula's eye was caught by a sturdy man who held a curved tool in his hands. "What is he shaping?"

"The keel. And those men over there are shaping the bow and ribs." The merchant shouted a sharp command, and the men returned to their activities.

Nicaula pointed to a group who stood at the back of the structure, chisels and wooden hammers in hand. "And those men?"

"They're removing the bark from the dwarf palms, preparing the wood for planking."

"And all of this has been commissioned by your king?"

"Yes. Eloth has become a shipbuilding center upon the king's orders."

The queen smiled with satisfaction. *The king of Jerusalem is a powerful monarch, indeed.* She moved outside and, with the merchant at her side, they walked to the shoreline. Up close, the sea vessels were magnificent, rising from the turquoise water with elegant strength.

"I can take you to a ship and show you the interior."

Nicaula nodded and waited as the merchant called to one of his men and brought a dhow made of imported teak for their party. They climbed in, and the small boat soon reached the anchored ship, the bottom of which had been sealed with thick, black bitumen. The merchant steadied the rope ladder, hanging from the port side, so the others could embark.

As the queen reached the top deck, she stood for a breathless moment, gazing over the tranquil swelling of the waters below. A warm breeze tugged at her clothing, lifting the hair from her neck, creating a shiver across her neck as she realized she was standing on one of the fabled king's treasured possessions. She closed her eyes briefly against the brilliance of the sun-dappled planks, visualizing the king standing nearby, his scarlet robes a startling contrast to his copper hair. She imagined that he extended a jeweled hand toward her.

"Come. I've been waiting for you."

Nicaula opened her eyes and spun around. The voice had been deep, warm, and familiar, yet she'd never heard its tone before. Her servants stood with the merchant on the other side of the deck.

Who had spoken?

Her gaze darted about the ship, but no one else could have said the words. *The gods of the wind, the sea, and the sun?* She looked to the sea below as another thought entered. *Had the great king spoken to me across time and land?* Nicaula drew away from the stout railing and wrapped her arms around her torso. Her soul had been touched by a man she had yet to meet, and she hoped this new king might repair the hole in her heart left from Batal.

✤✤✤

NICAULA AWAKENED IN THE sultry tent, droplets of perspiration soaking her back and staining her silk tunic, evidence that the wet season had begun. The threads of a disturbing dream slipped away just as she opened her eyes. She sat and tried to remember the details. It hadn't been the now-familiar one of the great king. It was something further into the future, something she couldn't quite grasp. Her heart was heavy with sorrow, but she wasn't sure why.

Rising, the queen crossed to the tent opening and lifted the flap. It had rained during the night, and beyond the traveling party, thunder rolled atop the distant hills. The queen could almost distinguish the line where the desert floor transitioned into scrubby green. They had been traveling for ten days now since leaving Eloth. They were almost to Jerusalem.

Preparations were already underway for their traveling day, and a short time later, as Nicaula sat upon her horse to lead the procession, a whisper filtered throughout the caravan.

Jerusalem is near.

It had been several weeks since Azhara had left with the others to prepare for her arrival in Jerusalem. As the caravan set out, Nicaula's sense of foreboding increased. When the midday sun had waned and in its place, tiered clouds of fiery orange and pink blanketed the sky, the wind picked up. It swirled the sand around the camels' feet, yet the great beasts plodded faithfully without protest.

Nicaula's hands tingled in anticipation. Against the first hillside, black tents perched stoically next to one another, forming a small community. Naked children ran from their shelters toward the approaching caravan, and several women, clothed in black robes, followed, their tongues clucking sharp reprimands. The children—their eyes liquid brown, hair matted with wriggling lice, and stained teeth bursting through wide grins—heeded no one and arrived at the first camel.

Batal urged his camel to the ground and disembarked. He met the children and joined them in their rapid dialect. Nicaula watched with amusement, focusing mostly on the children so that her gaze wouldn't stray to Batal's broad shoulders, or the hands that had caressed her . . .

"We have reached Ophel," Batal announced. "The children say this wall begins the kingdom of Jerusalem."

Nicaula gazed along the wall as excitement coursed through her body. The children ran alongside the camels for several minutes then eventually drifted off, their tiny chests heaving with exertion. The mothers stood grouped together, watching the travelers, periodically calling to their children.

The young boys reminded her of the child, David, she'd met just outside of Sa'ba—the child who first told her with all the wisdom his small body could muster of the great king of Jerusalem. She had provided young David a home, and now he lived within Sa'ba's walls with his ailing mother.

As the caravan moved along the sloping hill leading to the city, she noticed an old olive tree. A soft glow surrounded it, as if the sun shone through an opening in the clouds and illuminated only the tree, but the sky above was clear. A few clay lamps sat at the base of the trunk, as if it were a point of worship. She raised her hand in the air, and the caravan stopped.

Batal reached her side. "Has something happened?"

"I don't know." She had the sudden urge to touch the tree. Batal helped her down, and she walked to the silvery trunk. The rustic leaves rattled in the breeze, welcoming her and warding her off at the same instant.

She reached out and ran her hand along the roughness. An image jolted through her mind: a man hanging from a rudimentary cross, his hands and feet nailed to the wood. She drew her hand back with a gasp, stepping away from the tree. Her body trembled. The vision had been horrible, yet fascinating at the same time.

The queen turned to face those watching her. They spoke quietly among themselves as they adjusted the camels' baggage and appeared not to have noticed any change. "Batal?"

He hurried to her side, his expression curious.

She pointed at the gnarled trunk. "Do you see the man on the cross?"

"No." His eyes searched hers. "Are you feeling well?"

"I am well. But just now I saw a man nailed to a wooden cross."

"I do not see anything," he said, his brows drawn in concern as he looked from the tree back to her.

The queen couldn't deny the image she'd just witnessed. It was clearer than any dream she'd ever had. Her toes tingled, the sensation spreading up her legs to her other limbs. Had it been a dream? Perhaps, yet she had been awake.

"The sun is strong today," Batal said in a gentle voice.

"Yes, and so was the image upon this tree." She turned away. "Come. Perhaps the great king will have an answer." She knew her retort stung Batal, but she could not be doubted. The image had burned itself in her mind, and she wouldn't rest until she found out why.

The gates of the city were flung open in welcome, and an army of at least fifty lined the entrance.

The queen nodded to the soldiers, keeping her lips pressed together as the men bowed at her passing. On the other side of the wall, Nicaula joined Batal as he waited on the rocky path. Pulling her horse next to his, she laid first sight on the great city of Jerusalem.

"Mount Moriah and the temple of Yahweh," Batal said. His gaze was not on the city, but upon the queen, when he said, "Splendid."

Nicaula's face warmed, and she looked away to scan the valley spread before them. Because of the young boy, David's stories, she was familiar with the names of the great city.

The ivory buildings echoed the golden sun, nestled against the green escarpment. To the west, another hill arose, crowned by a temple. She drew in her breath as she marveled at the elegant structure. Next to the temple of gold was a palace fit for a very wealthy king. The legends preceding the king did him little justice.

Jerusalem was like a hidden emerald in the desert. There appeared to be some construction taking place surrounding the temple. Four towers flanked the adjacent palace, but she could not tear her gaze from the panorama spread before her. White tendrils of smoke curled from some of the lower shelters, most likely cooking buildings. Nicaula assumed that each day a feast was provided for so great a king. She wondered about his many wives and concubines. Did they live in the homes at the base of the hill? Or did they live in a vast compound on the opposite side of the palace? It would take many fields of crops to feed so many women and, undoubtedly, so many children.

The sound of horse hooves brought the queen from her revelry. A thick man approached them, his large, hairy hands guiding his animal with precision. His smile was broad as he climbed off his horse and bowed low to the ground. "Welcome to our land. Our king desires an audience with you."

"Tell him it is my pleasure." Nerves twisted in her stomach.

After all this time and all the travel, she had arrived at the day in which she would meet the man who haunted her dreams.

"I am Yigal, faithful commissioner to the king." His deep voice resonated through the afternoon air. "We are honored to have the queen of the South as a guest in our land."

Nicaula held his gaze for an instant longer then let a slow smile creep to her lips. "Thank you." She motioned to the camels behind her. "I have brought gifts for your king and his god."

Yigal's eyes shifted to the bags of bulky wealth. "Our king sends you his blessings and will be pleased to give you audience. We have also prepared quarters for your use, and you will find your servants waiting for you there."

Nicaula bowed her head in acknowledgment then raised her eyes to meet his. "Take me to the king first."

Chapter Twenty-six

Oman

THEY'D DRIVEN ALL DAY in silence, and Omar sensed that Mia's mood was no better. He spent the time vacillating between complete disgust with himself and wondering how he could have let David Levy have so much control. It was bad enough listening to his boss at work, but worse to have the guy invade all his thoughts. Omar would be thirty-seven in the fall, and though Mia was a few years younger, it wasn't as though they were lovesick teenagers, flying into jealous rages. Well, at least she wasn't.

Mia suddenly straightened, pointing. "There's someone up ahead."

Omar saw a billow of dust coming toward them from the north. "Military?"

"Can't tell yet."

"Any ideas?"

"We've done nothing wrong. Why should they pick on us?"

"They don't need a good reason." Omar let off the gas pedal and tried to catch a glimpse of the driver. The truck up ahead stopped, and someone jumped out of the back. It was a veiled woman—carrying a rifle.

Then a man climbed out of the driver's side and caught up with the woman. They appeared to be arguing. Both clutched rifles.

"What do you think they're arguing about?" Mia asked.

"Let's find out." Omar threw his door open. Several long strides put him within shooting distance of the two people. He stopped, surprised to see that the man looked European. Omar decided he had nothing to fear and waved Mia over.

"Do you have any medical supplies?" the man asked in accented Arabic when he reached Omar.

"A few of the basics. What's wrong?" Omar said in English.

The man switched to English. "A botched sacrifice. An African man—hasn't told us his name, but he's pretty bad."

Alem! Omar sprinted toward the truck, ignoring the shout from the French guy. He reached the passenger side of the truck and wrenched the door open. There, lying perfectly still, was his battered friend.

"Alem!" The markings along Alem's face and torso were hideous. Angry bile rose in Omar's throat, and he wanted to scream at someone. Instead, he whispered, "What did they do to you?" But his friend, with clumsy bandages across his chest and arms, didn't respond.

The French man and his companion arrived, staring through the driver's side. "You know him?" the woman asked.

Omar nodded. "Where did you find him?"

"Not far from here," the French man said. "We found him half-dead on a camel's back. It was a religious sacrifice," he continued. "See the markings on his face? The sun, the crescent moon, and the star inside the crescent? They are repeated on his torso. All were worshipped as pagan gods by early civilizations. This man was to be offered to the djinns of the desert."

Omar's stomach twisted in disgust. "Djinns? But those are myths, genies that young kids tell stories about."

"Myths to some," the man said. "Sure, there are good djinns, but there are also many powerful, evil ones. The ancient traditions surrounding worship obviously still exist. Even Muhammad worshipped the pagan gods before his conversion to monotheism."

Omar could hardly believe anyone would believe in djinns. "Who would still practice something so diabolical?"

"Those who believe the ancient legends." The man shook his head. "The sacrifice of a human guarantees the promise of greatness, the discovery of a wonder, or the resolution to conflict."

Omar shook his head in disbelief that some still practiced such perversion. "Ever hear of AWP?" the man asked.

Mia cut in. "We'll worry about all that later. He needs to get to a hospital."

Omar tore his eyes away from Alem and looked at Mia. "I'm taking him."

She seemed to sense that now was not the time to argue. "All right. Let's get out of here."

Omar ran to the jeep and drove closer to the truck. With the help of the others, they lifted Alem into the rear seat.

Omar extended his hand toward the French man. "Name's Omar."

"Lucas Morel. Try the hospice at Thumrait. If they can't help, Salalah has the closest hospital."

"Thank you—both of you. This man saved my life once."

After farewells were made, Omar started the jeep's engine and drove in the opposite direction of Shisur. The oasis would have to wait.

Chapter Twenty-seven

Shisur, Oman

THE RIDE CONTINUED TO be hot and uncomfortable, but Jade took reassurance in knowing the poor man was on his way to get help. She glanced at Lucas as he maneuvered through the barely perceptible road littered with dried roots, camel droppings, and an occasional thorny bush. She could see nothing else for miles—just endless stretches of sand and the changing colors of the landscape as the sun finished its journey across the Arabian sky.

She wanted to sleep, but her bladder hurt too much. Not wanting to ask Lucas to stop—*again*—Jade grimaced her way through it.

"Shisur."

Jade pulled her mind from its cobwebbed corners and looked at Lucas.

"See the rocks?" he said.

"I thought it was an oasis."

"It is. There's a well." He flashed her a smile.

The "oasis" consisted of a few palms crowded together as if they were gleaning off one another's shade, looking scraggly and bug eaten. Some pine trees rounded out the greenery, looking more robust than the palms. A short distance away sat a small settlement of buildings and homes. Jade spotted the awkwardly pitched tents and trucks from their group. The evidence of digging was apparent—lengths of yellow rope had been laid out, marking off certain areas.

The men came out of their tents and waved. When Lucas pulled the truck to a stop, Jade climbed out and greeted the men.

After the formalities were over and some animated discussion about the border patrol finished, Lucas said to Jade, "They've curtained off a section of palms over there that you can use at your convenience. Or you can walk beyond those homes, where there is another grouping of palms, if you need more privacy."

She thanked him and walked quickly to the curtained-off section.

Later, Lucas showed her the different areas of Shisur. They walked through the scant village and greeted the curious children. When they reached the larger ruins, he said, "These structures are at least three thousand years old, maybe more."

Jade touched the stones with reverence, trying to imagine the caravans that had stopped here to water their camels. Was it possible that the queen had touched these very walls?

Lucas continued, "This area was a lot more fertile, and groups of people camped here for weeks, perhaps months—especially during the dry season when crossing the sands would have been unbearable." Lucas leaned over and picked up a broken piece of stone. "If only something more remained of their history."

He led her to a low wall. "Here are the inscriptions Dr. Lyon studied."

Jade crouched and inspected the letters. "What do they say?"

"It's a prayer, and interestingly enough, the Hebrew god,

Yahweh, is mentioned."

"No wonder Dr. Lyon was interested."

"Exactly." Lucas crouched next to her. "Solomon taught the queen of Sheba about the God of Israel."

Jade touched the engraved stone, tracing the foreign letters with her finger. "Yahweh." A gust of wind whipped through the site, stirring up the sand beneath her feet and loosening her ponytail. She didn't mind the wind as a thrill of pleasure coursed through her at being so close to the artifact. "It's really amazing," she said.

Lucas nodded, his eyes lit with amusement. Then he reached over and tucked a strand of hair behind her ears. "Yes, it is."

Jade looked away, afraid of getting lost in his eyes. "Isn't this evidence enough of her existence here in Oman?"

"No," Lucas said, straightening. "The carbon dating is disappointing."

Jade rose beside him. "Maybe the queen taught her people about Yahweh, and this inscription indicates that they continued those teachings."

"An argument I've heard from the professor himself many times."

She gazed at the low wall, but soon the sizzling fire and smell of cooking meat drew her attention.

"Let's eat," Lucas said, a smile in his eyes. He cradled her elbow as he helped her step over the rocks.

Jade tried not to shiver at the warmth his hand brought. It had been a long time since she had known a man to be such a gentleman, yet so appealing at the same time, and it was driving her crazy. She almost wished that he'd just kiss her and get it over with. If he were a lousy kisser, she could stop looking at him like a lovesick teenager.

She glanced at Lucas. His white shirt was untucked, olive

pants frayed at the hem, tennis shoes worn. But he walked with confidence and assurance. He was an experienced, pretty much brilliant, man of the world. Just because he'd paid her a couple of compliments and was extremely polite didn't mean he really liked her. After all, they were pretending to be engaged, so his guiding her by the elbow was really no big deal.

As they neared the circle of men, Lucas lowered his hand and slipped it into hers. Jade's thoughts tumbled as she realized how much she wanted him to hold her hand *without* pretending. The gesture had its desired effect. Every man noticed. She had nothing to fear at being the only woman among this crew.

When they reached the fire, Lucas spread a rug onto the ground and indicated for Jade to sit. Then he brought her a paper plate of rice and dark, aromatic meat. Looking around the group, Jade saw that she was expected to eat her first official meal in the desert with her fingers. Lucas, who now sat next to her, leaned over and whispered, "Eat with your right hand." He handed her a Sunkist.

She smiled. Classic modern mixed with an ancient setting. "Thanks."

The conversation during supper turned serious as Lucas told the men about the stranger they had found half-starved and half-dead on the camel.

The round-faced man named Ismail spoke first. "Human sacrifice is bad luck. We cannot sleep here tonight."

Jade stared at Lucas. They would be relocating on a moonless night? But he already had his hands up. "Leave the fire burning, and all bad djinns will stay away."

Ismail looked doubtful, but he nodded. "We'll take turns standing guard."

"I'll take first post," Lucas conceded.

When the others retired for the night, some in tents, others huddled near the fire on top of sleeping bags, Jade moved to her designated tent. Lucas had told her to check for scorpions and snakes with a stick first. She had. She spent a few minutes writing her observations about Shisur and typing the prayer inscription into her phone. Then she lay against the stiff earth and burrowed inside her lightweight sleeping bag. Thinking of possible creatures invading her tent, it took at least an hour for her to drift to sleep.

She awoke sometime later, her bladder urgent. She reached for her stick and swatted the top of her sleeping bag before climbing out. Her small flashlight illuminated the way to her draped facility. The fire had gone out, and any signs of smoke had disappeared into the cooling night. All was quiet, and the apparent concern for bad luck had fallen asleep with the men.

Jade crept around the wiry brush toward the palms. Her flashlight faltered then wavered bright again. She caught the scent of cigarette smoke. Someone was nearby. She spun and looked for the person, but couldn't see anyone. She left the palms and started walking toward the second group that Lucas had pointed out earlier.

She tried to push away the fear of venomous creatures by keeping her flashlight arcing across the ground in front of her until she reached the leaning palms.

On her way back, she stumbled against a protruding stone. She continued, slower this time, picking her way toward the tents. The glow from her flashlight wobbled then dimmed. She shook it, hoping to jostle the batteries just enough, but the light went out altogether. Glancing upward, she wondered why the one time that the clouds covered the moon in the middle of the summer had to be tonight.

She walked for several more minutes, surprised she hadn't reached the tents yet. Then her foot sank into a hole. She fell to the ground with a hard thud, twisting her knee and scraping her arms.

As she tried to sit up, her body started to slide, sharply downward into some sort of hole.

Jade reached for a root, a branch . . . anything to stop her slide. Rocks and sand tumbled around her. Then there was nothing below, and she pummeled through the dark emptiness. Her hip made the first impact on a hard surface, followed by her shoulder, and then her head. *The well*, she thought as her head throbbed and her mind spun into oblivion. *I've fallen into the well.*

The darkness wrapped around her like a cool ocean, making it difficult to know which way was up. She tried to stand, but dizziness made her stay put. Pain pulsated through her shoulder and hip, and when she touched her head, she felt the warm moisture of blood. She tucked her knees close to her chest and wrapped her arms around her legs.

A well should have water in it. She'd watched the men pull out buckets of water to boil. "Not even fit for a camel," Lucas had said. If she wasn't in the well shaft, where was she?

"Lucas!" she yelled, her voice breaking with exertion. "Help me, someone!" She waited, holding her breath, but she heard nothing. Logic told her the crew would miss her in the morning and then come looking for her. She burrowed her head between her knees and tried to find comfort in the little warmth her body gave off.

She eventually dozed, waking some time later. Scooting forward, Jade inched her way across the space, extending her hands in front of her—both curious and afraid of the first touch of rock or earth.

Her fingers came into contact with a light, feathery substance. She pulled away, her heart pounding. *An insect? No*, she decided, and reached out again. It felt like the leaves of a plant. *An underground plant?*

Her hands moved with more confidence as she stood. The plant covered an earth-hardened wall of some sort. The roots twisted, wrapping about each other. The wall crumbled away as Jade dug her fingernails into the surface. She felt for any protruding stones beyond the earth and roots—anything she could use to climb out.

Step by step, she moved along the wall, gripping the tangled roots. Then her knee collided with something sharp. "Ow," she muttered.

Reaching down, Jade felt the corner of stone. "At last." She placed both hands on the stone and felt along the edges. The length continued for several feet. She moved along the side of it, amazed by the size of the rock. It was probably a cleft or shelf. A dribble of dirt fell onto her head, and she flinched, realizing that she would be buried here alive if the ceiling caved in.

Something scuttled across her feet, and suddenly, Jade's chest heaved. She gripped the side of the stone, trying to steady herself as dizziness passed through her. She waited for the pain of a bite or sting to come—the impending piercing of flesh from a scorpion's pinchers, the sinking of fangs into her calf, the swelling, the nausea, the blood draining from her head, the poison coursing through her constricting veins as her white blood cells tried to fight against her demise.

A minute passed, then two, and yet death did not come.

"I'm still here," Jade whispered, as if hearing her own voice were the evidence she needed. "I'm not dead yet, but I think I'm going crazy."

She gingerly sank to the floor, taking comfort in the sturdy stone behind her back and the hard earth beneath her feet. Trying to calm her breathing and her heart rate, she attempted to think of something neutral . . . well, anything that didn't have to do with being stuck in a cave in the middle of the desert while a dozen healthy men slept in oblivion to her foolish terror.

What would my mother do? Her mother would simply find a place to climb out, brush off her starched capris, and continue on her way to the tents. *What about me? What would Jade do?* Cower like a child who is lost in the forest, jumping at every sound and sensation? *Yep, at least until daylight.* She felt the tears come. *But I'm not going to cry.*

Chapter Twenty-eight

Salalah Hospital, Dhofar, Oman

THE VEINS ON HIS grandmother's hands crossed each other like a termite trail on a piece of bark. She took his hand in hers and patted it gently. "Alem, it's time to go to sleep."

"Just one more story," he pleaded, his eleven-year-old voice sounding tinny in his ears.

With a soft chuckle, his grandmother released him and adjusted her shawl about her shoulders. "All right."

Sinking against his pillow, Alem grinned. He loved to watch his grandmother's face as she told him about the great queen, Makeda. His grandparents had come to live with his family because of his grandmother's ill health, and Grandfather couldn't care for her very well. But tonight her cough was quiet.

"After leaving King Solomon, the queen of the South gave birth to a boy, Bayna-le'kem. Everyone celebrated, and when she banned the gods of nature and proclaimed that everyone worship the God of Israel, everyone obeyed."

"Why didn't Solomon come to Ethiopia?" young Alem asked, feeling his eyelids grow heavy.

"He had his own kingdom to rule. The child grew until he was about your age, and he became curious about his father. His friends told him it was King Solomon, but when he asked his mother, she became very angry."

"Why? Didn't she want him to know?"

"She was afraid, as any mother would be, that her son would leave her." His grandmother smiled faintly. "Many years later, the queen saw that he looked so much like his father, and her heart softened. She finally told him about the land of Israel then begged him not to leave the country."

"But he went anyway?"

"Yes. He made an oath in the name of God that after he visited his father, he would return to his mother."

Alem pulled his coverlet to his chin, burrowing into the warmth. Although he'd heard the story many times, he was always anxious to hear the ending.

"After he left Ethiopia, the prince traveled to Jerusalem," she said. "There he was received by the king, and immediately the resemblance was noticed between the prince and Solomon. King Solomon thought his son looked like David, Solomon's father."

Alem nodded, his whole body content.

"Solomon wanted Bayna to be his successor to the throne of Israel."

"But he said no," Alem piped up.

"Right. Solomon tried to persuade his son to stay by telling him that Jerusalem was where the Tabernacle of Law and the House of God were. Also, the king told him that Israel was where God dwelt. But not even the gifts of gold, silver, and armor could influence the young prince. His devotion to his mother remained unshakable."

Alem stretched his arms and linked his hands behind his neck. He thought about his own mother—her cheerful busyness combined

with her strict rules. Could he be as loyal as the young prince of
Ethiopia?

His grandmother continued, "When Solomon realized he
couldn't persuade his son to live in Jerusalem, he decided to ordain
Bayna king of Ethiopia. Then Solomon renamed his son—David.
He sent a whole group of servants and dignitaries home with the
prince, along with horses, chariots, camels, gold, silver, pearls . . ."

Imagining what it would be like to meet the prince, Alem closed
his eyes, seeing a large caravan of people dressed in fine clothing.
He saw himself running up to David and touching his soft leather
sandals. David would look down and smile at him.

"Would you like to ride with me?" the prince would say.

Alem nodded eagerly.

"I can't tell you how long it will take." The voice was no longer
David's, but one of a woman.

"That's all right," Alem said, confused as David's happy
expression blurred.

The woman's voice came again. "He's waking up. I'll contact
you when I find out any more."

Alem's eyes started to focus in the brightly lit room. He was no
longer an eleven-year-old boy, but a man lying on a bed as stiff as
wicker. A woman who looked vaguely familiar stood over him, her
dark hair pulled back, covered with a silk scarf.

"Alem. I'm Omar's friend, Mia." The woman sat next to him.
He looked into her nearly black eyes.

"I'm here to help you. Can you tell me who . . . hurt you?"

"The crew boss," he said in a hoarse voice.

"Rabbel?"

"Yes. And another man—in a military uniform."

"Can you remember his name?"

Alem ran his tongue over the inside of his chalky teeth. "I

don't."

"Were there others?"

"Yes." His throat hurt with the intensity of a bad case of strep.

"Was this man there?" Mia tilted the cell-phone-like thing toward him.

Alem stared at the image of the smiling man for a moment. He did look familiar, but the throbbing in Alem's head made it difficult to know for sure. "Possibly."

"Thank you." Mia pulled away the phone and offered a smile, though her gaze conveyed disappointment. "I have to leave now, but the hospital has strict instructions to contact me if you need anything." She straightened from the bed. "And don't worry about the bill—it's been paid."

He tried to speak, but all that came was a guttural noise. He cleared his throat.

"It's the least we can do," she said with the wave of her hand.

"Wait," Alem managed to spit out.

Mia turned, her face pinched with concern. "What's wrong?"

"Who's Omar?"

"The man you worked with on the crew. Have you forgotten?"

"I mean . . . I found . . . his passports."

"Ah. That."

"There were several passports and an ornate cross. Isn't he Muslim?"

"What kind of cross?

"Coptic is my guess."

Mia's expression tightened. "Are you sure?"

"How well do you know him?" he asked, looking about the room. He needed a glass of water.

"Unfortunately, I can't answer your questions." Then her expression softened. "But I *can* tell you that you can trust Omar

and me. He said you saved his life, and he wants to repay you."
She placed a hand on Alem's shoulder. "What did you do with the
items?"

"They took everything when they stripped me for the
sacrifice—even a letter from my grandmother." The letter had been
like a connection to home during his trip. Now that it was gone, he
felt as if he'd somehow failed.

"I'm sorry about your things, but don't worry about Omar's
stuff," she said. "We'll get you healed enough to travel home in a
few days. Until then, rest as much as you can."

Alem watched the woman exit the room. He closed his eyes,
wishing he still had his grandmother's letter. It was an insult that
they took it. What could they want with an elderly woman's words
to her grandson? Then he thought of the poem his grandmother had
included at the end, something she'd written about the queen of
Sheba.

If he could just remember enough of it and write it down, he
could pass it on to Omar and Mia. He reached the bedside table and
opened the drawer and found a pad of paper and a pen. He lifted the
two items out, wincing as he caught his breath. Then he began to
write from memory.

O Queen of the South,
Death began your journey
To that night when seven women held one man.

Chapter Twenty-nine

Shisur, Oman

IT SEEMS LIGHTER, JADE thought as she rose gingerly to her feet, peering into the dimness of the cave. Her entire body ached, and her stomach grumbled with persistence, but at least morning had come. She let her eyes adjust before examining the stone that had supported her in her sleep.

The cavern she stood in was too big for a well, and there was no sign of water. She limped around the rectangular stone, disappointed to find only scaly earth leading to a dish-sized circle of light above—the hole where she'd stumbled. The men must be awake by now.

"Lucas!" she cried out. "Help!"

She waited, listening desperately in the silence. Then she scanned the ground for a rock to throw, but there was only sand.

Periodically, she called out as the time passed. Desperate with thirst, Jade stood and walked about the cavern, hoping to find a trickle of groundwater somewhere. Her hip throbbed as she moved toward the large stone, but her steps were steadier in the dim light.

Jade stopped in front of the stone and studied it. Maybe she could kick it. Moses struck a rock and found water. A giggle bubbled in her throat as she realized how ridiculous her thoughts were. *I'm getting delirious.*

A shiver chilled her spine as she touched the rock. It had definitely been carved into this rectangular shape. Why would someone hide his handiwork? She thought of the great monuments, statues, and tombs aboveground that people had created in antiquity.

Tombs.

A whisper of a thought entered her mind—*this is a tomb.*

Jade took a halting step backward, unbelieving. *Can it be?* She hobbled back to see the opening above her head. "Lucas! Help me, anyone!"

Jade spun around, her eyes seeing the cave anew. *What if?* The roots seemed to melt away until she could almost see the stone beneath the collected dirt. She moved to the closest wall and scraped away several layers of crusted earth with a dried root. Not more than two inches into the dirt was a wall, smooth like polished limestone.

On she plunged, digging, not caring that she was using precious energy. The earth crumbled away like fine pastry, as if it had been waiting all these years for the magical touch.

Jade could see the headlines now—*Archaeology intern makes discovery.*

Her father would give her a great bear hug and finally be proud. His little girl was not just studying the past and the dead, but contributing to the scientific world. She didn't realize she was grinning until a chunk of dirt hit her teeth. She spit out the offending piece and continued. She'd cleared over three feet of the wall. Then, too eager to wait, Jade brushed her hands against the surface. Her heart nearly leaped through her chest when her fingers touched the crevices of ancient writing.

She traced her fingers along the engravings—words that had been silent for centuries. She grabbed the root again and continued her mad pace. Feverishly she clawed at the dirt, watching with satisfaction as it cascaded into billowing heaps.

When the root drove through the wall, Jade nearly lost her balance. She pushed her hand through the opening and discovered empty space. Clearing the surrounding debris, she examined the small opening, maybe a two-foot radius. Inside was pitch-black.

Jade leaned forward, her hair filled with dirt, her face equally plastered, and gazed into the dark hole, trembling at the thought of what might be inside as the cool, stale air caressed her face. Another room? Another sarcophagus? The stale air turned putrid, and Jade stepped back. If she couldn't see anything, there was no use going in. What if the other room dropped off into oblivion? Dangerous images from action films plagued her mind.

Staggering back to the sun-dappled patch of earth, she called, "Help! Someone!" The dizziness returned. Her mouth and throat were coated with dirt, and the rawness in her stomach overpowered the pain in her joints.

She raised her arms in the air. "I found a tomb! It's right here!" After a moment, her shoulders sagged, and she crouched to the ground, energy spent. She reveled in the tiny patch of light on her head, shoulders, and back. She was so tired. *I'll just sleep for a moment.* As the sun's strength waned, she curled up on the earthen floor and closed her eyes.

৵৻ও ৶৻৹

SO THIS IS WHAT heaven is like. Jade let her lips curve into a smile. Very bright, very white, and warm all over. A soft flutter next to her ear made her sigh. There were even butterflies. Imagine.

"Jade." The voice was male. In fact, it sounded just like Lucas.

Was he in heaven too?

Jade opened her eyes, blinking at the white, even teeth suspended just above her. It was his smile, attached to his face. "How are you feeling?" the floating face asked.

Can I speak when I'm dead? Jade moved her mouth and heard herself say, "Fine."

Another perfect smile. "Great. That means the painkillers kicked in."

"I'm not dead?"

He laughed. "No, you're not."

"How did you—?"

"You'll have to thank Ismail."

A merry, round face the color of cinnamon popped into view. "Thank you."

Ismail dipped his head. "Anything for the fiancée of my friend."

"It turns out that Ismail has the nose of a camel," Lucas said.

Both men chuckled. "More like the eyes of a vulture," Ismail conceded.

Lucas leaned closer to Jade. "He tracked you like a lost camel—the most valuable commodity in the desert."

Jade blinked a couple of times. "Me or the camel?"

"Camel," Lucas said. "Did you know that he can tell if a camel is pregnant simply by the amount of sand that its hoof displaces while walking?"

Jade shook her head then inhaled sharply. Whatever they'd given her hadn't prevented a massive headache.

"Take it easy," Lucas said. "I'll leave you to rest."

"No. Stay with me."

Hesitation flickered in his eyes, but he settled next to her.

"What about the tomb?" she asked. "I dug away the dirt from the walls—"

"There was no tomb, just dirt and rocks. They found you in a natural cave about four or five meters underground."

Jade rose to her elbows, wincing at the pressure in her head. "Dirt that covered ancient *writing* carved into a *sarcophagus*?"

Lucas placed a hand on her arm, patting her like a small child. "You really need to rest. You've lost a lot of water, and it may have caused some delirium."

"But . . ." Jade's headache intensified. *Did* she imagine the tomb? Her chest deflated with disappointment. Lucas stood and adjusted the light blanket over her. She fought to keep her eyes open and to continue questioning him, but sheer exhaustion took over.

The remainder of the day was filled with strange dreams, disturbing nightmares, and an unquenchable thirst. Lucas offered water each time she awoke, pronouncing over and over that she had a fever and needed to rest. As the coolness descended with the night, Jade started feeling almost normal. Still, Lucas insisted that she take more pain medication and stay in the tent. When she fell asleep, it was only to be troubled by dreams of falling into dark caves.

A breeze picked up sometime in the night, stirring Jade awake as fingers of cool air lifted her limp hair. Her body broke out in goose pimples, and she burrowed deeper into her sleeping bag. Then her eyes flew open. The palms were glowing. Through the open tent flap, she saw the unmistakable glow of a flashlight—no, several flashlights. She crawled out of her bed and hobbled out.

The huddled forms of men were distinguishable against the dark night. They were inspecting the place where she'd fallen—the tomb. Jade ignored her painful bruises and started to walk toward the light. She hadn't gone more than a few feet when someone grabbed her arm.

"What are you doing?" Lucas whispered.

"I—" Jade stopped, taking in his disheveled appearance in the moonlight. "I want to see the tomb."

Lucas pulled her toward him gently. "There's no tomb," he said in a firm voice, like a father scolding his young daughter. "They're covering the hole so no one else falls through it."

"Why are you trying to keep this from me?" She pulled away, but his grip was strong. Panic rose in her chest. "Please let go."

"Jade," he said, his tone soothing. "Please rest. If you want to take a look in the morning, I'll accompany you myself."

She hesitated. The moment of animal instinct had passed, and, like a lamb, she let Lucas lead her back to the tent and tuck her in. She heard his breathing outside and knew that he would not leave his post again. Before falling asleep, she wondered if she'd made a very big mistake joining Lucas. Eventually she drifted off, despite his watchful presence.

Chapter Thirty

Salalah, Oman

THE TICKING OF THE clock on the whitewashed wall reminded Omar of the dripping IV in Alem's hospital room. He focused once again on the hook-nosed police officer with a unibrow, who was standing in front of him. Omar had explained several times where Alem had been found, and he turned over the pictures of the injuries.

The satellite phone buzzed to life in Omar's pocket. He glanced at the officer, who excused him.

"Thank you." Omar shook the man's hand and then left the police station.

Stepping outside brought a rush of freedom and relief.

As soon as Alem was well enough, Omar would arrange his transport back to Ethiopia. Mia had to return to San'ā in Yemen to follow up on a lead sent by David Levy, but not before she handed him a couple of alternate IDs.

As he walked to the jeep, Omar read the brief instructions from Levy illuminated on the small screen.

What's the delay? You haven't finished your assignment.

If Omar could have reached through the phone and strangled his boss, he would have. He started texting with a furious pace. *There's been an attempted murder—connected with AWP.*

Another message beeped in, and Omar clicked over to it.

I'm in San'ā. Meet me at The National Museum tomorrow. –M.

Mia was already in San'ā? Omar switched over to his original message and deleted the contents. Levy would just have to wait for a response. Omar jumped into the jeep and started the engine.

The wind riffled through his hair as he drove to the airport, allowing some of the tension of the past several days to slide off his shoulders. His phone buzzed again, bringing the weight thudding back. A glance at the phone told him that Levy's patience had ended too.

Omar caught a late flight, using the time to sort through the pictures he'd taken of the tomb in Jerusalem. He zoomed in on the strange diagram on the cave wall. It was a drawing of a collection of trees—seven in all. The center tree was unusual, to be sure, the trunk looking like a snake and a flower. Was it the clue to the queen of Sheba's tomb? He drew a picture of the trunk on his airline napkin. Then he turned it upside down. Nothing. He flipped it over and held it up to the overhead light, staring at it in reverse. *If the queen is the flower, who is the snake?*

Leaning against the upholstery, he closed his eyes, trying to remember where he'd seen the symbol before.

The flight was short, and he arrived in San'ā before the sun. In the predawn hours, he walked through the streets of the capital city, soaking in the buildings and modern conveniences, though no matter how long he spent in this country, he couldn't get used to the intense heat.

He crossed Tahrir Square just as the loudspeaker on the al-Mutwakil mosque came to life. The wailing became more insistent—as if beckoning him to worship. *I would be considered a heathen within those revered walls.* His worship had included only a few synagogue visits with his mother on holidays.

Omar closed the last hundred meters to the National Museum. A quick glance told him Mia wasn't waiting outside, so he went in and paid the entrance fee. The nice-looking receptionist smiled brightly at him, and Omar returned the pleasantry.

He crossed to a set of bronze statues and read the museum inscriptions of the two Yemeni kings, one Dhammar Ali Yahbar, the other, his son, Tharan. For a moment, Omar stared at the second king. The name reminded him of those he had seen on the tomb wall beneath the Jerusalem border. He took out his phone and filed the name away.

Someone stepped close to him. "Meet me on the second floor."

Omar turned and saw Mia's retreating figure move through the reception hall. Although her curls were covered with a conservative scarf, there was no mistaking her walk. He waited a few minutes then followed.

On the second floor, six halls branched out—each one devoted to a different era. Omar moved to the first hall but didn't see Mia. He passed the Al-Masnad hall containing ancient writings—one he'd like to explore when time allowed. Passing the Marib hall, he arrived at the Sheba Hall. Mia stood by a case containing weapons and ammunition.

He crossed to her and stared at the dilapidated weaponry, but nothing remarkable stood out. "What am I looking for?"

"You're looking for what's *not* there."

Omar tried not to breathe in her fresh scent. She'd obviously had a chance to shower and change.

"Artifacts have been found in Shisur over the past few months—at least, that's what AWP claims. I've read their files and the descriptions of their findings. Several weapons were discovered, examined, cleaned, labeled, and displayed *here*." She waved a hand toward the case. "But they *aren't* here."

"Are you saying AWP has stolen its own findings?"

"No. I think . . ." She hesitated, as if unsure of her own theory. "I think AWP hasn't been excavating at all—or at least it hasn't made any discoveries."

"So what have they been doing in Shisur all this time?" Even as he asked the question, the answer was obvious. "Human sacrifice— for entreating the djinns?"

"Among other things." Mia's soulful eyes met his.

His stomach tightened. This operation was getting larger than he expected.

"We need Alem to identify his captors," she said.

"So what do you want me to do?" he asked.

"Find out who originated the reports of the fake artifacts. I also need the name of the man who approved them."

"It would have to be someone high up, someone with an influential position in GOAMM." *The General Organization for Antiquities, Museums, and Manuscripts.*

Mia raised a brow. "From what I've heard, they treat their jobs like a religion."

"Exactly. Perhaps finding out who is the most 'religious' will lead us to the right person."

A group of students entered the hall, and Omar and Mia drifted apart, each pretending to be lost in study. Question after question pulsed through Omar. How deep did the corruption go? He could only assume the amount of money it took AWP to bribe someone as devoted as a member of GOAMM. Hundreds of thousands? Millions?

When the student group filed out, their whispers fading, Omar moved to Mia's side. "I should make a call to the hospital. It was probably a long night for Alem."

Her hand rested on his arm briefly. "I'm sorry about your friend."

Omar nodded. "Do you have dinner plans?"

"We still have a lot of work to do."

"It will be work related." He winked at her.

"All right. I'll call you later."

He grinned. "I'll be waiting." Then he shoved his hands in his pockets and strode away. When he passed the front desk, he met the receptionist's eyes. She smiled at him, and he returned it. In that instant, his plan became laid out. All he needed was one document and one name. And all museums kept documents.

Exiting the museum, Omar cursed the Yemen heat. Then he cursed David Levy for making his relationship with Mia so complicated. Maybe over a very long, relaxing dinner, he could somehow prove he wasn't really an idiot. But first, Omar had to do everything possible to get the information she needed—and fast.

He put in a call to Salalah Hospital to ensure that Alem was comfortable. The man continued to sleep peacefully, the nurse reported, pain medication coming in regular doses.

Omar took a taxi to **Ali Abdulmoghni Street** and checked into the Taj Sheba Hotel. Paying for one night courtesy of David Levy, Omar requested a toiletry package. Then he visited the sundry shop and purchased a pair of reading glasses and a sari-like scarf with a tag that said, "Made in India."

Once in his room, he showered and dressed, and then removed the nose-hair trimming scissors and razor from the toiletry pack. For a moment he gazed at his reflection in the fluorescent-lit mirror with the steamy drops sliding along the glass. With slow clips, he lopped off his wavy hair and watched the chunks coil in the sink.

He lathered the cheap shaving cream and rubbed it onto his stubbly head.

No going back now. With careful strokes, he used the razor to remove the rest of the hair. Then he rinsed the cream from his scalp and surveyed the damage. "Not too bad. Now for the mustache."

Ten minutes later, he exited his room and started down the hall. With a Koran clutched in his hands, he walked slowly, keeping his eyes to the ground. The sari draped about his shoulders loosely. He took the stairs to the lobby floor, and as he passed through the exit doors, he caught a glimpse of his reflection. *Just like a Buddhist monk. A Buddhist carrying the Koran. Not even Mia would recognize me.* He kept the book pressed to his chest, covering the gold-embossed title.

Again he entered the National Museum and adjusted his glasses, the cooled air causing his freshly shaven scalp to tingle. Although he wanted to hurry, he shuffled slowly to the reception desk. The same girl hardly gave him a look as she asked for the entrance fee. When he paid, she let out a yawn and checked her watch.

He knew without a clock that it was almost 4:45, and the museum would close in fifteen minutes.

"My name is Govind Dhatri." He pushed up his glasses again and placed a hand on the counter. "I have an appointment with the curator to look at some manuscripts."

The woman met his gaze, her fire-red lips drawn in a disapproving line. "The curator doesn't come in on Thursdays."

"Yes, I know. But I have a special appointment with him at 4:45. Please tell him I'm here."

"You'll have to come back in the morning."

In his best Indian accent, Omar continued, "No good. I leave on the plane in the morning. I must look at the manuscripts today so

I can write a report for my monastery. My organization will not be able to donate funds if the report is incomplete."

The woman's eyebrows shot up. "You're a donor?"

"We're in negotiations. If my report is favorable, the donation will be quite large." He lowered his voice. "You wouldn't want to be the cause of losing a sizable donation."

"Let me try his home."

"Of course."

She dialed the number and waited for a moment. "No answer."

"Alas, I will have to leave empty-handed." Omar sighed heavily and turned, shaking his head.

"What exactly do you need to do?"

Omar hid a smile and faced her. "Just take a few photographs."

The woman hesitated only for an instant. Then she reached for her walkie-talkie and spoke with security. "I'm sending a man up who needs access to the document room. He's been authorized." She smiled at Omar. "It's been arranged."

He glanced at her name badge. "Thank you, Ms. Addeen. I'll not forget your kindness."

Her eyes glowed with satisfaction as he bowed and moved away.

A few minutes later, Omar met the security guard. He kept his gaze lowered and the Koran clutched to his chest as if he couldn't bear to part with the revered words. He stepped into a long, narrow room with tables jacked into each corner. Hesitating, he glanced about the space, distinctly aware of the security guard's presence. But Omar couldn't very well ask the man to leave.

Adjusting his glasses, he moved to the first table of documents and extracted a metal chair from underneath. The legs scraped painfully against the tiles. He took out a small notebook he'd purchased from the sundry shop and began to scribble notes. Then he snapped a picture of the document in front of him. Leaning forward, he examined the content for a moment, waiting. The security guard remained.

Moving to the next table, Omar repeated the procedure again. Security or no, nothing had yet caught his interest . . . until he reached the third table. The documents spread across the working area were still covered in crusted sand—an obvious sign that they hadn't yet been examined for content. *Were they from Shisur?*

He snapped a couple of pictures before the guard's radio came to life. The guard barked a few orders into the receiver then stepped out of the room.

Omar flipped off the lights and crossed the room. Crouching in a low cabinet he'd noticed earlier, he pressed against the bulky frame of an old microfiche machine and waited in the cedar interior.

Several minutes passed. Then the door was thrust open. Light flooded the room, reaching through the cracks in the cabinet doors. Omar heard the heavy tread of shuffling feet pass the cabinet and then pass again.

The seconds creaked by. Finally the lights clicked off and the door closed.

Still Omar waited, not daring to crack open even one side of the cupboard. When his watch read 5:30, he pushed the cabinet doors ajar. Then he crept out and stretched his jammed limbs. As his eyes adjusted to the dimness, he realized that it wasn't so dark after all. At the far side of the room was a high window through which the late-afternoon sun riddled.

Omar turned on his flashlight and moved to the third table. He brushed his sleeve against the dried sand particles. He propped his glasses on his head and squinted in the thin beam of light. The language was definitely archaic; he leaned close to analyze the script.

The faint smell of ink reached his nostrils. A document more than a couple of thousand years old should not smell of ink. Scanning through the papers, he saw the name of Nicaula sprinkled throughout. It was obviously a story written about her, or, if the forgers were really brave, a log written by the queen herself. It wasn't too far-fetched that a woman with enough power to be a queen would have known how to pen the written word.

His phone buzzed.

What time are we meeting for dinner? –M

Omar smiled and messaged Mia. *If I don't end up in jail before dark, I'll let you know.*

What are you doing?

Breaking and entering. Want to come?

Where are you?

Found some forged docs.

Are you at the museum? Get out of there! You could be arrested.

I already said that.

There was a long pause. Then Mia's reply came: *There's a rumor that a secret room exists behind the statues at the front entrance. Maybe you can try your luck.*

Any pointers?

Sorry, you're on your own. But it might give you what you need to finally prove AWP is linked with GOAMM. Everyone leaves a trail.

You aren't going to tell Levy, are you?

I thought you knew me better than that.

Did he? *Let's talk about it over dinner. 8:00 at the Graze restaurant, Taj Sheba Hotel?*

If you aren't in jail.

Omar smiled and moved to the next table. He took a few more snapshots, but the idea of a hidden room nagged at him. Omar entered the hallway, finding the air still and smug as if it held a secret that not even a deceitful Buddhist monk could uncover.

He descended the steps to the main level and walked to the receptionist's desk, looking around. A small panel of lights blinked against the pale wall next to the front doors—a security system that looked as though a high school student had put it together. He could disarm it within seconds, though maybe he wouldn't need to.

He walked toward the statues. "Hello, Dhammar and Tharan. No offense, but you're in my way." Omar moved behind the statues and knocked along the wall. The studs were consistently twenty-four to thirty centimeters apart. But without a jackhammer or a chisel, he saw no way to penetrate the wall.

Then he found a hollow spot.

Mia had been right. For at least two meters, there were no two-by-fours. He tapped downward. Nothing. His continued knocking told him that at about eye level, a stud ran horizontally—like the top of a door frame.

Turning, he moved to the reception area, looking for any object that was hard enough to smash through Sheetrock when his gaze rested on the plaque announcing Dhammar and Tharan to the world. "Sorry, boys."

He lifted the plaque, stand and all, and rammed it into the wall.

Omar grimaced as he threw his weight against his battering device over and over until the wall caved. *This better be the only entrance.*

He surveyed the damage. There was no covering up the crumbled Sheetrock and fine, powdery chalk now. The hole was just big enough to climb through. He landed with a thump on the other side onto a cold, concrete floor, and flipped on his flashlight.

Déjà vu.

Although it wasn't a three-thousand-year-old tomb, the

atmosphere could have been identical. The place had been built with no modern architecture considered. The stone room was a lopsided trapezoid. Chunky cement protruded from between the roughly cut rock, and the dank smell reminded Omar of something long dead and rotted. Oddly enough, a metal file cabinet stood in the center of the room. No table or chair or dangling lightbulb—just a lone cabinet for paperwork. "There's your trail, Mia."

On the dust-thick floor were unmistakable footprints from various shoes or boots coming from the right. He shone the beam above his head and examined the ceiling. A metal grate was wedged between the ceiling stones. "Ah, there's the second entrance."

The cabinet was locked. *Of course.* Omar checked his watch—6:30 p.m. He wondered if there was a night inspection from police or security, or even from the curator himself. Omar set to work quickly, and it took only a few seconds to jimmy the file lock and open the first drawer.

A row of red folders met his eye—each labeled with a sequence of numbers. He removed the folder in front and found a memo of some sort from the Ancient World Piracy organization. Omar's heart rate doubled. He snapped a picture and went onto the next. Folder after folder contained documents that, if each one stood alone, could incriminate some of the highest officers in the government.

The second drawer proved even more informative, containing several memos written by the director of GOAMM, Dr. Abdallah Saleh al-Qadi. A quick scan told Omar that he was the contact with AWP. Some of the other documents looked like articles or press releases. Not having time to read through each one, he simply snapped pictures and moved on.

One hour passed, and Omar kept taking pictures. His throat ran dry as he worked on the third drawer. Its files consisted of photographs taken at archaeology sites. Included with the photographs were field reports, and after reading the first one, Omar knew that the world he was familiar with was about to change.

"The queen of Sheba knew King Tambariah? Impossible." Yet as Omar breathed the words, puzzle pieces began to fall into place. He flipped through the final files, madly searching for any reference to Solomon but found none. In the last folder, he removed a printed article authored by a man named Dr. Lyon. Behind the article was a sketch of the same diagram he'd seen on the tomb wall, but this one was labeled. Omar was about to snap a picture when he heard a sound above him.

Light flooded the room.

Chapter Thirty-one

Salalah Hospital, Dhofar, Oman

THE PALE WALLS SURROUNDED her, the smell of antiseptic threatening to burn her nostrils, but Jade felt clean again. The last few hours had been a blur—Lucas insisting that she needed immediate medical care for dehydration, the drive across the desert to Salalah, and the transfer into the hospital bed.

The headache had never left. Jade raised her hand to her temple, feeling the bandage that covered several stitches. Lucas hadn't taken her to see the cave . . . or tomb, either. As soon as she had awakened in the morning, there was a flurry of activity just to get her loaded into the truck and transported far away from the pitfalls of Shisur.

A nurse entered the room now, pushing a metal trolley with a food tray on top. Jade eyed the items suspiciously, her stomach already rumbling in protest, but she was hungry enough to eat almost anything.

The nurse propped her up with pillows and flashed a dimpled smile. She said something that sounded very sweet in Arabic, and Jade nodded.

When the nurse left, Jade sampled the salad containing barley, tomatoes, and parsley. It had a strong, heady flavor and was quite good. Then she tried the half pita stuffed with some sort of a meat sauce. Spicy. But the guava juice felt like velvet sliding down her throat, counteracting the zesty meal.

She felt better now than she had in days, even before the fall. She reached for her bag, thankful that her phone was among her belongings, and for several minutes browsed through her notes, thinking of all she'd seen so far at Shisur. Then she wrote every detail that she remembered about the tomb.

When she finished, she rose from the bed, pulling the IV tower along with her. Lucas said he'd return the following day, so there was no one around to give orders. She opened her door and walked slowly to the lobby. Sitting on one of the chairs was a young African man sketching on a pad of paper. *Therapy, perhaps.* Her pulse sped up as she suddenly recognized him as the man she and Lucas had discovered on the back of a camel.

"Excuse me, sir?" she said, not sure what language he spoke.

The dark head turned, and Jade inwardly winced at the mass of stitches across his face. She held out her hand. "Remember me?"

He stared at her for a moment, his eyes rimmed in red, and then patted the chair next to him with a bandaged hand. "Who are you?" he asked in English.

"We found you in the desert."

The man nodded, his gaze seeming to go in and out of comprehension. He turned away for a moment, and when he looked at her again, tears glistened against his lashes.

Jade touched his arm. "You're safe now."

He looked down at his hands. "I found an ancient sword, and I thought they were taking me someplace else to dig."

His voice trembled, the pain evident as it swelled with his words. "They bound me and . . ." He licked his lips and shuddered.

"Started singing and chanting."

"You don't have to tell—"

His gaze met hers. "I felt sick when I realized what they were saying was evil, but I couldn't do anything. They held me down, next to the fire, and cut my skin." He moved his hand toward his face.

Jade put her hand on his shoulder. "I'm so sorry."

"They said that my sacrifice would bring about an important discovery." He closed his eyes, his long lashes resting against his ebony cheeks.

Jade noticed the drawing he held. She stared at the intertwined flower and snake for a moment, her heart rate doubling. "What's that a picture of?"

"My grandmother used to tell me stories of the queen of Sheba. She loved the legends so much that this symbol was engraved on her gravestone. I think it represents the queen and her lover."

"What lover?"

"King Solomon, of course. My family is descended from King Menelik of Ethiopia." He flashed a tentative smile. "My grandmother took her connection very personally." He traced the outline of the snake with his pencil. "So when I found that sword, and it had the same symbol, I thought I'd discovered something important—a link to the queen."

Jade's throat tightened. "So if this symbol was someplace else, say, inside a tomb, what would that mean?"

The man raised his eyebrows, crinkling the white tape holding his stitches in place. "If this symbol were to appear inside a tomb, I'd say that the tomb belonged to the queen herself."

Jade stared at the symbol as the Ethiopian traced it over and over. Silence ticked between them as her hazy recollection grew clear. "I've seen that symbol someplace else."

The man nodded absentmindedly.

"Inside a *tomb*," she whispered.

His pencil stopped its motion, and he raised his head slowly. "What did you say?"

"I found a tomb in the desert . . . but they told me it was only a cave and made me come here and . . ." Her voice trembled as she looked away, embarrassed.

The Ethiopian extended his large hand. "My name is Alem Eshete."

Jade took his hand, avoiding any pressure on the heavy bandage. "Jade Holmes."

His gaze had cleared, losing its wildness. "Tell me where you saw this symbol. Was the tomb in Sa'ba? Marib?"

"Shisur."

A faint shudder passed through Alem. "The *oasis*? No tomb has been uncovered there." His eyes flickered with painful memories. "That's where I was nearly sacrificed."

Jade nodded, her throat thick with pity.

But his eyes held no sorrow, only excitement. "Tell me what you saw."

"I was trying to make my way to the bathroom in the middle of the night when I fell into a cavern. When morning came, I noticed strange features."

"Such as?"

"A stone cut into the shape of a rectangle—large enough to be a sarcophagus. I dug the dirt away from the walls. Beneath the layers of soil was smooth stone, carved with writing and symbols." She pointed to the sketch. "That was one of them. I remember it because it reminded me of the possibility of snakes sharing the same space with me."

"Are you sure this was the symbol?"

Jade nodded. "I also found an opening in the wall—to another room, I think, but it was too dark to see inside."

Alem leaned back in his chair, letting out a low whistle. "It's probably all over the newspapers now."

"No. You see, when I was rescued, I was told there was no tomb . . . but I know what I saw."

"I believe you." He pointed to his drawing. "This proves it. So who rescued you?"

"A group of Yemeni excavators led by a man names Ismail. I was traveling with the Egyptologist, Dr. Lucas Morel." Jade shifted uncomfortably in her seat. She hadn't expected to be interrogated.

"Do these men have permission to excavate?"

"Yes, and they told me I'd been mistaken about the tomb." Her voice heated with emotion. "Even though I was probably half out of my mind with fear and thirst, I know what I saw."

"What else did these men tell you?"

"Nothing, really. Lucas was so worried about my health, he rushed me here."

"A little dehydration was a convenient way to get rid of you."

"Do you think—?"

"I do. You may have made one of the greatest archaeology discoveries of the century. I think those men, Lucas and Ismail, were trying to get you out of their way. This is an archaeologist's dream." His dark eyes were intent on Jade. "You may have found *her* tomb. Men and women alike have been searching for centuries, spending millions, and now . . . it was found by a young lady from America."

Jade felt a strange sensation creep along her skin. She was both elated and horrified at the same time. "But why would Lucas try to get rid of me? Doesn't he know that I'll eventually find out?"

"Not if he makes you disappear."

The same way Dr. Lyon disappeared? Is Lucas linked to the professor's death?

"Ms. Jade Holmes." Alem's tone was formal, serious. He stood awkwardly and bowed. "We have an oasis to find."

She let out a nervous laugh. "We're a couple of invalids."

"You look healthy to me," he said with a wink. "As for me . . . each day gets a little better." He tilted his head and smiled. "And I know just the person who can take us there."

Chapter Thirty-two

Yemen

OMAR SHOVED THE PAPERS down his shirt and moved toward the hole in the wall, his eyes watering from the sudden light.

"Stanis!" someone shouted as the ceiling grate slid open.

Omar scrambled through the broken Sheetrock, wondering why the security person, or whoever it was, hadn't come through the front doors of the museum. Then he realized that they probably thought he'd entered through the grate. *If I'd known it was there, it would have been much easier than punching a hole in the wall.*

He hesitated in the reception hall. Was someone running to the front doors right now? Should he hide in the museum? *No.* It would be only a matter of time before they found him crouched behind a statue, and it would take too many precious moments to disarm the security system. Decision made, he grabbed the trusty plaque stand and plowed it through the glass doors, sending a spray of shards both inside and outside the building. The alarm blared, momentarily stunning Omar. With a sharp intake of breath, he crawled through the shattered opening. His hands split as they rubbed across the fallen glass, but he scuttled to his feet and started a dead run.

He thought he heard shouting behind him, though he didn't slow to find out. Running through the streets of Yemen had now become a regular activity. Omar's breathing came hard, but the crinkle of paper against his chest urged him on, in addition to the collection of incriminating photos he'd just taken.

When he was sure he wasn't being followed, he slowed and continued toward the hotel. He skirted the entrance and found a back door. Once in his room, he rinsed the blood from his hands. He then retrieved a pair of tweezers from the toiletry bag and removed the shards one by one, wincing at the pain. Nothing looked too deep.

With shaking hands, he pulled out the papers and stared at the sketch in disbelief for a moment. It was identical to what he'd seen in the tomb, but this sketch had names written next to each tree. And the language was old. *Great. Give me something I can interpret, like Latin or Greek.* He stared at the letters, knowing that they had to make sense. Then he realized it was Aramaic. Although its form was more ancient than modern Aramaic, it was still very similar to Hebrew.

He picked out some letters—*Dālath, Zain, Mim* . . . His gaze focused on the name next the center tree. The letters, *Semkath, Hē, Bēth,* Ālaph . . . spelled *Shba.*

Sheba.

He looked at another name then translated it carefully. *Batl. Batel or Batal?*

Then one name stood out. The translation was plain: *David.* There was only one David connected to royalty during the tenth century, but he would have been dead by the time the queen met his son, Solomon. Omar slowly deciphered the remaining names: Ashara, Marib, Mother, Father . . .

The names floating in his head, he left the sketch and article on the bed table, and then stepped into the shower, letting warm water cascade over his tense shoulder muscles as he tried to compile the tons of information he'd stumbled upon. Then he remembered. *Dinner with Mia.* It was well after 9:00 p.m., and she'd probably left the restaurant by now. He shut off the faucet and toweled off. With the towel still wrapped around his waist, he grabbed his satellite phone and sent a message.

He waited for a few minutes. No answer.

Omar dressed, thinking of Mia. It seemed he could break through walls of Sheetrock or stone, but not through the barrier that existed between them. He called her again. Nothing. Omar picked up the sketch and settled beneath the scratchy sheets that smelled faintly of mango. The fruit bowl in the room sported various edibles, most overpowering the mango fruit. He'd ignored his growling stomach long enough, so he rose from the bed and snagged a kiwi, peeled it, and bit into the juicy flesh. The tiny seeds crunched beneath his teeth, bringing some satisfaction. Then he grabbed his camera and settled back onto the pillow. He found the picture he'd taken inside the tomb and compared it to the sketch. The trees were identical. So who had written these names on the copy?

He skipped through the pictures and slowed at the final ones.

The small screen made deciphering the document photos impossible, but it was gratifying to see that he had the proof now— proof that could probably get him in a lot of trouble, or killed. *That's nothing new.* He grabbed the article from the nightstand and turned it toward the light, reading through the contents slowly. It was a study by a man named Dr. Richard Lyon—a professor at Brown University in America. Halfway through, Omar sat up, tightening his grip on the pages. The study had obviously never been published, or at least had yet to be printed. If it had been published, everyone would know about it—even in the remotest parts of Yemen.

Lyon believed the queen of Sheba's tomb was at Shisur. According to the professor, the diagram in the Jerusalem tomb proved it.

Omar slept fitfully, and when morning came, he packed his bag, left his room, and walked to the hotel lobby. Down the corridor was a small conference room. He slipped inside and logged onto the Internet. Then he googled Richard Lyon and watched as dozens of links popped up on the screen.

Omar's gaze settled on a recent one—an obituary in a small newspaper in Providence, Rhode Island. The man had died less than a month ago. Stunned, Omar continued to search and found an article that was dated just a few weeks before Lyon's death.

The article boldly claimed that Shisur, an oasis in eastern Oman, was part of the region of Ubar—and that was where the hunt for the queen of Sheba should begin. And that was before the tomb in Jerusalem was discovered. The diagram on the wall solidified his theory in progress.

Omar stood and left the room, dozens of questions on his mind. He checked out at the front desk and stopped at the gift shop to buy cigarettes. Then he passed through the hotel doors, where he stood in the early morning damp and stared at his phone, willing it to ring. *Where is Mia?* He leaned against a tree and pulled out the pack of cigarettes. His nose wrinkled as he smelled the fresh nicotine. He lit the cigarette and was almost tempted to inhale, but thought better of it. It had taken him six years to kick the habit in the first place. However, holding a lit cigarette made a man standing alone in the dark seem less suspicious. Everyone understood a smoke break.

Fifteen minutes passed, and the city slowly came to life, but he couldn't wait for someone to recognize the guy with the cut-up hands. Maybe Mia was just ignoring him for standing her up at dinner. But didn't she want to know how his break-in went? She should at least be concerned about his health. He'd nearly been sliced to death by shattered glass. But the detailed message he'd sent to Mia had obviously garnered no sympathy.

He let the burning butt drop to the ground, crushing the glowing embers with his shoe. The final, acrid line of smoke reached his nostrils, sending his saliva into overproduction. He shoved his hands into his pockets and walked down the sidewalk, spotting a taxi. The sleepy driver slowed to a stop, and Omar climbed in. "To San'ā University."

As the taxicab hummed through the nearly vacant streets, Omar listened to the radio. The news, interrupting the Fathi music, filled the musty cab air. He strained to hear any mention of the museum, but there was no breaking report of a bloody monk, covered in Sheetrock powder, escaping the museum.

When the university gate came into view, Omar leaned forward in his seat. A few early risers walked the campus. These were the studious, the insomniacs, the students who couldn't finish a day without piling in as much work as possible. Omar recognized his former self in the faces of the Yemeni students dressed as if they were attending a board meeting in a few minutes.

He paid the driver and walked beneath the stone arch then hailed the closest student and asked for directions to the library. The Internet service in the hotel was too public, and Omar needed to access his information without creating undue interest.

He avoided colliding with a young woman and nearly froze when he noticed the bright lipstick. She wasn't the receptionist from the museum, was she? *No . . .* This woman was broader, darker—not the receptionist. Then another woman passed him, her lips a bright red. Had there been a sale on devil-red lipstick? Omar shook

his head. The receptionist from the museum wasn't following him.
It was like a recurring panic attack—except without an official
diagnosis.

Under a lot of pressure lately, Mr. Zagouri?

Omar would nod his head as he turned his pleading eyes to the
psychiatrist. "No more than usual—except for stealing cars, running
into my ex-girlfriend, finding my friend brutally sacrificed, and
confiscating evidence from a hidden room . . . Oh yeah, did I tell
you I was kidnapped?" If nothing else, that deserved a ninety-day
supply of Xanax.

The faces passed in a blur as he followed the directions given
by the student, but when he reached the library, the doors were still
locked. *Open at 7:00 a.m.* He checked his watch. 6:49.

Pulling out his phone, he emailed Mia again.

A thin man with a naturally bald head unlocked the doors four
minutes early. Omar walked casually through the front entrance,
glancing at the signs along the way. First he found a copy machine
and made four reproductions of the study by Dr. Lyon.

He logged onto a computer terminal and typed: *Queen of
Sheba, Batal.*

After a few seconds of searching, the computer offered several
dozen references. "Well, there are a lot of horses named after both
of them," he muttered. "And *Batal* means hero, the word *battle*
being derived from the Arabic *Batal.*"

He leaned back in his chair, staring at the screen. Batal was
also a village in the Indian Himalayas. Omar rubbed his bald head,
feeling the first signs of sandpapery hair growth. *Batal is just a
name.* Although, it was the name of someone who was important
enough to be mentioned with a queen.

Next he googled *mother and father of the queen of Sheba.*
"According to Ethiopian history, the queen of Sheba was born in

1020 BC in Ophir. Her mother was Queen Ismenie. Her father was the chief minister to Za Sebado. When her father died, she ruled at the age of fifteen."

Omar pulled out the sketch and studied the names. Nothing was close to Ismenie. He read on. "The queen's only son was Menyelek." He stopped and looked at the names on the palm tree sketch. If the queen had a child with Solomon, she hadn't named him David, at least according to the Ethiopians.

He googled the next two names on the sketch. Azhara— meaning *flower* in Arabic, but there was no historical significance.

Marib was a city in Yemen; he already knew that. "The ancient civilization of the Sabaeans lasted from early second millennium to the first century BC. The capital was Marib—the ancient city located 3.5 kilometers south of modern-day Marib." Omar stretched his hands behind his neck. Was Marib where the queen was buried? It seemed too easy.

But how did they all fit together? And how did the seven palms with the seven names lead to her tomb? Feeling more dissatisfied than ever, Omar returned to the computer and typed *Tambariah*.

Nothing.

Turug.

Turug was a city in Sudan. But what Omar saw next piqued his interest. The Turugs were a people living in Sudan and were responsible for introducing Islam to the region. Then another website caught Omar's attention—a press release detailing Turug statues throughout Mongolia.

A message came in on his phone. At last, Mia. *Sorry I didn't make it to dinner. Ran into a glitch.*

What happened? Omar typed.

Rabbel is here in Marib.

Omar took a deep breath. *What are you doing in Marib?*

I'm tracking a lead to AWP headquarters.

By yourself? I thought we were working together on this. Even as he typed the reply, he felt guilty for not keeping Mia informed of all *he* knew.

Levy wants us to split now. He'll be sending you new instructions.

Omar stared at the screen. Something was wrong. He could feel it.

Chapter Thirty-three

Jerusalem
960 b.c.

AS THE CARAVAN TRAVELED the narrow streets, the people fell
to the side, bowing before the queen and calling out good wishes.
Several threw flowers, littering the streets.

When the caravan rounded the final corner, Nicaula stopped
the procession. The king's palace spread along the green of Mount
Moriah. The palace's nearly white stone foundation supported the
great pillars that flanked the entrance, inlaid with gold.

Nicaula's pulse pounded at the majesty, the greatness. She
recovered from her awe and ordered the caravan forward. When
they reached the outer courtyard, Nicaula couched her camel and
climbed off. Batal moved stiffly at her side as they walked up the
polished cedar steps.

The queen had never seen anything so grand in her sixteen
years. She lowered the veil on her headdress and nodded to those
who bowed to her. The palace was built of cedar and fir trees, and
the massive doors were carved with palm trees, cherubim, and
flowers, all inlaid with gold. Nicaula and her procession walked

through the doors to see an interior that was even more luxurious. Inside was a crystal-blue pool with stone-carved animals, leafed in gold, spouting water in all directions. The cedar floor echoed their footsteps in the sunny enclosure.

The main hall was packed with onlookers. On one side, the women gathered, their colorful robes clinging to their shapely figures. *Are these the wives or the concubines?* The queen wondered if Azhara was among the women.

On the other side of the room, the men of the court gathered, postures erect in elegant robes, their animated eyes scanning every detail of the queen and her ensemble.

At the end of the hall was the throne. Reverence pierced Nicaula's heart as she took in the details. Six inlaid-pearl steps rose to the height of the base of the throne. The great chair itself was made from ivory and covered in gold leaf designs. Two crouching lions etched from stone stood guard, their inanimate teeth ferocious. Several girls sat around the chair, waving palms to cool the air. They were young, perhaps twelve or thirteen, their eyes holding a coyness that encouraged the pleasures of man.

But it was the king who sat upon the throne who was the most arresting of all. Nicaula recognized him immediately—his round, youthful face, copper curls, piercing eyes—all as she'd imagined. As he stood, a rush of energy passed through her body. This was the man whose glory preceded his name across the continents. This was the man she had dreamt about.

The king descended from his throne, the women flanking his sides. He stretched out a jeweled hand in greeting. Yet she kept her hands to her side and merely inclined her head to one side.

His power and confidence were tangible, and the queen took a deep breath before she spoke. "I am Nicaula, queen of the South, ruler of the kingdoms of Ubar and Sa'ba."

A smile convulsed against his lips, and Nicaula knew that he was surprised at her boldness in speaking first. King or no king, she was royalty in her own right. Although her intentions were friendly, she refused to be subservient to another who was her equal.

"Welcome, Queen of the South."

The warm timbre of his voice washed over her, sending shivers to her toes.

"Welcome to my city of Jerusalem. Your gifts have been received and pleasure derived from them. I am amazed at the quantity of spices you delivered. Your wealth must be great."

"My wealth is but plain compared to yours," Nicaula said.

The king shooed away the doting women, and his gaze soaked in the Arabian woman before him. "I have waited many weeks for your arrival." He paused, humor in his eyes. He circled her then stopped in front again. "Tell me what has detained you."

"I delayed in Eloth to inspect the fine fleet of ships," Nicaula said, watching the king from the corner of her eye as he walked around her.

He seemed to be deep in thought, but she knew he was assessing her. He stopped, standing very close to her, his russet eyes displaying streaks of gold. "And your family travels with you?"

"My throne is my family."

A troubled look flitted across his face, but his smile remained warm. "Come and join me. We will eat."

The people in the hallway beyond murmured in excited voices.

"We will have a feast," the king called out, and the people cheered. He raised his hands and laughed. Then he looked at Nicaula, his eyes filled with delight. "You may call me Solomon."

"Hail King Solomon!" the crowd chanted.

Nicaula followed the king into another room, larger than the grand hall. Low tables extended across the entire length, piled with tomatoes, cucumbers, olives, grapes, goat cheese, sour milk, breads, jugs of wine, and steaming meats. Most noticeable of all were the gold cups set at each place.

The queen sat on a pile of cushions between Solomon and Batal. Before the meal began, the king stood and praised his god in quiet, beseeching tones.

When he finished, Nicaula asked, "You do not worship the sun goddess?"

"Yahweh is the god of all—he is the supreme ruler of human, animal, and substance. He created everything a pair of eyes can see."

Nicaula sensed conviction in his words, but even more, she basked in his radiance, his youth and exuberance, his power and wealth. "Is he a jealous god?"

"Very." A smile touched Solomon's lips. He took a swallow of wine. "Have you done something to incur his wrath?"

"Not I," Nicaula assured him, venturing to smile back.

"Bel is like a rock compared to the God of Israel, who is a mountain. Yahweh will bless those who worship him, praise him, and believe in him." Solomon lifted his goblet and tilted his head toward her. "He gives to those who love him."

Nicaula was taken aback by the king's powerful statements. It was as if he'd spoken to God, or God was a friend. She thought about the image on the tree outside the walls. As the others around her continued to devour their food, she said, "I saw a tree outside the city walls. Incense plates and oil lamps were set around it. Is Yahweh found in the trees of olive? Or do your people worship more than one god?"

Solomon set his goblet down and leaned forward. "Some worship several gods, but in time, they will all be converted to the true God. I do not punish those who wish to worship otherwise.

Yahweh is the only one who will save us all. He is the supreme being."

Nicaula was startled by his sure knowledge, and a deep shudder pierced her soul. The image from the tree flashed through her mind again. "I have seen God's death."

A hush fell over those surrounding them, and Solomon placed his cup down.

"On the way into the city, I stopped at an old tree, and I was compelled to approach it." She closed her eyes and reached out a hand as if mimicking what she'd done. "When I touched it, an image passed through my mind. Immediately I knew what I saw was wonderful, even in its awfulness." The entire crowd was quiet now. "The man I saw was no ordinary man."

"Was he in a dream, or could you touch his flesh?" Solomon asked.

"I could not touch him, but it was as if I could." She opened her eyes and brought her fingers to her necklace, absently tracing the engraved design. "His scant garments were soaked with dried blood as he hung upon a cross made of wood."

"Tell me what else you saw."

"It was so brief, so sudden." She placed her fingers to her temples. Suddenly, a burst of knowledge shot through her. "The tree . . . the tree will become the cross from which Yahweh's son will hang."

"Show me this tree."

❧❦❧

THE QUEEN SPENT NEARLY every moment with Solomon for the next several days. He taught her about the one true God, and she told him about life in Arabia—the harvesting of spices, the tribal communities, and the harsh clime. She told him about her father and the brutal way he died. She finished by summarizing the fall of Sa'ba, the rescue of Azhara, and the revenge upon the marauders. Then she told Solomon about the little boy, David, whose mother was badly burned.

At this, Solomon paused in their walk along the perimeter of the temple of Yahweh. "David was only a babe when his mother fled. She thought she'd been cursed and refused to seek treatment within the city walls."

"Could you not have sent your guards after her?"

"She left word that she was returning to her family."

"It was only to appease you, then."

They fell into silence for a moment. When they reached the far side of the temple, she showed him the ring on her hand, the intertwining snake and flower, seemingly dependent on each other.

Solomon took her hand and slowly lifted it to his lips. "You entrance me, O Queen of the South."

Nicaula looked into his dark honey eyes. "I have dreamt of you since the day I heard about you from your son, David."

He pulled her hand to his chest and placed it over his heart. "You are a prophetess."

"No." Nicaula tried to draw away. "I do not hear God's voice nor see his face."

Solomon would not release her, but held fast to her hand. "Only a woman such as you, with your knowledge, wealth, and beauty, can rule with a man like me."

Nicaula's breath came shallow. *What does he mean?*

"You are as the lily of the valley that grows near the sweetest water. If I had a woman like you to love—"

Nicaula turned away. It was sudden. But wasn't it what she'd imagined in those lonely nights of restless sleep? Wasn't it what she had hoped for? He stood close behind her, his breath on her hair.

"You have suffered much and deserve your joy to return in full. Stay in Jerusalem, and serve as queen by my side." He placed his hands on her shoulders and turned her around. She was drawn into his gaze, but it was awe she felt, not love.

In time. No one could help but love such a young, handsome ruler who was more powerful than any throughout all the land.

"Your people can continue the spice trade in your kingdom while you live here in comfort." He fingered her hair, lifting it gently from her neck. "We can be together always in my city of Jerusalem. Surely our love is stronger than any other—better than wine, better than all the flowers and spices." He leaned forward, his lips hovering above hers. She could almost taste his sweet scent.

"Come to my bed of spices, and what I have will be yours." His hand traveled along her neck and then toward her breasts.

Before Nicaula could decide whether she'd accept his kisses, the sound of voices reached them. The queen drew away just as a group of women rounded the corner of the temple. There were seven of them, all dressed in fine linen and wearing bracelets and necklaces of gold. Two of them wore nose rings. They cast longing eyes at Solomon, and he smiled in return.

After they passed, Nicaula asked, "Wives?"

"Oh no, concubines. My wives stay in their homes with their children."

Nicaula turned toward the temple, thinking about this man and his vast arsenal of women. It was fascinating, yet dismaying at the same time.

He reached for her again. "We are meant for each other, beautiful Queen of the South. None of my wives can claim to be my queen. Only you will have that honor."

A small smile reached Nicaula's lips as she let him move closer, his hands settling at her waist. Pleasure shot through her and collided with the hot envy of the other women. An image of every woman she'd seen since arriving in the city flashed through her mind. They all looked at the king the same way. He was a man who would bring them pleasure and wealth.

There was nothing real. Nothing to be valued. Was she to join the line of hundreds of women to be seduced by the king?

The day she'd arrived in Jerusalem, she might have agreed that she and Solomon should marry. After all, what did all the dreams mean? Weren't she and Solomon destined for each other?

"I will build you your own palace," Solomon said in her ear, his body pressing against hers, "and every luxury will be at your disposal."

Nicaula's pulse raced. The only other man she'd been this close to was Batal . . . but that had been so brief, and he had been far less knowledgeable in the ways of women. Solomon's hands had no such reservations. His fingers moved up her back, and his lips pressed against her neck.

Wild thoughts tumbled through her mind, confusing what she was feeling for the moment with the man who was touching her. It would be so easy to let him take her here . . . now . . . But what would happen after? How many women were waiting their turn?

Her passion turned to irritation. She wasn't sure about Solomon. Not anymore. She placed her hands on his chest, pushing him away. "And how often will I see my husband? Once a year, when he can fit me in between his other wives and concubines? A man such as you has no need for love from another woman. You will choke and die on so much affection."

Solomon chuckled and caught her hand, pulling her against him. "You cannot mean what you say," he said, his breath hot on her face. "Remember your dreams, your visions. I am king of Jerusalem."

"Yes, but you are not *my* king." She pried his arms from her, and he released her, stepping back. "I am but a trinket in your eyes," she continued, "something to be gained so that you can boast of your success to your playmates."

Solomon's face reddened. "What you say is treason. I will not be denied my wish."

They stared at each other for a moment, anger pulsing between them. "Nor I," she said. "As soon as the next harem comes by, you can soothe your wounded soul." She turned away and left the king standing alone.

"You will return to a desert with *nothing*," Solomon called after her. "In Jerusalem, you can have everything, and I will dispel your loneliness."

Heat spread to her neck as she continued to walk. "Dispel? Is that all I deserve? Even a slave earns the right for more." Nicaula hurried from the temple. If she couldn't have a king to herself, did she really want one?

But still she doubted. There were no other men of equal rank whom she could marry. His power intrigued her. He would not bow to her as a lamb, but fight with her like a lion. Her heart thudded as she thought about what a union between her and the greatest king might mean. Her children would have their pick of which lands to rule. Just because he had so many wives and concubines didn't mean she wouldn't always get her wishes fulfilled. She would still be a queen—just not his only love.

She felt her legs weaken as she descended the hillside. A couple of her servants rushed to her side. "Go find Azhara," she commanded.

The men scurried away to fulfill the mission. Nicaula refused to turn to see if Solomon still stood near the temple, although she was certain he watched her.

She made it to her quarters and found Azhara waiting for her. The girl was dressed in a fine robe of silk, her black hair neatly plaited, gold earrings on her ears.

"Welcome, O Queen," the servant said, bowing to the floor.

"Rise." The queen gazed at the girl before her. Something was different, and it wasn't her clothing. "Where have you been?"

"I heard of your arrival while I was in the city of Megiddo. I started traveling immediately."

"Why were you in Megiddo?"

"In the weeks that separated us, I met a man who wants to marry me." She lowered her head. "I have given him no promise because my first loyalty is to you."

"Does he know you are a slave?"

"Yes, but he promised to buy my freedom. I've come to ask the price."

The queen walked to her bed and sat down. "Do you *want* to leave me?"

"No. I wish to serve you, but I also love Tambariah."

"Who *is* this Tambariah?"

"A great man. He is strong and acts as governor of Megiddo. Many say that he should have taken the throne after the death of King David."

Nicaula looked at her slave in surprise. "Who is this man to make such a claim?"

"He is Solomon's cousin. He served as one of David's closest advisors and was trained in law and government long before Solomon inherited the throne," Azhara said. "An army is being formed to make an advance on Jerusalem."

"How do you know this?"

"Tambariah—"

"A great commander would tell a female slave his plans?

Impossible. Did you trick him?" The servant flinched. Then Nicaula knew. "You shared his bed, didn't you?"

Azhara buried her face in her hands.

The queen stood and paced the room. "I must deliver this news of the army to the king immediately." She whirled around and faced the servant. "Don't you see? You have become a traitor by not revealing this information right away."

"But I've only just arrived in the city—"

"How long have you known about the plot?"

Azhara wiped the tears streaming down her face. "A few days."

"You could be put to death for this."

Azhara began to tremble, shaking her head. "But if I tell the king, Tambariah will surely be killed."

"Yes, he will." Nicaula started to pace again, thinking. Just a short time ago, the king had accused *her* of treason. He was not going to take this news of Tambariah well. She stopped and eyed her servant. "I have been accused of treason myself."

"What do you mean?"

"I have refused an offer of marriage from Solomon." The queen brought a hand to her heart, realizing the impact. She'd have to gather her people and leave as soon as possible. She didn't know the reach of the king, but war was probable. "If I can relay the information about Tambariah's advance, perhaps we will be restored into Solomon's good faith again."

"I cannot." Azhara fell to her knees. "Please. I cannot betray the one I love."

"You love this man more than your country . . . your queen . . . your own life? How can you give all that up for a man you have only known a few short weeks?" she asked. In her heart, she understood the burning infatuation, but if she'd overcome it, so could a mere servant girl.

Nicaula rose to her full height, disgusted by the sniveling woman at her feet. "You have known me your entire life. I conquered a city to rescue you. Do not forget to whom you owe your very life."

Azhara sank to the floor and lay prostrate on the ground, sobbing. "I beg you not to reveal Tambariah's plot, for I carry his child."

Chapter Thirty-four

San'ā, Yemen

STAY AWAY FROM THE compound. Let Levy handle it, Omar typed. He had a general idea where AWP headquarters lay near Marib, but it was no place for a lone woman—even someone like Mia.

A long pause.

They don't know who you are. Just do what Levy says.

Mia, talk to me.

The wait was torture. No matter how much they had loved, or hated, each other, he was still her friend, still her comrade in battle.

Finally she replied. *Where are you?*

The university library.

Normally she would have questioned him and wanted to know why he was there. He waited as students entered in small groups, milling about, greeting each other. "Come on, sweetheart," he muttered.

No answer. The minutes ticked by, each one longer than the last. Finally, she wrote, *You're in the library?*

Yes.

Open my email account and find the one titled "UBAR." Print off the PDF attachment.

Omar went to the front desk and asked for the printer key. By the time he was back at the computer, Mia had sent the user name and password. As he started the document printing, he scrolled through the pages. First he saw several satellite photos scanned into the PDF. At the bottom was the label—in Mia's handwriting—*Ubar.*

Ubar? Omar had read articles on the fabled city. But nothing significant had ever been uncovered to prove its existence, unless one counted stories handed down from generation to generation.

He clicked to the next page and saw the same satellite photo, only with a tighter zoom. *Shisur.* The document finished printing, and Omar changed the password and logged off the account. He returned the printer key and paid for the copies. Then he took the stack of papers and walked to a vacant aisle in the library, where he leaned against a bookcase and leafed through the pages.

Inspecting the pictures more closely, he made out several trucks and signs of an excavation going on. *When were these taken?* He turned over another page and nearly gasped. It was a picture of a dead man. It looked as if the elderly man was in his office chair with his head cocked back, mouth gaping, eyes open. There was no blood or vicious trauma evident. Below the picture of the dead man, Mia had scrawled, *Dr. Richard Lyon, murdered.*

The professor. Omar stared into the vacant eyes in the photo with revulsion. Just below the man's chair was something that looked like a white envelope with some words written across it. Omar turned the next page slowly, his heart drumming. The scanned email detailed the writing on the tomb walls that was uncovered in northern Jerusalem. Omar sank to the floor, crossed his legs, and read every word. As he reviewed the dates, he knew that if this new genealogical chart proved authentic, there was no way Solomon could have ruled the same region.

The next page nearly stopped his heart.

The tomb had been bombed about the same time he'd been enjoying his kidnapping in a storage room. All that evidence, all those artifacts . . .

He turned the page, feeling sick. The page was reminiscent of the crayon rubbings that children make of dinosaur fossils in a museum, though this rubbing appeared to be of charcoal, its image not exactly clear on the PDF. But it was clear enough.

The cuneiform letters stood out, searing themselves into his brain—the ancient script familiar and haunting at once.

Ancient Aramaic.

But it was the first line that stalled the breath in his throat. Translated it read, "O Queen of the South, Death began your journey."

Omar read haltingly through the ode to the queen. Was it a poem? A legend? Across the top of the page, Mia had written: *Mysterious Hebrew king—Tambariah—lover of the queen of Sheba?*

Omar turned the page upside down. Nothing appeared to be hidden, encrypted. A mysterious Hebrew king and an Arabian queen—lovers? Joined in marriage? Questions tumbled through his mind, each more fantastic than the next.

Omar folded the pages in half, his head feeling as though it would burst. Here he sat in a university library, two thousand miles away from a city that might be changed forever with the knowledge contained in a single document that he held in his hand.

He pulled out the sketch and stared at the center palm trunk— the snake and flower intertwined. Did they represent Tambariah and the queen? Eyes bleary with fatigue, he emailed Mia. A couple of minutes later, her reply came.

I'm almost there. Won't be able to talk for a while. We'll discuss the info later.

Mia, stay out of the compound.

I can't. If it makes you feel better, I'm wearing a bulletproof vest.

Don't feel better at all.

Looks like some trouble up ahead.

Get out of there! Omar typed then waited breathlessly. One minute passed. Then five. He paced, willing his phone to buzz.

Hotel room 18. Check carpet.

Omar stared at the email, waiting for something else to come through. He dialed her number . . . waited . . . sent an email, dialed again. Nothing.

She'd been staying at a hotel near the National Museum. He pushed through the front doors, nearly sprinted across campus, and hailed a taxi.

A message came in from Levy. Perfect timing, as always. *Return to Salalah. The Ethiopian needs to be extradited to his country before AWP can get ahold of him.*

I thought you had a security team in place, Omar typed.

Hired guns. Not trustworthy like you. A flight leaves in two hours. Be on it.

Sorry. Something's gone wrong in Marib. Mia's in trouble.

I'm already on it. She's taken care of.

By whom?

An operation is in the works right now. She'll be out of there in no time.

More hired guns? I thought they weren't trustworthy. I'm going in, Levy. You can fire me if you want.

It's too risky to go alone. Even if you were the best we had, you'll be killed before reaching the first outpost.

Unfortunately for you, Levy, I am the best you have.

If you go in, you leave me no other choice.

I said you can fire me if that makes you feel better.

Nothing would make me happier than to do it in person.

Come on down and join the party. Drinks are on me. Except you'll have to get off your skinny ass and get on a plane.

Done.

The taxi jerked to a stop. He paid the driver and climbed out. The seedy hotel was squashed between two apartment buildings, the Arabic letters a faded blue against a bleached-white backdrop. Omar's pulse raced with anger. He was going to hold Levy to his promise, just as he would keep his promise to find Mia. The hotel door swept open, and a man with wiry hair stepped out. Leaning against the crumbled plaster wall, the man lit up a cigarette.

Omar nodded to the man as he passed by and entered the building to find the musty lobby empty. A couple of salvaged leather chairs stood near a table littered with yellowed newspapers. The subscription looked to have run out years before. Perhaps management held on to the papers to keep up appearances. A phone jangled on the service desk, its hollow ring going unanswered. *Business must be too good to answer the phone.*

Then Omar realized that the man smoking out front was the employee. Sure enough, the door jangled again, and the man reentered. Omar greeted him and asked for a room. After paying, he requested room eighteen. The employee narrowed his haze-filled eyes—the man had been smoking something more than just nicotine.

"My lucky number," Omar said, placing more riyals on the counter.

The employee grinned, displaying missing teeth, and took the bills then handed him a key with ١٨ handwritten on the dangling, orange tag. The employee motioned to the right, and Omar followed his directions down the long corridor.

When Omar reached number eighteen, he unlocked the door, not knowing what to expect. What he saw exceeded even his wildest imagination. There was not one thing left untouched, overturned, or unopened. Even the pillows were slashed, the matted stuffing strewn about the bed. The faded green wallpaper had been stripped, and pieces of crusted glue littered the floor. The ancient television and its aluminum-wrapped antennas had been dissected.

Omar waded through the rubbish and tugged open the drapes, letting the early sunlight pierce the chaos behind him. *Under the carpet . . . under the carpet.* He started in one corner and ran his hands along the carpet, feeling for any inconsistency. Then he stood and moved his hand along the curtain rod. It was then that he saw it. Spray painted above the window—between the drapes and the ceiling—was the message:

VENITE, DILECTI FILII, EGREDEMINI IN HORTUM.

Omar pulled out the PDF pages and scribbled the Latin words down.

Hortum was "garden"—that he was sure of. And *venite* meant "come." *Come to the garden?* It must be a pretty important garden. Then he paused. The Garden of Eden was theorized to exist in Iraq. Were the men who destroyed this room from Iraq?

Venite, dilecti filii, egredemini in hortum. The words reverberated inside his head. He needed a Bible. Something in his gut told him that the message was linked to the Song of Solomon.

Omar moved to the next corner, ready to rip the carpet up when he noticed a lump. He picked at the edge of the carpet and found it loose. Seconds later, he held a white envelope sealed in a plastic bag in his hands. The word "cyanide" was scrawled across the plastic in big black letters. Through the plastic, Omar saw an envelope with a set of words written across it, printed in block letters.

VENITE, DILECTI FILII, EGREDEMINI IN HORTUM.

Then he realized why the words seemed familiar. The same words were on the envelope in Dr. Lyon's office.

Voices sounded from the hallway.

"Oh, hell," Omar said. Standing, he faced the window and searched for a latch. The thing was virtually painted to the glass, but the adrenaline coursing through his veins made it easy to pry open the stubborn handle. Whether or not the voices were destined for room eighteen, Omar was taking no chances. He maneuvered through the open window and closed it behind him.

Outside, the sun glistened off the wet clumps of wild grass in the hotel's scraggly, what-seemed-to-have-once-been-a-garden patch of cracked earth. The sun had offered no mercy to this former oasis. Omar walked briskly, keeping his eyes lowered. The wailing prayer began just as he passed a mosque, nearly causing him to jump out of his skin.

He waited until he'd been walking about ten minutes before looking around for another taxi—one to take him to the airport.

A taxi pulled to a stop, already carrying passengers—an ancient woman holding a squawking chicken and a bearded man reading the day's newspaper. Omar climbed in at the teenage driver's promise that he would be dropped off first. The odors coming from the chicken were noxious. He hadn't realized how much a hen could stink.

Omar stole a look at the front-page headlines, scanning the Arabic and searching for information of a break-in at the museum. Nothing.

The envelope. When the taxi lumbered forward, he took out the PDF and flipped to the picture of the deceased professor, holding the image out of the driver's view as he squinted for a better look. He avoided the professor's vacant gaze and focused on the envelope.

The writing was barely legible on the plain exterior, but the first word was clear: *Venite*.

An invitation of death.

"Or salvation."

Omar stared at the taxi driver. The words had been spoken by someone—he was sure of it. Letting out a sigh, he turned to the window, his reflection framing the passing scenery. *Now I'm hearing voices.*

Chapter Thirty-five

Jerusalem
960 b.c.

NICAULA CLASPED HER HANDS together then unclasped them. She stared into the polished length of brass, studying the servant's clothing covering her body. Slowly the queen lowered the dark veil, making the disguise complete.

Azhara stood stiffly by the bed, awkward in her royal attire. Everything from her jewel-encrusted shoes to her embroidered silk headdress made her appear as a queen. Nicaula had not realized how similar their body shapes were until they switched their clothing.

The queen extended her hand to her servant. "Come and see for yourself."

The two women stood side by side. The similarity was astonishing.

"Tonight you will marry Solomon in my place," Nicaula said. "And I will tell no one about your beloved Tambariah. He will be spared a traitor's death. The kingdom of Sheba will be forever favored." She raised Azhara's veil and smoothed a lock of hair. "On our way out of the city tomorrow, you will have a chance to bid farewell to your love."

Azhara nodded as a tear trailed down her cheek.

"We will leave Jerusalem as we found it." The queen tilted her servant's chin upward and gazed into her eyes. "We will leave Tambariah to his conquests and Solomon to his wives and concubines. Your kingdom awaits you at the end of the journey. I have made it known to Solomon that I will spend only one night—the wedding night—with him. Then I leave. You must ensure that he does not guess our trickery."

Azhara swiped at the fast falling tears, and Nicaula lowered the veil again. "Although the separation from your lover will be bittersweet, the rewards will far outweigh your broken heart. Remember that you will leave Jerusalem as a queen inside your heart, and no man or master will ever be able to take that from you. Your loyalty to me has brought you a lifetime of power and wealth."

The women entered the temple of Yahweh together with servants in tow. Through her veil, Nicaula spotted Batal standing in the corner, surrounded by several women. He paid them no attention, but focused his gaze on the dressed-up Azhara.

Azhara bowed as Solomon approached in his purple robes and white turban laced with colorful jewels. Flung over his shoulders was a tightly woven shawl, white with indigo fringes. A twinge of doubt passed through Nicaula. If he should learn of the deceit . . . He extended a hand to Azhara and led her to the altar. Nicaula's heart thumped as she watched Azhara stand in her place. The queen forced herself to melt into the crowd, yet stay within view. From across the room, she saw Batal turn away and leave the temple. More than anything, she wanted to leave with Batal and tell him that it wasn't really her marrying the king.

The surrounding crowd fell into a hush as the high priest stepped forward. The dignified man blessed Solomon and Azhara as they knelt before the altar. Then he led them to the huppah.

Those around Nicaula broke into a strange song of foreign words. Then abruptly, the singing stopped.

"King Solomon, son of David," the priest's voice rang out. "Will you take Nicaula, queen of the South, to wife according to the law of Moses and Israel?"

"Yes," Solomon said.

"Nicaula, will you take King Solomon as your husband, according to the law of Moses and Israel?"

"Yes," Azhara said, her voice barely audible.

A second priest presented a cup of wine. Solomon sipped from the cup then passed it to Azhara, and she carefully raised her veil to reveal only her mouth. She sipped the wine and returned the cup to the king.

The high priest presented the ceremonial ring and gave it to Solomon. He placed it on Azhara's finger, saying, "Behold, thou art consecrated unto me with this ring according to the law of Moses."

"From the beginning, Yahweh created male and female," the priest said, raising his arms.

Azhara circled around Solomon seven times. Then she stopped and waited for Solomon to lift her veil. Nicaula watched in anticipation, hoping that the second veil her servant wore would still conceal her identity enough.

The high priest removed the shawl Solomon wore over his robe. Then Solomon lifted Azhara's veil, placing the hem on his shoulder.

The priest said, "What Yahweh hath joined together, let no man put asunder."

A cheer rose from the crowd, and the king smiled. His smile seemed genuine for a man who must have heard the same words hundreds of times.

The lower priest placed a garland each on the heads of

Solomon and Azhara. Then a bowl of holy water was presented, and the bride and groom dipped their hands into it.

The high priest stepped in front of the couple and read the marriage contract. A word from Solomon had him skipping to the marital blessings. "In the words of Jacob," the priest said, "'Let my name be named on them, and the name of my fathers Abraham and Isaac; and let them grow into a multitude in the midst of the earth.'"

"Amen," thundered around Nicaula, bringing the ceremony to a close. Many of the guests began to dance, while others moved to the feast laid out in the nearby garden.

The queen gripped her veil tightly as she moved through the thronging people and returned to her living quarters. Her servants ignored her since she was dressed in Azhara's clothing, and they assumed she was cleaning the queen's room. Once alone, Nicaula stripped off her rough clothes and pulled on a robe. She climbed into her bed and closed her eyes, replaying the events in her mind. Solomon was with Azhara right now, and if Azhara was careful, he would never know he'd married a servant.

Before the light of morning, Azhara was to leave the king's bed and return to the queen. They would switch places—Azhara turning to menial duties, and Nicaula pretending as though she were newly married. She hoped to make a graceful exit from Jerusalem.

The queen turned over in bed as Batal's pained expression came unbidden to her mind. Had she made the right decision? Was she a fool to think she could be happy without him?

Could she keep the secret from him? Batal was the only man whom she'd truly kissed, truly desired. What if . . . in his melancholy . . . he turned to one of the beautiful courtiers? He surely had his pick of at least a dozen. She thought about the seven women who had made eyes at Solomon when *she* stood in his presence.

A shudder passed through her body. To be married to a man like that would have been worse than a loveless marriage. She had tasted the bittersweet of love, and she had to be grateful for at least that.

Batal would continue to grow in his commandership and would someday take a bride, but Nicaula wanted no more from men. She would remain a virgin and die a virgin.

◦◦◦

THE RED CLIFFS TOWERED over the queen's camp, offering shade in the blistering afternoon heat. The queen's caravan had left Jerusalem several weeks before, and now they camped at Eloth. Nicaula paced back and forth inside the tent, knowing that at any moment her servant would enter, and she would have to tell the woman the truth. In the morning, she'd send Azhara on her way to her new life in a foreign land, and Nicaula would return to her old one. Azhara had made the ultimate sacrifice for her mistress, and now the queen was about to change the woman's fate yet again.

The heat was suffocating, and Nicaula's mind wandered. It had been a hot day like this one when she'd been summoned to her father's side, just days before he left on that final journey. The king had gripped her hand and sent the servants away.

"Daughter, hear me now," her father had whispered. "There is something you must know now that you are a young woman and will be queen someday . . ."

The breeze outside picked up, and the raised tent flap fluttered, bringing Nicaula from her long-ago memories.

Azhara appeared at the entryway. She bowed before she stepped inside. Then she took her usual place, sitting on the rug at the foot of the queen's reed chair. The woman wore the clothing of a servant still so that the others would not know what had transpired.

Azhara kept her eyes lowered, and Nicaula noticed the fleshy rose of the girl's cheeks. Her thin hands had swollen, and her belly had rounded.

"Are you well?"

"Yes, thank you," Azhara said.

Nicaula had spent long days wondering what had transpired between Azhara and Solomon on their wedding night. "How did you conceal your identity from King Solomon?"

The servant turned her head away, a lock of hair falling into her face. "I asked him to extinguish the oil lamps and insisted that all Arabian women wear their wedding veil on their wedding night."

"You are sure he did not guess the change?"

"No," Azhara whispered. "Each time his hands moved to my neck, I changed position. He did not mind my avoidance in kissing. After he fell asleep, I stained the bedcover with the blood from the vial you gave me."

The queen let out a breath of air, satisfied. "You have served me well, and I know you grieve for Tambariah. Perhaps one day he will join you in your new home."

Azhara lifted her head, hope shining in her eyes.

"But you may change your mind after hearing what I have to say." She produced a roll of papyri from the waistband of her robe. "I received this scroll delivered from Solomon this morning." She crossed to Azhara and knelt beside her. "I told him about the child, and, of course, he thinks I am carrying it. I also told him that I would not return to Jerusalem to raise a son among his other wives."

"A son? How can you know?"

"I know," the queen said. "Solomon has promised a new kingdom, a new life in another country. The country is south of Egypt, called Abyssinia."

"And this is where we'll dwell?"

"This is where *you* will live, with your son." Nicaula touched the woman's shoulder. "You have done me a service that I may never be able to repay, except in this small way. You will be the queen of Abyssinia, under the blessing and order of King Solomon. You will bear your son and live a life of prosperity and honor. This will replace the sorrow in your heart."

Astonishment covered Azhara's face. "You are giving me a kingdom? I cannot be a queen . . . I haven't the heritage, and I don't know how to make decisions like a monarch. I cannot read or write."

The queen smiled benignly. "All these things can be learned." She straightened and looked past her servant. "As for your heritage, there is one more thing I must tell you before we part ways."

Confusion lay in Azhara's eyes, and she gripped her trembling hands together, holding them against her swollen belly.

"Royal blood runs through your veins. You were born to my father by the way of a servant girl. Father made me promise never to reveal this secret, or civil disputes might arise. You were born sickly, and although he didn't educate you, he protected you by bringing you to the palace." Nicaula took a deep breath, feeling her own emotion surface. "The best way I knew to ensure your safety was to keep you as a personal servant."

Nicaula pulled Azhara to her feet and embraced the girl's trembling body. "Sister, you have served me more than any woman can serve another. You deserve to represent your heritage now and forever. Go and rule your country. Rise to the queen within you." She drew away and touched her sister's chest. "Within your heart, greatness lies, waiting to be uncovered."

Tears streamed down Azhara's cheeks as she nodded and took a shaky breath. "Where do I begin?"

"First, you will learn what all men know—how to read.

Chapter Thirty-six

San'ā, Yemen

"PULL OVER HERE," OMAR told the taxi driver.

The small bookshop near the airport had a couple of tables set outside displaying shiny copies of tourist books. Omar entered the dim store and greeted the shop owner. The heavyset man looked up from his tea.

"I'm searching for a Bible," Omar said.

The shop owner waved him toward a stack of dusty books piled on a table. Omar walked back and sorted through them quickly, sneezing a few times in the process. After he'd spent several minutes in fruitless searching, the shop owner stood. He shuffled into a back room and a moment later appeared with a box. He set it on top of a stack of books and returned to his tea without a word.

Omar started emptying the contents of the box. At the bottom was a well-worn copy of the King James Version of the Bible. He'd never actually read this version, but as long as it contained the Song of Solomon, it would do.

He paid for the Bible then hailed a taxi and ordered the driver to the airport. He put the Bible into his bag and sorted through his things. When he dialed the hospital number in Salalah and asked about Alem, the receptionist transferred him to a nurse.

"Hello, madam. I'd like to check on Mr. Alem Eshete."

"Mr. Zagouri? Mr. Eshete has been asking for you."

"He's awake? Can I speak with him?"

"There's no phone in his room, but he needs to see you as soon as possible." She lowered her voice. "He's quite agitated over it."

"Tell him I'll be there in the morning."

The taxi stopped. Omar tossed the driver a few bills and climbed out. A narrow-faced, bird-thin man sat at the reservations desk and looked up when Omar approached.

"I need to charter a helicopter today."

"We're booked."

"How much to book a helicopter to Marib right now?"

He motioned for Omar to come closer. "How much do you have?"

Omar removed a stack of traveler's checks from his bag and handed over a dozen. "You get this now and more when we get to Marib."

The man smiled and extended his hand. "I'm Zabid." He shouted over his shoulder something about going to dinner. Then he grabbed a blazer from the back of his chair. "Let's go."

"*You're* flying me?"

"Yes, yes." Zabid grinned again, leading the way through the crowds and then out into the blazing heat on the tarmac.

They stopped before a helicopter that had seen much better days. "This is it, huh?" Omar asked.

Zabid whistled as he checked a few things then rushed Omar into the chopper. "We must hurry . . . before the boss returns."

Omar laughed aloud. He liked this guy already. "We're picking up another passenger. There's another thousand in it for you if you wait."

The man reddened. "All right. All right. I'll say we had engine trouble."

Omar wondered if the man's lie wouldn't be far from the truth. At least he hoped a little rust wouldn't impede the helicopter.

The flight wouldn't be long, but Omar took the opportunity to thumb through the Bible. He stopped at 1 Kings and skimmed the verses that chronicled Solomon's early reign as king. The man had it all—women, gold, unimaginable luxuries, the confidence of God. Omar slowed his reading at chapter 10. As he scanned the verses of the encounter between Solomon and the queen of Sheba, he tried to picture the grand meeting that must have taken place between two great regents.

He skipped to the Song of Songs, or the Song of Solomon as it was titled in this Bible version. By the second sentence, he was entranced. "For thy love is better than wine . . . he shall lie all night betwixt my breasts . . ." *And this was three thousand years ago?* Omar read on until he reached chapter 5. "I am come into my garden, my sister, my spouse . . ."

He thought back to the envelope: *Venite, dilecti filii, egredemini in hortum.*

Come, beloved sons, go into the garden.

Did the garden equal love? Ecstasy? Bliss? The words had been written on the envelope and on the hotel window—both places of destruction. Somehow he didn't think that the garden represented innocent love. But palm trees were green. In the desert, palms signified an oasis—a garden? If the sketch of palms was a map for the queen's tomb, maybe the garden was her tomb.

This is getting absurd. Jesus Christ was buried in a garden tomb hundreds of years later. Was the queen of Sheba's death a precursor to Christ?

"There's Marib," the pilot shouted over the roar of the helicopter.

Omar looked at the towering ruins. "Five kilometers to the north is a guard station in front of a complex of low buildings. Drop me there."

Zabid banked the chopper left. Moments later he brought the helicopter down. Omar grabbed the pistol from his bag and slid it into his pocket. "Wait here. A thousand extra for you."

Zabid grinned. "Yes, yes."

Omar climbed out of the helicopter and made his way the couple hundred meters to the outpost, where several guards had already exited. Just beyond the guard station was a series of low-lying buildings—the top of the massive underground complex. Someone here knew where Mia was.

One of the guards raised a hand, signaling Omar to stop. The guard wore a dingy white shirt, unbuttoned to the navel, with a black military-style beret perched on his head of dark, curly hair. He had two rifles slung over his shoulder. *Must be a former Boy Scout. Always prepared.*

"We're in lockdown. Come back tomorrow," the guard stated as if he were a recording.

"Impossible," Omar said in a clipped British accent, mentally sizing the guard up. Although a long scar ran the length of the guard's pockmarked cheek, Omar wasn't intimidated. He could easily take him, even with the two guns. It was the other three or four guys inside the guard post that he worried about. "I was told to come today or blood would be on someone's hands."

The guard stared at Omar, fiddling with a radio attached to his belt. "What's your name?"

"Diya Al-Ghabiry, secretary of Abdallah Saleh al-Qadi, who is the director of GOAMM." Omar presented his fake government badge.

"I know who the director is," the guard said, sounding annoyed.

"There's a woman here . . . We have a meeting scheduled."

"All right." The guard stepped into the post for a moment, and after gesturing to the men inside, he came out. "Follow me."

Omar followed, trudging through the sand to the next building. The interior was cool and dark, and the concrete floor sloped downward. At the bottom of the incline sat a wide pair of gates. "Wait here. Someone will meet you."

The compound opened into a huge cavern—an underground parking lot, containing several vehicles. Omar walked along the parking garage looking for another entrance. At the far end, he found a heavy door and a surveillance camera mounted above it turned in his direction. He walked to the door and banged on it. Sure enough, the door slid open, and another guard emerged, his hand on the AK-47 slung over his shoulder.

Omar showed his badge to the guard. "I have a meeting with the woman and Mr. Rabbel Al-Omda," he said, keeping his accent.

The guard's eyebrows lifted. "Al-Omda said he's not to be disturbed."

"And the woman?" Omar pressed.

The guard spoke into his radio then listened to the reply. "She's not available."

"I'll just wait in Al-Omda's office."

"No one waits in his office."

"I have a delivery from the director of—"

"Shhh." The guard's face hardened. "Come in."

Omar stepped into a dim hallway. The unmistakable odor of frankincense oozed from the cement walls. Cameras dotted the ceiling, making Omar wonder if the surveillance room rivaled Israeli government headquarters.

The passage veered to the right and sloped downward, taking them deeper into the complex. A cool rush of air came from up ahead and with it, the scent of cleaning chemicals. A small sign next to the door they passed had a stick-figure picture of someone swimming. *The place had a swimming pool?* He noticed that all the doors had a keyless entry system like a hotel.

The guard stopped, waved a card in front of a monitor, and held the door open for Omar. "Wait here."

Omar entered, and the door slid shut behind him. He scanned the room. There were two windows—too high to see out of—a bookcase, an overstuffed chair, and a halogen lamp. The floor was bare except for a small rug at the foot of the chair.

Two minutes passed and then another. Rabbel wasn't going to meet him after all, Omar decided. He'd have to find Mia on his own.

Omar opened the door, looking both ways along the corridor. Then he chose the opposite direction from which he had come. When he heard someone approach, he lowered his head, avoiding eye contact. But the person stopped. From the corner of his eye, Omar saw that he was a large man wearing a long, white tunic, head covered with an embroidered cap. Hopefully the guy carried only one of those long knives.

Omar raised his head just as the man drew a gun. He didn't have time to second-guess himself, so he lunged to wrestle the gun away. A sharp elbow to the man's head gave Omar an instant's advantage, and he grabbed the gun and slammed it against the man's temple, knocking the fellow out. Then Omar riffled through the man's pockets and found what he needed.

An identification key.

Hang on, Mia.

Omar sped through the hall, trying one door after the other. He waved the ID to get into the rooms. The first looked like a science lab—full of long tables, equipment, and stacks of books. Shouting reached his ears, so he slipped into the next room—a junky office. The light was dim, but Omar scanned for a storage closet. Nothing but books lined the walls, and a couple of half-dead plants stood in the corner. He waited on the other side of the door with his gun ready until the voices faded along the hall.

Cracking the door open, he found the hallway empty. He moved out and skidded to the next door. Waving the badge, he opened it and slipped in. The voices were back. Omar closed the door with a soft click and stared into the pitch dark as footsteps thudded down the hall, slowing nearby. They had entered the office.

Omar crouched, trying to force his eyes to adjust. Tall shapes rose in front of him, and he put his hands out, feeling the angles. It was a storage shelf of some sort. Voices erupted just outside the door. Angry—searching for him. Omar dropped to the floor and crawled around the shelf unit, concealing himself in case the door opened.

He waited, his gun poised, when something moved behind him. Omar nearly pulled the trigger. He turned, swinging the gun around, staring blindly into the dark. *Rat or human?*

"Matan?" the voice was faint. A shape moved.

"Mia?"

Suddenly the door flew open. He froze. Now he could see Mia huddled in the corner—mouth taped, hands and feet bound.

Her eyes, wide with fear, met his.

The man took a step inside the room. After a long minute, the man backed out, shouting to someone running down the hall. The door remained open.

In a silent instant, Omar was at her side. He tore the tape off her mouth. Her eyes were crusted with tears, her lips raw with abrasion. He had never seen her so helpless . . . so weak. As he cut into the ropes that bound her hands, he saw with a sickening feeling that her clothing had been torn. If he stopped now to think of the implications, anger would control his actions and get them both killed. "What did they do to you?"

She shook her head and wrapped her arms around his neck. Omar held her for a moment, but then the voices returned.

"They're not giving up yet," he whispered, lifting her in his arms. "Let's go, sweetheart."

"No," she said, her voice guttural. "They'll kill you."

"We'll discuss that another time." Omar gritted his teeth and moved to the door. The hallway was empty, but he could hear voices coming from another passageway—or was it the rage throbbing against his temple? He set off toward the right.

Mia leaned her head against his chest. "Go left."

"But I came from the right." Omar looked at her pale face, her dull eyes.

"I didn't get the ring yet."

"What are you talking about?"

Her grip tightened. "That's why I came."

"Mia—"

"I can't leave without it."

"How long will it take?"

"Minutes. Just follow my directions."

"All right, you're the boss." He moved as fast as he dared, racewalking, on the verge of running.

A door opened down the hallway, and two men emerged. The first one to see them started to shout. Omar braced Mia against the wall as he fumbled for his gun.

The men started running toward them, guns raised. Omar pressed his body against Mia, shielding her. He aimed and shot first. One man cried out and dipped to a knee, but the other still charged forward. Omar pulled the trigger again, aiming for the second man.

The man returned fire at the same time, and Omar waited for the searing pain. Nothing came, and he watched the other man crumple to the ground as if in slow motion.

Lifting Mia again, he charged forward, passing the dead guy and the one who screamed in pain, holding his knee. Perspiration soaked every inch of Omar's body as he came to a crossroads.

"Still want that ring?"

"Turn left again." She tightened her grip around his neck. "Hurry."

He ran.

"Here. Stop here," Mia said.

Omar spun to a stop and set Mia down. He waved his ID in front of the door. Nothing.

"It won't work on Rabbel's private offices."

"Stand back." He shot the door handle, and an alarm blared through the complex. He kicked the door open. "Now what?"

Mia limped inside and pulled up the corner of the rug. Beneath was a small safe set in a concrete hole. With trembling fingers, she dialed the combination and pulled out stacks of cash. Then she lifted a small black box—small enough for a ring. She peeked inside then closed it.

"Got it."

Omar stooped and grabbed a stack of money.

"What are you doing?"

He stared at her. "Same thing as you."

She started to protest, but they heard more shouting.

"Let's get out of here." He picked her up.

"I'm fine."

"No, you're not. Hang on."

Mia directed him to the exit. The keypad against the wall was camouflaged, but when he swiped the stolen ID, the door rolled open. He plunged ahead, gripping Mia as he passed the parked vehicles. At the gate, the badge did the trick again, and the gate obediently swung open. Sunlight hit him full force in the eyes, momentarily blinding him, but he stumbled forward, balancing Mia's weight in his arms, and ran past the guard post.

He came to a dead stop. The helicopter was gone.

Chapter Thirty-seven

Israeli Intelligence Headquarters—Northern Command

"SOMEONE'S GOING TO PAY for this," David Levy muttered under his breath, staring at the screen. "That American woman will screw everything up."

"Screw what up?"

Levy turned, startled to see the deputy chief of staff standing behind the console. The chief's pale-blue military shirt stretched almost to a snapping point across his wide girth.

"Nothing." Levy stood and casually stretched. "Need more coffee."

He brushed past the chief and walked the lime-green hallway to the break room. The blasted woman had fallen into a shaft, which just happened to be a tomb—in the middle of the Shisur oasis. Of all things. Of all places. Of all *people*. The American media whores would most likely broadcast the woman's interviews all over CNN before the day was over.

Automatically, David checked his watch—a Yacht-Master—one of his few indulgences. He'd told his buddies that his Rolex was a fake. The only thing fake about it was that there were no decent ladies to impress with it. The pickings were slim since Mia went on assignment.

Levy turned into the break room and wrinkled his nose in distaste. Discarded paper cups overfilled the trash bin, and the coffee pot held just a few ounces of murky liquid. He filled the pot and sat on the torn vinyl chair to wait. Then he pulled out his phone and texted Omar again. Where was he? Levy didn't believe his threat about finding Mia for one moment. The man would be killed before he even passed through the first gate of the Marib compound. David had been studying the satellite photos for the past hour. The operation he was developing would launch at midnight, and if all went as planned, Mia would be sharing more than a drink with him in celebration.

Footsteps slapped against the cement floor outside the coffee room. Levy kept his focus on his phone, hoping that whoever it was wouldn't bother him. After a moment, he was rewarded with the fading sound of footsteps.

Omar, he typed. *Where are you? Your flight to Salalah leaves in thirty minutes.*

He waited a full ten minutes with no response. An uneasy feeling slipped across David as he pocketed the phone. Something was going down, and he had to find out. Fast. The coffee timer went off, and he stood to pour himself a fresh cup. Then it hit him. He knew what he had to do next. He dialed the security number on his phone and booked a jet for immediate departure.

Sorry, Omar, he thought as he reached for a paper cup. *I tried to warn you.*

Chapter Thirty-eight

Marib, Yemen

"I'M GOING TO KILL you!" Omar screamed at the empty sky. Mia wriggled in his arms. "Sorry, sweetheart, not you."

"Put me down," she said, her voice strained. Omar lowered her to the ground, steadying her for a moment.

"Stop where you are," a voice commanded behind him.

Omar spun on his heels, coming face-to-face with a young kid not more than fifteen. The kid wore no shirt, only black cutoffs and a colored scarf around his waist, securing a jambiya knife. The kid's unruly curls parted in the wind as he tried to stare menacingly at Omar. The bulky rifle he carried weighed nearly as much as he did.

Omar smiled and reached into his pocket, pulling out a chunk of cash. "Money—for your rifle."

The kid's gaze wavered, and Omar knew he had him. "This lady is hurt, and I need to get her to a hospital." He pushed the cash toward the kid. "Trade me. I'll tell no one."

The kid grabbed the cash and then handed over the rifle. Omar left him counting the money and, pulling Mia with him, ran full tilt back to the compound. The gates were still open. "See, I wasn't stealing money—just redistributing."

When they reached the first truck, he settled Mia into the backseat.

The door to the compound slid open, and three men came running toward him. He jumped into the driver's seat and reached to hot-wire the thing . . . "You've got to be kidding." The keys dangled from the ignition. "Here we go!"

He threw the truck into reverse, scattering the men who'd just reached the vehicle. He gunned the truck past the guard post, noticing that all the guards were inside the building. *Probably counting their money.* They'd be after him soon enough.

Dust billowed behind as he cleared the compound, but through the rear window, he saw the dark silhouettes of the pursuing trucks. He scanned the sky, hoping that the helicopter was circling, waiting. "Where the hell is Zabid?" Omar shouted to no one.

"Who's that?" Mia said.

"I swear I had a better plan than this."

Mia pulled herself up. Omar glanced over. Her face was still pale. "You don't look so good."

"Neither do you."

Omar's hand automatically went to his head and touched his bristled scalp. "Oh yeah—that. I'll explain later."

She eyed him. "Can't wait."

He held her gaze for an instant. "You know, if you wanted a ring so badly, I could've bought you one—someplace a little nicer."

She rolled her eyes.

"Well then, I hope I didn't ruin your shopping experience."

Mia glanced behind them at the pursuing vehicles. "I wouldn't have expected anything less."

He laughed and grabbed her hand. Pulling it toward him, he kissed it. It didn't taste quite like the wine described in the scripture, but just looking at Mia was better than drinking the finest wine. "Ever read Solomon's Song?"

"From the Bible?"

"Yeah. It's really sexy. Solomon was quite the ladies' man."

"Too bad he screwed it up."

"What do you mean?"

She tugged her hand away from his. "Well, when you get past all the 'sexy' stuff, it's just plain reality. You don't listen to God, you get cut off, and it all goes downhill from there."

Was she speaking about him or Solomon? "So listening is the key, right?"

"Yeah." Mia's eyes narrowed. "And you'd better listen now. We're going to die in a few minutes if you don't have a plan to get us out of here."

Omar didn't need to check the rearview mirror to see that two vehicles flanked their tailgate, rifles pointing out the windows. He looked ahead for anything—a tree, a building—to give them cover. *Oh yeah, forget the cover. We're in a desert.*

Mia tapped his shoulder and pointed. "Is that what you were looking for?"

He turned his head. A helicopter hovered a couple of hundred meters in front of them. "Zabid!" He started honking like mad—not that the pilot could hear him, but it worked out his extra adrenaline. "Hang on!" he shouted just before slamming on the brakes. Mia hit the back of his seat with a thud. He veered sharply to the right and drove straight toward the helicopter that was slowly landing.

"You're a maniac!" Mia screamed.

"I'll take that as a compliment." Omar floored the gas pedal, making the truck whine as it accelerated. "When I stop, I'll run you to the helicopter, covering you. If something happens to me, tell Zabid to lift the chopper and leave."

"No."

"Yes!"

"You got us into this mess, and I'm going to get us out of it," Mia yelled, grabbing his arm with a death-like grip. "Or at least get *you* out of it. I'll give myself up, and you can finish the job you came out here to do."

"Last I saw, *you* were the one trapped in the complex needing to be rescued."

"I never asked to be rescued, damn it!" Mia said. "Levy was creating an entire operation to get me out with *real* pilots flying *decent* helicopters and men who would be carrying more than a *pistol*."

"Sorry I didn't get the email." Omar slammed to a stop. The helicopter was just a dozen paces away, its blades pumping in the hot air. He jumped out of the truck and swung her door open. Then he grabbed her arm, his face inches from hers. "We either die together or live together. Your choice."

She stared at him, but Omar saw the wavering in her eyes. He pulled her into his arms and lifted her from the seat.

"I hate you!" she shouted above the roar of the chopper blades.

"I hate you too."

Omar ran to the helicopter, his thighs burning with the effort in the deep sand. He couldn't hear if any shots were fired above the sound of the blades, but he zigzagged until he reached the chopper. He helped Mia into the helicopter and then climbed in after her. Zabid's eyes were almost as big as his face.

"Go! Go!" Omar screamed.

The pilot shifted the controls with shaky hands, and the chopper lifted, bullets spraying the metal. Omar shielded Mia from the onslaught of bullets. He twisted in his seat and tried to get in a couple of good marks before the helicopter was too far away.

A few minutes into the flight, when they were out of range and apparently undamaged, Omar finally started to relax.

"Ouch," Mia complained. "You're crushing my hip."

Omar shifted over. He'd practically been sitting on top of her leg. He turned and grinned at her.

"You planned this."

His grin widened. "I did." Then Omar slid his hands around her waist and pulled her toward him. Her eyes closed just as their lips touched. He kissed her long and hard, knowing that she might not let him do it again.

ာ၇၃ ၃၇ာ

OMAR WATCHED MIA SLEEP next to him on the plane. Her expression was peaceful now, but he still had yet to ask about her torn clothing. Zabid had been most helpful and found her new clothes when they'd reached the airport. He'd also booked them on the next flight out of San'ā. Now, in less than thirty minutes, they'd be landing in Salalah. They were headed to Shisur.

Omar didn't care that Rabbel was illegally excavating or had maybe tried to kill a pope, but sacrificing Alem and then kidnapping Mia . . . It was personal now.

Mia stirred and cracked open her eyes.

"Hi, sweetheart." He waited for her to thump him, but she just blinked. *Good sign. Maybe that kiss wasn't so bad after all.* "How are you feeling?"

Mia took a deep breath. "Better."

"What happened at the compound?"

"I had some inside information about Rabbel. He had a stolen artifact from the tomb that was discovered in Jerusalem."

"The one that was bombed?"

"You already know about that?"

He nodded. "So you went alone . . . to get this ring?"

"You were busy breaking in to the museum." She cast him a half smile. "And Levy seemed to think it was safe enough."

"Lousy decision," he said, trying to keep his voice low.

"Omar—"

"It's not about being *politically correct*, Mia. You're a woman. How could you be safe going someplace like that by yourself?"

Her face flushed. "I can take care of myself."

"If you call tied up in a storage room, half-dressed, taking care of yourself."

"You should have seen the other guy." Mia's eyes flashed.

Omar shook his head. "It makes me sick that anything could have happened to you." He eyed her, gauging her reaction. She seemed calm enough. "Do you want to talk about it?"

"Nothing happened," she said.

He wasn't sure if he believed her. "Tell me about the ring."

"I can't disclose that information."

"Oh, come on. I won't tell Levy."

Mia shook her curls. "This doesn't have anything to do with him."

If it didn't have anything to do with Levy, then what was it? "I can help you," he ventured. "I can hire a helicopter and storm another compound in the middle of a desert if that would make a difference."

A faint smile reached her eyes. "You've done . . . more than enough."

"Or I could kiss you again, but only if it would *really* help." He winked at her, but was surprised when her eyes filled with tears. "I'm sorry," he whispered. She was scaring him. He wasn't used to the vulnerable Mia. "If I knew it would upset you—"

"It's not that. The ring is very important to someone I care a lot about."

Omar felt stung. Mia turned away and looked out the window. The seat belt light flashed on just as the plane started to descend.

He didn't know what to say. But if it was so important to Mia, it would be important to him too. Even if he were hurt in the process. He stared at his hands, thinking. This must be what people mean by selfless love. He blew out a breath of air. Maybe it was time he tried a little of it.

Chapter Thirty-nine

Sa'ba
960 b.c.

THE IMAGE OF AZHARA'S forlorn figure, riding atop a camel, burned itself into Nicaula's mind. The queen had dressed her sister in a robe of tightly woven flax, dyed indigo. The good-bye at Eloth was brief, but Nicaula had been choked with emotion.

Now, as her caravan approached Sa'ba, she proceeded with mixed feelings. The story of her marriage to Solomon would have certainly reached her kingdom, as well as news of the expected child.

She glanced down at her flat abdomen, her hand absently touching the space where no child grew. Or would ever grow. She would live out the remainder of her years as barren as a scorched wheat field. The gods had seen fit to curse her in matters of love. Her sister, Azhara, would be the one to carry on their father's name.

"O Queen," a voice spoke behind her.

Nicaula reined her camel and turned. Seeing Batal's face in the moonlight, she longed to share her secret. But would he think she was a coward, a temptress, a deceiver? She couldn't return to Sa'ba.

The people would know of her treachery when no child arrived.

Batal grew closer, and she suddenly knew what she had to do—if only to protect the name of Solomon and Yahweh. She pulled her camel next to Batal's horse and reached out her hand.

His eyes curious, he clasped her hand.

"I cannot return to Sa'ba," she whispered. "I will explain later, but we must continue to Ubar."

Batal nodded, unquestioning trust in his gaze. Then he turned swiftly from her. He commanded a few men to stay with the queen. The rest were to continue on to Sa'ba with the camels and supplies. The queen would return to her birth land for a brief stay.

After the caravan separated, Nicaula urged her camel ahead. She was grateful for the darkness so the others couldn't see her consternation.

Batal came up next to her and rode in silence for a few moments. "Are you unwell?"

"My soul is beyond repair."

"I cannot believe that, O Queen," Batal said, his voice soft. "You have the favor of the great king of Jerusalem and carry his royal child."

After a brief hesitation, Nicaula made her decision. "I do not carry his child."

Batal arched a brow. "Have you lost it? Is that why you are ill?"

"I'm not ill. I never carried his child. I never went to his bed. I never pledged to be his wife."

"I saw you marry him . . ."

"That was Azhara dressed in my clothing."

Batal stared at Nicaula, emotions crisscrossing his face. "You're not married?"

"No."

He looked ahead then back to her. "You're not married?"

"You already asked that."

"I . . ." Batal fell into silence. He pulled his horse alongside the queen's camel so that their legs touched. He placed his hand over hers. "Can you claim the child was lost?" His palm was hot against her skin.

"I have lived this lie too long, and to reveal it will desecrate the king's name." She looked beseechingly into his eyes. "I need your protection, and I'll find that only in Ubar. I need to go into hiding until the baby is supposed to be born. Then I'll have to fake a tragedy."

He squeezed her hand. "We'll ride through the night and not stop until you are home."

She nodded, a lump closing her throat. She wanted to throw her arms around him and thank him for not judging her.

He kept his horse close to her. "Come onto my horse. It's much faster than your camel, and soon we'll leave the city of Jerusalem in your past."

Nicaula held on to Batal's arm and switched over to his horse, sitting in front of him. A servant scurried forward and took the camel's reins. Batal wrapped his arm about her waist and held her tight. "Aiyah!"

The horse leapt forward, its hooves thundering through the empty desert. Nicaula leaned against Batal and closed her eyes as the desert wind rushed by. Nicaula's headdress loosened until it was lost in the wind, and her hair streamed out behind. What would become of her? Would she have to live as a recluse the rest of her life?

Through the sand and clay they rode, stopping only for sleep and refreshment. The hours and days passed, and slowly, the distance increased between the queen and Sa'ba.

When they arrived in central Ubar, it was the middle of the

night after the fourth day of traveling. The streets were quiet and the structures dark.

Batal and the other men led the way to the palace situated on the top of a small hillside. The sleeping guards were startled awake by the approaching group. They bowed in embarrassment and scurried to make preparations. Then several female slaves appeared, quickly lighting a fire and heating water for tea. One approached the queen and removed her outer cloak. A cushion was brought, and Nicaula sank into it, trembling with exhaustion.

"The bedchamber will be prepared immediately," one servant said before hurrying away.

When her chamber was ready, Nicaula rose to her feet, cup of tea in hand, and walked to her rooms. They seemed plainer and smaller than she remembered, but they were delightfully familiar. The oil lamps had been lit and the old coverlet replaced with a new one. The only thing missing was Azhara.

Nicaula fell onto the bed, kicking off her sandals. Two servants lingered at the entrance, and she waved them away. When the door closed, she hovered between sleep and awareness until, quite completely, she fell headlong into her dreams.

Chapter Forty

Salalah, Oman

OMAR SLAMMED THE DOOR on the Nissan truck after seeing that Mia was settled safely in the passenger seat of the rental. She wanted to make a stop before they went to check on Alem. Then they'd head to Shisur and get ready for Rabbel's grand entrance.

As Omar walked around to the driver's side, he scrolled through the latest message from Levy. *See you in Shisur.*

Omar smiled to himself, inhaling the warm sea air. *I knew he couldn't stay away. Plus, he probably wants to stake his territory with Mia again.* Ever since the kiss in the helicopter, Omar had renewed hope, and being in this beautiful coastal town wouldn't hurt. Not that Mia had exactly warmed up to him, but at least she hadn't slugged him in the last hour. Progress.

"So where are we going?" he asked as he hopped into the truck.

"I'll tell you where to turn," Mia said.

"Are you sure you're up to this?"

Mia had practically hobbled through the airport to the rental car desk. "It's my job."

He grimaced. She could be such a pain when she wanted. "So

who's the lucky guy?"

"The who?"

"You know, the guy who gets the ring?"

She lifted a shoulder, keeping quiet.

Great. This day just keeps getting longer. His head started a dull throb, and he grabbed a couple of aspirin from his bag and swallowed them dry.

Through the winding streets of the city, Mia navigated, seeming to know her way quite well. Omar focused on the driving, the image of the ring box burning in his mind, until she told him to pull over. He straightened and took in his surroundings—they had stopped in a very nice neighborhood. The streets were wide and quiet, bordered by mature palms, and behind the ten-foot walls of the properties sat large compounds built for wealthy families.

Popping her door open, Mia said, "I'll be back in twenty minutes."

"No, you don't." He reached over and grabbed her arm. "I'm going with you."

"Sorry." She tugged from his grasp. "I have to do this alone."

"The last time you did something alone—"

"Twenty minutes. Then you can call in the forces."

"At least tell me the house number."

Reluctantly she said, "341." Mia pulled a scarf over her head and melted into the neighborhood, looking like just another Omani woman going about her errands.

Omar waited as long as he could stand it. He'd be an idiot to let Mia walk into some snake pit alone—even if the snakes were of the harmless garden variety.

Exactly three minutes passed before he climbed out of the truck. He walked quickly, but not too fast, keeping his nose buried in a newspaper. He passed a tall, metal gate, and a casual glance confirmed his earlier assumption—large homes built for the rich.

The street ran on an incline, and soon Omar's calves burned. *Been sitting on my rear too long; need another good chase through the streets*, he thought as he looked for 341.

He slowed his pace when he reached the house sporting ٣٤١. He found a rock under a nearby bush and continued to the next estate. Stopping in front of the security box, he opened the cover and used the rock to smash the inside panel.

Although the alarm was silent on the outside, it certainly blared throughout the house on the other side of the gate. He hurried to 341 and hid in the bushes, knowing that any good neighbor would help a friend in need.

Seven minutes later, sirens blared from all sides, and three police cars pulled up and screeched to a stop. The women and children in the other house ran to the gate. Omar stayed in position until he saw a person emerge from 341.

Perfect.

The man who looked like a butler approached the gate, chewing something and wiping his bushy mustache with a cloth napkin. He withdrew a key from his pocket and unlocked the large metal divider. Omar watched him rush to the neighbors and speak to the police. At that instant, Omar rose from the bushes and walked through the gate in plain view of everyone.

He figured he had at least ten minutes to locate Mia and get out of the neighborhood. He walked around the boxy house, staying close to the foliage, when he saw the servants' entrance. Moving through the door, he paused.

Mia's voice came from somewhere inside the house.

He inched down the long hallway, careful to keep his footsteps on the Turkish carpets silent. He stopped in front of a closed set of double doors.

Mia's voice was clear now. "No. That was not the arrangement."

The hairs on the back of Omar's neck stood.

A male voice said, "This deal is no good. I can pay right now— no paperwork, and here's extra for the personal delivery."

Mia uttered a small yelp, and something crashed to the floor.

Omar pushed against the doors, but they were locked. "Mia!"

Silence.

He aimed his pistol at the door and cocked it just as the door swung open. Mia's flushed face stared at him.

Omar lowered the gun. "Are you all right?" He moved forward as she backed away.

"I told you to wait in the truck," she hissed. Behind her, a chair was tipped over.

Then a hand snaked around her shoulder, and a face came into view. A heavyset man with slicked-back hair placed his cheek against Mia's head. His mustache was long and droopy, as if he'd oiled it into place.

For the second time, Omar nearly pulled the trigger. "Get your hands off her," he growled.

The man laughed, deep and rich. "Who's this boy you bring to my home? One of your pets?"

"He's leaving now." She pointed toward the door and jerked her head to the side.

Then Omar realized why the man looked so familiar. He was the director of GOAMM, none other than Abdallah Saleh al-Qadi himself. His picture had been in the PDF file, and he couldn't keep his hands off Mia.

Omar felt sick. Obviously the director wouldn't be acting like that if Mia hadn't welcomed it, and a woman like her wouldn't do what she didn't want to. She'd made that plain enough.

"This is part of the plan, then?" Omar asked, his gaze searing into his former girlfriend. Images of Mia with David, and now al-Qadi, etched into his mind.

"This is none of your concern," she said, her voice clipped.

"But the ring—"

"Was a very generous gift," al-Qadi said. He placed his hands on Mia's shoulders possessively, his eyes greedy. He wiggled his middle finger, and Omar noticed the heavy metal ring on it. "Just trying it on for size before I have to put it in the museum." He winked at Mia.

Omar stared at the ring. He'd seen it before. No, it wasn't the ring itself that he'd seen. He moved closer, ignoring Mia's death-wish glare directed at him. The ring had a design—a snake intertwined with a flower.

The symbol from the sketch . . . the tomb. Then it hit him. *Mia's tattoo.* She'd had it done just before their breakup. Her tattoo matched the design on the ring.

Omar raised his gun again, aiming at the director. Something was terribly wrong. Either Mia had completely lied to him, or he was in the worst nightmare imaginable. "Hand over the ring."

"Knock it off, *Omar*," Mia said. "You're making a very big mistake."

Omar kept the gun leveled at al-Qadi.

Mia flinched, but didn't relinquish her position. In fact, she leaned against the man, seeming to take comfort in his closeness. After a couple of tense seconds staring down Omar, Mia turned her face toward the well-oiled director and pushed her lips into a pout. "Maybe we could let him have a look, sweetie."

The director's face softened as he smiled at her. "Only if he puts that thing down."

Mia glared at Omar. "Put the gun down." Then she looked at al-

Qadi with a sickening puppy-dog gaze, her hand caressing the back of his neck. "Sorry. He's just ornery."

The director's reserve melted. He twisted the ring off and walked to Omar, placing it in his hand.

Omar fingered the weight of the object. So this was the artifact in the mysterious package. "Where'd you get it?"

Mia rolled her eyes, sighing with exasperation. "Shisur, of course. I 'borrowed' it from the tomb that was just discovered. When it hits the media, it will be big news."

Relief flooded through Omar as he clued into Mia's lie. She was playing this guy, or at least playing at *something*.

The director laughed—a big belly laugh. "*Borrow.* You're funny."

"I just wanted to show it to my sweetie before I take it to San'ā," she said, playfully nudging the director. She blinked her long lashes at him. "Remember when I told you about my crazy half-brother?"

He flushed with pleasure and smiled, revealing a couple of gold teeth. "Of course." He turned to Omar and held out a beefy hand. "Nice to meet you."

Disgust and anger pulsing through him, Omar managed to shake the man's moist hand. He itched to pile drive the guy. Whatever game Mia was playing, he couldn't wait to find out.

Mia swatted the director on the arm. "We'd better get back before someone notices it missing." She kissed his cheek, and when he leaned in for more, Mia pulled away. "Another time, perhaps?"

"I'll be waiting here." He smiled a greasy smile.

She took the ring from Omar, waved at al-Qadi, then linked arms with Omar and practically dragged him from the room.

He followed Mia out of the front entrance, with one last look behind at the massive pillars framing the wide porch. Police lights from the neighbors' reflected off the outside garden wall. Mia put on her scarf and walked briskly to the gates, ignoring everyone.

Once they passed the commotion of the police at the neighboring house, Omar started in. "What was that all about?"

"Just doing my job."

"Your job?" The skin around his neck boiled. "*Kissing* that man?"

She ignored him and hurried to the truck. Without waiting for him to catch up, she climbed into the driver's seat and started the engine.

Omar flung the passenger door open and jumped in just as she pressed the accelerator. He grabbed her arm as she drove. "Look at me!"

Mia yanked her arm away, her face reddening.

"Who else is there?" Omar yelled. "Is this how the female operatives work? Was al-Qadi on your list after David? Did you sleep with him as part of your cover?"

Mia slammed on the brakes and turned her furious expression to meet his. "If you even have to *ask* me that . . ." She tossed the ring into his lap. "Take the stupid thing. It's just a fake."

"A fake? I risked my life for a *fake*?"

"If you want to see it that way," Mia spat out. "It's not really from Shisur, but it's a replica of a ring found at the tomb in northern Jerusalem. The real one is in protective custody."

Omar examined the ring again. "But this is the emblem of the queen of Sheba. That would prove—"

"I know," Mia said. "And it will, but not yet."

He thumped the back of his head against the seat. "Why is the same emblem on your ankle? You had that tattooed before the Jerusalem tomb was discovered."

She looked over her shoulder before pulling onto the street

again. "It's a long story."

Omar folded his arms. "Try me."

She hesitated, and Omar groaned. "You're driving me insane. Forget our undercover work, forget that we ever dated, forget Levy, al-Qadi, and whoever else . . . If we haven't been through enough together to warrant a little friendship and trust, I'll get out right now. You won't have to hear from me again. Take your fake ring and your double life—I've had enough."

Mia's jaw tightened, but Omar saw that she was thinking. "The ring was sent to me from the patriarch," she said.

"What patriarch?"

"The Coptic pope—the one Rabbel tried to assassinate. The patriarch's also the one who sent those people we met by Shisur— the French man and American woman."

Omar's mind reeled. "I thought you were sent here by Levy, like me."

"Levy's working with the patriarch. This was the most direct way of proving that al-Qadi is guilty of embezzling stolen artifacts."

"So you bring him a fake and talk him into buying it."

"I tell him I'm working for AWP and talk him into placing an order for whatever comes out of the tomb."

Omar shook his head. "So the stuff about the tomb in Shisur was also a fake?"

Mia smiled. "That just happened to be a nice coincidence. The American woman we met fell into a tomb while we were in San'ā. It hasn't hit the media yet, but al-Qadi knew about it—which just proves his involvement even more."

"Buying a few artifacts off the black market will only get his hand slapped," Omar said.

"You're right, but *someone* paid for the assassination attempt," Mia said just above the hum of the engine. "And someone set off the bomb in Jerusalem."

"You think it was al-Qadi?"

"Yes. And I think he used Yemeni government money. He came to Oman to set up a secret alliance with AWP—away from his government colleagues. Keeping the information found in the tomb a secret is AWP's priority. The two men in the world who could interpret the map without so much effort are the best of friends. One is dead, the other in lockdown."

"Dr. Lyon?"

"How did you know?" she asked.

"I have some things I need to tell you too. But first, explain to me how Levy got ahold of this ancient ring, and why is he keeping it a secret?"

"He didn't share that information." Mia stared ahead, a strange look in her eyes.

"So you couldn't have asked him?"

"It's not that easy."

"Enlighten me."

She met his gaze. "The boss takes his name very seriously. He thinks he's descended from *the* David, father to King Solomon. It's given the man quite an ego, I'd say." She maneuvered along the main street. "He'd protect the Bible with his life."

"A lot of people would, so *why* wouldn't he want the ring shown to the world?"

"It's all part of the plan. He's using the ring as bait. Let's just say he wants me to find the highest bidder," she said.

Omar thumped the dashboard. "Ah, I knew he was crooked."

"Not for *himself*. He'll dangle it in front of a few notables and see who takes the first leap."

"It sounds like a great way to build a retirement fund."

"Omar . . ."

He exhaled, shaking his head. "It's unbelievable. You have evidence of the queen of Sheba's very existence in Jerusalem, evidence that King David and King Solomon reigned . . . but you're putting your trust in Levy, risking your life, and pretending to find a buyer?"

"This artifact might draw out the illicit collectors, but it's not going to prove that David or Solomon were true kings." She paused. "How much do you know about what was found in the tomb?"

Now it was Omar's turn to come clean. "I was in the tomb."

Her eyes widened.

"On my last assignment, I was on a digging crew, and we broke into the tomb."

"So you know about the lineage of kings outlined on the walls."

Nodding, Omar said, "I don't have an answer for Tambariah or the others yet." He pulled the PDF papers from his bag. "What I want to know is, who is Dr. Lyon, and how is he connected?"

"As I said, he and the patriarch were . . . close friends," she said. "They were old colleagues and brilliant scholars, each in their own right. In the archaeological world, they were known as the experts on the queen of Sheba. So when the attempted assassination of the patriarch happened, Dr. Lyon demanded that the tomb be sealed off from the public. Rumors flew that he had some pretty potent information about the queen's tomb. Putting the information together—"

"It's quite plain why Dr. Lyon was murdered," Omar finished, leafing through the pages and ignoring Mia's incredulous stare. "I did a little research on my own." He knew he was taking a risk by telling her this, but she had to understand the ramifications of the game that was being played. He told her about the study written by Lyon that he found in the museum. Then he removed the sketch of the seven palms, the one with the seven labeled names, and handed it over to her.

She took it, and at the next traffic light, she looked at the names. "What do they say?"

"Translated from Aramaic, these names appear to be those with whom the queen was closely associated." Omar pointed to the center of the sketch, where the symbol of the snake intertwined with the flower. "This flower-and-snake symbol is somehow associated with all these palm trees—leading me to suppose that this map has something to do with a garden. The queen is in the center of the garden."

Mia nodded, but didn't look too surprised.

"So, I'm very interested to know more about this tomb in Shisur. Did Levy fill you in yet?"

"No. The patriarch told me."

"You have a Coptic pope calling you?"

Mia smiled. "Sounds strange when you put it that way."

"What do you know about the Shisur tomb?"

"Practically nothing—just that the American woman stumbled into it and excavation has already started."

Omar turned over the ring, looking at the symbol. "What does it mean?"

"The flower is a canna lily—an elegant flower with exotic-colored blossoms. The petals are known for their reflection," she said. "And you can probably guess what the snake is."

"Satan in the garden?"

"No." Mia smirked. "Anciently, snake goddesses were believed to have psychic powers like a female oracle. The female oracle is also fearless and can handle snakes with confidence. Some legends that surround the queen of Sheba say she had snake blood in her, making her a seer. A snake goddess is the symbol of female justice and equality, and through the ceremony of controlling a snake, the social power of women is recognized."

"All the things that the queen represented," Omar mused.

"Exactly." Mia turned onto the main road that led to the hospital. "With the rise of male-dominated religions around the world, women lost their social and economic power. In this century, they're finally starting to gain it back."

"Do you think the queen charmed snakes as well as you do?"

Mia shrugged, pursing her lips.

"Is that why you tattooed the symbol on your ankle?"

She shook her head, her curls bouncing against her neck. Omar reached over and lightly touched her shoulder.

"What are you doing?" she asked.

"Nothing."

A faint smile reached her face as she pulled into the hospital parking lot. "Let's leave it at that."

"Let's not."

She turned off the truck and let her hands fall to her lap.

Omar leaned close to her, breathing in her fragrance. He trailed his fingers up her neck then to the back of her head. She stiffened, and he pulled away. "What?"

"I just . . . I don't want you to think that I enjoyed how I acted around al-Qadi." She looked at him, her eyes imploring.

"I understand. Part of the job."

She grabbed his hand. "No, really. Listen to me."

Omar straightened and nodded. "I'm all about listening. Shoot."

"Being a woman in this line of work basically sucks. Half the time, I'm not taken seriously; the other half, I'm just plain used." She released his hand and folded her arms. "If having a tattoo that reminds me of who I really am helps me, then it's nobody's business. You know, sometimes a woman just wants a friend she can trust. She doesn't want to worry about the whole relationship thing.

Will he hold my hand? Will he kiss me? Will he call me? Will he leave me?"

He watched her, his stomach in knots.

She rubbed her arms, staring out the window.

"Am I your friend?"

She didn't respond for a long moment. "I hope so."

Omar put his arm around her, and she laid her head against his shoulder. "No matter what, I'm your friend." He pretended to check his watch. "It's been at least ten minutes since we've argued. I call that a good start."

Mia laughed, and Omar's heart thumped at the sound. He kissed the top of her head. "Let's see if we can double it." Reluctantly, he let her go, telling himself to take it slow. This was too precious to mess up now. He eyed the hospital. "Better get in there."

"I'll wait."

Chapter Forty-one

Salalah, Oman

OMAR CLIMBED OUT OF the truck and strode to the hospital doors. He wanted to hurry back before Mia changed her mind about him. He'd check on Alem; then he and Mia could leave for Shisur. He entered the hospital just as a message came onto his phone. Omar shook his head at the string of instructions from Levy. The man wasn't going to make his arrival easy.

"Omar!" someone said.

He whirled around, expecting to see a stern-faced doctor. It was Alem—stitches, gauze strips, and all. "What are you doing down here?" Omar asked.

Next to Alem stood a tall young woman, her sandy hair pulled into a loose bun, wisps of blonde framing her pretty face—the American.

He stared at her. Hadn't Mia just told him this woman found a tomb in Shisur? So why was she in Salalah?

She took a step forward and offered a hand. "Jade Holmes."

"Yes . . . uh . . . Shouldn't you still be in bed?" He looked from one to the other.

"We need a ride to Shisur," Alem said, his face twisting into a smile, contorting the ugly welts on his cheeks. If Alem had said "the moon," Omar couldn't have been more surprised. Was the American woman a mad shrink, trying to get Alem to face his demons?

Omar eyed Jade. "And why are you here?"

"I became dehydrated at Shisur and was brought here. I met Alem in the process," Jade said.

"Look, the police haven't caught the men who did this to you," Omar said to Alem. "I think you should leave the country until the men are caught and safely put away. I'll be happy to take you to the airport if the hospital has released you."

The look in Alem's eyes told Omar that this argument wasn't going to be easy. But how could Omar tell these people that his orders came from Israeli Intelligence or that Alem was part of an international crime?

Alem shook his head. "It's *very* important that we leave for Shisur as soon as possible."

This must have something to do with the tomb. He thought about Mia in the truck. She'd be furious. Two extra people meant more danger for everyone when Rabbel's crew showed up at the site. But if Jade and the French man had been commissioned by the patriarch to excavate Shisur, she had just as much right as anyone to be there.

It was Alem who was the problem.

Omar looked from one to the other, debating. He doubted Alem would stay behind, but it would directly defy Levy's orders. *And why do I care?*

"All right."

Jade stepped forward and embraced Omar. "Thank you so much."

He stiffened and patted her lightly on the back. *If only Mia could see me now, maybe she'd appreciate me more.*

"I was just about to trade in my truck for a more comfortable SUV."

Jade smiled, her eyes bright with excitement. "Thank you for this."

He'd never known a woman who was excited about traveling into a decimated land of nothing. Except for Mia, maybe, but she was a nut. "Do you need to check out?"

"Already done," Alem said. He took Jade's arm and started toward the doors.

"Here we go," Omar muttered to himself, following the chirpy pair outside. He saw Mia's head snap to attention. She climbed out of the truck and walked to Alem.

"They're coming to Shisur with us," Omar announced. Mia threw him a pointed look, but she didn't argue.

Jade loaded her bag into the bed of the truck.

"I'll sit in the bed, you guys up front," Omar said.

First stop—car rental agency in town. As Mia pulled next to the rental lot, Omar saw that the pickings were slim. There was one Toyota Land Cruiser and a couple of smaller trucks like the one they already had, and the rest were sedans.

Omar hopped out of the bed. "Pull around the side, out of sight," he told Mia.

"Don't do anything stupid," she said.

Omar watched the truck leave the lot and turn right. Satisfied, he removed a fresh ID and a military-style cap from his bag. He was going on a hunch, but if it worked, he would be killing two birds with one stone.

He strode to the rental counter, ignoring the few people waiting in line. Slapping his ID onto the counter, he said, "I have a reservation."

The woman behind the counter flinched. "Please wait your turn."

"This is urgent government business. I'm picking up that Land Cruiser over there."

The woman looked apologetically at the waiting customer then typed something into her computer. "The reservation was made under another name, sir."

"Of course it was, and I'm here to pick it up."

The woman excused herself. Moments later, she returned with a short, nervous-looking man sporting round spectacles on his nose.

"Are you my driver?" Omar demanded.

The man's face reddened. "No, I'm the manager. Come with me."

Omar followed him into the back room—an office cluttered with years of disorder.

The manager turned to face him. "No one told me you were coming."

Omar swore. "The director of GOAMM sent me to deliver a package. I need the Land Cruiser right away."

The manager's face paled as he blurted, "We've done nothing wrong."

"It's not a death warrant," Omar said, flashing his badge again. "I just need the SUV."

The man nodded, beads of sweat popping onto his forehead. "I guess I didn't get the message."

"Just hand me the keys, and I won't mention the mistake."

"All right." The manager wiped his brow with his sleeve. He pulled the radio from his belt and spoke into it.

Three minutes later, a young kid, no more than sixteen, entered the office and handed over the keys. After the boy left, Omar turned to the manager. "I also need a copy of this month's deliveries authorized by Mr. al-Qadi."

The manager dabbed his forehead then walked to the desk and shuffled through a stack of papers until he produced a legal pad with times, dates, and addresses scrawled across the page. "It will just take me a minute to make the copies."

The phone started ringing on the manager's desk, and when he turned to answer it, Omar snatched the legal pad, hurried out of the office, and sprinted to the Land Cruiser. Just as he started the engine, the manager came flying out of his office, shouting.

"Sorry, sir, can't hear you." Omar punched the accelerator and sped out of the parking lot.

He spun the car around the corner and screeched to a halt next to the waiting truck that Jade, Alem, and Mia were leaning against. Omar flung his door open and jumped out, yelling at them to hurry. He grabbed their bags from the sidewalk, made the transfer, and peeled from the curb just as the others shut their doors.

"Hang on," Omar shouted over the roar of the engine.

"I thought I said not to do anything stupid," Mia said.

"Guess I misunderstood." Omar careened through traffic. Then he made a hard right, catapulting them through an alley.

"Don't tell me you stole this." Mia's voice was furious. "That's all we need."

"Not exactly. Al-Qadi will get the bill."

"You could have used my credit card," Jade said.

"I didn't have time to go through the formalities." He waved the notepad he'd taken from the manager in the air. Mia snatched it.

"According to these papers," Omar continued, "we're only hours ahead of another excavation crew getting to Shisur. Several vehicles have been reserved by al-Qadi for Rabbel, who is part of AWP."

"Ancient World Piracy?" Jade said.

Omar nodded, glancing at Alem. "Rabbel is scheduled to go to Shisur."

Alem stiffened but said, "I'm still going."

"That's what I thought." Omar looked at Jade. "What else do you know about AWP?"

"Lucas said they were competition for us, and I don't think he liked it."

"Competition?" Omar paused as he rounded a corner at a high speed. "Sorry," he muttered, slowing down again. "'Competition' is an odd word to describe a corrupt agency that is undoubtedly bribing government officials to get away with murder and stealing."

"Murder?" Jade's voice sounded very small.

"Ever heard of Dr. Richard Lyon out of—"

"He was my professor," Jade said. "Lucas thought Lyon was murdered."

"This Lucas character has his fingers in everyone's dish." He grunted, slowing the truck as they neared a military checkpoint. He glanced at Alem and Jade. "Can you both hide behind the seats? We don't want the military to give anyone else our stats."

A guard had already exited the post. Omar cursed under his breath when he saw two more exit. There were enough to get nosy and peer inside the Land Cruiser.

Omar glanced at Mia. "We're going to need a little sweet talk."

"My pleasure."

As soon as the guard approached the window, Mia leaned over Omar. She waved two new packs of cigarettes.

The guard smiled and thanked her, and Mia laughed pleasantly. Then she offered a few bills. The guard accepted the cash and took a step back from the Toyota. Omar tried not to grin as the guard waved him through. "Excellent," he said under his breath. "Tell me one thing: Where'd you get those cigarettes?"

Mia crossed her arms, keeping a straight face. "Compliments of al-Qadi."

Behind them, Jade and Alem rose from their crouched positions.

Omar drove a few kilometers and then noticed that Mia was starting to drift to sleep. He was getting tired as well. He brought the SUV to a stop and rotated to look at Jade. "Feel up to driving?"

"Sure."

Omar and Mia traded Alem and Jade places. "Just stay on this road," he said. "If you have any questions, wake Mia up."

Mia threw a glare at Omar before settling into her seat and closing her eyes. He watched Jade, who drove the Land Cruiser along the road of sand. Her hair had escaped its clip, and the flyaway strands whipped against her shoulders in the wind that poured through the open window. Next to her, Alem's head bobbed as he drifted in and out of sleep. The wounds on his face had begun to heal, but they still had a long way to go.

Omar was exhausted, but wanted to talk to Jade without the others overhearing. When he was sure Mia was asleep, he leaned over the seat and said in a quiet voice, "I hear you found a tomb."

Jade jerked her head to the side and looked at Alem. He didn't stir.

"He didn't tell me, if that's what you think," Omar said.

"Yes, I fell into a tomb." She glanced over her shoulder at Mia.

"She knows too. What's wrong?"

"It's just that . . . some people didn't believe me. They told me it was just an empty cave. Then they took me to the hospital."

"Was Lucas one of those people?"

She nodded.

"Interesting," Omar said. "I guess we'll find out soon enough. I wonder if you've read the professor's work."

"Well, his textbook and syllabi, of course. I've seen a few of his articles too. Lucas . . ."

Another Lucas story, Omar thought.

". . . the study Dr. Lyon wrote is missing, and the head editor of *Saudi Aramco World* said he can't find it now. Lucas thinks Dr. Lyon was killed because of the information in it."

"I've seen it," Omar said.

"Where?"

"Well, I actually have a copy of it with me."

Jade's hands tightened on the steering wheel as she brought the SUV to a slow stop. She turned, her eyes fiery with interest. "Can I read it?"

Alem stirred and opened his eyes as Omar dug into his bag. Mia remained asleep. Omar handed over the article and watched Jade read it silently. When she finished, she said, "Lucas will know what to do with this information."

"What information?" Alem asked, taking the pages from her. He let out a low whistle. "He thinks the queen's tomb is in Shisur." He looked at Jade. "That might mean the cavern you fell into . . ."

She nodded, her eyes wide.

"According to the car rental agency, a whole slew of interested parties will be arriving at Shisur in the next twenty-four hours."

Jade stared at Omar. "Who *are* you?"

A chuckle came from Alem. "I asked Mia that very thing not long ago, but you won't get a straight answer out of either of them."

"I told you—" Omar started.

"No worries, man, no worries," Alem interrupted. "I'm just glad you're on our side." He waved away Omar's protest. Then he glanced at the article and asked, "But what does this part mean?" He cleared his throat and read, "*A finding that proves David and Solomon fictitious leads us to question the validity of the Bible. Will Israel's claim to Jerusalem be fraudulent and the Ethiopians'*

royal heritage turn out to be propaganda from the Middle-Ages?"
He turned to Omar. "Is it true about a tomb discovery in Northern Jerusalem?"

Even as Omar answered, "Yes," Jade was nodding her head. "You know about that too?"

"Lucas—"

"Ah. Self-explanatory, then . . . I saw the tomb in Jerusalem before the bombing."

"What did it look like?" Jade asked.

"Just like every other tomb, I suppose," Omar said with a smile. "It was quite ordinary. I was there with a work crew when we cut through the outer wall."

"Did you see the names of the kings?" Alem asked.

"Yes, but for only a few minutes."

"Were there symbols on the walls?" Jade asked.

"Some." Omar paused. "Now that I've told you my secret, tell me yours."

"What secret?" Jade asked, looked furtively at Alem.

"The tomb at Shisur."

Jade's face turned pink. "The cavern I fell into had writing on the walls. There was a stone that could have passed for a sarcophagus, but more significantly, I saw a symbol that Alem said is on his grandmother's tombstone."

Alem pulled out a piece of paper and held it up. Omar looked at the rough sketch of a snake intertwined with a flower—the canna lily, no less.

Omar took the paper and studied it for a moment. "Who have you told about this symbol?"

"No one," Jade said, confusion crossing her features.

"And Lucas sent you away?" Omar asked.

"He convinced her that she'd only imagined the sarcophagus,"

Alem cut in. "That's why we needed your help."

"As a taxi?"

"No," Alem said. "For your many skills."

Omar cracked a smile. "If it involves a tomb belonging to a queen, I'm at your service."

Alem pulled out another piece of paper. "When I was . . . tortured . . . they took a letter that I always carried with me. My grandmother wrote it, admonishing me to try to find the queen's tomb."

Omar nodded. He remembered seeing Alem read the well-worn letter.

"I couldn't understand what the crew boss would want with the letter—until I remembered the poem she included at the end." Alem passed over the paper. "I think I remembered most of it. A word or two might be reversed."

"Poem?" Omar took the page. He stopped dead at the first lines. They were the same verses he'd read on Mia's PDF.

> *O Queen of the South,*
> *Death began your journey*

He paused on the third line.

> *To that night when seven women held one man.*

"I just read this—it's from the Song of Songs. No, wait. Only some of this comes from Solomon's accolade." He grabbed his bag and took out the Bible he'd purchased in Yemen. Flipping to the Song of Solomon, he scanned the words. "Here it is: 'His cheeks are as a bed of spices, as sweet flowers: his lips like lilies.'"

He turned back to Alem's poem.

> *The feast of seven days brought him from your dreams,*

But your heart melted for another like incense spread gold upon cherubim

Until your desire became as bright as precious stones

Against your bed of spices, O Queen of the South.

Your lips are lilies; your chaplets of flowers fill palms of love.

Yet your virgin flower faded as the face of the serpent appeared.

As sunlight wasted, six branches closed, and flowers wilted.

Now the seven devils hide beneath the tomb,

Waiting as seven lamps still burn above,

Waiting for the queen of the South.

Omar looked at Alem. "What's the origin of this poem?"

"I assumed my grandmother wrote it."

"I don't think so." If Mia had a copy of the original etching, it was impossible that Alem's grandmother was the author. This poem was ancient, translated from Aramaic. Omar ran his finger along the lines, muttering, "Seven women, palms of love, six branches, seven lamps, virgin flower, serpents, waiting for the queen of the South."

Omar grabbed the sketch and started to count the branches of the palm trees. "Each tree has six branches." He looked from Alem to Jade. "I don't know what this is, but I think we have something here."

Alem eyed the sketch in Omar's hand. "How did you get ahold of that?"

Omar hesitated. "In an unorthodox manner."

"I can very well imagine that," Jade said.

"So you are telling us this is hot property?" Alem asked with a laugh.

Omar winked at Jade. "It's hot no matter how I obtained it."

The three of them laughed, and Mia stirred with a soft moan.

"Let's go," Omar said. "We can fill Mia in later. But right now, I think we'd better get to Shisur as fast as we can."

Chapter Forty-two

Shisur, Oman

"WE'RE HERE." OMAR'S VOICE pierced through Jade's drowsy state.

She lifted her head, feeling the dull ache brought by trying to sleep upright. The oasis looked beautiful in the orange-red glow of the setting sun. The palms swayed majestically in the evening breeze, the tents dotting the earth as if they had since antiquity. A chain of smoke billowed from a campfire on the perimeter, and several men had gathered in a circle around it.

Jade's stomach twisted as she anticipated seeing Lucas again. As soon as their Land Cruiser was noticed, the men rose to their feet, and two men strode forward to meet them. One was Lucas.

Seeing him brought it all back with a hard slap, and his betrayal burned hot in her breast. He'd lied to her about the tomb. Anger flushed her face as she prepared to ask him why he deceived her.

As plain as midday, she saw that excavation work had taken place in the area where she'd fallen. She took a deep breath and twisted her ring furiously. It had dulled to amber. *Nervous.*

The four of them climbed out of the SUV. Their footprints

immediately filled with sand as the wind swirled around them. Jade shouldn't have been surprised to see both Lucas and Ismail carrying guns—ready to defend their claim, even if it resulted in violence. Was this Luc's true character? Did it take the discovery of a tomb to reveal it? She bit her trembling lip to keep her emotions in check. She was usually a mess when she was mad—and she didn't want to turn into a blubbering idiot in front of all these people.

She focused on her new friends. Omar's eyes flashed like a jaguar ready to pounce as his hand moved to his pocket and brandished a pistol. At least she had Alem and Omar on her side— two seemingly loyal guys.

Lucas scanned the group, his gaze settling on Jade. "Are you all right?" His unmistakable accent cut through the tension. His hand tightened on his Kalashnikov as he finished surveying the others. "Hello, again." He nodded to Omar then to Mia. His eyes settled on Alem. "You're looking much better."

Why is he being so normal? So cordial? Jade wondered.

"Alem, this is Lucas Morel," Omar said, throwing the politeness right back. "He was with Jade when she found you in the desert."

With a smile, Alem said, "I can't thank you enough. I wish I could repay you in some way."

Don't smile at him, Jade wanted to shout. *Lucas is the one who forced me to go to the hospital. He lied to me about the tomb.*

Lucas acknowledged Alem then moved his focus back to Jade. He took a step toward her, but she shrank back. "Why did you leave the hospital? I was going to check on you in the morning."

To make sure I didn't *leave the hospital.* She forced a smile and glanced between Lucas and Ismail, her insides crawling with uncertainty. Surrounded by people who believed her story, Lucas was acting far from the tyrant she'd conjured up in her mind. In fact, he looked quite handsome as the desert wind blew his hair across his face. "The doctor seemed to think I was just fine," she managed.

Lucas nodded, hesitation in his eyes. "Great news. I think you should still take it easy, though."

He just wants to get me out of the way again. "I will when I finish my research."

Lucas looked at her sharply, and Jade wondered if anyone else had noticed.

"You must join us for supper," Ismail cut in. His broad smile welcomed the entire group. "Are you passing through?"

Omar answered, "We've come to do some of our own excavation, although we'll set up away from your roped-off area."

Lucas's smile was amiable enough, but Jade recognized a steely glint in his eyes.

They unloaded a few things from the SUV and joined the crew for supper. Omar presented fresh tomatoes and cucumbers purchased from a roadside stand, which the Yemeni men eagerly accepted. Jade stayed by Mia, avoiding Lucas.

"Omar said you were stuck in Marib," Jade said as they both ate their rice.

"Yes. I was working on a contract project when things went wrong."

Jade noticed a haunted look in her eyes. Omar had told her and Alem about hiring a helicopter to rescue Mia. Jade could very well understand Omar's near obsession with making sure the woman was all right . . . not to mention that it appeared he'd rescued her from a dangerous situation. "Omar seems like a really decent guy."

Mia raised an eyebrow. "He can be impulsive, so I'm surprised he didn't charter another helicopter and fly us all here."

"Impulsive?" Jade tried to hold back a laugh. "More like

reckless."

"That too," Mia whispered with a smile. She turned her attention to the men's conversation.

Omar had wasted no time in confronting Lucas. "Even under conditions of severe dehydration, it's still possible to be coherent in your surroundings."

"Undoubtedly," Lucas responded in a smooth tone. "Ismail examined the cavern, found nothing, and it's now sealed off to prevent further danger."

Omar's eyes were dark, doubtful, and Jade felt her heart rate pick up.

Luc's gaze locked with Jade's across the sparking fire. His expression burned through her, and for a moment, she wouldn't have been surprised if her hair spontaneously ignited. She couldn't deny the attraction, yet she was starting to hate herself for it. It was as if he had some power over her, and now, he seemed to be willing her to back him up.

"Take me there," Alem said. "I want to see the place."

A reverence fell over the Yemeni crew. Surviving a human sacrifice made Alem a legend. Ismail stood and bowed. "We would be honored."

Lucas leaped to his feet, his face dark in the fire's glow. "I cannot allow it. Your safety is in jeopardy."

Slowly, Alem removed some of his bandages and spread his arms. Gasps echoed around the circle. Reflected against the light of the fire, the carvings of his skin stood out, gory, yet fascinating. "I have returned to this place of death, and it is my last wish before leaving this oasis to see the cavern Jade speaks of."

The others waited in silence, seeing how it would play out. Lucas relaxed his shoulders and held up his hand. "At first light, then."

Omar nodded with approval, and Alem looked pleased. Jade felt the tension flee from her limbs, knowing that her questions would be answered once and for all. She wondered: If it hadn't been for Ismail's obvious move to please Alem, would Lucas have allowed the exploration?

Supper had disappeared, and the work crew reclined, sharing stories of previous excavations in other sites. Omar moved to unload the rest of the SUV, and Jade joined him. She couldn't just sit around the fire and try to avoid Lucas's penetrating gaze. She still had questions for him, but she hoped her answers would come in the morning.

"Satisfied?" Omar asked Jade when they were alone. He spread a tent cloth on the sandy ground.

"I know what I saw, but at times I doubt."

Omar straightened, and Jade felt him surveying her in the moonlight—unnerving her to the very core. "I don't doubt you."

"That's what Alem said. How long have you known each other?"

"Just a few weeks. Toiling under the hot sun for long stretches with someone reveals his character in no time." Omar threaded tent poles through the slots of the canopy. "How did you hook up with Lucas?"

"Through Dr. Lyon." Jade lifted the sleeping bags from the SUV and carried them to Omar.

"I'd be careful around Lucas," Omar said. "He seems to know an awful lot about Dr. Lyon. And considering that the professor was murdered . . ."

"I honestly can't believe Lucas is involved," Jade said. "I know he can be brusque and piously intelligent, and I don't understand why he's lying about the tomb, but to *kill* someone?"

"Seen it multiple times." Omar grunted as he bent over to

hammer the stakes into the crusty ground. As the sound pinged through the air, Mia rose to her feet and crossed over to them.

Jade noticed Omar's change in demeanor as Mia approached; it was like a fierce protectiveness. She guessed there was some sort of history between them.

"I'm almost finished," Omar said.

Mia nodded then turned from Omar and looked at Jade with curiosity. "Tell me about the cave you fell into."

Jade studied the woman in the rising moonlight. It looked as if she owned this desert—her beautiful olive skin, dark eyes, and soft, curling hair falling to her shoulders. "Alem showed me this sketch at the hospital," Jade said, withdrawing the page from her pocket. "This is what I saw on one of the walls."

Mia moved to her side and examined the simple drawing with a flashlight. She glanced at Omar and motioned for him to join them. In two strides, Omar was peering over Jade's shoulder.

"The symbol of Sheba," Mia breathed.

A shiver passed along Jade's neck. "So you recognize it too?"

"It seems that tomorrow is going to be a banner day," Mia said.

"You mean *tonight*," Omar corrected.

Mia and Jade both looked at him.

Omar lifted a shoulder. "Think about it. If Jade really did find a tomb, which I wholeheartedly believe, and Lucas really did try to get rid of her, do you think he'll allow us *near* the site?"

"But he said first thing in the morning—" Jade protested.

"I know what he said." Omar glanced at the dwindling fire and the group of lazing men surrounding it. "My bet is they collapse the opening tonight, or they create some sort of tragic diversion to get us out of the way."

"You think they'd kill one of us first?" Mia asked, her tone sarcastic.

"Either way, they're not going to let us near that tomb," Omar said.

Jade twisted the ring on her finger. What if Omar was right? Lucas did know a lot, maybe too conveniently. Why would he lead her all the way out here, though? He could have dumped her in Cairo. Whatever the answers, she felt as if she were slowly spinning into a living nightmare.

"What's your plan?" Mia's businesslike tone inspired Jade to try to think more rationally.

"Can't we just have an honest conversation with Lucas?" Jade asked. "The three of us against him should give us enough influence."

Omar snorted, looking up at the infinite stars spread across the night sky. "These men are experts, whoever they are, whomever they work for. Plus, they outnumber us three to one."

"Are you thinking AWP?" Mia asked.

"Possible," Omar said.

"Are you certain those men are Yemeni?"

"Does it really matter?" Omar sounded annoyed. "Do they know about the sketch on the Jerusalem tomb wall?"

Mia arched a brow. "Let's take this conversation somewhere else."

"Jade knows, Mia," Omar said. "I told her and Alem about the sketch and the names. I told them we know about the tomb. And Alem gave me a poem that came from his grandmother that I think you'll find *very* interesting."

Mia looked angry, but Jade guessed that Mia was probably surprised he had shared so much information.

Mia folded her arms, eyes narrowed. "Why don't you just take over, then? You ignore what Levy says; you ignore what I say. You don't care about anyone but yourself." She pushed a finger into his chest. "And now there are innocent people involved. We shouldn't have brought them back here. As soon as the AWP louts show up, it will be dangerous for everyone. You should have left me in Marib and let Levy handle Shisur."

Omar scoffed. "You were practically stripped and tied up in an underground storage room in the middle of nowhere!"

Not knowing whether she should be hearing all of this, Jade took a step back.

"An operation was being planned, and you knew that," Mia said, her voice harsh. "Besides, *I* am none of your business. You tell me to trust you . . . and now this. You don't trust *me*. It's like you're trying to get everyone on your side so you can show them what a great hero you are."

Jade saw the hurt displayed on Omar's face.

"'Thank you for rescuing me' would have been nice," he said, turning from her.

Both women watched him walk away.

Jade started to say, "I know it's not my business, but—"

"You're right," Mia said, deadpan. "It's none of your business."

Chapter Forty-three

Shisur, Oman

MUDDLED SHAPES LEERED ABOVE him—foul, chanting. He shrank from the knife, but the cuts continued, one after another, until he was mercifully numbed from the pain.

Opening his eyes with a start, Alem realized he'd been dreaming. He exhaled in relief, trying to block out the images. From where he had slept in the open desert, he saw Omar leaning against the Land Cruiser. A cigarette butt extended from his mouth, the dull glow a point of light in the dark, competing with the canopy of bright stars.

Alem stood and crossed to Omar. "How long did I sleep?"

"A couple of hours. I was just about to wake you."

Nodding, Alem looked toward the tents of the Yemeni workers. "Any sign?"

"Not yet," Omar said, flicking the cigarette to the ground.

"I didn't know you smoked."

"I don't." Omar kicked sand over the smoldering cigarette. "Let's go." He handed Alem something cold and hard.

"What?" Alem looked down at the pistol. "I don't think I—"

"Pray you won't have to use it then." Omar grabbed a length of rope from the Land Cruiser and slung it over his shoulder then gave Alem a backpack.

They moved to the line of palms and the roped-off excavation area.

"Wait!" Alem grabbed Omar by the sleeve. "There's someone sitting on the other side." The men stood for a moment, gripping their guns.

The figure rose, silhouetted against the moonlight. "Jade?" Alem said. She brought a finger to her lips.

"What are you doing here?" Alem asked.

"I was waiting for you. Isn't Mia coming?"

"No." Omar unwound his rope, secured one end to the closest palm, and then handed a flashlight to Jade. "Don't lose it."

She nodded. "Thanks for doing this, guys."

"Alem, you go first," Omar said.

Alem was surprised at how little effort it took to go down the rope. As he descended, he thought of the lecture Omar had given him about the signs of a cave-in, how to keep himself oriented to which way was up, and how much time he'd have to dig himself out before running out of air. His feet touched solid bottom. Then he pulled the rope taut and waited for Jade's descent. Soon, she came down the rope and joined him. Omar was next.

The three of them stood in a circle, each shining flashlights in different directions.

"There's the stone," Jade said, her voice sounding hollow.

Alem swung around and arched his light over the rectangular shape. He sucked in a breath of air as he realized the magnitude of what he was seeing.

"Amazing," Omar said as he walked toward the rock. He ran his hands along the top and the sides. "Just as I thought." He focused his light on the top of the sarcophagus. "See the inscription to the left?"

Alem nodded.

"The ancient cuneiform lettering predates Aramaic. *Wila'at.*"

"Wila'at was one of the many names used for the queen of Sheba," Jade said.

Her words sent prickles along the back of Alem's neck.

"What does the rest of it mean?" Jade asked.

Omar studied the ancient lettering for several moments. "I don't believe it."

Alem moved closer. "What is it?"

"I don't know if Wila'at is the name for the person in this sarcophagus because there's another name here—Batal." He looked at Alem. "The names on the sketch of palm trees—one was Batal."

Alem's breath caught.

"Let's have a look around," Omar said. They walked deeper into the cave, brushing away the dirt along the walls as they went. "Whether or not this is the queen's tomb, you certainly didn't imagine anything," he said to Jade.

She exhaled slowly, a smile on her face as she stopped next to him.

He tore away some dried roots from the stone wall. "Look at this." They stood in silent awe as he slowly deciphered the cuneiform lettering. "The queen of the Sabaeans."

Omar lowered his flashlight, his face glowing in the artificial light. "It appears, Ms. Holmes, that you may have discovered the queen of Sheba's tomb."

"Bravo!" a voice boomed behind them.

The three turned and found themselves gazing into the barrel of an Uzi.

Alem instinctively moved in front of Jade.

"What a surprise," Omar said in a cold voice.

"Indeed." Ismail grinned. "You just couldn't stay out of this place, could you?"

To Alem's astonishment, Ismail spoke flawless English.

"Why?" Jade asked, her hand on Alem's arm as she maneuvered to stand next to him.

Ismail's gaze moved to her face. "Do you really think I'd let someone like you, an *American woman*, come to *my* country and find *my* queen's tomb? I've been seeking to find Bilqis's resting place my entire life. I inherited that right from Dr. Lyon and the patriarch. I've done the research, made the sacrifices, and worked years in these conditions. I have paid my dues." His grin appeared again. "Too bad you had to involve so many."

With a trembling hand, Alem pulled out his borrowed pistol, seeing Omar do the same.

"Ah, this looks interesting," Ismail said. "Unfortunately, by the time you pull your triggers, my baby will have obliterated all three of you."

"Your glory will be short-lived, sir," Omar said. "You may be credited for discovering a tomb, but it will be only a matter of time before you're left to rot in prison."

"Very unlikely." Ismail raised the Uzi. "After I finish cleaning your blood off the walls, I have the perfect place to bury you. Not a soul in the world will have guessed what happened." He shone his light on Omar. "And your pretty lady out there will join you. In fact, she may already be meeting her maker, if the others have followed my instructions."

"What about Lucas? Is he with you?" Jade asked.

Ismail cocked his head to the side. "I'm very close to persuading him. It turns out that he has some serious financial concerns—a couple of his grants fell through after Lyon's death. I believe a healthy million will convince him." He glanced upward. "If he refuses, he'll be the offering to show our appreciation to the djinns and the god Bel."

In the instant that Ismail lifted his face, a flash of memory crossed Alem. *This* was the man who worked with Rabbel to mutilate him. Alem's body grew clammy all over as though he were going to vomit. Rage welled up from the deepest recess of his soul, and he moved forward, his pistol aimed dead center at Ismail's forehead.

"No!" Jade shouted.

Omar collided with Alem, shoving him against the wall. "What are you doing?"

"No one move!" Ismail shouted.

Alem took a shaky breath, his trembling body pinned between Omar's frame and the rock wall. "*He's* the one."

"Move back, all of you!" Ismail's tone bordered on alarm.

Omar raised his hands. "Relax, man." Another glance at Alem. "Right now we're going to do as he says."

Alem nodded, feeling as though his chest would burst with the swollen anger.

"All right, we're putting our guns on the floor." Omar backed away from Alem, hands in the air. "We surrender."

"How convenient for you," Ismail said, his lip curled in a sneer.

Alem noticed a hump on Omar's back as he bent to put his gun down. *Another weapon?*

"Come here, woman." Ismail shifted the Uzi so it was level with Jade's heart. She clenched her fists together as she stepped forward.

"You don't have to," Alem said, moving toward her protectively.

"One more move, and you'll be wearing her blood," Ismail said.

Alem glanced at Omar—whose face was unmoving, as hard as the stone surrounding them.

Jade walked to Ismail, who promptly grabbed her and turned her around, then wrapped his muscled arm about her neck in a headlock. She gasped, her chin trembling.

"What do you want with her?" Alem yelled, receiving a warning glare from Omar.

"The same thing any man wants from a piece of chattel," Ismail said. He spat on the ground—his eyes wild, fanatic. "Before the prophet Muhammed put restrictions on the lusts of man, women were in the place they were born to be—creations for man's pleasure. It's time all things were restored to their proper order."

Alem looked again at Omar. But he continued to stare straight ahead as if he had fallen under a trance.

It's up to me. Alem couldn't stand by helplessly. He'd come through the valley of death and risen to the other side for a purpose. Perhaps it was for this—to sacrifice his life for Jade. Being shot couldn't be much worse than what he'd already suffered.

As Ismail forced Jade to her knees, Alem dove for the pistol he'd abandoned. At the same moment, Omar lunged toward Ismail and Jade.

Several shots rang out, but Alem didn't have a chance to discover who had fired before everything went black.

Chapter Forty-four

Ubar
959 b.c.

AS THE MONTHS PASSED quietly in Ubar, Nicaula secluded herself, away from the eyes that might notice her flat stomach. The only visitor she received in her private chambers was the commander of her military.

Today she had summoned him and waited until he knelt at her feet to ask her question.

"Have you found her yet?"

Batal's steady gaze seemed to pierce through her. "Yes. She is about your age and will give birth very soon."

"Husband?"

"None. Her parents have hidden her in their shame."

Nicaula looked past him, knowing she had no other choice. "Smuggle her into the palace tonight."

When Batal bowed and left, she slowly rose. It had become an obsession—to hide her deceit. She could not turn back now.

Nicaula stood at the window opening, overlooking Ubar from her room. She watched the people scurry about, a pet goat bleating in the street, a child crying. It was her world, yet she no longer felt a part of it. She stood there as the sun moved high in the sky then watched as it descended beneath the west dunes. The evening deepened into night, and still she waited. When the moon had risen, the knock finally came.

The queen threw open the door and ushered the two people inside. Batal tried to say something, but Nicaula ignored him and stared at the girl. She looked very young and very afraid.

"How old are you?"

"Thirteen with the next monsoon."

Nicaula took in her appearance—scrawny arms and face, dark hair neatly plaited, thin, pointed chin, belly overextended. She looked at Batal. "Leave us."

He held her gaze for a moment, his eyes darker than his black cloak. Then he bowed and turned on his heel, leaving the two women alone.

⚬⚭⚭⚬

THREE DAYS LATER, THE girl gave birth to a daughter. The queen named her Marib. The queen refused visitors or gifts. Batal was the only one allowed to deliver food outside of her door. He told the people that the queen rested peacefully with her midwife, who cared for both the queen and the new child.

The girl never wept, never complained, but the night Batal came to take her away, the queen embraced her. "You will have a nice home in Sa'ba in exchange for your sacrifice. You will claim to be the widow of a wealthy merchant."

The girl's lower lip trembled as she nodded.

"You will yet have many children, and you may take comfort that your first child will be brought up as a princess."

The days passed slowly as Nicaula waited for Batal's return and report. Even when he was away, she thought of him.

Her nightmares of betrayal were replaced with dreams dominated by the commander. In each person she spoke to, she saw Batal's eyes, his hair, or his broad shoulders. He knew she could not marry, or her deceit would be made obvious. Still, she knew he watched her, and she watched him.

The obsession had never died.

And his absence had made it even worse.

As she prepared for the day, she tried to ignore the fire of longing in her chest. If she stopped seeing the commander everywhere she turned, he'd eventually leave her dreams and someday become a distant memory.

As soon as Batal delivered his report, she'd send him back to Sa'ba to train the military there. The queen dressed quickly, drawing courage from the resolve she'd made.

A sharp knock sounded at the door.

"State your name."

"Batal."

The queen composed herself by taking a deep breath and offering a quick prayer to her new god, Yahweh.

She opened the door. Batal towered against the door frame, his eyes extraordinarily dark in contrast to his light brown robe.

Nicaula touched her throat, suddenly unsure of her grand plan. How could she bear not seeing this man every day? She blinked rapidly against a hint of tears. She stepped aside and motioned for Batal to enter her chambers. He stepped inside and bowed.

"Is she settled?"

"Yes."

The queen motioned for him to sit on a cushion. He didn't move but gazed into her eyes.

"Batal . . ."

"I have news. The Bedouin boy, David, lost his mother. I brought him to Ubar."

Nicaula nodded. "Very good. He will live with me here." She looked away. "Perhaps I can make some retribution by raising a son of Solomon's."

"Nicaula . . ."

She held her breath—he had used her name again. She should reprimand him, but when she met his eyes, it was the last thing she desired.

Slowly he reached for her hand and brought it to his lips. "Why didn't you marry him?"

She knew he meant Solomon. She gazed into Batal's eyes and saw the raw hope there.

"Can I change your mind about marriage?" he asked.

"No." Her throat constricted, and she pulled her hand from him. "I cannot. I have imparted vast lies, and now I must spend my days alone to pay for them."

"Remember what King Solomon taught about Yahweh?"

"I remember every word, but I have betrayed Solomon and his god."

"The God of Israel does not expect us to suffer our entire lives for one wrong deed. A sin sacrifice can be made, and the sin that grieves you will transfer to the sacrificial animal." He paused, waiting for her to meet his eyes again. "How can you forget the image you saw when you touched the tree?"

She blinked back her tears.

"One day in the future, the son of Yahweh will come and be the ultimate sacrifice." He moved closer, too close. "But you can be happy *now*. You can have marriage and love too. A queen should have more than any other. She should not be forsaken."

"You expect me to find pleasure in life after I betrayed Solomon and persuaded Azhara to take my place? Now she raises her child alone in a strange land."

Batal touched her cheek, tracing his fingers along her jaw, stopping at her neck.

Heat from his touch spread through her, and she knew she should pull away, but she didn't.

"Azhara made sacrifices, yes. But yours are far greater. At least Azhara has known love and will be a mother with a son to carry on her name."

A tear splashed against Nicaula's cheek. "Azhara will be a good queen—"

"And she'll be very happy in Abyssinia . . . with wealth, power, and a healthy son," Batal finished.

She looked away from his gaze. "I want you to take the post of chief military commander in Sa'ba. In time you'll forget me."

He didn't say anything for a moment, but she was afraid to look at him. "Don't let happiness escape you," he whispered.

Batal dropped his hand, but they were still close enough to touch. "I can be happy without marriage, without a child of my own. You'll see."

"I'm not happy." His voice was quiet. "But if you say you can be happy without me, I'll accept the post in Sa'ba."

Nicaula stared at her twisting hands. "I don't care about my happiness. But I care about yours, and that is why I must ask one more thing of you."

"What?"

"Find a good woman in Sa'ba, and marry her."

He pulled her hands into his. "Do not command this of me, Nicaula," he said. "I cannot do this, not even for my queen. I have loved only one woman in my life, and if I cannot have her, I'll have no one at all."

Tears burned her eyes, looking at their intertwined hands. "You must find a wife," she said, but her voice trembled with doubt.

"Please." Batal leaned his head close to hers so that his breath touched her ear and neck. "O Nicaula," he whispered. "You are not listening to your heart. Marry me in secret. You'll be married to Solomon by day in the eyes of the people, and by night, you'll be mine. We'll be joined in heart and body as true husband and wife."

The queen closed her eyes and allowed herself to breathe him in, if even for a moment. Then she pulled away from his intoxicating touch, shaking her head.

But he wouldn't release her hands. "Tonight . . . meet me at your father's tomb. We will marry beneath the stars with Yahweh and your father's spirit as our witness."

Her heart pounded as she thought about marriage to Batal. Would it work? In Yahweh's view, she was not truly married. She lifted her gaze to meet Batal's. His eyes danced with hope, excitement . . . love.

She saw the different colors in his eyes—deep brown with streaks of fine gold. She knew that if she were blind, she'd still feel his presence each time he entered the room. Suddenly, her legs felt strange, as if they would no longer support her.

"Think on your answer." Batal kissed each of her hands. "I will be waiting. If you do not appear, I will know your final answer and leave for Sa'ba at the morning's first rays."

Nicaula nodded, not trusting herself to speak. She watched him leave the room, and as soon as the door shut, a wave of emptiness replaced his presence. Running to her bed, she threw herself upon it and wrapped her arms about her torso. It might work. It just might.

Chapter Forty-five

Shisur, Oman

ISMAIL'S BODY COLLAPSED ON top of Jade's, thrusting her to the ground. Something in her shoulder popped. I've been shot.

By Ismail's groans, she knew he was not dead . . . yet. His labored breathing resounded next to her ear. He struggled, not to move off her, but to reach for the nearby Uzi.

Jade's arms were pinned beneath her, so all she could do was watch helplessly as his hand inched closer to the weapon. The dropped flashlights cast odd beams about the tomb, and Ismail's face looked garish in the uneven glow. His teeth protruded over his lip.

"Omar! Alem!" Jade called. No one responded. Were their bodies lying lifeless just feet away?

Ismail's other hand locked around her neck, and the pressure prevented Jade from crying out again.

Suddenly, Ismail rolled off her, and Jade gulped for air. A scream curdled the air, and when Jade realized it wasn't her own, she scrambled to her feet.

Someone stood over Ismail, straddling his torso, a gun aimed point-blank at the center of his forehead.

"You have ten seconds to say your last prayer." Mia's clipped voice bounced off the walls.

"Please—don't kill me—"

"Say it," Mia commanded, her grip steady on the trigger.

"In the name of Allah, the Most Compassionate, the Most Merciful," Ismail said, his voice choking on his own sobs. He broke away from the traditional words and shouted, "O Allah, spare my life. Have mercy!"

Jade scooted away until her back collided with the wall. She had no doubt Mia would shoot the man in a matter of seconds. Her eyes scanned the tomb, looking for the others. Omar was crumpled against the far wall, and Alem lay just a few feet from her, flat on the ground. With relief, Jade saw that he was breathing. But Omar didn't look so lucky.

"Turn over." Mia's harsh voice sent a chill along Jade's back.

Ismail complied with Mia's order, and with a few deft strokes, she had tied his wrists together and then his ankles. She fastened another rope that dangled from the hole at the top of the cavern. "Pull him up," she called to someone above.

The rope slowly lifted Ismail's weight. Mia glanced at Jade. "If you aren't hurt, come help me."

By the time Jade reached her, Mia had turned Omar on his back and torn the fabric of his shirt. Pulling it off, she wadded the material and pressed it against his right shoulder. Blood immediately soaked it.

"Hold this in place," Mia said.

Jade slid her hands beneath Mia's and pushed against Omar's flesh. The blood oozed warm between Jade's fingers, and she felt dizzy.

"Look away if you must, but keep the pressure." Mia's voice

sounded far away. She took Omar's opposite arm and felt for a pulse, counting the throbs against her illuminated watch. "He's fighting."

A tear slipped down Jade's cheek as she took a shaky breath. "How did you find us?"

"It wasn't too hard to guess when three men tried to wrestle me from my bed. I kind of assumed the rest of you were in danger as well."

Just then, Omar's eyelids fluttered.

Mia bent over him, but he relaxed again and held still. "Don't do this to me, baby." She kissed his forehead then his cheek. "If you get out of this alive, I'm going to kill you for being such a stupid fool."

Mia's tears dripped onto Omar's neck. Then she straightened suddenly. "We have to get him out of here now! His heart rate is slowing."

"What about Alem?" Jade asked.

As if on cue, Alem stirred and spoke in a drowsy voice. "What happened?"

"You fainted," Mia said in a matter-of-fact tone. "Now get up, and help us with Omar."

A voice from above ground called down to them. "Mia, is everyone all right?"

Lucas.

Jade's heart nearly burst into a thousand shards. He wasn't responsible for all this deception—the shooting—the horror. He was good, honest . . . right?

"Take his legs." Mia's voice cut into Jade's revelry.

She bent over and grasped Omar's ankles, resting his heavy boots on her hips. Her knees buckled as she tried to support his weight. With Mia and Alem carrying his torso, they made their way to just below the opening of the cave.

"More rope," Mia shouted. Additional rope tumbled down.

"How are we—" Alem started.

"You'll see." Mia wound the rope about Omar's waist and tied his hands together. "Good thing he passed out, or this would be quite painful." Finally she lashed his hands to the main rope. "Ready."

Slowly, Omar was raised to the surface, and the rope cascaded down again. Mia insisted that Alem and Jade go ahead of her. Then she followed.

At the surface, Jade blinked in the morning light, hardly believing that this was the second time she'd been rescued from the same place. And both times Lucas had been there to greet her. She stood at a distance as Lucas and Alem assessed Omar.

"We'll have to dig the bullet out immediately," Lucas said, his expression grim. "Transporting him to the hospital will take too much time." His stern gaze alighted on Jade for a brief instant then left.

Jade wanted to run to him and embrace him. She wanted to thank him for being himself, for being normal and good, and to tell him she was sorry for doubting. But his withering glance had suppressed her compulsion. He was concerned about life and death right now, not her roller coaster doubts.

Mia crossed to Omar and, bending over him, stroked his head.

Looking away, Jade swallowed at the lump in her throat, realizing she'd had it easy. Lucas instructed that Omar be moved inside Mia's tent for the surgery.

The women waited outside the tent, saying nothing as the sun slowly rose in the sky, making everything hot and sticky. Ismail sat in the bed of the truck, a rope connecting his bound hands to the axle. It was then that Jade noticed the camp seemed deserted. Where were all the others?

An hour crept by. The early sun was just starting to dissipate the last of the shade when Lucas exited the tent. Flies immediately congregated to his unwashed hands. Mia grabbed a liter of water and poured it over them.

"I took out the bullet and cleaned the wound as much as possible," Lucas said, rubbing his hands under the water, "but the next couple of hours will tell us if there's an infection."

"Can I see him?" Mia asked.

"Of course," Lucas said, lifting the tent flap. After Mia went inside, Lucas stood over Jade. "Are you all right?"

She nodded, too exhausted to answer. He left to check on Ismail, and a couple of minutes later, Alem exited the tent. Jade rinsed off his hands with water.

Lucas had settled beneath the fragmented shade of a palm, leaning his head against the trunk and closing his eyes.

Jade hesitated then made her way over to him—if nothing else, just to thank him. She at least owed him that. She didn't know all the answers, but she did know he wasn't the bad guy.

He cracked an eyelid open as she approached. Then he patted the spot next to him.

Jade settled in the cool sand and was surprised when Luc's calloused hand closed over hers.

"Alem told me what happened down there."

She nodded, not trusting herself to speak as the memory surfaced.

"I'm sorry about saying the tomb was just a cave. I wanted to get you away from Ismail as soon as possible. The night before you fell into the tomb, he said a few things that made me suspicious of his character." Lucas squeezed her hand. "I wanted to get you someplace safe. Ismail told me there were more AWP crew on their way, and I didn't want you exposed to such a dangerous situation . . ."

"I understand," Jade said.

But he shook his head. "I can't believe I didn't see through Ismail earlier. I've known him for a decade and even worked with him over the years. It seemed the hospital was the perfect place to keep you safe until I could figure out what to do next." Lucas wrapped an arm about her shoulder and kissed the top of her head.

Never in her whole life—regardless of the fact that she was thousands of miles away from home and literally in the middle of nowhere, with an angry criminal only paces away—had she felt so secure. Yet even now, she dared not hope that Luc's attention was based on more than concern for another's well-being. He was just trying to comfort her.

"When I saw you step out of the SUV, I'd never been so scared in my life," Lucas continued as he pulled his arm away. "By then I knew what Ismail was capable of. The situation was about to blow."

"I should have trusted you," Jade said. "I'm sorry."

Lucas remained silent for a moment. "It's always hard to completely trust another person."

Jade thought about men she'd dated—no relationship lasting long. "I know what you mean."

Lucas smiled. "I never thought I'd truly enjoy another woman's company again."

"As opposed to a man's?"

"No." Lucas laughed. "That's not what I meant at all."

Jade felt her shoulders relax, but her mind was still fuzzy with confusion.

"After my divorce, I swore off relationships with a female counterpart."

"I didn't know you were married." Jade pulled her knees to her chest.

Lucas touched her shoulder, his hand skimming the surface of her back. Jade inhaled at the sensation as she gazed across the rippled sand.

"It was a long time ago. I didn't think I'd ever really care about another woman again. But when I saw you come out of that tomb, alive, covered with dirt, but otherwise unharmed . . . I changed my mind."

She knew if she looked at him now, she'd be captivated forever. Forcing herself to keep her gaze forward, warmth spread through her body anyway.

His fingers touched her hair, and she held her breath as she looked down at her hands, willing them not to tremble. She absentmindedly played with her ring. It was dark blue. She didn't know if she could speak, but Lucas had leaned toward her, as if waiting for her to respond.

"Tell me about your ring," he said.

"It's a mood ring. It changes color according to my emotions."

"Interesting." He took her hand and examined the ring. "From a boyfriend?"

"No," Jade said. "I bought it at a flea market."

"Flea market?"

"A bazaar."

"Ah." He was so close to her. "What does this color mean?"

Jade bit her lip, feeling embarrassed. "Passion."

"So you're feeling passionate?"

Jade was sure she was bright red. She couldn't even think straight enough to reply. The corners of her mouth turned up.

Lucas grinned, tugging her arm until she was leaning against his chest.

Safe. The nightmares of the underground cave seemed to be

from another lifetime, Jade thought as she nestled against Lucas. It was strange that it seemed so *normal* to be in the middle of a desert with a man she'd met only a short time ago. She gazed in the direction of Mia's tent. All was quiet, except for Alem, who walked around the excavation site.

She straightened from her relaxed position, reluctant to pull away from Luc, but she was starting to feel nervous. What if he kissed her? Thoughts of her nasty hygiene leaped to her mind. But perhaps he'd be so enraptured he wouldn't notice. Jade laughed at herself. If he ever *did* try to kiss her, would she be ready?

If she'd met Lucas on campus at Brown, he wouldn't have given her a second glance. He was the type who would have every girl over the age of eighteen pining for him. But now . . . here . . . he'd gone from someone who had been obligingly civil to a man who was *interested* in her.

She tried to focus on the excavation and what it might reveal. "Is there a curse?"

"On me and women?"

"No." Jade let a smile reach her lips as she looked at Lucas. Then she had to look away quickly to keep from drowning. "On the tomb."

"Ah, a subject I'm a bit more comfortable with." He let out a long breath as if he were glad the conversation had been steered someplace else. "It's very likely." He pulled a piece of paper from his pocket. "Mia showed me Alem's poem."

"What do you think?"

"The last few lines are reminiscent of other curses placed on ancient royal tombs. Listen. 'Now the seven devils hide beneath the tomb, Waiting as seven lamps still burn above, Waiting for the queen of the South,'" he said.

"What does it mean?"

Lucas pulled out another page, which Jade recognized as the sketch Omar had shown them. "I think what you discovered is just the beginning."

She looked back and forth between the sketch and poem. "I still don't understand."

"I think there's possibly another tomb. Perhaps . . . seven of them."

Jade let the words sink in. "Are you sure?"

"Anything is possible at this point," he said. "If this is proven to be the queen's tomb, I'm sure all types of stories, lore, and conjecture will come forward. They will naturally explain why the tomb was here—in Shisur, of all places—and it will seem absolutely logical that it had been here all along." He paused, resting his hand on her shoulder. "I think you've just had a bit of bad luck mixed with incredibly good luck."

"Mostly good luck," she said in a quiet voice. For a moment they gazed at each other.

He leaned forward until his face was inches from her. "You're making me lose my concentration. We'd better get back to work . . . sooner than later."

Jade saw the mischief in his eyes. She could almost see the sparks flying. "You're right. Let's go." She made a move to rise, but Lucas beat her to it. He extended his hand and pulled her to her feet. He kept her hand clasped in his as they walked to where Alem crouched over a low wall.

If Alem was surprised at seeing the two of them holding hands, he didn't show it. Jade was silently grateful for this, since her excitement was mixed with insecurity all in the same moment.

"Anything new?" Lucas asked.

Alem straightened and shook his head.

"Once we have Omar out of danger, we'll open up the cave,"

Lucas said.

Jade looked at Luc. "With just a few of us?"

"Several of the men who left will return. I've no doubt,"
he said. "They made themselves scarce when Ismail started
brandishing his weapon." He released her hand and walked toward
the fateful opening. "Just think of the secrets that have been buried
for so many years."

Jade joined him near the opening, incredulous at what lay
beneath their feet. She caught Alem's eye, and he gave her a big
wink.

"He's gone," a voice shouted behind them.

It felt as if a knife had plunged into her chest when Jade turned
and saw Mia running toward them. *Omar?*

"Ismail escaped."

Not Omar.

"Can we catch him?" Alem asked.

"Ismail knows the desert better than any of us," Lucas said. "It
would just be a mission of disaster."

"Then what? We let him get away?" Mia's face was scarlet
with anger. "He nearly killed Omar. What's going to stop him from
coming back?"

"He'll be punished enough by his employer," Lucas said,
scanning the oasis.

"How?" Mia asked.

"What happens in your line of work when someone fails in their
mission?"

"Fired, or maybe jailed, depending on what went wrong," Mia
said as she crossed her arms, clearly not amused with the question.

"It's different for Ismail," Luc said. "A failed mission for him is
a fate worse than death. It's dishonor, humiliation, a separation from
his tribe—a spiritual death. His right hand will be cut off, and he'll

live the rest of his life as an outcast from his own people."

Mia's expression didn't soften.

"Look at that," Alem said, pointing. "You were right, Lucas."

All heads turned, and Jade saw the dark forms of something moving on the horizon.

"The crew is returning," Lucas said. "Luck is with us. We won't have much time as it is."

"Let me guess—Omar told you about AWP too?" Mia asked, her expression still stubborn.

"The Coptic patriarch told me."

Mia let out a breath of understanding. "I see."

"The patriarch also leaked the news about the tomb discovery to the media." He offered a wry smile. "Ironically, if the media can get here before AWP . . . they might actually be useful for once. Unfortunately, we're going to need the military to protect so many people."

"Can we hold off the media?" Mia asked.

"I don't think anyone can hold off the media," Lucas said. "So, as long as Omar continues to progress, we'll all remain here to work."

Alem's eyes lit with excitement. "What's the plan?"

"Excavate as much as possible until we are elbowed out by someone with more guns than us."

Chapter Forty-six

Salalah, Oman

ABDALLAH SALEH AL-QADI CLOSED his cell phone
and squeezed the thin plastic as he leaned against the leather
upholstery in his den. Taking a few days away from the office had
given him a chance to orchestrate matters of more importance.
And until about seventy-five seconds ago, everything was running
smoothly.

The phone call from Ismail brought al-Qadi back to the reality
of the present at lightning speed. One part of him rejoiced that a
tomb had finally been found after many months, even years, of
delving through the latest research and bribing others in ways he
never thought possible to discover the gem of Dr. Lyon's theory.

Then there was the ring that devil of a woman, Mia, had
brought.

It verified that the legend of the queen was real. It had been
too good to be true.

Israel would remain secure in their claim to the Holy Land—
for now. But before al-Qadi threw the phone against the wall and
shattered it, he dialed one last number.

"My friend," the voice on the other end of the line said after the first ring.

"Rabbel. There has been a problem."

A ragged intake of air could be heard. "I'm already working on it, sir. We're sure it can be fixed."

"No, I'm afraid this is beyond repair." Al-Qadi's temples throbbed with fury. The line was dead silent on the other end. "Ismail has been exposed in Shisur, and undercover operatives are waiting at the tomb site right now. He said a female student from *America* fell into a tomb shaft."

"I already have men on the way to Shisur."

"It's not enough. You need to go."

"No problem," Rabbel soothed. "We've set up a preliminary excavation there. My convoy can make it there in no time, and the woman won't know what hit her."

"There's more," al-Qadi said. "She's with a group—organized by the patriarch."

"Impossible," Rabbel said. "We have him dangling from our strings like a puppet."

"Apparently, the patriarch doesn't share your view," al-Qadi said. "The Omani government is behind this operation and is no doubt informed of the group's progress."

"As I said," Rabbel continued, "my people will be there before the Omani military—"

"Forget your operation. Call Levy right away, and tell him plans have changed. I want the patriarch dead by midnight. Tell Levy to be more discreet than he was with Dr. Lyon's death. And this time, don't screw it up. The breaking news of the assassination will be a diversion, and it will buy us time."

"Time for what?"

"To destroy Shisur. If we can't have the queen, no one gets

her." Al-Qadi broke the connection and, with a single swift movement, sent the cell phone crashing to its demise.

Chapter Forty-seven

Shisur, Oman

THE SHADOWS GREW LONGER, casting much-needed shade over the excavation site. Alem worked alongside the crew as much as his body allowed. Jade and Mia even joined in, lifting rocks and transferring wheelbarrows of sand. Mia alternated between keeping vigil by Omar's side and working out her frustration in a physical manner. Every hour or two, Lucas paused to phone the patriarch— apparently the purse strings behind the excavation.

Alem was just as excited as the others to investigate the tomb, though he wasn't entirely convinced that it belonged to the queen of Sheba—even with the name of Wila'at engraved on the sarcophagus. After all, his country referred to her as Makeda, and the Yemenis called her Bilqis, while Josephus had written about her as Nikaule.

"The ramp is ready," Lucas said, arriving at Alem's side.

Mia wiped her dirty hands against her pants. "I'm coming too."

Lucas, Alem, Mia, and Jade made their way down the steep ramp, Lucas leading the way. The crew perched around the expanded opening, their dusty faces lit with excitement. Whatever history arose from this burial ground, they were part of it.

As they descended into the darkness, Alem noted how different this burial site was from the proclaimed one in Ethiopia. His people believed the queen was buried in a hillside tomb in Aksum.

Did the thousands of years of sand and wind merely cover the great edifice built to the queen? Or did she want to be buried below the ground, something unfit for a person of her rank and notoriety?

The group moved to the sarcophagus first, and Mia murmured in admiration. Lucas began to take pictures, snapping photos from all angles of the walls, the ceiling, and the floor surrounding the stone block.

Alem ran his fingers along the walls, knowing that after this day, probably no one but an archaeologist would be able to get this close. He found the symbol Jade had told him about. "Come here."

Jade and Lucas moved to his side, and he said in a hushed voice, "The symbol of Sheba—etched on the stone."

Jade touched the design. "No one can doubt this is her tomb."

"This symbol has become universal in representing a woman's power combined with a man's authority," Lucas said. "Although we connect it with the queen, there's no way to know where it originated."

Mia cleared her throat behind him. "The most eminent scholars in the world would argue that this symbol originated with the queen of Sheba."

Alem moved from the three and continued inspecting the wall. He came to the small opening in the rock, the one Jade had told him about. Sticking his flashlight through the hole, he peered through the dank darkness and let out a low whistle as his flashlight's beam reflected off something shiny.

"It's another room," Alem said, feeling the hairs on the back of his neck stand on end. "A treasury, I think."

The others joined him, alternating turns looking into the adjacent cavern.

"Give me a leg up," Lucas said. Alem hoisted him through the opening.

They heard the muffled thud of Lucas's landing on the other side. Alem, Jade, and Mia put their heads together, trying to see into the room.

"Are you all right?" Mia called.

Lucas's voice echoed. "Yep."

Jade turned to Alem. "Help me?"

He helped her through the wall then looked at Mia. "Do you want to go through too?"

She shook her head. "Someone better stay on this side, just in case . . . But you go ahead."

Alem wriggled his way through the opening, taking extra care with his bandages. Jade guided his safe landing. Alem swept his flashlight around the new room. It was quite different from the first. Shelves had been carved into the rock, filled with items that looked decayed and unrecognizable.

"There's gold here, gemstones . . ." Lucas said as he walked about the room. "I can't believe it was never looted."

Alem searched the walls, finding the same writing as in the other room. "Look, here's that name of Batal again. Do you think it's a place?"

Lucas came up behind Alem. "Most likely a man. *Batal* means 'hero' in Arabic."

"Who was he to the queen?" Jade asked.

"Maybe a brother or son?" Alem suggested. He raised his light to join Lucas's, and the wall was flooded in brightness.

"Or her husband," Lucas said. "I know that's not what you want to hear, Alem."

"She was never officially married. Ancient Ethiopian law states that a queen can reign only if she's a virgin," Alem said.

Jade looked at him. "Then why did they accept her after she conceived with Solomon?"

"Because Solomon tricked her, and she was not to blame. Therefore, it must have been God's will that the queen bear a son to carry on her name," Alem said.

"Do you think Batal was a king?" Jade asked Lucas.

He lifted a shoulder. "Nothing here uses the title of king, although he must have been privileged because of the manner of his burial." He waved his hand toward the artifacts. "And to have so much buried with him, he must have been in a position of power."

"Are there dates?" Alem asked.

Lucas walked along the wall, searching. "Not dates in the sense that we would write them down. But I would guess this person died before the queen," he concluded. He snapped several more photos then moved to the shelves.

Jade sidled up to Alem. "What are you thinking?"

Although he knew she meant well, Alem felt himself bristle. "It looks like the country of Oman may have won."

"Whether the queen of Sheba was buried here or someplace in Ethiopia, that doesn't tarnish the heritage she left behind." She touched his arm gently. "Think about it. Scholars will conclude she was a valid person, a real part of the Bible. The debates and uncertainties will be put to rest. Even if it is disappointing that her tomb is not in Ethiopia, this finding can bring only enlightenment."

"You don't understand," Alem said. "There's archaeological proof of a monarch family that reigned in the tenth century B.C. If it wasn't Makeda's family, who was it?"

"Azhara." Lucas's voice echoed through the cavern.

"What?" Alem asked.

Lucas walked toward them. "Before coming to Oman, Jade and I took a detour to Ethiopia. There we saw a statue of a woman that had just been discovered. Her royal heritage was plain, and the name on the statue was Azhara." Lucas put a hand on Alem's shoulder. "It may also interest you that a second name appeared, that of *Tambariah*."

Alem stared at Lucas. "Tambariah is my middle name." His thoughts tumbled. "I was named after my grandfather, who was named after his. Tambariah has been a family name for generations."

Chapter Forty-eight

Shisur, Oman

HE FELT HER PRESENCE before he saw her, so when Omar opened his eyes, he knew Mia sat next to him.

She smiled. "Welcome back, Matan."

Without moving his head, Omar looked about the enclosure and recognized they were inside a tent. That would account for the stuffiness. He licked his dried lips. His mouth felt cottony, bitter. Mia offered him water.

"How did I get to be in the care of such a beautiful woman?"

She pulled a face. "If you hadn't just been shot, I'd smack you."

Through the haze, he saw the dampness of the hair around her face and smelled her perspiration. "Is there danger in opening the tent a little?" His tongue felt thick against the roof of his mouth.

"Flies," she said.

"How did I get here? Did you rescue the man in distress?"

Mia fought hard not to smile. "Something like that. I was pretty ticked off at being awakened in the middle of the night by groping men. One thing led to another, and I followed Ismail to the cave, attacked him, and saved you all."

"That's my girl. I wouldn't have expected anything less."

"Oh, and Lucas helped a little." She wrinkled her brow. "I should have shot the man."

"Lucas?" he asked.

"No," Mia said, delivering a light jab to Omar's good shoulder. "Ismail."

The cobwebs were drifting from his memory. "Ah . . . he did seem a little eager to let us see the tomb. Maybe he wanted to bury us in it."

"Maybe." Mia's voice sounded disconcerted.

"What's wrong?" he asked, trying to focus on her face. "Were you hurt?"

"Not physically."

Their eyes met for the briefest moment, and Omar haltingly raised himself up on one elbow, wincing with the discomfort. "Mia, I think you're becoming soft."

"Hardly," she said, folding her arms. "I just don't like failing on a mission."

"So that's it. All about the mission, huh?"

She nodded emphatically, but he wasn't convinced. "Who took out the bullet?"

"Lucas, with Alem's help."

Omar settled back on the folded sleeping bag. "It seems I owe Lucas a great deal, as well as an apology."

"You did nothing wrong."

"I *thought* wrong." He took pleasure in gazing at her, glad that she was here. He noticed that the light coming through the weave of the tent had faded somewhat. *It must be early evening.* "How long have you been here?"

She shrugged. "Off and on. The workers returned after they had fled from the commotion. We dug out the opening of the tomb and built a ramp. Lucas, Jade, Alem, and I explored the cave and took a lot of pictures."

Omar felt the interest burn within. "Anything significant?"

"We found a second room—a treasury. On the walls, it mentions Batal again, and Lucas thinks it's maybe her husband or brother."

"I know that name. It was written on the sketch I found beneath the museum." Omar fell silent for moment.

"Lucas said it means—"

"Hero," he said. "Did you update Levy?"

"Yes," Mia said, narrowing her eyes. "He's coming to Shisur. Did you have something to do with that?"

"He just wants to put me in my place."

"Meaning?"

"Just guy stuff. You wouldn't understand." Ignoring her glare, he said, "Did you tell the patriarch?"

"Lucas keeps him updated. I alerted the military, though."

He arched a brow. "Good for you." Mia calling for backup was unusual. She must really be worried about AWP. "Why are you being *Ms. Nice* all of a sudden?"

Mia turned her gaze from him, her face flushed.

"Had a change of heart?" he asked it in a joking manner, but inwardly he hoped it was true. Maybe something good would come from being shot. *Maybe.*

"What's wrong?" he asked when she didn't look at him.

"Ismail got away."

Omar let the information sink in. "He'll get his dues."

Mia faced him, her cheeks flaming. "He needs to pay for what he's done to you. It's wrong that he's getting away with it." Standing, she removed her gun from her belt and checked the ammunition. "I'm going to find him before everything else goes down, even if—"

"Whoa," Omar said, straining into a sitting position. He grabbed Mia's arm. "You're not going anywhere. You didn't see what he was about to do to Jade. The bastard's not worth it . . . Besides," his tone softened, "I know you're just trying to show how much you still care for me."

"I am not," Mia nearly shouted. She jerked away from him, but Omar caught her with one hand, as painful as it was to move his shoulder. He tugged her toward him, and she stopped struggling, finally letting him hold her.

After a moment, she raised her eyes, still seething with anger. "He needs to pay."

"He will. As soon as I'm healed, we'll bring him in together."

"But our assignment will be over by then."

"Perhaps yours will. I'll have plenty of time, since I'm retiring."

Mia scoffed. "You can't retire at thirty-six. What do you have, a stash of gold somewhere?"

"I'm not retiring from working—just from working for the government. I'm tired of people like Levy telling me what to do and how to do it." He let out a frustrated sigh. "I'm not cut out for this job."

"You're perfect for it," Mia protested.

"No, *you're* perfect for it."

Their eyes met for a long moment. Then she leaned toward him and kissed him.

"Ow!" Omar said.

She moved away, her expression apologetic.

"Never thought I'd be telling you to take it easy."

A timid smile reached Mia's lips. "I think you need a little more rest before we chase down Ismail and you retire."

"You're telling me what to do?"

"Yes, Mr. Zagouri, and you're going to have to accept it." Mia gently pushed against him, forcing him to lie down. Then she rose and left the tent with a final backward glance.

Omar stretched his good arm behind his head, wincing slightly. He liked what he'd seen in her eyes. *Reconciliation.*

Chapter Forty-nine

Shisur, Oman

THEY SPENT HOURS INSIDE the tomb, taking pictures and recording information. When Jade and Lucas climbed the ramp, Jade felt exhausted and exhilarated at the same time. Mia and Alem sat together beneath a group of palms, undoubtedly poring over the poem.

Lucas grabbed Jade's arm and pointed upward at the approaching helicopter.

"Take cover!" Mia shouted.

Everyone headed toward the ruins and hid next to the groups of fallen stones.

"What's going on?" Jade asked Mia after the noise of the helicopter faded.

"That helicopter was private, probably doing surveillance," Mia said.

Lucas stood, pulling Jade with him. "Not military, not media, so that leaves only one conclusion."

"AWP is on their way." Mia took out Omar's satellite phone and dialed. "I'll find out how close the military is."

"When you're finished, meet us in Omar's tent. We need to make a plan," Lucas told her.

Just then, like a horde of locusts, the desert rumbled with approaching trucks, vans, jeeps, and busloads of people. The first to arrive was a television crew from Salalah. A thin man with a khafiya wrapped about his head climbed out of his van. The sliding door opened, and two more people hopped out, one with a camera perched on his shoulder. A neatly dressed fellow with a trim mustache ran forward, holding a microphone out to Jade.

"Ready for this?" Lucas asked Jade. "It looks like we may have just been saved by the media."

"What about that helicopter?"

"It undoubtedly saw the approaching trucks and will report."

"Can I defer the questions to you?"

He chuckled. "Only the technical ones."

She glanced in the direction of the tomb opening. The Yemeni workers stood guard, their weapons in easy sight.

The newsman broke out in rapid Arabic until Lucas interrupted, "English, please."

Jade was astonished when the man switched languages as if he were turning on a light.

"Madam, are you the one who found the tomb?"

"Yes."

Several pictures were snapped. "Who is buried there?" the reporter asked.

"We don't know yet," Jade said.

The cameraman finished setting up, and he said something in Arabic to the interviewer.

"Okay. We begin again, eh?"

Jade smiled. The questioning lasted only another minute when they were interrupted by another vehicle approaching.

"Everyone woke up early this morning," Lucas said. A Land Cruiser stopped, and the cameras turned toward it. A man exited, wearing Western clothing. He was tall with dark hair, his short beard nearly gray. He carried an air of authority and was obviously someone used to being respected. He waved at the camera crews and strode over to Lucas and Jade.

"I don't believe it," Lucas said.

"Who is he?" Jade asked.

Before Lucas could explain, the man stopped in front of Jade. "Ms. Holmes? I'm Dr. Izzy Stein. It's a pleasure to meet you."

Jade was dumbfounded. This man was one of the most notable archaeologists in the world. She shook his hand, thinking of the books he'd authored, his many articles, his words quoted in history classes—and he knew *her* name.

Next he shook Lucas's hand. "Dr. Morel, nice to see you again."

"And you, Dr. Stein."

The archaeologist smiled. "It seems there's a tomb to date."

Lucas laughed. "Thanks for coming. I didn't know if you'd receive my message or if your schedule would allow you to come."

Stein shrugged. "Nothing much was happening in Meggido, so here I am."

Another bus arrived, filled with eager reporters. Lucas waved off the media, saying, "We'll make statements in about an hour. Make yourselves comfortable."

Lucas turned to Stein. "Let's talk in private. Jade and I have a lot to share with you."

Less than an hour later, Stein had been fully briefed. Alem sat with the men as they dissected the poem. Jade alternated between hovering inside the tent to checking on Omar. Mia had mellowed considerably and seemed to appreciate Jade's efforts. But every time Jade went outside, the media would scramble for her. So finally, she just stayed inside the tent and listened to the men.

"You've found one tomb already—two, if you count the one in Jerusalem," Stein was saying.

Lucas nodded. "I don't know if the seven tombs are right here in Shisur or if they span the globe."

"Let's find out." Stein rose to his feet and looked at Jade. "Can you tell the press we'll have a statement before nightfall? Then join us if you can."

Jade nodded and hurried outside with the message. On her way, she spotted a convoy of vehicles approaching from the horizon. The dust billowed behind the lead SUV, and flags rose from each side of the black Land Rover.

She ran to find Lucas, who was fielding off a variety of questions from several media personnel on his way to the tomb. "Who's that?" she asked, pointing.

He squinted against the sun. "The sultanate of Oman, Sultan Bakarat ibn Murshid."

And the vehicles kept coming. "It looks as if he's brought some assistants," Stein said.

Jade watched with fascination at the protocol taking place. Bodyguards stepped out of their vehicles before escorting the sultan to the site. Lucas tugged Jade along with him to greet the man, and Stein followed. All eyes focused on Lucas as he stepped forward with a slight bow.

The sultan nodded to Jade then turned to Lucas. "Tell me of this discovery."

Lucas said, "The tomb dates to possibly the tenth century B.C. at the latest. We won't know for sure until we do carbon testing. Dr. Stein is here—"

"Is it the queen of Sheba's tomb?" the sultan asked.

"The names of Batal and Wila'at appear many times on the

walls. We are not sure which name represents the person within the sarcophagus."

"Wila'at is the Omani name for the Sabaean queen," the sultan observed.

"Yes, but that only raises more questions."

"Of how she came to rest at Shisur?"

"Exactly."

Jade was impressed with the sultan's knowledge.

"When will you know if she honored our country with her last repose?" the sultan asked.

"As soon as we have the proper equipment to date the artifacts. The equipment is on its way. In the meantime, Dr. Stein will be able to make some fairly accurate observations."

The sultan stroked his chin as he gazed at Lucas. "I have read some of your studies and findings in other places. The Coptic patriarch called me last night and told me of the discovery, reiterating the faith he has in your ability. I'll consider putting you in charge of this excavation." He turned to Jade. "Please let my advisors know if there is anything you require."

"Thank you," Jade said, self-conscious about the attention.

After a few more minutes of discussion with Lucas, the sultan said, "I'll let you do your work, Dr. Morel and Dr. Stein. I look forward to your findings."

Jade watched the man leave then was surprised to see Mia approach her. By the expression on her face, Jade knew something was terribly wrong.

"Come with me," Mia said. She remained silent as Jade followed her to Omar's tent. They stepped into the stuffy interior.

Omar was propped up on his bedroll. His ashen color had faded. He looked healthy, but his expression was grave. "Tell her."

"All right. We know . . ." Mia cleared her throat. "I know how

Dr. Lyon died."

Jade felt as if she'd been punched in the stomach. "How?"

Mia produced some papers. One was a picture of an envelope. Jade read the Latin words. "How long have you known this?"

"The patriarch sent me the information a few days ago. This envelope was delivered to Dr. Lyon in his office. It contained cyanide."

Hot tears burned against Jade's eyelids.

"Go on," Omar said, his voice sounding angry.

"The people . . . the *man* we think is responsible for this is on his way here."

Jade stared at Mia. "Is he going to be arrested?"

"Well, it's kind of complicated."

Jade felt the back of her neck heat up. "How?" She hoped this wasn't a case of a murderer being let off because of a technicality.

Mia pursed her lips, but Omar's voice boomed in the tent. "Because he's our boss."

Jade looked at Omar. "You *work* for the guy who killed Dr. Lyon?"

"Technically, he just *ordered* the killing—" Mia said.

"Mia," Omar interrupted and then looked at Jade. "The man who's responsible for the attempted assassination on the Coptic patriarch and the successful murder of Dr. Lyon is David Levy, senior intelligence officer of the Northern Israeli Command."

He produced a small electronic device. "Mia placed a bug in a high-ranking official's office before we picked you up at the hospital. This recording just came in. The man who's speaking is the director of the General Organization for Antiquities, Museums, and Manuscripts." He turned up the volume.

Jade listened to the chilling words with horror. *Forget your operation. Call Levy right away, and tell him plans have changed. I want the patriarch dead by midnight. Tell Levy to be more discreet than he was with Dr. Lyon's death. And this time, don't screw it up. The breaking news of his assassination will be a diversion, and it will buy us time.*

Time for what?

To destroy Shisur. If we can't have the queen, no one gets her.

Omar switched it off. "Ten minutes ago, Mia received an email from the patriarch. He told her to plan on receiving him at Shisur today."

"The patriarch's coming *here*?"

"Yes," Mia said in a faint voice, looking as if the news had come as a shock.

"What should we do?" Jade asked. "We need to warn him."

Omar stood with some effort. "You have to talk Lucas into leaving Shisur. We need to weave a good tale to get the media out of here. This place is going to be a battle zone."

"What about you and Mia?"

"Levy doesn't know we know," Omar said. "We'll find a way to protect the patriarch and play along with Levy until we have an opportunity to either expose him or get away ourselves."

"How long do we have?" Jade asked.

Mia glanced at her watch. "Less than an hour."

Jade's head started buzzing, and she wondered if she'd be sick. Then she realized the buzzing was coming from outside.

Mia pushed past her and lifted the tent flap. "It's too late."

Chapter Fifty

Shisur, Oman

"DAMN," OMAR SAID, HOBBLING out of the tent.

He stopped by Jade and Mia, staring to the south. Clouds of dust rose from the desert floor as the distant buzzing turned to loud rumbling. A convoy of vehicles approached from the horizon, dust blooming behind the lead SUV, flags perched on each side.

The lounging media crews frantically gathered their stuff, trying to move it out of the way. Omar looked toward the excavation site. A massive tent had been set up to shade the sultan. His military personnel stood at attention, their rifles poised.

One by one, the vehicles arrived.

A heavyset man stepped out of a Lexus, and bodyguards surrounded him as he strode to the sultan's tent. "Who's that?" Jade asked.

"Dr. Abdallah Saleh al-Qadi, the director of GOAMM," Omar said.

"Is he . . .?"

"The voice on the recording," Mia said. "I'd love to hear what he says to the sultan."

"Does the sultan know?" Jade asked.

Mia shook her head. "As far as the sultan is concerned, al-Qadi is just doing his job—investigating the new tomb for the General Organization for Antiquities, Museums, and Manuscripts."

More men poured out of the vehicles, all of them armed.

One of the last men looked familiar. "There's Rabbel," Omar said.

Mia turned away.

"Are you all right?" Omar asked.

"I want to kill him." She swiped at her cheeks.

"Me too." Omar put an arm around her. "This will all be over soon. Alem will go ballistic when he sees Rabbel."

Omar walked the women back to the tent. He grabbed a khafiya from his bag and wrapped it around his head. "I'll see if I can bring Alem over here without Rabbel noticing. Are you going to be all right in the tent?"

Mia reached for her rifle and checked the ammo. "Of course." She smiled thinly at him. "If anything happens, I want the first shot."

"You got it." He turned to Jade. "Mia will hook you up with a gun."

Jade nodded, her eyes wide.

Omar left the women and kept to the outskirts of the action. His shoulder was on fire, but he moved quickly, scanning for Alem as he walked around the tents and media vehicles. The media crews started to assemble again, strangely quiet. It was as if they sensed something important was going on.

Just about the same time Omar saw Alem leaning against a news truck, Lucas and another man emerged from the tomb shaft. The media reporters rushed toward them. Omar kept one eye on the sultan's tent, where al-Qadi and Rabbel were, and the other on

Alem.

The Ethiopian seemed oblivious to Rabbel's presence. As Omar drew closer, he understood why. A pretty brunette was exclaiming over Alem's bandages, and Alem had a grin plastered on his face. Omar chuckled. His friend seemed to feel a lot better.

Before he could vie for Alem's attention and warn him about Rabbel, the sound of a helicopter filled the air. Omar looked up, adrenaline surging through him. The helicopter that approached was neither military nor commercial. The chopper landed, and the doors opened. The pilot stepped out first, and Omar's insides lurched.

It was David Levy.

The passenger joined the pilot, and Omar narrowed his eyes, trying to make out the figure. A large Coptic cross shone against the man's billowing, black robes. *The patriarch.*

Welcome to the party, men. Then, unbidden, another thought entered his mind: *Come, beloved sons, go into the garden.* The words echoing in his head, he hurried to find cover, stopping next to a media truck to watch.

Palms swayed gently in the breeze, and several torches flamed against the gathering dusk. Omar studied the terrain, paying close attention to the groves of palm trees dotting the oasis. He twisted around, counting the separate groves. *Six . . . seven. Seven groves. Seven tombs. Seven devils.* Well, there were more than seven devils present right now. Maybe it meant seven curses. Or seven djinns.

Was this the queen's garden? The breeze ruffled Omar's clothing, and he involuntarily shivered. The media crews positioned themselves with cameras and microphones. It appeared that Lucas and the man with him were about to make a speech.

"A press conference?" Omar muttered. "Now?"

The patriarch, accompanied by Levy, made his way to the sultan's side and was given a hearty greeting. The two men sat together on rugs, front and center.

All eyes trained on Lucas as he started speaking, and Omar moved in closer. He tried to keep his breathing under check as his shoulder ached, making him feel slightly dizzy. On the outskirts of the group, he stopped, close enough to listen but far enough to keep a nonchalant eye on the patriarch.

A slight movement came from behind Omar, and he turned. Mia and Jade stood there, both of them wearing veils. It would take an astute eye to know they weren't Bedu women.

Mia whispered, "I don't believe it. Levy's going to kill him in the middle of all these people."

"Impossible."

"Look at his eyes."

Omar focused on Levy. The man's gaze was cold and hard, but that didn't mean he'd try to assassinate the patriarch in public.

"Impossible . . ." He turned. Mia had disappeared. He looked at Jade, but she just shrugged. The bulky shape beneath her clothing told him she was armed.

At the front of the group, Lucas introduced the other man as Dr. Israel Stein.

"Let's get straight to the information. Then we'll take questions," Lucas said. "The sarcophagus clearly states that the tomb belongs to a Sabaean queen." Murmuring erupted in the crowd.

"But that doesn't mean she's Bilqis, the woman we refer to as the queen of Sheba," Stein added. "As always, in a preliminary investigation, we have to entertain more than one explanation. A man by the name of Juris Zarins suggested that Ubar was not a city, but a region, and Shisur was one of the seven oases of this legendary Ubar."

Omar stared at Stein. *Seven oases?*

Next to him, Jade whispered, "That was in Dr. Lyon's article."

Stein continued, "It wouldn't surprise me if this area was a pleasant one in antiquity. Perhaps it contained crystalline pools, refreshing groves of palms, and elegant, sturdy structures." He looked at Lucas, who nodded. "Its geographical position provides an exclusive location—yet it is accessible to the frankincense trail. The ships bringing goods from Africa and the Eastern countries unloaded in the coastal town of Salalah and brought their luxuries by caravan by detouring the one hundred and seventy kilometers to Shisur for water supply."

"A queen as great as she would have had a mausoleum built in her name," Lucas said. "So it's a mystery why the tomb is underground."

"The reason may be twofold," Stein said. "First, she may have died grieving in some way. In that case, the queen could preselect this method of burial. She also may have done it for protection—to prevent looters from finding her." He leaned forward, his eyes intent on the crowd. "Whatever the reason, those who built her tomb would have been put to death by one trusted man. That man took the secret of her burial place to his own grave."

The scholar waved a hand toward the excavation site. "It's a highly plausible conclusion, and that's why the tomb is intact and artifacts teem along the walls." He rubbed his hands together. "Questions?"

Every hand shot up.

Stein pointed to one.

"If she had died 'grieving,' as you say," the reporter said, "could this place have been something other than what you described? Not a resort at all, but a desolate, forgotten town—making her disguise all that more complete?"

Stein stroked his bearded chin. "Perhaps."

"Another name was found in the second tomb—that of Batal," Lucas said. "We know the name derives from old Arabic, meaning 'hero.'" He looked beyond the circle of people out into the darkening desert. "But to the people of Oman, there's more meaning."

"As some of you may be aware," Stein said, "even in our modern world, Batal represents a warrior, commander, or competitor. Video games, comic books, and music have incorporated the name to represent strength and power. Much as the queen of Sheba has come to represent power in womanhood, *Batal* is connected to powerful manhood. The English word *battle* derives from the Arabic *Batal*. *Batal* is also another word for conqueror."

"So the name Batal on the sarcophagus may not be a name at all, but a title," Lucas added.

Dr. Stein nodded. "Exactly. It could also be a female."

Hands shot up, but Lucas waved them off.

"Batal is feminine *and* masculine," Stein continued. "In Arabic, it's masculine, but there are many cities, feminine in nature, named Batal—in the Himalayas, Pakistan, Chile, and Serbia. Although carbon dating still needs to be done, so far the artifacts match with the tenth century B.C."

Some of the reporters clapped, and the sultan and the patriarch smiled. Omar shivered. Dr. Stein had all but confirmed his suspicions, and the stakes had just risen.

"Wait," Stein cautioned. "There's an incredible amount of Aramaic writing to be translated and interpreted. It will give us the greatest clarification. At this time, we believe we have discovered the tomb of a royal prince named Batal." He looked at Lucas. "My colleague will now brief you on another discovery made not long ago in Ethiopia."

Cameras flashed as Lucas stepped forward and cleared his

throat. "A royal statue was found in Aksum, Ethiopia, recently. Two names were engraved on it: those of Azhara and Tambariah. The statue dates to the tenth century B.C."

A collective gasp went up from the audience. Omar shifted on his feet, feeling goose bumps prickle his skin. Another Tambariah had been found?

Lucas continued, "In a tomb found in Northern Jerusalem that was recently bombed, a lineage of three kings appeared on the walls: that of Melech Turug, Melech Amariel, and Melech Tambariah. These three ruled in the region of Israel. The third—Tambariah—lived during the same era as King Solomon."

Buzzing ran through the attendees. Omar walked around the group. He still hadn't spotted Mia, and Alem was nowhere to be found either—he'd been missing from his original spot for ten minutes.

"Is Azhara the true name for the queen of Sheba? Was the queen an Ethiopian queen, an Egyptian princess, or a Hebrew bride?" Lucas asked the audience. "We don't know the answers. But we do know that a ring was found inside the Jerusalem tomb that belonged to the queen of the South. It was later stolen in transit."

Omar froze. He didn't think anyone else but those in his undercover operation knew about the ring.

"The symbol upon the golden face is that of a flower intertwined with a snake. Undoubtedly many of you will recognize the symbol as belonging to the queen of Sheba. But the question becomes: Is it her ring?" Lucas paused, then said, "Perhaps the location where this ring was found will provide the answer . . . It was found *inside* the sarcophagus of King Tambariah."

Hands shot up, and reporters spouted questions.

But Lucas waved away the questions. "This same symbol was found etched on another tomb wall, not a dozen meters from where we are."

The entire audience started talking at once.

Stein spoke above the noise, and the voices hushed. "The serpent and the flower is the ultimate symbol of a powerful queen, with her womanhood represented by the flower and her masculine reign represented by the snake. Throughout time, antifeminists have called the queen of Sheba a devil incarnate, a demon, and an evil spirit born of a djinn mother come to torture the neat hierarchy of man's dominion, her hairy legs and cloven feet reminiscent of the devil's own. A 'Devil's Dame.'"

A few people laughed. *The seven devils*, Omar thought, the hair on his neck prickling. A shadow passed behind Lucas and Omar focused on it, sure it was Mia. *I need to stay close to her so I can stop her from doing anything foolish.*

Lucas and Stein started taking questions. Omar turned his attention to the patriarch, His Holiness. The man looked rather young for a pope. He was maybe in his early sixties. Omar was surprised the religious leader came with no bodyguards other than David Levy. The man must have a lot of faith.

Omar tuned in to the reporters' questions. "What's been done to recover the ring of Sheba?"

"Rumor has it that it's up for sale. Every effort is being made to recover it," Lucas said.

Omar's gaze was drawn to Levy. He could have sworn his boss's face went a shade darker.

Stein looked surprised at Lucas's comment. "But that's illegal. Selling an ancient artifact belonging to Israel, or any other country of origin, would be violating international law."

"There may be some here who differ in opinion," Lucas said with a smile.

Omar stiffened. Lucas was taking this way too far.

"I'm only bringing up a debate that has already been started," Lucas said. "If the ring were taken by the queen to Jerusalem, does the ring belong to Israel or to Oman?"

"Or Yemen?" shouted a reporter.

The audience started talking all at once. The sultan of Oman leaned toward the patriarch and said something. Omar watched the pair closely then moved his gaze to al-Qadi. The director of GOAMM sat only a few paces from the sultan.

"How much?" another reporter called out over the din.

Lucas chuckled, looking a bit uncomfortable. "I don't have the answer." He looked at Stein, who shook his head.

Then the sultan of Oman stood, and everyone fell silent. "Perhaps our very own director of GOAMM can give us an idea of the value of such an artifact."

Al-Qadi's face went red, and Omar moved behind a group of people as the man turned to survey the crowd. He stood and fidgeted with his turban for a moment. "An exact price, I couldn't say without analyzing the ring itself. But if one country were to purchase the ring from another, I'm sure the price would be more than fair with a large share of goodwill."

The sultan beamed. "Very well said."

Omar saw Rabbel stand up. Two men accompanied Rabbel as he left the media crowd. Omar scoured the perimeter, trying to see what had caused the men to leave so abruptly, and then he spotted Alem walking toward one of the SUVs.

What are you doing? Omar wanted to shout. Rabbel had obviously seen Alem and was now closing in. Omar slid out of place and made his way to the opposite side of the crowd.

The media droned on as Alem made a beeline toward the fleet. Omar's heart sank. There was no way he could intercept Alem without attracting the attention of Rabbel.

Reaching the edge of the crowd, Omar walked from vehicle to vehicle, pausing behind each one. Alem hesitated at the first SUV then walked around it. In a couple of minutes, he'd be surrounded by the men who'd nearly murdered him once before.

Just as Rabbel and his men approached Alem, Omar ran to the last vehicle—stopping a few meters away. By the time he peeked over the hood, all of the men, including Alem, had their guns drawn, and Rabbel was speaking. Omar held his breath and listened.

"Who else knows about the poem?"

"No one," Alem answered, his tone angry. "I want my grandmother's letter back."

Rabbel laughed and turned to his men. "He wants the letter from his nana." His gaze turned steely as he focused on Alem. "Sorry to disappoint you, but the letter is gone, and now we must make sure that anyone who has seen the queen's poem can never tell a soul." He lifted his rifle, aiming straight at Alem's head.

Alem's hand shook, but he kept his pistol leveled.

"Three against one," Rabbel said with a scoff. "I'll give you one more chance, and I might spare your life. Who else knows about this poem?"

Alem's hand wavered, but he didn't speak.

"This can be very quick or very painful. Your choice," Rabbel said.

Omar leaped from behind the vehicle just as Rabbel's finger curled around the trigger. "Drop your guns. Then put your hands in the air."

The three men whirled around, their guns still raised.

"Get behind the truck, Alem," Omar ordered.

Instead, the Ethiopian scurried to Omar's side. "We're in this together," Alem said.

"Omar?" Rabbel asked. "I should have known. I've never seen

a Yemeni worker who could faint as you did."

"Why, thank you. I've never seen a man who needed two men to back him up before."

Rabbel's face twisted into a smile. "You must be a loyal friend to come all this way and be willing to die for Alem."

"No, I just wanted to tell you that I've read the poem about the queen. So have at least four other people in that crowd over there. You'll have to kill a lot more than just Alem to keep your secret."

Rabbel covered up any surprise by taking a step closer. "In that case, we have some work ahead of us."

"I try to be a gentleman in most situations, but tonight it's *me first*." Omar raised his gun and pulled the trigger. Screams exploded from behind him. It took an instant for Omar to realize two things: first, his gun had jammed, and second, someone was popping off shots at the press conference.

"Run," Omar shouted at Alem.

The media crews were in chaos. People were running everywhere, tripping over each other, some getting trampled. Omar grabbed Alem by the arm, and together they headed straight for the press tent as the others streamed in the opposite direction.

"Find Jade," Omar yelled. "I'll find Mia."

Alem broke away from Omar and was instantly lost in the mayhem. Omar pushed his way through the panicked crowd. Then someone slammed into his injured shoulder. Pain seared through him, and he struggled for control while he scanned for Mia. Then he spotted Lucas coming toward him.

"Have you seen Jade?" Lucas shouted.

"No. Mia?"

"No."

Another round of shots went off, and both Omar and Lucas dove for the ground. Omar looked up to see a man with a mask standing where Lucas had delivered his press conference.

Levy. In one hand, Levy held an assault rifle, in the other, Mia. Several meters to the left, the Omani sultan and al-Qadi huddled together, surrounded by a few bodyguards. The director was obviously playing it safe. He wasn't going to acknowledge any of his seedy connections in front of the sultan.

"What should we do?" Lucas said.

"Find the patriarch." Both men gazed across the prostrate forms.

"Who's the guy in the mask?" Lucas asked. He buried his head as another shower of bullets erupted from Levy's gun.

Levy screamed at some men to gather everyone together and to dump all the weapons in a pile.

"He's the one who ordered Dr. Lyon's death," Omar said.

Lucas snapped his head around and stared at Omar. "How . . . who . . . ?"

"Everybody shut up!" Levy yelled. "I have only one demand. Then this will all be over."

The noise stopped, and the only sound was the wind rattling the overhead tarp. "No one will be hurt tonight if you follow my instructions very carefully." He nodded to the AWP fellows surrounding the patriarch. "His Holiness will stand."

Slowly, the Coptic patriarch stood, his fine robes rumpled and layered with dirt. His face looked ashen.

"Search him for a package."

The patriarch raised a hand. "No need." He dug into a deep pocket and produced a small, square box. "Here it is."

That's the fake ring, Omar thought. *Maybe Levy doesn't know it's a fake.*

Then Levy said to Mia, "I saw you hand it over earlier, my love. I thought you would have been more discreet." He shoved her forward. "Go get it."

Omar's stomach dropped as he watched Mia stumble, regain her balance, and walk with her chin lifted to the patriarch. She reached for it, and then the most extraordinary thing happened. The patriarch kissed Mia on the cheek.

Levy smiled as Mia returned. He yanked her next to him. "You're coming with me too." He pocketed the ring.

Mia struggled beneath Levy's grasp, but he only tightened his hold. He shouted a final order to the crowd: "No one moves until my helicopter is out of sight."

As if to answer, a low hum erupted in the distance, and Omar strained to see in the darkness. At least half a dozen helicopters approached. A murmur ran through the crowd.

Out of the corner of his eye, Omar saw Rabbel moving along the perimeter, his rifle in hand. Time was running out. But whom was Rabbel searching for?

Desperately, Omar searched for Rabbel's target. Alem? Where was he? Rabbel stopped in the shadows just outside the tent and took aim. Omar twisted his head around and stared at the person he was targeting. *The patriarch.* Two thoughts flashed simultaneously through his mind: Mia saying, "The ring is very important to someone I care a lot about," and the patriarch gently kissing her on the cheek as if in a heartfelt farewell.

Omar plowed through the jumble of bodies, throwing himself at the stunned patriarch. Omar covered the pope as a splay of bullets peppered all around them. There were more screams mixed with the approaching sound of the helicopters. But before Omar succumbed to his second bullet in less than twenty-four hours, he twisted around to see a large black man fire in the direction of Rabbel.

Time seemed to stop as Omar watched Alem charge through the sand, shooting not once but several times. The AWP men reacted after a second's hesitation. Firing erupted from all directions. Levy's voice rose to a high-pitched scream above the shouting and the helicopters that were nearly on top of them now.

Omar sensed the life of the man beneath him still pulsing, but as Omar raised himself from the patriarch, Levy turned and started running straight for them. *If I'm not dead yet, I will be now.* Omar raised his hands in weak defense of the sure fire of accurate bullets, but to his surprise, Levy pitched forward and fell onto his face. Then the flurry of two female attackers subdued him. By the time Omar struggled to his knees, Jade and Mia had the man pinned to the ground, forcing him to inhale plenty of sand.

As Omar tried to stand, pain and shock echoed through his body. Then his knees gave way, and blackness closed in.

Chapter Fifty-one

Ubar
959 b.c.

NICAULA OPENED THE ORNATE metal box with her key. Inside lay the ring of Sheba. She lifted the heavy piece from its enclosure. The gold gleamed in the filtered sunlight of her room, and the intricate carving of the snake and flower seemed to move with fluidity.

When she met Batal tonight, she would give it to him as a symbol of their marriage.

Yes. She would marry him. In the eyes of the God of Israel, she'd finally marry her love.

The pleasure started at her feet and radiated through her legs. She closed her eyes, imagining what Batal might wear tonight—a jeweled turban, alabaster robe, and gold dagger hanging at his belt. Her heart constricted with anticipation. She missed him already.

Nicaula smiled as her pulse increased its throbbing. She was ready to give her heart—at last. After replacing the ring in its box, she left her chambers and called to her servant. "Prepare my horse. I want to see the progress on the temple."

A short time later, she sat astride a mare and made her way to the temple site. It might pale in comparison to King Solomon's temple, but it at least honored the name of his god—the god who helped heal her heart and the god to whom she owed her new happiness. Batal had been right. She could find forgiveness.

The site was situated on a rise, and although the work looked as though it had barely started, the crews had been working for over a month underground. Beneath the holy structure, Nicaula was having her own tomb built. When she died, she wanted her earthly body to remain in peace, hidden from marauders who plundered graves.

Nicaula reined her horse to a stop a short distance from the temple site. The workers had been sworn to secrecy, promising never to reveal the location of her tomb. Their families would be executed if the information left their lips.

The queen climbed off the horse and pulled her robe tightly around her shoulders as the blowing wind kicked up the sand, just enough to reach her eyes. Lowering her veil, she approached the site, admiring the muscled backs of the men hard at work. They shaped and moved the rocks, brought from a quarry in Upper Egypt. With the aid of ropes and donkeys, the stones were dragged, lifted, and put into place. Another team of men used a mixture of dirt, water, and gummy plant matter to seal the crevices.

Entering the temple, Nicaula gazed at the innermost holy room. The altar of limestone sprang from the tiled floor, ready for its first animal sacrifice.

"Leave me," the queen commanded, and her servants scurried out into the sunshine. She moved behind the partially constructed holy of holies and lifted the tiles that concealed her tomb opening. Sitting, she drew her knees to her chest and felt the cool air escape the deep hole. She would not visit the place of her burial, in case it brought ill foreboding, but she wanted to connect her birth, her life, and her death all together in this new temple.

She heard the crewmen call to each other as they worked, and she took comfort in their physical labor and routine. As soon as the temple was completed, she would instruct them to build a second tomb on the other side of the city. She replaced the tiles and walked to the temple entrance.

Hope and happiness filled her chest as she looked over her kingdom. Soon the sun would set, and she would marry. She smiled to herself, knowing that on this day, her soul soared with God.

Chapter Fifty-two

Shisur

THE FIRST THING OMAR saw was a set of gigantic white teeth. He blinked several times, and the teeth shrank to normal, human-sized ones.

"Welcome back, my friend," Alem's thick voice boomed.

"You're alive? I thought . . ."

Alem chuckled. "Got lucky, I guess."

Omar turned his head to take in his surroundings. He wasn't in a hospital. That would account for the throbbing pain in his shoulder and most of his body. No morphine IV was in sight. It was early morning, if the weak glow penetrating the tent was any indication. "How many times was I shot?" he asked.

"Counting the time in the tomb? Once."

"Only once?" Omar lifted his head, staring at his body. "That's all?" He let his head fall back. "Are you sure? Feels like at least three or four. Did you check everywhere?"

"Not *every*where."

Omar started to lift the covers when a female voice said, "I checked everywhere."

He turned his head. "Mia." Looking at her, alive, was the most beautiful thing he'd ever experienced.

She sat by him. "Glad to see you decided to wake up."

"How did you all get away?"

"Well, after you threw yourself against the patriarch, nearly getting killed *again*, Oman's finest took over," she said.

"I heard the helicopters coming. I think that's why Rabbel decided to take action."

"Probably," Mia said, smiling.

"Why are you smiling?" Omar asked.

She lifted a shoulder. "Someone wants to meet you."

"If it's someone important, I need to brush my hair first."

Mia rose, a smirk on her face. She crossed to the tent opening and lifted the flap. "He's awake."

Omar's eyes widened as the patriarch stepped inside the tent, clad in dark robes with a large Coptic cross hanging from his neck. He greeted Mia by saying, "Thank you, Miriam."

The Coptic pope knows Mia on a first-name basis? The patriarch crossed to Omar. Then, even more surprising, the man leaned forward and kissed each of Omar's cheeks. The man must be grateful for Omar's valiant leap in front of a loaded weapon.

The patriarch pulled away, and Omar decided he'd probably get a blessing of some sort. Then Omar would go back to playing on Mia's sympathy for an injured man.

Instead, Mia moved to the patriarch's side. "I'd like you to meet my father, His Holiness, Pope Stephanus II."

Omar opened his mouth, but nothing came out. He tried to sit up and soak in the stunning information. "But I thought . . . you said your father was a . . . herpetologist."

"That's my *step*father. My natural father is—"

"A pope?" Omar finished. Both Mia and her father, none other than His Holiness, Pope Stephanus II, grinned. "I think I see the resemblance now. One is just a little more hairy than the other."

Before he could feel embarrassed at what he'd just said to a world religious leader, the patriarch laughed. "Miriam told me you were spunky."

Spunky? he mouthed to Mia.

The next few moments were surreal as the patriarch sat cross-legged on a rug. Omar decided to let Mia's father take over the conversation before he made any more blunders.

"Miriam tells me you have a lot of questions."

Omar nodded, flashing her a glare. *How much has she told him? Did she leave out the part about what an absolute idiot I am?* "Yes, but first, I want to know what happened after I went down," he said, looking at Mia. "I saw you and Jade jump Levy."

"That was an easy takedown," Mia said, "since I'd just shot him in the leg."

She said it so matter-of-factly that Omar wondered if he'd heard her correctly. "You shot him?"

"He forgot to disarm me."

The patriarch put a hand on his daughter's shoulder.

"So all that time I thought I might never see you again . . ." Omar shook his head in disbelief. "You were armed, and you knew things would turn out all right?"

"I only hoped for an opportunity."

Omar exhaled, gazing at her. "You saved my life."

She cocked her head, half-smiling. "You saved my father's life."

"Touché." He smiled back. "Where's Levy now?"

The patriarch answered for her. "Locked away for a long time."

"And the fake ring that caused all the fuss?" Omar asked.

"Right here." Mia patted her pocket. "But it's not a fake. It was real all along."

"Part of the plan, I suppose," Omar said. He couldn't stop staring at her. He loved it when she was nice . . .

"Of course."

"Can I see it?" Omar held out his hand.

Mia took out the small box and handed it to him. He opened it carefully and gazed at the heavy gold ring inside. "Amazing." He looked at Mia. "*You're* amazing."

She leaned forward, her mouth less than an inch from his. "No, you are."

The patriarch cleared his throat.

Mia pulled away. "Sorry, Father," she mumbled.

Omar's heart thumped. She'd almost kissed him in front of her father—a Coptic pope, no less. *A very good sign.*

"Al-Qadi has been arrested," Mia said, focusing on the conversation again. "I turned over the recording between him and Rabbel. He awaits trial in Salalah."

"And Rabbel?"

Mia looked at her hands for a moment. "Alem . . . shot him. Rabbel died on the spot."

Omar thought of Alem—his friend with the large stature and easy smile. "How's Alem?"

"You saw him. He seems to be handling it very well. He was questioned but released, and he'll probably have to make a formal statement at the police station once we return to Salalah."

"Now the real question I have," Omar said, waving his hand from Mia to the patriarch, "is, how did *this* happen?"

The patriarch chuckled. "I never knew Miriam's mother was pregnant until years after Miriam was born. When I found out, I'd already entered the priesthood. Miriam's mother refused to let me have contact with my daughter until she reached adulthood."

"When I found out, I guess I fell apart," Mia said, looking at Omar. "Things were shaky between you and me, and it seemed easier to break things off so I could figure out who I really was. I tried to tell myself that my father hadn't knowingly abandoned me for religion."

The patriarch put his hand on Mia's shoulder.

"Did Levy know this? Is this why he was involved?"

"He found out who my father was," Mia said as her eyes met his, pleading. "And, since a patriarch is required to live a life of celibacy, Levy tried to use that information to control us. He thought if the news reached the media that the Coptic pope had a daughter, my father might lose his position because of simple politics. No matter that he's been celibate since entering the priesthood." She glanced at her father then back to Omar. "I'm sorry you were caught in the middle, and I'm sorry for my behavior."

Omar felt the old protectiveness return, and this time it was stronger than ever. He was no saint, so how could he deny the woman he loved forgiveness when she asked for it? Besides, she'd shot David Levy. It couldn't get any better than that. "You are completely forgiven."

She breathed out slowly and reached for his hand.

He squeezed it, seeing one thing in her eyes that he'd been waiting months for. *Promise.*

"Venite, dilecti filii, egredemini in hortum," the patriarch said.

Omar turned to the patriarch. "What did you say?"

"'Come, beloved sons, go into the garden,' as stated by Thomas Aquinas on his deathbed." The patriarch leaned forward. "It's believed that St. Thomas had a vision of the queen of Sheba and knew where she was buried—beneath a garden. Ubar used to be a garden with groves of spice trees, flowering plants, dams of irrigation water, and a system of complex canals.

"David Levy was a member of DiscoveryArch," the patriarch continued. "Through a series of emails, he started to suspect that Dr. Lyon and I knew a lot more about the queen of Sheba than we were telling. He questioned us extensively, and it became a battle of intellect. He asked about the legendary poem, but I'd only heard of it at the time and had never read it. Dr. Lyon had seen some watered-down forms of it. When the tomb in Northern Jerusalem was discovered, along with the sketch, Dr. Lyon sent out an extraordinary observation."

Omar tightened his grip on Mia's hand, soaking in her father's words.

The patriarch dabbed his brow, his forehead wrinkled in concentration. "Lyon said, 'The sketch and the poem hand in hand will reveal the final resting place of Bilqis.'" The patriarch paused. "I called the professor and asked him to explain what he meant. That was the day I was nearly killed and the day before Dr. Lyon was murdered."

Omar shook his head. "What did he say?"

"Lyon had a theory . . . simple, really. He had written an article, but at that point, I was the only one he told."

"So they tried to assassinate you just for that?"

"No. They wanted to get rid of me because I *wasn't* going to keep it a secret. The world—Ethiopians, Yemenis, Jews, everyone—deserves to know the truth. To AWP, I was a billion-dollar risk." He smiled as if attempted assassinations didn't bother him. "Why don't you ask the others to join us? I've had a chance to study the translation of the poem Alem received from his grandmother, and I think they might find my conclusions rather captivating."

Mia released Omar's hand and left the tent. No fewer than five minutes later, the tent flaps were flung open and propped with sticks. The warm desert breeze entered on the heels of Lucas, Alem, and Jade.

The small group gathered around the patriarch as he laid out a copy of the sketch and the poem side by side. Omar glanced at Alem and received a confident smile in return. His good friend had been through a lot, but his countenance radiated. The worst was over.

The patriarch pointed to the sketch. "You'll notice that the palm tree in the center has a trunk in the form of a snake and flower—the canna lily."

Omar nodded. Mia had told him as much.

"Surrounding the center palm are six others, each representing someone in the queen's life. Now there has been speculation that each of these palms represents another tomb."

That's what I think, Omar thought. "More tombs right here in Shisur?"

"I think the chance of that is very slim," the patriarch said. "With the discovery of the statue of Azhara in Ethiopia, it's very possible that one of these palms represents her tomb."

"So the tombs might be scattered about the world," Jade said.

"Or one tomb at each of the seven oases of Ubar," Lucas said.

The patriarch smiled. "I like those ideas, although the Ubar theory might rule out Azhara as one of the seven palms. And I must say, Dr. Morel, your colleague, Dr. Lyon, would favor that theory too."

"Seven tombs linked together in seven oases," Omar said. "Fascinating."

Nodding, the patriarch continued, "But it's only a theory right now, and it makes me wonder who authored the sketch. Who drew this seven-palm diagram on the tomb of King Tambariah?"

Jade raised her hand. "Maybe Tambariah is one of the seven tombs?"

"And that would be my guess too," the patriarch said.

"So if the tomb Jade discovered is Batal's, where does that put the queen of Sheba?" Omar asked.

"Ah," the patriarch said. "That's where I think the mapmaker made a mistake." He clutched the edges of his robe and looked upward for a moment. "The queen of Sheba—whether we call her Bilqis or Nicaula or what have you—was a very intelligent woman. And like all high-minded royalty, she didn't want her tomb to be looted."

"Didn't she have the tomb builders put to death?" Jade asked.

"It wouldn't have really helped, since someone had to bury *her*."

"And whoever wrote the poem knew the true location," Alem said.

"He didn't necessarily write it," the patriarch said. "He probably handed down the story verbally, and it passed from one generation to another. Someone wrote it down much later, so the version we have is likely altered."

"What do you think it means?" Alem asked.

The patriarch smiled. "I've given it my best educated guess, and you can each decide for yourselves if you agree."

Omar scooted a little closer to Mia, concentrating on every word.

The patriarch began to read the poem. "'O Queen of the South, Death began your journey.'" He looked up. "It seems that death caused her to leave her home and travel to another location."

"Like Jerusalem?" Jade asked. "It would fit the next line of 'To that night when seven women held one man.' Solomon had plenty of women."

Everyone laughed.

"But the poem takes a turn on the very next line," the patriarch said. "'The feast of seven days brought him from your dreams,

But your heart melted for another like incense spread gold upon cherubim.' Although it sounds like a description written about Solomon, I think the queen had another love."

"Batal," Mia said, glancing at Omar.

"But the next lines are similar to the Song of Solomon," Lucas said. "'Until your desire became as bright as precious stones. Against your bed of spices, O Queen of the South. Your lips are lilies; your chaplets of flowers fill palms of love.'"

"And what about 'Yet your virgin flower faded as the face of the serpent appeared?'" Jade asked.

"Something must have happened to her lover," Lucas said.

"How can he be a lover if she's a virgin?" Jade asked. When everyone snickered, she blushed red.

"Perhaps the relationship was never consummated," Omar said as Mia jabbed him in the ribs.

"Always possible," the patriarch said. "But what's more interesting is the next line that speaks of her death. 'As sunlight wasted, six branches closed, and flowers wilted.'"

"How sad," Jade said.

The mood within the tent turned somber.

"'Now the seven devils hide beneath the tomb, Waiting as seven lamps still burn above, Waiting for the queen of the South.'" The patriarch finished reading the poem. "This is the most troubling part. But I have an idea." He rose to his feet. "Follow me."

The group followed the pope to the tomb site. Members of the media still hung around, and Dr. Stein rushed over to greet them as they approached. The patriarch invited the archaeologist to join them.

They descended into the tomb and turned on flashlights when the interior dimmed. For several moments, the patriarch studied the cuneiform lettering on the walls and the sarcophagus. He said,

"Nothing here. Let's have a look in the treasury."

The others squeezed into the small room and waited in silence for several minutes.

"Here." The patriarch pointed to the wall he'd been examining.

They all crowded in, shining their lights on a small drawing. "It's an oil lamp," Lucas said.

"'Waiting as seven *lamps* still burn above,'" Omar quoted.

"Bravo," the patriarch said. "There should be six more just like this one."

The group examined the walls, the ceiling, the floor. Soon they'd found six more drawings of oil lamps.

"What do they mean?" Jade asked.

"If it means what I think it does, we'd better start looking for those devils," the patriarch said.

"The what?" Jade asked.

"Djinns—or fiery spirits. They are made of fire," the patriarch said.

"Why are they called devils?" Jade asked.

"A common misconception—and easily mistranslated over time and through different languages. Some interpret a djinn as a genie, but they are not the same. There are three classes of djinns: those who guard graveyards, those who can appear in any form, and those who are just plain evil spirits."

"Let's hope these djinns are the ones that guard the graveyard," Alem said. Everyone nodded in agreement.

"So we're looking for fire-like creatures?" Mia asked.

"Something close to that," the patriarch said.

The group separated to the walls and started looking again.

"Now the seven devils hide beneath the tomb," Omar whispered to himself. He shone his flashlight on the floor and slowly moved the flashlight to the left. He stopped the beam on a strange shape.

Is it a cloud? Omar crouched to the ground and saw a rudimentary drawing of what appeared to be a thin, wavy set of lines. *The fiery spirit of a djinn.*

"I think I found something," Omar said, and the others crowded around.

The patriarch clapped him on the shoulder. "I believe you have." He traced the outline of the flame with his finger. "If the last three lines of the poem are accurate in any way, the queen of Sheba is buried *beneath* this floor."

Chapter Fifty-three

Shisur, Oman

THREE HOURS HAD PASSED since the patriarch had led them all into the tomb and found the seven lamps and the seven djinns. The work crews had labored without breaks as they dug out a large hole in the floor. Each shovelful of dirt had to be analyzed before the next one could be removed. The process was slow and agonizing, and as each hour passed, Jade grew more anxious. Was the patriarch's theory wild?

Lucas supervised the digging with Dr. Stein. At times they even pitched in to relieve the excavators. Jade rose from her perch on a low rock beneath a palm tree. The air was electric, tense, as if at any moment the place would burst with the media crews ready and the Omani military surrounding the oasis.

Alem, Omar, and Mia kept close watch on the progress. Jade was the only one who couldn't sit still. She fidgeted with her ring, thoughts churning through her mind. For the first time since leaving Rhode Island, she thought about the day she would go home and about leaving Lucas and the others who had become her friends. She thought about leaving the arid desert with its flies, snakes, and deep shafts. She would miss all of it—the heat, the never-ending perspiration, the unpleasant smells, Luc's easy smile and engaging eyes.

She gazed at the endless horizon. Its vastness made her feel as though she lived in a world all her own. What would happen when she returned to the bustle of university life? She closed her eyes and let out a breath. Spending the last several days with Lucas showed her how different her life could be—how happy. Even if she never saw Lucas again . . . She opened her eyes, hating the possibility.

Jade looked at her mood ring. Orange. *Daring. Just perfect.*

A shout echoed through the site, and Jade raised her head. The media crews scrambled to their feet and left their coveted shade to run toward the tomb. Even the military edged closer, their intense guard temporarily forgotten.

Jade ran. She reached the edge of the crowd just as Lucas emerged from the tomb. Dr. Stein and the patriarch already stood before the crowd, grinning. Dr. Stein raised his hands for silence, and the excited murmuring quieted. He motioned for Lucas to begin, but first Lucas scanned the group until his gaze stopped on Jade.

"Just a minute," he said and pushed through the crowd until he reached Jade. He took her hand. "Come with me."

Jade almost melted on the spot. Lucas pulled her to the front of the group, and they stood next to Dr. Stein. "We're ready to reveal the results of our second dig," Lucas said. He still held Jade's hand, and it was as if fire pulsed between them.

"Thanks to Mademoiselle Holmes's timely fall a few days ago," Lucas said as a few chuckles surrounded them, cameras snapping like mad, "and His Holiness's insightful interpretation of an ancient poem, we have made another discovery."

The blood rushed to Jade's head. *Was it possible?*

"There is indeed a second tomb beneath the treasury room," Lucas said in a tremulous voice.

Jade looked up at him and was caught in the emotion herself. She swallowed against the thickness in her throat and squeezed Lucas's hand. He squeezed back.

"Dr. Stein and His Holiness have some interesting observations to make," Lucas said.

Dr. Stein waited until the excited buzzing dimmed. "We wanted to be sure, and we didn't want to make the world wait a moment longer than necessary. So, with the help of the work crew, we opened the sarcophagus found in the second tomb."

A collective gasp arose.

The patriarch stepped forward and withdrew a folded piece of cloth from his robes. "We found this on the preserved skeleton." He held up a square of fabric and carefully lifted one side. Within the folds was a thick, gold chain. At the end of the chain was a large pendant.

Jade covered her mouth. The pendant held the Sheba symbol identical to the ring found in the Jerusalem tomb—the snake and the flower intimately intertwined.

Cameras snapped pictures as the patriarch rotated and displayed the necklace for all to photograph.

"We now believe," Lucas called out above the murmuring crowd, "that Her Royal Highness, the legendary goddess known as the queen of Sheba, has been found!"

❧

AFTER NUMEROUS INTERVIEWS, LUCAS was free to speak with Jade. She'd waited quietly on the sidelines, her hand still burning from his touch. When he turned and caught her gaze, her heart leaped. He crossed to her and grinned.

"Let's go see the queen."

Jade inhaled sharply. "Are you sure it's all right? I'm not an archaeologist."

"Neither are the others. Mia, Omar, and Alem went down a few minutes ago with the patriarch."

He led Jade down the ramp, and the light grew dimmer as they entered the tomb of Batal. When Jade shivered at the sudden temperature change, Lucas put an arm around her. "Come on."

They climbed through the opening in the wall to the treasury room. Jade immediately saw the gaping hole in the floor. Light flickered in the dark pit. Lucas called down to the others to let them know they were coming. Then he held the rope ladder steady for Jade to go first.

She put her flashlight back in her pocket and gripped the rope as she slowly descended into the musty air. Jade pulled out her flashlight and scanned around the space that was about the same size as the treasury room above. On the walls appeared several drawn figures, looking royal in nature.

"This is the antechamber, or the tomb entrance," Lucas said, coming up behind her. He arced his beam of light along the wall. "Beyond this room is a second area that serves as the queen's burial chamber. You'll see there's no other entrance. This tomb was completely sealed off after she was buried."

"So the queen meant for someone to dig through the treasury floor to find her?"

"No, the queen meant for no one to find her," Lucas said. "Just as the patriarch said, the poem was likely handed down verbally from generation to generation."

"Wow." Jade walked to one of the walls. "Who are these people drawn on the stone?"

"We'll be able to figure that out in time. But first, I want to show you something." Lucas led her to the next room just as Mia and Alem exited. They greeted each other in hushed tones. Then Jade followed Lucas into the burial room. A huge sarcophagus took up most of the space.

This was it.

The final resting place of the queen of Sheba.

Jade stepped forward and touched the cold stone coffin. A shiver traveled through Jade's entire body. She walked around the sarcophagus, trailing her fingers over the ancient rock.

Her stomach flipped with disbelief and excitement at the same time. Lucas stood back, letting her take her time as she examined every inch. After a while, he joined her, saying, "I have something else to show you."

He guided her to the closest wall and fixed his light on the lettering. "The most incredible find so far is the amount of Aramaic writing. The author apparently knew the queen quite well, as the writing chronicles her life." Lucas pointed to a series of words. "Here her story begins."

Jade listened in awe as Lucas translated. "Her father died when she was in her fifteenth year, and that's when she took the throne." He moved his beam along the wall.

"'Death began your journey,'" Jade quoted.

"Exactly." Lucas moved his light. "Her journey north to Jerusalem."

"And she met Solomon, just as it says in the Bible?"

"Yes. But look at this." He pointed to a drawing of a man who looked as if he were ready for war. "See the name?"

She nodded, but didn't understand the lettering.

"Batal."

A wave of understanding passed over her. "He was the one she truly loved."

"The one for whom her 'heart melted . . . like incense spread gold upon cherubim.'"

Lucas's body heat seemed to radiate toward her, making her heart pound and throat grow dry.

"It's a love story like no other. 'Until your desire became as bright as precious stones Against your bed of spices, O Queen of the South,'" he whispered.

The poem is about me, or any woman who has ever forgotten herself for a man. Jade folded her arms, pressing them tightly against her chest, as if she could calm her thudding heart. "So she didn't marry Solomon?"

He moved a few steps away. "Not according to this. Here are two women: one, the queen, and another named Azhara."

Azhara.

"It seems that the queen bestowed some royal honor upon this Azhara woman. I'm not exactly sure what it all means yet, but the woman left the queen and traveled southwest . . . possibly to Abyssinia."

"Modern-day Ethiopia," she breathed, looking at the drawn figures. "Amazing."

"But then something tragic happened." Lucas moved his beam along the wall. "The final portion of her story begins here . . ."

Chapter Fifty-four

Ubar
959 b.c.

NICAULA STOOD IN FRONT of the polished metal, staring at her appearance. She was no longer a girl of fifteen—as she'd been when she had first met Batal.

She smoothed her tunic over her breasts and stopped her hands when they reached her narrow hips. Looking at her reflection in the metal, she imagined Batal standing next to her, his strong arms encircling hers. "Soon," she whispered. "Soon I will be joined with him."

The sky had turned to violet, making Nicaula even more impatient. In a few hours, she would be with Batal. A servant brought in a meal, but she couldn't eat anything.

She paced.

But she did not doubt.

At midnight, she left her rooms and found her way to the stables. There she readied her horse, whispering soothing words. Moments later, she was riding full speed to the west.

She saw him standing at the top of the hill near her father's tomb, illuminated in the moonlight. Nicaula spurred her horse forward, breathless, laughing. He was waiting for her. He met the horse and helped her down, his touch almost singeing her skin.

Before she had a chance to speak, he swept her in his arms, nearly crushing her against him.

"You came." He pulled away, staring at her.

She smiled.

His face turned serious, and he reached for her hand. Without a word, he led her to the entrance of her father's tomb. Together they knelt in respect and paid homage to the king of Sheba.

Then Batal rose to his feet and extended his hand toward Nicaula. "Are you ready?"

She grasped his hand and rose to her feet. "I am."

He poured a goblet of wine from the wineskin he'd brought. Then he set it on a nearby rock.

Looking at Batal in the moonlight reminded her of the first night they spent tracking the marauders and the sacrifice he made to defend her.

He wrapped her hands in his. "Nicaula, queen of the South, will you take me as your husband?"

Her voice was tremulous as she spoke. "Yes."

He smiled and squeezed her hands.

"Batal, will you take me as your wife?" she said.

"With all my heart."

Batal released her hands as he reached for the goblet. He took a sip from the cup then handed it to Nicaula. She sipped and then put the goblet back on the rock.

Nicaula removed the ring of Sheba from her hand. "With this ring, we are consecrated together." She slipped it on his finger in reverence, her throat constricting with emotion.

She circled him seven times then stopped in front of him.

Batal removed the cloak from his shoulders and wrapped it around her, pulling her close. "What Yahweh hath brought together, let no man put asunder."

He pulled a scroll from his waistband. "I have the marriage contract, although nothing is written on it yet."

Nicaula smiled, her pulse thudding. "We can do that later."

Batal tossed the scroll onto the rock, where it landed and rolled next to the wine goblet. Then he turned back to her.

His gaze drew her in, and she forgot to breathe. He reached for the cloak that hung from her shoulders, but instead of removing it, he pulled her closer and bent his head until their lips touched.

Her heart thundered as their bodies melded and his kisses turned passionate. This time the queen didn't need to worry about propriety. This time he was her husband. She slid one hand around his neck, her fingers gripping his curls. The other hand trailed along his shoulder, chest, arm.

Batal moaned as the kissing intensified. She wanted him closer, and when he lifted her, she wrapped both arms around his neck. He set her on the rock, and she tugged him against her, knocking the goblet of wine over.

Batal lifted his head as the scarlet liquid splashed across the rock.

"Leave it," Nicaula whispered, pulling his head toward her again. Kissing him and feeling his warm, strong body pressed against her was better than a thousand dreams combined. She thought she might faint if he weren't holding her upright.

"I love you," he breathed in her ear. "Always."

She was about to reply when he jerked away, his expression confused.

"Batal?"

He released her and stepped back, looking down.

Then she saw it. A cobra.

Before Nicaula could react, Batal snatched up the snake and flung it out into the desert.

Nicaula took a deep breath, trying to calm the panic in her heart. "You could have been bitten doing that."

Batal turned toward her, and she saw it in his eyes. With horror, she looked down. Two rivulets of blood ran along his left shin.

No.

Not this.

Somewhere, deep inside, a strange calm overtook her. "Sit down on the rock."

Batal wordlessly obeyed.

Nicaula tore off her headdress and tied it just above the puncture wounds, cinching the knot as tight as possible. Batal silently handed over his dagger. The queen made a quick incision above the wound.

Batal sucked in his breath, but didn't pull away. Their eyes met, and Nicaula stood, flinging her arms about his neck. "We must get back to the palace."

By the time she helped Batal mount his horse, his leg had swollen. She climbed on behind him and swatted the horse forward. Nicaula wrapped her arms around Batal's body, but with each passing minute, he became more and more slack.

"Stay with me, please," Nicaula said, tears burning her eyes. His arms hung limply at his sides, and it took all her strength to keep him from sliding off. "The healer can assist you. You just need to hold on."

When they reached the palace, Batal was practically sideways on the horse, his eyes glassy, staring at nothing.

The queen shouted across the deserted courtyard for help. Several harried servants appeared and helped transport Batal to her rooms. "Fetch Nabil!"

Moments later, Nabil entered the room. The man hadn't bothered to change out of his sleeping garments, and the usual turban he wore had been left behind. Nabil located the site of the wound almost immediately. With his dagger, he made a second incision on Batal's leg and let the blood.

This time, there was no reaction to the pain. Sitting on the other side of Batal, Nicaula touched his hot face. His skin was so pale. She tried to cool him with wet cloths, but his skin wouldn't cool.

"O God of Israel," Nicaula pled. She took Batal's hand and caressed his palm. "Heal him."

The queen closed her eyes and prayed as the healer made incisions into Batal's flesh and saturated cloth after cloth of blood. Batal's leg was now severely swollen, and Nabil continued to find places to let blood.

When the healer finished, he cleaned up the handiwork. "I have done all that I can."

"You may leave now," Nicaula said. "I'll send for you if I need anything else." After Nabil left her chambers, she climbed onto the bed next to Batal. She lay parallel to him, not touching his swollen leg, but lying close enough that she could hear his every breath. Tears slipped along her face, soaking the bedding beneath her head.

She watched him until her eyes slipped closed, only to awake a short time later by someone whispering her name.

"Nicaula."

The queen rose on an elbow and stared into her beloved's face. His eyes were barely open, yet his face was radiant.

"I wanted to see you again."

"Of course," Nicaula said, stroking his cheek. "You will be healed soon, and then we'll live together as husband and wife at last."

Batal gazed at her for a long moment. "No. It's my time to depart this life." He moved his hand slowly until it touched hers. Nicaula grasped it, desperately.

"Do not be angry with Yahweh. Remember Him. Worship Him." Batal took a ragged breath. "I want my love for you to be written on the walls of my tomb." For a moment, his breathing stopped.

"Batal!" Nicaula cried out.

He took a breath and closed his eyes. "I will always love you." His fingers pressed against her hand as his breathing grew fainter. "Always."

Then he was still.

"Batal!" she screamed. She placed her hands against his chest, searching for his heartbeat. His body was warm, yet there was no pulsing. She stared at his face, wondering if he had fallen unconscious. Laying her head against his chest, she held her own breath, waiting for his body to move again.

It did not.

She wrapped her arms about his torso, burying her face against his neck, and sobbed. "O God of Israel, give him back to me!"

The moments passed, quiet as the death that permeated the room. Nicaula raised her head and looked through her tears at Batal. He was perfect, even in death. She rose from the bed, her tears still coming fast. She took a basin of scented water and gently cleaned the dust and perspiration from his body. After she washed the dried blood from his leg, she set the basin on the floor.

She climbed onto the bed with him again and gently kissed him on the cheek. "This is for our child who will never be."

She hovered over him for a moment, disbelief pounding through her chest. She kissed his other cheek. "And for the years we will not share." She moved her lips to his forehead as a sob caught in her throat. "And for making you wait so long." Tears burned her eyes and dripped onto his face. She placed both hands on his cheeks and stared at his closed eyelids. "With this kiss, you are my husband forever." She kissed him on the mouth, his lips salty from her own tears.

She collapsed against Batal and clung to his clothing, sobbing, wishing she were dead instead of him. "O God, why did you take my beloved?" The pain coursed through her, faster than a snake's venom, as she clung to him, praying, cursing, and grieving until the first light touched the horizon.

Only when his body had grown rigid and the coldness had set in did Nicaula pull away. She moved to the door and summoned Nabil. He entered quietly and prepared the body for burial while Nicaula huddled in the corner of the room.

Before the sun crested the dunes, Batal was buried in his tomb below the temple of Yahweh. The procession was small—David, Queen Nicaula, Nabil, and four guards to carry the shrouded body.

While the rest of the city slept, Batal's body was lowered into the cavern. The guards descended by rope and placed him in the sarcophagus. Nicaula knelt at the opening when the task was complete and bowed her head.

"Farewell, Batal," she whispered. "My husband and my only love. Thank you for loving me as a man loves a woman. Please wait for me. Wait for the queen of the South."

In the late morning, the queen announced Batal's death. A body made of wood, wrapped in linen, was brought forward, and the queen led the procession to the tomb prepared on the other side of the city. No one would ever find the true burial place of her beloved and desecrate his body.

That evening, Nicaula requested little David to visit her. When he arrived in her private chambers, the queen tried to put him at ease. "Come here, child."

The young Bedu boy stepped forward.

"Have you had a chance to see the city of Ubar?"

The boy nodded, and the queen smiled gently. "And what did you think of it, son?"

"Very . . . beautiful."

She nodded. "It *is* very beautiful. And one day, it will all be yours."

David's large black eyes gazed at her.

Nicaula removed a metal box from the folds of her garment. She lifted the lid and took out the heavy gold ring from inside. "Tomorrow I will declare you my son, my heir to the throne." She waved her hand around the room. "Everything you see will be yours someday." Nicaula crossed to him and knelt by his side. "Tell me what's wrong."

"If I am your son . . . then . . ." His voice faltered.

"Then I will be your new mother," the queen finished. She drew the small boy into her arms. "In return for all the riches and power a boy could dream of, I ask only one thing in exchange." She pulled away and looked firmly into the boy's eyes.

He set his jaw straight and blinked back his tears.

"You must write my true story upon my tomb walls then never tell a soul where I am buried." She smiled. "When you're grown, you will return to the land of your birth and give this ring to a man named Tambariah. Tell him I am sorry."

The boy nodded.

"Good son," Nicaula whispered and drew him into her arms again.

Chapter Fifty-five

Salalah, Oman

JADE SAT IN THE Salalah airport, the chair hard beneath her. She was uncomfortable—yes, tired, very, but her heart ached. She had just finished reading David Levy's confession printed in the newspaper—English edition. Next to it was the last article Professor Lyon had written, which had apparently been found in his email draft folder. Lyon had indicted the head of AWP, now confirmed as the deceased Rabbel Al-Omda, and Abdallah Saleh al-Qadi, ex-director of GOAMM, but he had failed to realize his real enemy: the senior intelligence officer of the Northern Israeli Command, David Levy—the one who admitted to sending an envelope laced with cyanide, intercepting the article submitted to Saudi Aramco, and concocting a long trail of cover-up.

The ring and necklace were currently being studied by Dr. Stein and his colleagues, Jade read. The tomb had turned into a full-blown excavation site, and predictions estimated that it would take nine to twelve months before everything was excavated, identified, and preserved. She scrolled through her recent notes on her phone about the queen's burial chamber. The story of the queen's life on the tomb walls had been only a brief outline of what must have happened to her.

Jade tried to imagine the trials and tragedies the woman faced. She was buried beneath the tomb of Batal—a man whom she obviously loved, but who had died tragically. Jade lifted her gaze to see Lucas crossing to her, a steaming cup of coffee in one hand and a freshly squeezed glass of juice in the other.

A twinge of sadness crept into her heart. He'd come to see her off. She was headed back to the States, and he would remain in Oman trying to tie all the new artifacts together.

"Here you are," Lucas said, handing over the juice and settling next to her. "They should be calling your flight soon."

Jade nodded, sipping the fresh juice and making a mental note to find the nearest health food café once she returned home. She didn't think she could drink processed stuff after this.

"Well, we've accomplished a lot, haven't we?" Lucas said.

"And Lyon's killer—David Levy—is behind bars." Jade looked out the airport windows at the drizzly rain that had crept in over the past hour. The summer monsoon was in full swing.

"One man's evil heart affects many."

She turned. "You're sounding poetic, Luc. Are you sure you don't believe in the Bible?"

He chuckled and draped his arm around the back of her chair, meeting her gaze. "Do you honestly think I would be in this line of work if I didn't?"

She smiled. Butterflies invaded her stomach when he smiled back. She would miss those amber eyes. One part of her wished he'd invite her to stay. She could make herself useful during the day then dream about him at night. In fact, she might even stop comparing him to Photoshopped heroes.

The announcement came over the intercom, first in Arabic, then in accented English. Boarding had started. Jade finished the last of her juice and rose to her feet. Lucas stood too. He took her cup from her and leaned forward to kiss her cheek. "Until next time, mademoiselle."

You don't even know how much I hope to see you again. Jade pulled away, trying to memorize the electricity of his touch. "Until next time, then." She hesitated, wanting to hug him. But he held his coffee and her empty juice cup, and she didn't want to make it awkward—especially in the middle of an airport where the local men and women didn't show public affection.

She turned and walked to the desk. She handed over her boarding pass, and with a final glance behind, she saw Lucas staring after her—watching her as if he were the king of his own jungle.

She waved, and he lifted his cup of coffee.

Au revoir.

Chapter Fifty-six

Shisur, Oman

OMAR SLAMMED THE PASSENGER door shut then leaned through the window, looking at Alem, who sat in the truck, a crooked grin on his face.

"Thank you for everything, my friend," Alem said.

Omar gripped Alem's hand. "Thank *you*. Without your grandmother's poem, we may never have found the queen's burial chamber."

Alem tapped his forehead. "I'm glad it was still up here."

Omar laughed. "Me too." He sobered for a moment, thinking of what Alem had been through. Alem's skin was nearly healed, although his face was still lined with red scars. "I'll never forget this."

Alem nodded, a far-off look in his gaze. "Each time I look into a mirror, I'll remember Arabia."

"Think of the queen, my friend," Omar said. "Think of your part in finding her. Your scars are evidence of that sacrifice." He blinked against the sudden stinging in his eyes. Allergy season must be coming early to the desert. He placed a hand on Alem's shoulder.

"I'll do all I can to see that everyone associated with Rabbel is behind bars."

"Thank you."

"Ready?" Mia spoke behind Omar.

He turned. Mia was personally escorting Alem to Ethiopia. They didn't want to take any chances with Alem's passage back home since Ismail was still at large.

"Do you need me to come with you?" Omar asked.

"No. It's all routine."

He hated to see her leave. "And your father? Is he leaving too?"

"I think he'll stick around for another day or two, just to see how things unfold with the excavation."

Omar nodded slowly, searching Mia's eyes. If she left now, when would he see her again? She'd probably be swept into another undercover assignment before he could return to Jerusalem.

"Hey, I have a question for you." Mia led Omar a few paces away from the truck. "Alem told me he found a Coptic cross with your possessions. Was it yours?"

"It was a gift from an elderly neighbor when I was a child. I used to walk her dog each day, and she left it to me in her will. I guess I thought it was good luck, so I kept it with me."

Mia looked skeptical. "Is that all?"

"Yes, and I wish I had it back."

A slight smile turned up the corners of Mia's mouth. "I might be able to get another one for you."

Omar eyed her for a moment. "Just don't tell my mother. She'd kill me."

Mia drew an imaginary line across her lips then asked, "So what are your plans?"

· "I'm going to stick around here for a few days too. Lucas might need some help with translating that Aramaic." Omar winked.

She laughed. "I'm sure he will."

"If nothing else, it will give me time to . . . uh, think about what I want to do next."

She gave him a knowing smile. "Levy's job is available."

"I already tried that route, and look what happened."

Mia folded her arms and tilted her head. "Enlighten me."

"Well, I interviewed for the job, and they hated me so much that they found the worst possible person to hire." He leaned toward her. "That person came between me and the woman I love more than anything in the world. Then the guy killed a renowned historian, tried to assassinate a patriarch, *twice*, was thrown into jail, and . . . got fired." He stared at Mia, enjoying her flushed cheeks as the wind tugged at her hair. Omar reached out and tucked a lock of curls behind her ear. "And I thought *I* had bad luck."

Mia took a step closer. "What if I asked you to come back?"

"Nope. That job is cursed." He dropped his hand.

"What if I *begged* you?"

He rubbed the back of his neck and gazed at the sky. "She's going to *beg* me?" He looked at her. "Then I would say my luck is starting to change."

Mia threw her arms around his neck and pressed her mouth against his.

Omar nearly lost his balance, but quickly recovered and wrapped his arms about her waist, pulling her even closer. Kissing her was something he never wanted to retire from.

After a moment, she released him, laughing at his dazed expression. "Let me be the first to say that your luck has definitely changed."

Chapter Fifty-seven

Ethiopia

THE DRONE OF THE tires nearly lulled Alem to sleep, but when the taxi slowed, he was fully awake as the driver stopped at the small cemetery just outside of Aksum. After asking the driver to wait, Alem hopped out and walked toward the broken gate. The metal hung on its hinges, squeaking in the light breeze.

It was a scorching day in Ethiopia, and Alem wore his white tunic shirt and linen pants. His sandals fit neatly over his healed feet, and although the scars were still evident, he didn't draw quite so many stares.

He gripped the bouquet of flowers he held in his hand, searching for signs of another lone person on the property, since his grandfather had promised to meet him. Alem walked slowly among the grave markers, imagining he heard the rich history of the people's lives whispered beneath his feet. A hunched form sat near his grandmother's tombstone, and Alem crossed to meet the elderly man. His grandfather looked up as Alem approached and held out a trembling hand.

Alem sat next to him and waited quietly as the old man touched the scars on his face. Clicking his tongue, his grandfather said, "Your sacrifice was great."

Alem nodded, struck with the age of the man, the wrinkled blackness, the nearly all-white beard, and the arthritic hands.

"My wife was a great woman," his grandfather said. "After her death, I found a record of her life—a diary of sorts. She fervently believed the legends of Queen Makeda."

"That's what I want to ask you about," Alem said. "Where did Grandmother hear the stories that she used to tell us about the queen?"

His grandfather shrugged. "Passed down from her grandmother. She told me the same ones when I first met her, although I was never quite drawn in."

His confession surprised Alem. "What do you think about the discovery of the Azhara statue and the name of Tambariah?"

"Oh, there's been talk," his grandfather said. "The one thing I've always found interesting is your grandmother's name . . . Ahara. Spelled A-h-a-r-a."

"Very close," Alem mused. "And my middle name is Tambariah . . ."

"Yes."

Alem fell silent as the wind picked through the blades of grass. The names on the Azhara statue were part of his family lineage. There was no doubt his family descended from someone great—royalty, for that matter.

"Have you heard about the Sheba ring?" Alem asked, watching his grandfather's expression.

"There's been talk . . ." his grandfather began. "I suppose Azhara could have known King Tambariah in Jerusalem and given him the ring. He might be the father of her child."

Nodding, Alem plucked a blade of grass and twisted it between his fingers. "Why would she come here? Where does King Solomon fit in?"

"Those are questions that may never be answered, son, until the *next* coming of Christ." He patted Alem on the shoulder. "Tambariah seemed to be a contender with Solomon, and Solomon won more than land and power. Perhaps there *was* a woman involved." He chuckled. "I smell a love interest. Two princes, one queen? But whom did the queen really favor? And who was Azhara? And why would a woman who was in love with Solomon leave Israel and come to Ethiopia?"

"Maybe her true love followed *her*."

"Tambariah? Very possible . . . Or maybe Azhara was another princess."

Alem stared at his grandfather. That would certainly explain a lot.

"I believe everything happens for a reason," his grandfather said. "Life continues on, pain lessens, and new legacies are born." He touched Alem's chest. "Look inside yourself, and you'll see who you really are. What's important is how you represent your *own* name."

Alem thought about his grandfather's words as he let the warm breeze wash over him, drying his perspiring skin. He rose to his feet and placed the flowers at the base of his grandmother's tombstone. With a finger, he traced the outline of the Sheba symbol. The snake and the flower. Man and woman intertwined.

He let his hand fall away, thinking about the turmoil and excitement the new discoveries had brought to the outside world. But here he was, in a quiet graveyard with just his grandfather, his grandmother's grave, and dozens of memories.

And today, in honor of his grandmother, he—Alem Tambariah Eshete—would believe.

Truly believe.

Epilogue

Rhode Island
Five months later

DRAWING THE GOOSE DOWN coat about her, Jade made a mad
dash to the Brown University library. She was nearly done with her
master's thesis on the queen of Sheba, and she planned to turn it in
before Christmas break. It was hard to believe that five months had
passed since she'd left the hot sands of Arabia. Five rather boring
months. Compared with the adventures of traveling throughout
Arabia, Providence was bland.

The only thing she looked forward to were two interviews the
first week of December—both for associate teaching positions. At
least when she graduated at the end of the year, she had a chance of
being employed.

She entered the library, noticing that it was nearly deserted. Not
many college students spent their Saturday nights studying. She
crossed to the row of monitors and, logging onto the Internet with
her student ID, she pulled up her emails before diving into more
research. A couple of emails were from fellow classmates trying
to plan a barbecue for a pre-Thanksgiving bash. *Crazy.* She didn't

understand why her friends insisted on doing ridiculous activities such as winter cookouts.

She typed a return email. "I'll meet you at the barbecue. Count me in for chips."

Jade knew that most of the students would stay inside anyway, sipping that nasty, dark beer. *Gourmet*, they called it. Another email came in just as she was about to log off. Not recognizing the sender and seeing an attachment, she selected the email to send it into the junk folder. Yet something in the subject line made her hesitate.

Looking for a fun adventure?

Always, Jade thought. It was definitely spam, but then her eyes widened as she dissected the sender's name: LMorel.

Lucas.

She opened the email, and a grin spread across her face.

> *Jade,*
> *Hope all is well. Just received a grant to excavate the Pharaonic sun temple found under an outdoor marketplace in Cairo. Speculation says the large statues are of King Ramses II. I'm sure you've read the theories that King Ramses II was possibly King Solomon and that a floor of gold dust, discovered in 1999, sixty centimeters below Nile mud, belonged to the first temple of Solomon. Perhaps the excavation of this temple will provide new evidence. How about it?*

It took her only seconds to type her reply.

> *Dear Luc,*
> *I'd love to.*

ACKNOWLEDGMENTS

FINDING SHEBA WENT THROUGH various stages, from adding in Omar Zagouri, who ended up becoming a main character, halfway through the novel to completely revising the ending, which made the book a hundred pages longer, to having my agent tell me I needed to cut a hundred pages . . . somewhere, somehow.

As you can imagine with any manuscript having evolved so much, there are many people to thank. First, I'd like to thank Julie Wright and Josi Kilpack. At the time I wrote *Finding Sheba*, I was just getting to know these ladies, and they have since become close friends as well as coauthors in my Newport Ladies Book Club series. I also want to thank Loree Allison and Phil Allison. Loree has read more than one draft of some of my books, and her friendship is priceless.

Thanks to S. Kent Brown, my father and biblical scholar extraordinaire, who first brainstormed the idea for this book with me, and to my mother, Gayle Brown, who, unlike most moms, will tell me what she doesn't like. I also appreciate author Gordon Ryan, who tragically passed away in 2012, but had been a mentor and confidant as we both navigated along the writing path.

I want to thank Laurie Liss, a friend and agent who has amazing patience and great wisdom. Thanks to author Richard Paul Evans, who introduced me to Laurie and inspired me in many ways. I also appreciate Crystal Liechty, who gave me excellent comments, and agent Elaine Spencer, who told me to change the ending (and I did).

Thanks to Karen Christoffersen, who wouldn't allow this manuscript to sit around, and to Eric Swedin for our great debates over historical details. Also, many thanks to members of my critique group who plowed through the story: Stephanni Meyer, J. Scott

Savage, Lu Ann Staheli, Lynda Keith, Annette Lyon, Michele Holmes, and James Dashner (who has gone on to hit the *New York Times* list).

Special thanks to Kelli Stanley for her sweet friendship and for referring me to James Rollins, who gave me great advice, and thanks to David Sylvian-Czajkowski, who is too smart for his own good but is willing to help a friend in need.

I'm extremely grateful to my publisher, StoneHouse Ink, and to Aaron Patterson, who is doing something extraordinary in the industry. Thanks also to Kate Neal for all of her work, copyeditors Melissa Marler and Tristi Pinkston, and cover designer Cory Clubb.

A final thanks goes to my husband, Chris, and my children, who have always been number one.

ABOUT THE AUTHOR

HEATHER B. MOORE IS the award-winning author of nine historical novels which are set in Ancient Arabia and Mesoamerica. She is not extremely old and doesn't remember the time period, thus Google has become a great friend. Although she has spent several years living in the Middle East, she prefers to forget the smells. Heather writes her historical thrillers under the pen name H.B. Moore so that men will buy her books. She is also the author of two non-fiction books and several women's novels—these are written under her real name so that women will buy her books. It can be confusing, so her kids just call her Mom.

For updates, visit Heather's website www.hbmoore.com or her blog http://mywriterslair.blogspot.com